NUCLEAR NATION

A PROSECUTION FORCE THRILLER

LOGAN RYLES

SEVERN RIVER
PUBLISHING

Severn River Publishing
SevernRiverBooks.com

ISBN: 978-1-64875-624-5 (Paperback)

ALSO BY LOGAN RYLES

The Prosecution Force Series

Brink of War

First Strike

Election Day

Failed State

Firestorm

White Alert

Nuclear Nation

Fallout

The Reed Montgomery Series

Overwatch

Hunt to Kill

Total War

Smoke and Mirrors

Survivor

Death Cycle

Sundown

To find out more about Logan Ryles and his books, visit

severnriverbooks.com

For Andrew, Cate, and the entire Severn River Publishing team —
Thanks for everything.

1

Sticky gray diesel fumes bubbled from the tailpipes of a trio of armored Mercedes SUVs as they raced through the high steel gates of the facility and navigated to the headquarters building. It was tall and wind beaten, bleached by the sun and petrified by decades of brutal Russian winters. Black windows stared over the parade ground as the lead vehicle ground to a halt and a trio of men in black suits rolled out.

They were members of the Federal Guard Service, the elite Russian counterpart of America's Secret Service, and they made zero effort to conceal the SPS handguns affixed to their hips or the PP-2000 submachine guns strapped to three-point harnesses over their chests. Another three men in matching attire bailed out of the tail vehicle, and together the six FGS agents spread into a natural security perimeter as the compound's gate closed, and the middle vehicle shifted into park.

From the edges of the parade ground and the tops of guard towers staffed by Russian army personnel, all eyes turned to that middle vehicle, and the air itself seemed to stand still. The driver remained behind the wheel, but the man riding shotgun got out. He wasn't tall, overly muscular, or physically remarkable in any way. Gray eyes and a grizzled beard were joined by an ill-fitting overcoat and smudged black boots in need of cleaning.

He looked like just another plumber or St. Petersburg mechanic. A nobody. And yet everyone in the compound knew the face of Anton Golubev, the Ghost of the Kremlin and the right-hand man of the president, as well as they knew that of his boss. Where a physical trademark was lacking, a reputational signature had taken its place.

A signature signed exclusively—and frequently—in blood.

Golubev lit a cigarette and took a moment to survey the perimeter, muttering a word or two to the FGS agent in charge. Then at last he approached the rear door of the middle vehicle and tugged it open.

President Makar Anatoly Nikitin was everything his right-hand man wasn't. Tall, muscular, and handsome, he kept his black hair trimmed and styled to perfection, an iron face discreetly manicured to hide the lines and creases that had invaded over the long decades of public service...and public dominance. As much as the rumble of a Russian T-90 main battle tank or the scream of a Sukhoi Su-57 fighter jet, Makar Nikitin demanded attention as brazenly as he demanded respect.

It was as much his not-so-secret weapon to success as Golubev's bloody signature.

"Is he here?" Nikitin asked, accepting a cigarette. Golubev held out a flame and nodded once in way of reply. Never one to waste words.

Nikitin dragged on the smoke, then turned for the headquarters building. The FGS agents fell in behind, maintaining the security perimeter. Not trusting any one of the six thousand Russian military personnel occupying the base, or even the fifteen thousand additional infantry stationed in the Caucasus valley beyond it, to do their job for them.

The security of Russia's preeminent leader was their responsibility alone.

The headquarters door burst open as Nikitin approached. The army infantrymen stationed there saluted. Nikitin ignored the salute and marched straight inside. Down a hall, into welcome warmth. Around a corner and straight to a conference room where shouts in Georgian—the most common Kartvelian language spoken in the region—were already audible.

Angry, obstinate shouts. Objecting shouts. Defiant shouts.

Nikitin shoved through the door with one muscled heave of his big hand, cigarette still clenched between his teeth. Only two of the FGS guards followed him and Golubev inside, the rest remaining in the hallway. On the far side of the heavy doors, a conference room was occupied by a long table strewn with documents and computers, chairs resting at random around it, a single projector screen displaying a map of the Caucasus region.

A dashed red line marking a border only five kilometers south of the outpost's location.

Two men joined the conference table. The first was tall and well built, much like Nikitin. Bald, dressed in a Russian military field uniform, with three stars on his shoulder patches to signify his rank as a colonel general —only two ranks down from the supreme rank of Russian military leadership. His features were set in hard, emotionless lines as he confronted the second man—a much smaller, middle-aged male in a disheveled black suit. Tangled black hair, sweat-stained shirt collar. An inflamed red face. The short man in the sweaty black suit turned instantly at the sound of the doors blowing open, his eyes widening as Nikitin barged in.

"Good evening, Giorgi. How was your trip?"

Nikitin spoke in Russian, knowing that everyone present would understand. Even as the Russian president walked easily to the tea bar and poured himself a porcelain cup of bitter dark tea, Giorgi Meladze seemed unable to speak. He sputtered, looking from Nikitin to the colonel general, then to the doors—now closed—and finally to Golubev.

When he saw Golubev, blood drained from his face. His mouth closed, but the outrage in his gaze remained.

Nikitin turned from the tea bar, stirring his beverage with a silver spoon as the cigarette smoldered on from the corner of his mouth. He sipped. Nodded once. Then took a seat at the head of the table without further comment. As he dragged on the cigarette, Meladze finally seemed to collect himself.

"Mr. President," Meladze began in Russian. "I do not know where to begin. I am *deeply* alarmed by—"

"The reports of unrecovered Soviet-era nuclear weapons?" Nikitin asked. "As am I. Hence my speedy response. We'll have the situation under control shortly."

Meladze's eyes widened. He jabbed a finger toward the window. "With *them*?"

It was an accusation as much as a question. Nikitin didn't respond. The colonel general, Golubev, and the FGS guard stared on in silence.

"As we previously agreed," Nikitin spoke slowly. "This security measure is for the safety of the entire region. Nothing may be left to chance."

Meladze's fingers tightened into a fist. He slammed it against the table. "There are twenty thousand Russian troops and heavy armor over that ridge. This is not what we agreed!"

Nobody spoke. Nikitin extinguished the cigarette in a waiting ashtray. He set the tea down and faced Meladze. But he didn't speak. The moment lingered closer to a minute as Meladze's wild eyes snapped from one person to the next, waiting for anyone to acknowledge his complaints.

Then Nikitin tilted his head toward Golubev, and the stone-faced man reached into his jacket. He produced a cell phone. He passed it to Meladze without comment.

Meladze took the device with a splutter, lips already parting in objection. Then he stopped. He faced the screen and the flush of his cheeks faded into ashen white. His mouth closed.

Nikitin broke the silence. "So you see, my friend, it is not what we agreed, but what the situation demands. Do you have any further questions?"

Meladze looked up from the phone. The outrage returned, but it was joined by fear now. He closed his mouth. Golubev stepped around the table and took the phone back, then he extended his hand toward the door. Meladze followed him with slumped shoulders, stopping only a moment next to Nikitin's chair. His lips pursed. His fingers clenched. He spoke through his teeth.

"This was your plan all along, wasn't it?"

Nikitin sipped his tea.

"Will you give me your word?" Meladze pressed. "Swear to me."

"They will live," Nikitin said simply.

Meladze's teeth clenched. His chin rose. Golubev took him by the arm and led him through the door and down the hallway. The door closed.

A single gunshot cracked, and a body crashed against the floor.

Nikitin finished the tea, enjoying the burn on his throat. Enjoying the juxtaposition of harsh, angry things contrasting a future so sweet he could already taste it.

Then he looked to the colonel general.

"Begin the operation."

2

Joint Base Andrews
Maryland

The Special Activity Center Gulfstream was unmarked, touching down on the darkened tarmac ten minutes before five a.m. and taxiing directly to one of the large metal hangars reserved for the use of the CIA. The engines died with a whine, and giant steel doors were rolled shut by Air Force ground personnel. Then those personnel departed, leaving the jet, a black Chevrolet Suburban with tinted windows, and an otherwise empty hangar alone in the predawn chill.

The rear doors of the Suburban popped open as soon as the room was clear, and three men piled out. All dressed in subdued dark clothes with handguns only semi-concealed beneath black jackets. Reed Montgomery shook a cigarette from a pack and lit up before passing it to the bigger man on his right—his longtime comrade in arms, right-hand man, and best friend. Rufus "Turk" Turkman.

Nobody offered Wolfgang a smoke. He never smoked. He was what Turk liked to call a "viceless gimp," a jab at Wolfgang's prosthetic leg, and a compliment at the same time.

As Reed approached the door of the plane, he signaled with two fingers to a shadowy figure behind the cockpit window. The figure disappeared, and a moment later the Gulfstream's door swung slowly open, deploying a set of steps.

Reed and Turk automatically shifted their jackets to the side, gripping Glock and SIG sidearms. Wolfgang held up a hand.

"Easy...he's not a threat."

"So he shouldn't mind a little precaution," Reed retorted, taking another step forward.

Two men appeared at the top of the steps, both dressed in all-black operator gear with sidearms on their hips. One advanced to the hangar floor and turned back.

Then the third figure appeared—a mountain of a man, all bulky muscles and thick limbs, walking with his head covered in a black bag and his wrists constrained by cuffs. He advanced down the steps with ease, breathing like a bear behind the hood. As soon as he reached the ground, his escort released him. Awkward silence filled the hangar. The CIA operators turned a question on Reed.

Reed tilted his head, and one of the black-suited men stepped forward to sweep the hood off with a rush, revealing a tangle of graying black hair and a heavy, scarred face with a thick nose and deep, black eyes.

And a sinister smile. Toothy and subdued, but impossible to ignore. The prisoner looked straight to Wolfgang and nodded once.

"Greetings, Amerikos."

"Ivan." Wolfgang returned the nod. "Welcome to America."

"Is this your man?" Ivan asked, turning to Reed. "He's shorter than I expected."

Reed ignored the comment, measuring the steady steel in Ivan's eyes. The depth of mystery, hostility, and potential alliance. A cocktail of confused intentions and a sincerity—or lack thereof—that was impossible to judge.

Ivan Sidorov had played at the outer edges of the Prosecution Force's activities for years now, usually by feeding intelligence through Wolfgang. It was the first time Reed and Ivan had ever met face-to-face, but the magnetic effect was impossible to ignore.

Not the pull of opposite poles drawing near to each other, but the hostile resistance of two matching poles being forced together. A reverse magnetic effect.

"You take it from here?" one of the men in black asked.

Reed nodded. "Put him in the truck."

Ivan lifted his hands, rattling the cuffs. He looked a question at Wolfgang, and Wolfgang opened his mouth. Reed cut him off.

"Cuffs stay on. So does the bag."

Ivan snorted. Wolfgang put a hand on Reed's arm. Reed ignored him, advancing to within a yard of Ivan and locking gazes with him. The big Russian stared right back, unmoved and unimpressed, a challenge radiating from his weathered face. A question.

Reed answered it in blunt monotone: "We don't know you yet."

The men in black loaded Ivan into the rear seat of the Suburban. Wolfgang and Turk took their places in the middle, turned sideways to monitor the prisoner. Reed rode shotgun, and the CIA driver whose name Reed had already forgotten shifted into gear.

The doors opened after a call to the Air Force personnel. Nobody approached or questioned the Suburban as it rumbled down the tarmac, through a series of gates, and out into the Maryland countryside.

They turned south, skirting DC and driving into northern Virginia. Not headed toward Langley but out into the countryside—the foothills of the Appalachian Mountains, where miles of farmland and forests were easily secluded from highway view by low ridgelines. The heavy motor of the Suburban handled the hills with ease, surging onward for the better part of an hour before eventually turning down a rough gravel road that wound between the trees. There were No Trespassing and Keep Out signs. One cattle gate, where the driver bailed out to unlock it with a key. Typical rural security measures, but nothing to indicate that the little house buried in the woods, two miles from the nearest neighbor, was anything other than a personal, private retreat.

Nothing to indicate that the property was, in fact, owned by the same myriad of shell corporations who laid claim to the Suburban and even the Gulfstream.

Nobody spoke on the drive. Turk kept his watchful eyes fixed on their prisoner, and Reed swept the passing streets for any indicator of interference. Even so close to the heart of governmental power, he could never be sure that a bad actor wouldn't spring out of the woodwork to wreak havoc on the mission at hand.

In some ways, maybe that fear was only reinforced by working so close to the heart of governmental power.

At last the Suburban ground to a stop. Reed peered through the darkness at the little house situated in a clearing barely large enough to hold it. Maybe forty feet wide and half as deep, with a porch, rocking chairs, and a little gravel driveway that disappeared around back. He could see a bumper, barely visible around the corner. Another black government vehicle, this one a sedan. In the trees he noted shadows that conflicted with the natural curves of nature.

Hard lines to mark the presence of men armed with assault rifles. More CIA personnel.

"You can take him on in," the driver said. "I wait here."

Reed departed the Suburban without comment, enjoying the relative cool of the Virginia air. It was a refreshing change after so many months of long, brutal summer heat. Fall was approaching, but the intensity of the previous season had yet to leave his taut muscles and sleepless mind.

It burned like a bonfire, raging on even when it seemed to have consumed everything. It still consumed more.

From the back doors, Turk and Wolfgang bailed out. A seat was lowered to allow Ivan to pass. The bulky Russian grunted and cursed as he banged his bagged head on the roof, eventually landing in the gravel. Heavy boots crunched, and he snorted.

"Can we dispense with the hood now? I'm quite sure I have no idea where I am."

"I think we'll leave the hood," Reed said. "It kind of suits you."

Wolfgang shot him a look, but Reed ignored it. They ascended the steps to the front porch and were admitted by yet another CIA officer. Unlike the black-clad operators outside, this man wore a simple business suit, and drank coffee from a mug.

The inside of the safe house was simple and clean. Faded furniture. A small kitchen and worn linoleum flooring. The guy with the coffee pointed down the hall.

"She's waiting."

Reed led the way. Wolfgang and Turk followed behind, guiding Ivan. Past a bathroom and a linen closet lay a pair of bedrooms. The largest sat to the right. It was nearly empty. Just a table in the middle with a laptop, a half dozen chairs, and one occupant. She rose as Reed entered—tall and slender, with dark hair held up in a bun. The woman greeted him with a nod and motioned to a single chair sat against one wall.

Wolfgang and Turk guided Ivan into it. He sat with a tired sigh. The woman stood with her arms folded, regarding him with puckered lips. Not saying anything. Reed poured himself a cup of coffee from the pot on the table and sipped it silently.

Then the woman nodded. Wolfgang tugged the bag off, revealing Ivan's large, ugly face. The Russian shook his head to clear hair out of his eyes, then looked quickly around the room.

His gaze settled on the woman, and the sinister smile returned to his lips.

"Do you know who I am?" the woman asked.

"Da." Ivan nodded. "Dr. Sarah Aimes...longtime deputy director of the CIA. Recently promoted, I believe."

"That's right," Aimes said, tugging a chair back from the table and taking a seat, still facing her prisoner. "And you are Ivan Sidorov, longtime Russian soldier, KGB agent, and then ranking SVR officer. Recently *retired*, I believe."

The smirk widened. "Only if attempted assassination is what you classify as *retirement*."

Aimes tapped her finger slowly against the tabletop, not blinking or breaking eye contact. Then she lifted a pen and adjusted a notepad. The pen clicked open.

"We've got a lot to discuss, Mr. Sidorov."

3

"All right, Carrie. You're up first."

Vice President Jordan Stratton spoke even as the doors to the cabinet room banged shut behind him. A long table stretching the length of the room was surrounded by secretaries and officials, military personnel and aides. A full cabinet meeting. Everybody rose to their feet as he entered, but Stratton waved them down and took his seat. He directed his attention to a screen at the end of the room, where the stiff face of Ambassador to the United Nations Tracy Carrie was framed by American and UN flags. She was conferencing in from New York City, in her office at United Nations Headquarters.

"Good morning, Mr. Acting President."

Stratton acknowledged the greeting with a grunt, clicking a pen open. He turned expectantly to the screen. Carrie dove in.

"The meetings this morning are progressing well. We're receiving unilateral support from our allies in Europe and Asia. Even the Chinese are demonstrating unusual levels of cooperation. My gut tells me they're still rocking on their heels and scrambling for an angle of exploitation. It won't last long."

"Everyone is rocking on their heels, Tracy," Stratton said. "Where are we with the resolution?"

It was the question he'd called Carrie into the meeting to answer. The question he'd deployed her to NYC to ask in the first place. How would the global community respond to the first-ever use of a nuclear weapon at the hands of a terrorist?

It happened eight days prior, but the ripple effects of shock and fear were still crashing against shores around the globe. Even as the radioactive fallout from the Panama Canal bomb settled over two different oceans and nearly a dozen Central and South American countries, the nuclear community remained on full alert. The United States, France, the United Kingdom, Pakistan and India, Russia and China. Israel and North Korea. The nine nations who formed the most exclusive and deadly club humanity had ever birthed—the nuclear club.

They were all asking the same two questions: Whose nuke had been used by the terrorist Abdel Ibrahim in the Panama Canal attack? And how would everyone else respond?

The emergency session of the United Nations Security Council was designed to calm those nerves and bring order to the chaos before a catastrophic situation became the first domino in a chain of world-ending calamity.

"What about Russia?" Stratton asked.

It was the name Carrie hadn't mentioned. Stratton watched the muscles in her face tense as she braced to answer it.

"The Russians are...very alarmed, sir. I might even say they are panicky. Moscow is calling for full international access to the bomb sight. They want to know the origins of the weapon."

"Or to hide the origins." It was General John Yellin, Chairman of the Joint Chiefs, who broke in with his old-man growl. "We all know the odds are better than one out of nine that the weapon in Panama was Russian made. The Soviets put weapons everywhere. Did they collect them all?"

Stratton held up a hand. "We don't know, General. And we won't until the investigation is complete. Let's hold the speculation." He pivoted back to Carrie. "Have you spoken with the Russian ambassador directly? What are they saying about troop movements?"

The movements in question had occupied most of Stratton's morning. Reports pouring in from CIA spy satellites of Russian armed forces concentrating in the southern Caucasus—as many as twenty thousand, plus armor. It was likely nothing more than one of President Makar Nikitin's bizarre and often meaningless military exercises. Flexing his muscles in front of the mirror—or in front of his neighbors.

But so close to a nuclear detonation in the Panama Canal, it made the Pentagon nervous. It made Stratton nervous. He'd already deployed significant naval assets to the Caribbean Sea to help contain the blast site and provide aid to those impacted by the fallout.

So many shifting chess pieces on a global game board crowded by panicking players was never a good idea.

"I've been unable to book a private meeting with the Russian ambassador, sir," Carrie said. "I was reluctant to broach the subject in an open security council session."

"Stay on him," Stratton said. "Whatever it takes. I want an open line of dialogue."

"Yes, sir. I'll keep you posted."

Carrie's screen transitioned into a field of blue marked by the White House logo. Stratton pivoted back to the table. General Yellin was already drawing breath, but Stratton knew what he had to say, and he didn't have time for it. Not yet.

Instead, he pivoted down the length of a table to a slender Latina woman in a maroon pant suit, black hair swept back into a ponytail. She was younger than many of the members of the Trousdale administration, only thirty-four. Carmen Silva was a graduate of Yale, and a first-time politician. Stratton had questioned his boss when President Maggie Trousdale nominated this woman for the position of secretary of the Treasury.

He didn't question any longer. Silva was as brilliant as she was effective, always cutting straight to the point. He needed that now.

"Where are we, Carmen?"

"Dow Jones is down another two hundred forty-eight points as of ten a.m. this morning, sir. That brings us to a cumulative drop of eleven hundred seventeen points over the week. Overseas shipping stands at sixty-two percent over pre-blast numbers and is projected to decrease. Fuel prices are already up forty-eight percent and projected to increase another ten by the end of the week. Bear market indicators—"

Stratton held up a hand. "Summary, Carmen."

The room went dead quiet. The secretary lowered her pen.

"We're headed into a recession, sir. A severe one. I can't predict total fallout any better than any talking head on cable news, but forty percent of total US container traffic passes through the Panama Canal annually. Or it did, anyway. Until last week. There's not a market anywhere in the world that won't feel the loss of the canal, but we'll take the biggest hit by far. We were already fighting market instability and economic trepidation following the terrorist attacks. We were right on the edge. There's no way this doesn't push us over."

It wasn't the answer anybody in the room wanted to hear, but it was the answer Stratton expected. He sat clicking his pen slowly open and closed, staring at a blank notepad. It was like a mirror of his ideas. Complete emptiness. His brain was so overworked and overwhelmed that Stratton didn't know where to begin. Where to start unraveling the mess.

Media outlets all displayed the carnage. Supermarket shelves were emptying as panicked Americans rushed to hoard essentials, expecting the collapse of global trade. Schools were shutting down as parents pulled their kids, and teachers failed to show up for work. Offices were sending their worker bees home. Cruise lines were canceling sailings, major music acts terminating tours.

The fear in the air was palpable, and it wasn't just the murder of former president William Brandt, or the attempted murder of current president Maggie Trousdale, or the chaos in North Korea, or the terrorist attacks in Tennessee and Baton Rouge, or even the nuclear blast in Panama that brought the world to a screeching halt.

It was all of those things. All together, all at once, pounding like a kick drum in America's skull. Stratton could hear the threads popping as the nation came apart at the seams. See it in the skyrocketing fuel prices and abandoned shopping malls. Americans were afraid to go to work. Afraid to go to school. Afraid to gather to worship or to watch a football game.

This delicate democratic experiment was crumbling, right before his eyes, and *he* was the man the world looked to for an answer.

All he had was a blank notepad.

"Mr. Acting President—"

General Yellin started in again. Stratton held up a hand, ordering silence. The room fell still. Everyone waited with bated breath, hoping to see a rabbit pop out of a hat. A miracle out of thin air.

Choose, Jordan. Make a call. Pick your battle.

"Mr. Acting President, we *must* confront the issue of national security." This time General Yellin didn't wait to be given permission. He just barged ahead.

Stratton's gaze snapped toward him.

"The Russians are still at full nuclear alert," Yellin continued. "They're massing troops in the Caucasus and won't say why. China is deploying their fleet into the South Pacific. Our allies in Europe are standing by for us to lead a coordinated response to stabilize the globe, but they won't wait much longer. We need a plan, sir."

A plan. No kidding.

Stratton pinched his lips together. Secretary of Defense Steven Kline filled the gap.

"General Yellin is right. Our first priority has to be national security. We need to coordinate with our allies. Deploy additional forces into the Caribbean Sea to protect the bomb site while we talk Russia and China off the cliff. It's got to be our first priority."

Priorities.

It was an oxymoron to Stratton. You couldn't have *priorities*, plural. Not really. The very definition of the word meant *most important*. Multiple things couldn't all be most important. Only one thing could be, and that was the big question.

What would he pick? What battle would he bend the energy of a nation against?

"Sir?"

It was Jillian Easterling, Maggie's chief of staff, and now Stratton's chief of staff. His right-hand woman. The linchpin of the entire organization. Stratton pivoted toward her and made his decision.

"We focus on domestic issues first. I want the economy stabilized and people back to work. If we have to put National Guardsmen on every street corner in America, we'll do it. We can't keep our heads above water if our own people won't even leave their homes."

Easterling nodded once, about as great a sign of approval as she ever gave. General Yellin was already prepping his next argument.

"Mr. Acting President—"

Stratton held up a hand. "Save it, General. I've heard you. Assemble the joint chiefs and formulate a strategy for domestic security. I want our forces and our attention focused *here*. Secure our own borders. Protect global trade. We'll worry about everything else as it comes."

Yellin and Kline exchanged a look. Then Kline stepped up to bat.

"With respect, sir, I think what the general is trying to say is that we can't simply ignore international security threats in favor of prioritizing domestic issues—"

"If we don't prioritize domestic stability, we may not have a country left to protect. Stick your head out a window, Mr. Secretary. This nation is falling apart. Society is unraveling. It's been one blow after another after another since President Brandt was killed, and in every case, President Trousdale has prioritized global security. Where has that left us?"

Dead silence. Stratton stood.

"There's your answer. I want every department to formulate strategies to stabilize the economy and ensure domestic security. No idea is a bad idea. Put your undersecretaries, your aides, your freaking interns on the job. I need briefings by the end of the week. That is all."

Stratton turned from the table, and Easterling slid right into gear to manage the meeting. As Stratton neared the door, FBI Director Bill Purcell rose from his chair and intercepted him.

"A word, Mr. Acting President?"

The two men stepped into the hallway, Stratton headed for his office. He needed a moment to think. He needed silence, however brief, to clear his head and formulate his own strategy.

"Make it fast, Mr. Director."

"I'd like to talk to you about Director O'Brien, sir."

A cold chill ran up Stratton's spine. He stopped in the hallway and pivoted, glancing both ways. Nobody else was around. The West Wing was strangely quiet with so many of its daily occupants gathered in the conference room.

"What about him?" Stratton said.

Purcell cleared his throat, shifting on his feet. He seemed uncomfortable. Then again, he always seemed a little on edge.

"I just wanted to notify you of our unfolding investigation, sir. Into Director O'Brien's death."

Victor O'Brien had been the last director of the CIA prior to the confirmation of Dr. Sarah Aimes. Stratton knew the man well. He had positioned himself as an adversary of the Trousdale administration, particularly President Trousdale herself. He was difficult, obstinate, and ineffective.

Maggie had fired him during the aftermath of the terrorist attacks in Tennessee and Baton Rouge. She'd replaced him with Aimes, and by every report, O'Brien hadn't taken the adjustment well. He'd fired back, threatening testimony before the senate intelligence committee regarding evidence of illegal action on the part of Maggie Trousdale.

Of course, by then Maggie was in a coma, her life hanging by a thread as complications from her attempted assassination months earlier finally caught up with her. And O'Brien?

He was found face down in his backyard swimming pool. Dead.

"Cut to the point, Mr. Director," Stratton said.

Purcell wiped sweat from his forehead. He kept his voice low.

"The medical examiner just completed his autopsy. It hasn't been released yet, but I had a look. O'Brien was hammered just prior to his death. There was nearly a full bottle of gin in his stomach. Blood alcohol level of point *four*."

Stratton remained impassive. "So the man was wasted. He was known to be a drinker. He had too many and he fell in his pool."

"Yes," Purcell said. "Maybe. But there were abrasions found in the back of his mouth. Marks that appear to have been left by the mouth of a liquor bottle, as though it were jammed in."

Stratton waited. Purcell said nothing.

Stratton cocked an eyebrow. "What's your point?"

"My point, sir, is that we're not so certain his death was an accident. We think it may have been an orchestrated hit."

The chill returned to Stratton's spine. His brain went numb, and he forced a snort.

"You've lost the forest for the trees, Bill. You're the director of the FBI, for goodness' sake. This is petty local cop nonsense."

Stratton started back down the hallway, moving more quickly this time. He called over his shoulder.

"You want to investigate something? Find out who sold Abdel Ibrahim a freaking *nuke*."

4

Virginia

The sun was arcing toward the western horizon while the interview in the little house in the woods ground on. With the group seated in chairs around the bedroom, Aimes asked most of the questions, and Ivan Sidorov did most of the talking. Reed, Wolfgang, and Turk just listened as Ivan recounted his background as a Soviet soldier in the Red Army, followed eventually by appointment to the KGB, and then, when the Iron Curtain fell, an eventual transition into the SVR. The evolution of the KGB.

Ivan was one of its finest agents—or so he unabashedly claimed. He was a senior officer and quickly rose into a directorate role. He managed covert intelligence operations on behalf of Moscow all around the world, which was eventually how he met Wolfgang, in a bathroom in Paris. The meeting hadn't gone well. Wolfgang broke Ivan's nose.

Somehow the two became begrudging allies.

The story zigged and zagged a lot, sometimes trailing off into extraneous detail, but eventually it came to the meat of the matter. How Ivan had uncovered a connection between Moscow and a man named Fedor Volkov, an elite Russian sniper who took a shot at President Trousdale. That singular event set off a domino chain of investigations for Ivan, all orbiting around the Kremlin's association with a disgraced Russian oligarch and that oligarch's routine involvement in compromising the stability of the United States.

First with the attempted assassination of Maggie Trousdale. Then with a power play in Venezuela. The trail went dead there, but it was already too late for Ivan. His investigations had been discovered and his security compromised. Russian officials tried to kill him as he fled Moscow. Ivan eventually landed in eastern Europe, where he partnered with Wolfgang to continue his pursuit of the truth.

What exactly was the Kremlin up to?

At least...that was his story. He'd fed Reed Montgomery's Prosecution Force intelligence that helped them sabotage two-thirds of Abdel Ibrahim's planned chemical weapons attacks in the United States, and eventually led them to pin him down in the English Channel Tunnel. It was after the nuclear blast detonated over the Panama Canal that Ivan made the decision to finally commit the ultimate betrayal of his homeland. To turn himself over to Russia's greatest rival, and consort directly with the Americans.

Aimes made copious notes at first, fingers rattling over the keys of her laptop while Wolfgang grunted corroboration of Ivan's story whenever he was involved in it. Reed just listened, arms crossed, leaned against the wall, waiting for the bottom line. Whatever it might be.

"To be clear, Mr. Sidorov, you are here in the United States of your own volition, in no way prompted by your government?"

It was a stupid question at face value, but Reed guessed that Aimes was more interested in *how* Ivan answered it than what he actually said. The Russian smiled.

"If my government had sent me here, Madam Director, I would not be implicating them, would I?"

Aimes said nothing for a long while, just staring. Evaluating Ivan. Thinking three or four moves ahead, Reed guessed. Trying to play chess with a man who was clearly a master at the game.

"Take me back to the attempted assassination," Aimes said. "Clarify the connection. You're saying that the *Kremlin* was directly responsible for the attempt?"

A derisive snort. "Of course not. They wouldn't be so stupid. What I am saying is that Fedor Volkov was a weapon of the oligarchs. A problem solver. I'm saying that he worked at the behest of a certain disgraced oligarch whom President Nikitin banished from Russia. And I'm saying that the Kremlin was in direct contact with that certain oligarch at the time of your president's attempted assassination."

"So, in effect, the Kremlin was behind it."

"You will never prove it."

"Okay. Moving on to the terrorist Abdel Ibrahim. A Ukrainian arms dealer sold Ibrahim the land mines he used in Tennessee and the chemical weapon he used in Baton Rouge."

"Both of Soviet origin," Ivan clarified.

"And you found that arms dealer," Aimes pressed.

"We," Wolfgang said. "We found him. I was with Ivan."

"And you killed him," Aimes continued.

"I killed him," Ivan said. "But not before I confirmed details of the sale. From there, Wolfgang and I parted ways. I continued my investigation in Europe. I connected with some old associates. They provided clues that I followed into Georgia...That's the one with mountains, not peaches."

"I know where Georgia is," Aimes retorted.

"In Georgia I found an old Soviet military depot. The place where this Ukrainian arms dealer was said to have found the chemical weapons he sold to Ibrahim."

Ivan broke down the details of his investigatory trip to Georgia, describing an underground warehouse once used by the Red Army to store munitions for a third world war that never came. Artillery shells, small arms, and chemical weapons.

Reed had heard the story before. He fought to stay awake as Ivan droned on, ignoring the ache of overworked muscles and the incessant pound of a headache that never ceased. It had been eight days since his mad motorcycle ride into the English Channel Tunnel, the ride that had finally brought him face-to-face with Abdel Ibrahim. The man responsible for his wife's near death.

For his unborn child's brutal death.

The encounter was everything anyone could have expected. Reed killed

Ibrahim with his bare hands. He choked the life away, fingers coated in blood, vision narrowing with maddened rage. He didn't hesitate. He didn't regret.

He didn't...feel anything at all. He'd been numb ever since, as though his body was awake but his soul was unconscious. He couldn't feel any emotion. Not elation, not satisfaction, not the sweet taste of vengeance. Not even loss or pain.

He was dead inside.

"Mr. Sidorov, to clarify, you're saying that the chemical weapons used in the Baton Rouge attack were forgotten relics of the Soviet era?"

"No. I'm saying that this will be Moscow's position. This is what they will claim."

"But?"

Ivan narrowed his eyes. Arms folded, he looked to Wolfgang. Reed caught the exchange, the gentle nod of reassurance that Wolfgang offered. It did little to assuage the guardedness in Ivan's gaze as the battered old Russian turned back to Aimes.

"I have spent most of my life playing this cat-and-mouse game with America," Ivan said. "Hunting you. Spying on you. Watching your every move and working to outsmart it. Intelligence and counterintelligence, no? The dance of two superpowers locked in an icy embrace, one breath away from blowing each other into oblivion."

Ivan shook his head, eyes sad. He sucked his teeth. "I trust you, Dr. Aimes, about as much as you trust me. Which is to say, not at all. There are a million places I could enjoy my *retirement*, as you say, and none of them are anywhere near your country."

Aimes waited, hands folded on the table, unblinking. Nobody else in the room move or spoke.

They could all feel the punchline coming. Ivan leaned forward to deliver it.

"There is only one reason why I am here. It is because, at this very moment, the balance of global security is under threat of demolition at the hands of a single man. A ruthless, brutal, conniving fiend who has taken control of his country and will next take control of the world. A man without morals. Without decency. Without any fear of consequences or collateral damage. A man who is unwilling to dance any longer."

"Who?" Aimes said.

Ivan laughed. "Oh, you know, Dr. Aimes. You know."

"I'd prefer you to say it. For the record."

Ivan looked to Wolfgang again. Another reassuring nod. He turned back.

"Makar Nikitin has ascended to power in Russia with a singular purpose. It is his obsessive ambition to restore the glory of the Soviet Union in its golden years and to pursue those objectives which Soviet leaders were too weak to realize. In summary, global domination. It is his obsession. His one true aim. He will do whatever is necessary to make this dream a reality."

Reed noted a vein in Aimes's temple twitch. She remained perfectly calm as she spoke her next question.

"That's a monumental accusation, Mr. Sidorov. What proof can you offer?"

"How about a nuclear device detonated over the Panama Canal? Ostensibly in the name of radical Islamic terror but supplied to the terrorist by Russian authorities for the purpose of fracturing the American economy. Just as the attempted assassination of your president was meant to fracture your government, and the terror attacks in Tennessee and Baton Rouge were meant to fracture your society. The money, the leadership, the people. Three cornerstones that no nation, no matter how powerful, can survive without. A knockout punch, as you may say."

Reed's heart accelerated, a twinge of adrenaline rushing into his blood that finally drove back the exhaustion that clouded over him. He leaned away from the wall, interjecting himself into the conversation for the first time.

"What the hell are you talking about?"

Ivan turned to Reed. He nodded slowly.

"I'm talking about the end of the world, Prosecutor. And it's already begun."

5

James O'Dell stood in the built-in conference room adjacent to the private, presidential medical suite where the most powerful woman in the free world lay fighting for her life.

He'd stood next to Maggie Trousdale when the assassin's bullet raced between Chicago high-rises and ripped through her gut like an artillery shell. He'd rushed to her side as the blood pooled, and remained at her side as the Secret Service evacuated the president to a nearby hospital. He'd held her hand as she fought for her life, barely surviving surgery and struggling through weeks of agonizing recovery. He'd served her every need. Remained faithfully at her back, fending off White House aides and vulturous reporters who quickly branded her with the nickname "Lame Duck Maggie."

James O'Dell had pressed ahead sleepless and exhausted for his president. He abandoned time with his estranged daughter to remain at Maggie's side. He discarded his personal life and surrendered his very existence to lift this woman, this beacon of hope standing against a dark horizon, this swamp girl from Louisiana, out of the depths and back onto the pedestal where she belonged.

It shouldn't have surprised him when that dynamic of relentless devotion evolved into something more passionate. Something more intimate. He'd spent most of the last four years of his life so close to Maggie's side that he had memorized the smell of her perfume, working first as her bodyguard in Baton Rouge during her tenure of governor of Louisiana, then advancing to Washington when she ascended to the vice presidency.

And then the highest political office in the land—the Oval Office itself. James O'Dell served as a pseudo bodyguard, and when the truth finally spilled out and passion overtook them both, he hadn't resisted. Why should he?

Maggie needed him. He needed Maggie. It was as simple as that. But now this woman he needed, this woman he had devoted his very existence to protecting at any cost, was lying in a medically induced coma, fighting for her next breath. She'd recovered from the gunshot wound to the stomach, at least initially. But the regeneration of her shattered liver had stalled.

It was the stress, he knew. The pressure of the office. The turmoil of one domestic emergency and international catastrophe after another. They were enemies he couldn't protect her from.

Grenades he couldn't land on.

O'Dell's eyes burned as he dumped creamer into an oversized cup of coffee and stirred it with a silver spoon branded with the presidential logo. Everything in this place was branded as such. The suite was an extension of the White House. A private residence for the president and their family while undergoing medical care.

None of Maggie's family was here, however. O'Dell had made sure of that. He didn't want any stress or any noise anywhere in the building. Maggie needed perfect calm. He was her only visitor.

The door behind him swung open with a gentle groan, and soft footsteps landed on the carpet. O'Dell looked over his shoulder to see a tall, slender woman with short black hair step in. Dr. Cara Fletcher wore a white medical coat and carried an iPad, nodding once to him as she advanced to a seat at the conference table.

"Good afternoon, Mr. O'Dell. I hope you're well."

It was an empty comment that O'Dell felt no pressure to acknowledge. He took his seat next to Fletcher and sipped coffee. It was cold and tasted burnt. He drank anyway, hoping for a jolt from the caffeine.

He hadn't slept in nearly twenty-four hours. He'd been up all night, researching. Making phone calls. Digging.

Looking for that miracle that could save Maggie.

"I'll cut straight to the point, Mr. O'Dell," Fletcher said. "The president's liver has failed to regenerate and is actively failing. We've got her on a hepatic support system—a device to filter her blood in place of her liver— but it's a stopgap only. Not a solution. Without a transplant, she will die."

O'Dell didn't so much as blink. The words landed in his soul like bombs, blasting through his chest and turning his organs to mush. He felt as though he were on fire, burning from the inside out. He couldn't breathe.

He couldn't believe what he was hearing.

"Mr. O'Dell? Do you understand what I'm telling you?"

O'Dell swallowed hard. He blinked to clear his mind. Then he spoke the first logical thing that came to mind.

"Take mine."

"I'm sorry?" Fletcher squinted.

"Take my liver. I'm ready to go into an operating room now. I'll sign whatever."

"Mr. O'Dell...that's not how this works."

"Why not? I have a liver, she needs a liver."

"But you're *alive*. You won't be without a liver."

"Okay. So I'll eat a bullet. Just let me sign the paperwork first."

Fletcher gazed on in disbelief, then slouched back in her chair and removed her glasses. She folded them and placed them into her jacket pocket. Very slowly, breathing deep along the way.

"Mr. O'Dell, the process for procuring a suitable liver is extensive and complex. It involves a donor list and an allocation system administered by the United Network for Organ Sharing. Priority is given to patients based on medical need, time on waiting list, and compatibility of available organs. Currently, the president ranks third on the list."

"*Third?*" O'Dell's palm landed on the table. "She's the president of the United States!"

"Office, position, title, and last name are not factors in the allocation process, Mr. O'Dell. It's objective. As fair as possible."

"Fair? Are you serious? Doctor, if an alcoholic with a fried liver dies because his president is prioritized, that's not an issue of fairness. That's an issue of national security."

Fletcher folded her arms. "I don't make the rules, Mr. O'Dell. I comply with them. Availability of donor livers is an unpredictable thing. We may have none for a month, or five tomorrow. In the meantime, it's my job to keep the president alive as long as possible. That's what I'm doing. Please update the White House accordingly."

O'Dell clenched his teeth. Cajun blood boiled just beneath the surface of his dark skin, and he suddenly wanted to throttle the doctor. Pin her against the wall, put his fingers around her neck, and squeeze.

Demand the right answer. No matter the consequences.

O'Dell's vision blurred and he blinked to clear it. He saw Fletcher staring at him, confusion and concern clouding her exhausted eyes. He saw the lines in her face, the sag in her shoulders. The wrinkles in her lab coat.

She was just as exhausted as he was. Maybe more so. What was he thinking? What was wrong with him?

O'Dell stood abruptly, shoving the chair back. He drained the cold coffee and crumpled the paper cup. It fell into a trash can on his way to the door.

Dr. Fletcher called after him. "Mr. O'Dell?"

O'Dell looked back. The doctor was still seated.

"You have no medical background. No medical education or expertise."

"So?"

"So I find it peculiar that the White House would assign you as official liaison for the president's developing medical condition."

O'Dell waited for Fletcher to continue. She didn't. She didn't break eye contact, either.

"Is there a question in that statement, Doctor?"

"No. No question. Just a professional observation."

O'Dell turned back to the door. "Worry about your own expertise, Doctor. Keep the president alive. Whatever it takes."

6

Music Row
Nashville, Tennessee

"Are you...are you serious?"

Banks gazed at the document spread out in front of her across a polished cherrywood table and still couldn't comprehend the figure written at the bottom. A numeric figure, accompanied by a dollar sign.

Seven bold digits long.

The slick-haired dude bruh wearing a suit jacket and a pressed white shirt, unbuttoned at the collar, leaned back in the chair across from her and smiled. It was a flashy smile, as though he were posing for a billboard. All high wattage and somehow *too* white.

"Serious as a heart attack, Banks. You've got crazy talent, and we want to be the label that brings that talent to the big stage. We're willing to put our money where our mouth is."

Banks looked back at the page, still dazed. Still unable to completely comprehend. She understood the numeric value, but she couldn't wrap her mind around what it *meant*.

A dream. More than a dream. The twenty-six-page document spread out before her represented the hopes and longings of every waitress and barista in Nashville. That elusive, seductive, impossible goddess of *making it*. Becoming a signed music star with a fat contract, a recording deal, a tour schedule.

She had dreamed of this moment since she was a child. Since before she left a wealthy—if broken—family behind and moved to the big city to chase that fantasy for herself. Now it was finally here. And she couldn't accept that.

"It's..." She stopped.

"It's a lot of money," the dude bruh said, still grinning. "It's life-changing money. And you deserve it."

Banks's vision blurred. Her shoulder slumped, and she fought back the tears. The dude bruh's smile faded, and the seat next to Banks groaned as Jim Massilo, Banks's agent, leaned in to put a hand on her shoulder. He squeezed gently.

"Banks. What's wrong?"

Suddenly the room felt very hot. Banks pushed herself out of the chair. "Can I have a minute, please?"

She didn't wait for an answer. She turned for the door and barreled into the hallway. It was practically deserted this late on a Friday. From the floor-to-ceiling window at the end, she overlooked the Nashville skyline, the twin spires of the bat building glimmering in the sunset.

It was beautiful. Stunning. A view she never got tired of. But even in the context of the insane offer waiting for her on the table in the room behind her, it all felt somehow very stale. Empty.

Missing something.

She pulled the phone out of her pocket and tabbed to the text message menu. There were updates from the babysitter—a Belmont student who also dreamed of singer/songwriter stardom—confirming that her two-year-old son, Davy, had finished dinner and was playing games. Banks's mother, Sharon, had also texted asking for updates. So had one of her new friends she'd met at a coffee shop the previous spring.

But there were no texts from the number she cared most about. No missed calls or voicemails. No updates at all. Reed had ghosted his wife almost completely. She didn't even know where he was.

Someplace in east Tennessee, drinking beers with his best friend, Turk?

Already overseas again, getting shot at and returning fire? Sunbathing on a beach alongside a bikini-clad goddess of a different sort? Some woman who hadn't been nearly blown in two by a terrorist's bomb. Who hadn't lost their unborn child. Who wasn't a broken fragment of her former self.

Banks's face fell into one trembling hand and she fought back the tears. Reed had come home for only one night after his mission in London. Then he'd disappeared. Just loaded himself into the battered '69 Camaro his father had left him and driven off. He knew about her upcoming meeting with the record label. He knew that at any moment, she might land a deal. He had no idea—neither of them had any idea—that it would be this big.

But why should that matter? Shouldn't he be here, right at her side, to cheer her on? Her husband. The father of the child who *hadn't* been slaughtered. The only man she'd ever loved.

A door creaked open behind her, and soft footsteps thumped across the carpet. Banks knew who it was even before Jim Massilo reached her side. He put a gentle hand on her shoulder, and Banks quickly thumbed the tears away.

"You all right?"

Jim's voice was calm. Not at all pushy. Not at all desperate. Thirteen percent of the seven-figure contract waiting on that desk belonged to him, after all. Maybe he had a right to be freaking out.

"I'm sorry," Banks said. "Tough week."

"Reed?"

Banks looked up quickly, caught off guard.

Jim offered a sheepish smile. "Sorry...I overheard you on the phone with your mother. Didn't mean to eavesdrop."

Banks rewound her memories to what phone call Jim could have been thinking of, but in truth, it didn't matter. Sharon called a lot. Banks had learned to tolerate it. With Reed out of town, who else was there to talk to?

"He works for the government," Banks said. "He's gone a lot. It's just...it's messy sometimes."

Jim pocketed his hands, nodding with understanding. He suddenly looked a little awkward, and embarrassment twisted Banks's gut.

"I'm sorry. I'm a mess. This is so ridiculous."

"No...not at all. It's a big moment. You should take your time."

It wasn't the answer Banks expected. She dug into her purse for a compact. One look into the mirror and the embarrassment erupted into an absolute tidal wave.

"Oh my gosh. I look terrible. I'm so sorry."

She went to work fussing with her hair. Jim put a hand on her arm again, giving her a soft squeeze. When she looked up, his smile had returned, as soft as before.

He had kind eyes. Deep and brown, not at all overbearing. It relaxed her, a little.

"Look. Why don't you step into the ladies' room and freshen up? You'll feel better. Then we can duck back into the conference room and put some ink on this thing. Okay? Make you a millionaire. That's got to feel good."

Banks indulged in a bashful smile. "Yeah...when you say it that way."

Jim winked. He turned back for the conference room, calling over his shoulder. "There's a new place in the Gulch. Some fancy, exclusive bar. Drinks on me tonight...I won't take no for an answer."

7

A wife and two beautiful twin daughters waited for Stratton at the Naval Observatory, the official residence of the vice president, but he didn't want to see them. It wasn't that he didn't miss his daughters—he wouldn't even pretend that he missed his crazed, nerve-addled wife. He would give his left arm for a weekend away at some beach in Mexico, nothing but strong drinks, stronger Cuban cigars, and empty hours to play volleyball with Louise and Lindy while Carolyn Presley Stratton drank herself into a coma. It was the transcript from two summers previous, back when Stratton was *Senator* Stratton, not Vice President Stratton, let alone Acting President Stratton.

All that felt like an empty, distant memory now. He couldn't remember the last time he even held a conversation with either of his daughters. Mercifully, he couldn't remember a conversation with Carolyn, either. It wasn't exactly his wife's fault that she was a basket case, perpetually cycling through therapy, doped out of her mind, and incapable of an intelligent conversation. He'd married her for her family name, not her powers of intellect.

Despite the doors into political stardom that decision had opened, it sometimes felt like the dumbest thing he'd ever done. At least he had the girls, for what precious time he spent with them. There wouldn't be any books read or movies shared tonight. He'd departed the White House under the pretense of spending much-needed quality time with the family, but in truth he was headed straight to his study. Straight to his humidor and his bourbon cabinet. Straight to the problems at hand that threatened to drag America into the abyss.

He needed quiet time to unravel them. Insulation from the West Wing and all the strings that tugged on his attention there. He needed a moment to gather himself, to recover his strength.

To make *some* sort of plan.

Slouched in the back of his vice-presidential limousine, struggling to remain awake and so mentally exhausted he could barely remember his middle name, Stratton had no idea what that plan would be. He only knew that he couldn't return to the White House empty-handed. Americans needed reassurance. They needed leadership.

They needed hope.

The built-in, secure telephone rang from the console next to him, and Stratton almost ignored it. It was almost certainly Easterling, calling with questions or updates that Stratton lacked the mental bandwidth to address. But he answered anyway, because he'd asked not to be called unless it was important. This was the job.

"Yes?"

"Mr. Vice President, it's O'Dell."

Stratton recognized the Cajun drawl of Maggie Trousdale's longtime bodyguard and—most recently—covert lover long before he identified himself. It wasn't just the accent, it was the approach. O'Dell was direct, almost abrupt. He never called Stratton *acting* president, only *vice* president. He never wasted time with pleasantries.

None of that bothered Stratton. He appreciated James O'Dell for what he was—a tool. A blunt instrument. Maybe that was all the former bodyguard was to Maggie also.

"What's the update?" Stratton matched O'Dell's directness.

"Doctor Fletcher says the president's liver has failed. They've got her on some kind of filter to keep her blood clean. It's temporary."

O'Dell's voice wavered, and Stratton sat up. He shifted the phone against his ear. "What's the prognosis?"

"She needs a transplant. ASAP. I offered mine but—"

"Don't be absurd, O'Dell."

Stratton's voice rang a little sharper than he intended. His mind spun as he assimilated the implications of O'Dell's update and raced to the logical conclusion. There was a donor list, he knew. He'd already been updated on that process as part of his transitionary briefing, a default protocol put into place the moment Maggie collapsed at the end of a table.

Per the twenty-fifth amendment of the United States Constitution, Jordan Stratton was now effectively the president of the United States—the *acting* president, the Constitution called it. But an acting president held all the same powers and responsibilities of an elected president. The post would be temporary, of course, assuming Maggie recovered. Assuming her liver was able to regenerate or she received a transplant. Now the first of those two options was off the table. She would need the transplant. That brought him one giant step closer to maintaining this office for the duration of her elected term.

"Have you spoken to Secretary Whitmore?"

"I just got off the phone with her," O'Dell said. "The Department of Health and Human Services collaborates with the United Network for Organ Sharing, but they don't manage it. They have no direct authority over it."

"Meaning?"

"They say..." O'Dell swallowed audibly. "They say they can't do anything about the list. The president is currently third in line. It's just a matter of supply."

Stratton ran a hand over his face and felt two days of razor stubble. He'd forgotten to shave. He couldn't remember his last shower.

"Keep me updated," he said simply.

"Yes, sir."

"O'Dell?" Stratton caught him before he could hang up.

"Sir?"

"I had a conversation with FBI Director Purcell today," Stratton said slowly. "He asked about O'Brien."

A long pause. Both men knew it was a secure line. Neither man wanted to test that guarantee.

"I need to know that we're airtight," Stratton finally said.

"Completely." This time there was no hesitation in O'Dell's voice. Stratton nodded slowly, trying to decide if he believed O'Dell.

At this stage, he didn't think he had a choice.

"Keep me updated," he said again. Then he hung up.

8

Virginia

The CIA liked Marriotts. It was a lesson that became clear to Reed sometime around his fifth government-sponsored stay in one. The property in Leesburg was one of Marriott's smaller brands, but the room was clean. The bar served Jack Daniels. That was really all Reed cared about.

Seated out by the pool with an early fall breeze whispering out of the mountains, Reed held a cigarette in one hand and a plastic cup full of Jack in the other. He'd bribed the hotel bartender into filling it all the way to the top, but already the cup was half-empty. There was a dull burn in the back of Reed's skull that felt a little like consciousness, if he pretended, but in truth he was so completely vacant inside that he wasn't even sure if he was actually awake.

The only way to know for sure was to close his eyes, and Reed wouldn't do that, not unless he absolutely had to. The dreams were always there, ready to flood in and consume his very soul. Pictures of Abdel Ibrahim. Pictures of the bomb blast. The blood on the stage and Banks splayed out with shrapnel ripping through her guts.

Pictures of their unborn daughter, reaching out for Reed. Eyes pleading. Face consumed by flames and agony. The harder Reed fought to displace the images, the sharper they became. Denying their existence only increased their frequency. He could no longer sleep without seeing them on replay, like a cinema.

A cinema from hell.

The hotel's back door groaned open next to him, and Turk stepped out with a satisfied grunt. Reed didn't even look up.

"Been looking for you," Turk said, settling into the chair next to him with a sigh. "Got a smoke?"

Reed handed him the pack without comment. Turk shook one out and lit up. He inhaled with greedy energy and exhaled with a delighted sigh.

"Yeah. That's good. You know that's my first smoke in nearly a month? Sinju's gonna kill me."

The words reached Reed but he barely heard them. He thumped ash off his cigarette and stared at the translucent blue surface of the pool. It was so clear that it barely reflected the hotel lights, but what dancing images played across the surface looked like fire.

Like a bomb blast.

"I got a call from Aimes," Turk said. "She said she couldn't reach you. They're gonna keep Ivan at a safe house a few more days. They want to mine him for data on Nikitin...whatever he knows. She said we're good to head home."

Reed nodded once, accepting the message. He'd expected it. After Ivan's bombshell declaration that Nikitin was ready to instigate the next world war, Aimes's stress level had visibly shot through the roof. She'd asked a lot more questions. She'd taken a lot more notes. She'd stepped out to make calls, already working through the complex machinations of the CIA's intelligence verification apparatus.

Reed didn't care about any of that. He didn't even care about the nuclear weapon detonated in Central America or who had supplied it. Only one aspect of Ivan's testimony was relevant for him—that possible link between Abdel Ibrahim and Makar Nikitin. Because if Nikitin had provided the nuke for Panama, then he had provided the chemical weapons for Baton Rouge. And if he'd provided those, he had provided the land mines used in Tennessee.

And that made him culpable for the death of Reed's unborn daughter.

That made him a dead man walking—a reality that saturated Reed's mind and stained his consciousness just like Ibrahim's spilled blood had stained his hands.

It was rage so hot that he no longer felt it. Focus so strained that it turned all else into white noise.

"Reed?"

Turk's voice broke through the fog in Reed's brain, and he pivoted slowly toward him. He squinted. Turk had the look of a man who had repeated a question and was now concerned by the lack of a response. Reed registered no guilt for that.

"Are you okay?"

Am I okay.

Reed lifted the cup to his lips and swallowed Jack. It didn't taste good. It didn't taste like anything at all, but he felt a little heat when it landed in his stomach.

Heat, like the flash of fire on his face the moment the blast went off. The moment Banks was blown to the stage.

The moment April...

"I'm fine," Reed muttered.

"We should go home," Turk said. "I'll call Corbyn and have her pick us up in the morning. I need to get back to Sinju. Check up on Liberty."

Reed made no response, placing the cigarette between his lips and dragging. He tasted nothing, and then he realized that was because the cigarette had gone out. He stared at the tip and fought with his muddy mind to connect the next link in a chain of practiced events.

Did he relight it? Throw it away?

"Reed."

Reed's gaze snapped toward Turk, sudden and illogical levels of adrenaline rushing his system. He sat bolt upright.

"What?" he snapped.

Turk put a hand on his arm. "Let's get some rest. You know Corbyn will land early. Have you called Banks?"

Banks.

Reed hadn't called her. Not in a few days. He'd seen her messages and bumped her calls or simply ignored them. He wasn't entirely sure why.

He'd flown to Maryland without telling her where he was going—or even that he was going at all.

He didn't want to talk. He didn't want to answer her probing questions. Questions about why he had suddenly become so silent. About why he wouldn't touch her. Wouldn't talk to her. Wouldn't open up.

"Sinju said she had a meeting today," Turk said. "Some record label? Sinju said it was big. You should call her."

Reed thought he remembered something about a record deal. Banks's small-time singer/songwriter career had taken an unexpected turn after Ibrahim's land mine bomb. She'd become famous. Her tracks were streamed a few million times.

All the Nashville labels wanted a slice of the action. Banks was excited. But all Reed could think of when she discussed the future was the moment that had made that future possible.

The moment...and the brutal, inescapable *failure* that marked it. His own failure.

"Worry about your own wife," Reed snapped. "I don't need to be told when to make a phone call."

Turk withdrew his hand, eyes narrowing. He flicked ash from the end of the cigarette, then took a long drag. He stood and flipped the smoke into an ashtray, breathing between his teeth. He turned back to Reed.

"Look. I don't know what's happening with you. I don't pretend to understand. I want to help. But if you're not going to talk to me, I'm still gonna talk to you. That's what brothers do. And what you need to hear right now is that you have a *family*. You understand me? You have a wife and a son. And they need you. So suck it up, rub some dirt on it, and get your act together."

Turk's voice was low and stern, but not angry. Reed eyeballed him, unsure what to say. Hearing the words but not really registering them. Turk's shoulders dropped an inch.

"I'm here, Reed. I'm always here."

Reed stood slowly, carrying the dead smoke and the empty cup with him. He advanced until he stood toe-to-toe with the bigger man—his long-time battle buddy. The only friend he'd ever really had.

He stared into Turk's eyes and tried to feel something. Tried to connect with the pain he saw reflected there.

It all rang hollow. Reed felt nothing at all. He only felt the buzz he'd fought all night long to build slipping gradually away.

Without a word, he turned back into the hotel and headed for the bar.

9

The Naval Observatory
Washington, DC

The phone woke Stratton sometime just after one a.m. A loud shrilling ring that cut through the room and jarred him out of a sleep he didn't even realize he'd fallen into. He sat bolt upright in his office chair, choking on saliva as he fought to clear his vision.

The vice-presidential office on the second floor of the residence building was crowded with bookshelves and overwhelmed by paperwork. Stratton sat behind a sprawling mahogany desk, a computer shoved to one side, an open bottle of Pappy Van Winkle Family Reserve resting next to it.

The glass was missing. He found it on the floor next to a puddle. When he looked into his right hand, he found a half burnt Cuban cigar, now extinguished. He could still taste the flavor, sour on his breath. He swallowed, and the phone rang again, somehow sounding louder this time.

Stratton grabbed the bourbon bottle and took a long pull, swishing it like mouthwash. Like five-thousand-dollar mouthwash. Then he swallowed and lifted the receiver. The burn in his throat helped to drive the last of the fog from his brain.

"What?"

"Sir, it's Easterling. Are you near a computer?"

Straight to the point, just like James O'Dell. Stratton had noticed that it was a hallmark of the people Maggie surrounded herself with.

"Right in front of me. What is it?"

"I'm sending you an email. I need you to follow the link and watch the video. It's easier than me explaining."

Stratton rubbed his eyes and put the phone on speaker. He unlocked his laptop and navigated to his secure email server. Easterling's note had just arrived. She'd called him immediately after sending it.

That couldn't be good.

Tabbing open the message, he clicked the link. The internet connection at the Observatory was lightning fast, and a video loaded almost instantly. The thumbnail displayed a red carpet, a wood podium, and a backdrop of matching flags.

Russian flags. The title below the video read: "Executive Announcement from Russian President Makar Nikitin on the Panama Canal Bomb."

"What's this?"

"Press conference from President Nikitin. Twenty-five minutes old."

"About what?"

"You should watch it, sir."

Stratton mashed play and bumped up the volume. He recognized Nikitin instantly as the Russian president took his place behind the podium, dressed in an impressive black suit that clung close to his muscled frame. Smooth, dark hair accentuated with gray. A stern face.

Nikitin tapped the mic once before beginning his address. He spoke in Russian, but an English translator kept pace easily, overpowering his voice.

"Ladies and gentlemen, thank you for meeting me this morning. I have called this emergency press conference to announce to the world that Russia's efforts to assist the international community in the search for those responsible in the Panama Canal nuclear attack have reached a critical breakthrough. In cooperation with authorities of the Republic of Georgia, the source of the weapon used in Panama has been determined...to be Soviet in origin."

The metaphorical bomb fell from Nikitin's lips after a short pause, and it detonated in Stratton's chest like a lightning strike. He leaned toward the computer, breathing a curse as the crowd of reporters gathered around Nikitin's podium murmured exclamations. Cameras flashed. Nikitin held up a palm.

"Please. Allow me to continue. As I have stated, Russian investigators have made this determination in cooperation with authorities from Georgia. This is because the source of the bomb has been traced to a deactivated Soviet-era weapons depot outside of Tbilisi. It is not known how this weapon was neglected for collection by the Georgian government or how it was found by the terrorist Abdel Ibrahim. However, to proactively prevent possible further dissemination of abandoned Soviet weapons and to ensure the security of the region, Russia is taking immediate steps to take control of the site. As I speak, detachments of the Russian Armed Forces are deploying alongside the Defense Forces of Georgia to lock down this weapons depot and prevent any further spread of possible weapons of mass destruction. We will notify the public as we have updates. Thank you."

Nikitin ducked his head. A storm of questions erupted from the reporters gathered around. He ignored them all as he stepped off stage. Then the video ended.

Stratton snatched the phone back up, flipping speaker mode off. Easterling was waiting.

"This is twenty minutes old?"

"Half an hour now."

"And Russian military action?"

"I just received an update from the Pentagon. Russian armed forces and armor are rolling across the Georgian border as we speak, headed for Tbilisi. Georgian Defense Forces are showing no signs of resistance."

"How many?" Stratton pressed. It was the critical question.

"We're still gathering intel. But at first glance...at least twenty thousand."

Twenty thousand. A far stronger force than any military needed to secure a forgotten weapons depot. The implication was crystal clear.

Stratton stood, carrying the phone with him. He reached for his coat.

"Call an emergency cabinet meeting. Anybody who can make it. We'll gather in the Situation Room. I'm on my way."

10

Virginia

Turk's fist landed on Reed's hotel room door with a booming thud—not a repeated knock, just that same trademark bump that had wakened Reed in the middle of more dream-tortured sleep than he cared to remember. Eyes snapping open, he pivoted to the bedside clock.

Two a.m.

"Rolling out in three," Turk called. Then his booted feet thumped back down the hallway.

Swinging his legs onto flat carpeting, Reed grimaced past a thumping headache and stiffened muscles. Flicking on the bedside lamp, he spilled light over a bare chest and bare legs, all covered in scars from four different continents. Checking his phone, he saw two missed calls from a Virginia number.

Aimes.

Reed's heart rate quickened as he pulled jeans and boots on. A tight T-shirt, a loose leather jacket. His favored SIG P226 Legion slipped into a hip holster. Knife, wallet, and phone in his pocket. One splash of water on his face and half a bottle down his throat.

Then he was ready to go, just like that.

Turk and Wolfgang waited in the hallway, fully dressed and looking fresh in contrast to Reed's disheveled hair and sagging shoulders.

Turk passed him another water bottle and two little white pills without comment, then they were all headed for the stairs.

"Aimes?" Reed asked, swallowing both pills and guzzling water.

"Ten minutes ago," Turk said. "We're back to the safe house."

"What happened? Ivan split?"

Reed looked sideways at Wolfgang as he said it. Wolfgang didn't so much as acknowledge the jab, clipping along with a smooth stride that neatly concealed the prosthetic leg strapped to his right thigh.

"I don't know," Turk said simply. "She just said to get there."

The black CIA Suburban they had used to transport Ivan to the safe house waited for them in the parking lot. A new driver this time. They all piled in and the glimmering lights of northern Virginia metro faded quickly as they turned toward the mountains. Nobody spoke. Turk and Wolfgang were both zeroed in on their phones, and Reed was zeroed in on blocking out the building headache thumping from the back of his skull.

The meds hadn't kicked in yet, but his memories of the nightmares that had plagued him all night were already clear. Those dreams had flooded in on him despite his inebriation—the same haunted images that had played on repeat every time he attempted to sleep, drunk or otherwise.

The bomb. The hospital. Banks bleeding out and reaching a desperate hand toward him.

And then...the field. Swaying tall grass bathed in golden sunlight. The tree on the hill. And his daughter. Not a baby, but a young child. Seven or eight years old, a spitting image of her mother. Reaching out a hand to him.

"Daddy?"

Reed blinked hard to drive the images away, noting an acceleration of his own heartbeat as the little voice rang through his mind. *April's* voice. The name he had known his slain child by even though he hadn't even known that Banks was pregnant.

More layers of the mystery.

The CIA driver turned the Suburban up the gravel road and powered straight to the house in the trees. All the security staff were there. Aimes's car was there, as was another generic black CIA vehicle with government plates.

No sign of a manhunt. No sign of rushing gunmen blazing spotlights through the trees.

Reed bailed even before the driver shifted into park. He marched across the gravel and up the steps, letting himself in. The house was illuminated by overhead lights, buzzing with voices and footsteps. There were half a dozen personnel there that hadn't been before. Aimes marched down the hallway, dressed down to jeans and a subdued blouse, coffee in one hand. She looked right past Reed, her gaze settling on Wolfgang.

"Mr. Pierce. This way."

Reed and Turk invited themselves to join Aimes and Wolfgang in the house's second bedroom. Not the large, primary room where Ivan had been interrogated, but the smaller room on the other side of the hallway. It was occupied by empty bunks—no people. Aimes shut the door as soon as they were all inside.

"What happened?" Reed spoke first. Aimes looked right past him to Wolfgang.

"Mr. Pierce, I need an honest, one-hundred-percent blunt assessment. How reliable is Ivan Sidorov as an intel source?"

The room went quiet. Everybody looked to Wolfgang, and Wolfgang looked instinctually toward the room where Ivan—presumably—was still held. He took his time answering.

At last: "I would trust Ivan with my life, Madam Director. He's never lied to me. He's never sold me out. But..."

"But?" Aimes raised both eyebrows.

Wolfgang turned back. "But he's a creature of his own devices. We've only ever worked together when our priorities aligned. The one time those priorities conflicted, it was a problem. Ivan Sidorov is trustworthy only inasmuch as the thing you want is the thing he wants."

"So he would use us."

"Absolutely. He would use anyone. Your best bet in determining the veracity of his claims is to understand what he's after."

"And do you have any idea what he's after?"

Wolfgang thought about that a moment. He pocketed his hands.

"I only have one guess. Despite his problems with Moscow, Ivan is a patriot. Always has been. Whenever he's helped us in the past, his alleged motivation was always to investigate possible corruption in Moscow. He's obsessive about it. I think he views his fight with his old bosses as a patriotic campaign."

Aimes seemed to be considering. Reed took the lead.

"*What happened?*" he repeated.

Instead of answering, Aimes tilted her head and led them back across the hallway into the larger room where Ivan waited, still seated in his chair, a half-empty bowl of something that smelled like Indian food growing cold on the floor next to him. He didn't seem surprised to see Aimes, Reed, or any of the others. He simply watched as Aimes resumed her position behind the table and folded her arms.

"You think Nikitin is planning Russian expansion?" she asked.

Ivan grunted. "I know he is."

"And he'll start soon?"

"As soon as he can."

Long pause. Ivan squinted.

"What did he do?"

By way of answer, Aimes opened an iPad and set it on a stand. She pressed play, and the little speakers blared to life as everyone zeroed in on the screen. It was a press conference. Reed recognized the Russian president immediately. A translator kept up with his address.

The room dropped five degrees by the end of it. Ivan nodded once.

"Do you want me to say I told you so?"

"Is it *true*, Mr. Sidorov?"

"Is what true?"

"That there could have been a lost nuclear weapon discovered in that weapons depot?"

Ivan's lips bunched and he took his time answering, just zeroed in on the iPad as his already dark eyes turned somehow darker.

Then he looked up. "You will deploy your team to Georgia. I will go with them."

"What?"

"There are two possible realities, Madam Director. Either this claim is true, and Russia's actions are in everyone's best interests, or the claim is not true, and Nikitin is making an expansion play. In that case, the question of where the Panama bomb actually came from is more critical than ever. If Nikitin did indeed supply it to Abdel Ibrahim, this would constitute a direct attack on your sovereignty—an act of war. You will need evidence, one way or the other. I will help you. We will go to Georgia."

"You were already *in* Georgia," Wolfgang interjected. "You went to the weapons depot. You should already know what you saw."

"I know there was a locker built into the floor of the depot, painted with a Russian radiation symbol. I know that the locker was empty, and there were fresh tire marks on the concrete."

"That proves nothing," Wolfgang said.

"Which is why we must go back, before whatever evidence remains is erased. Nikitin is clearly using this emergency to annex Georgia. That fact is obvious, and it is of no importance. What you should be most concerned with is what comes next. If anything I have proposed is true—if Nikitin stands behind your president's attempted assassination or any of Abdel Ibrahim's attacks—you may be sure that Georgia is but the first domino. If you want any hope of stopping him, you must get ahead of him. I'm your best chance."

11

The West Wing
The White House

Only two members of Stratton's cabinet beat him to the situation room—
and they were exactly the two members he would have guessed. First,
General John David Yellin, Chairman of the Joint Chiefs, dressed in slacks
and a tight military button-down that looked ready to burst around his
bulldog muscles.

Second was Secretary of State Lisa Gorman, dressed in morning exer-
cise gear with a sweatband still wrapped tight around her head. Eyes
strained, crow's feet slicing toward her temples.

"What's happening?" Stratton barreled through the door with Jill Easterling at his elbow. A knot of aides were already occupying the room, scut-
tling about to arrange breakfast pastries and coffee, plugging in computers
and taking phone calls. Stratton ignored them all and addressed the question directly to Yellin—his connection to the Pentagon.

"Russia is invading Georgia, sir. It began two hours ago. Infantry and
armored divisions are still rolling across the border as we speak. They're all
headed south, apparently to Tbilisi."

"Resistance?" Stratton peeled his coat off and took his seat, gaze pivoting toward the primary screen at the end of the table. It displayed rotating satellite footage. Zoomed in close, the tanks were easy to see. The heavy trucks. The columns of Russian Tigr multipurpose vehicles, all kicking up dust as they roared southward.

"No apparent resistance, sir. At least not yet."

Stratton pivoted immediately for Gorman. She was ready with an answer before he even asked the question.

"My office can't get in touch with Tbilisi, sir. We're still trying."

"And Moscow?"

"We received an official statement from the Russian embassy thirty minutes after their troops were deployed. They're calling this a 'special military operation.' They claim that Russia is moving to secure the region following evidence of forgotten Soviet weapons."

Stratton gritted his teeth, looking back to the screen. He couldn't count the troops—not quickly, and not from grainy satellite photos. But it didn't take a genius to identify the presence of literally thousands of vehicles. Maybe tens of thousands of personnel.

A *lot* of firepower. Certainly for a "special military operation."

"I want Moscow on the line," Stratton said. "I want to speak to the Kremlin directly."

"I'll make it happen."

Gorman went to work on her desk phone and Stratton pivoted back to General Yellin just as Secretary of Defense Stephen Kline broke through the door.

"Where does this leave us, General?"

"We're still at DEFCON 2 following the Panama blast. All our naval assets in the Mediterranean and Persian Gulf regions are standing at full alert, but I'd directed them to keep their aircraft on their decks. If this is an attempted provocation, I don't want to risk taking the bait. At least not until we know what's happening."

"Oh, we know what's happening." Kline joined the conversation as he crashed into a chair. Dark bags hung beneath bloodshot eyes, and his suit jacket was wrinkled. He looked like he hadn't slept in days. "Nikitin is annexing Georgia, just the way the Chinese annexed North Korea following the attempted coup last year. This is a false flag op if ever I saw one."

"We can't be sure of that," Easterling interjected. "Russia claims they have evidence of a forgotten WMD cache in the Georgian mountains—"

"And we can't possibly believe them," Kline said. "*Special military operation? Really? Does that phrase not ring any bells?*"

Easterling flushed. Her small mouth parted, shoulders turning stiff. Gorman lowered a handset and called to Stratton before the argument could develop further.

"Mr. Acting President, I've got President Nikitin on the line."

The room went dead quiet. Everybody looked to Gorman.

Stratton raised both eyebrows. "*Nikitin?*"

"Yes, sir. Seems he was waiting by the phone."

Stratton looked to Easterling. The chief of staff's mouth had closed, pressed now into a tight line. He knew what she was thinking, and he couldn't help but think the same. There had been many moments of international chaos during the preceding two years. Several of those moments necessitated the White House to connect with the Kremlin.

But getting President Makar Nikitin on the line was easier said than done. It almost always required patience and persistence.

What was different this time?

"Put him through." Stratton guzzled water and sat up in his chair. The room remained still as Nikitin's voice crackled through the speakerphone on the desk.

"Good morning, Mr. Acting President. I hope our little disturbance didn't wake you." Nikitin's voice was calm, almost jovial. It struck Stratton all wrong.

"What are you doing, Mr. President?" *Straight to the point.*

If Nikitin was miffed by the bluntness, his voice didn't betray it. The relaxed tone continued. "I gave directions for our embassies to dispatch a memo. You will have heard of our discovery in Georgia?"

"You found a forgotten weapons depot?"

"This is correct, Mr. Acting President. Unfortunately, it seems that a Soviet-era cache may have been neglected in Georgia. A depot from which Abdel Ibrahim may have obtained a bomb. We are still investigating details, but rest assured that Russia takes this matter extremely seriously. We are working in cohort with the Georgian government to secure the location and complete our investigation. We will keep you updated, of course."

Nikitin spoke slowly, the words rolling off his lips so casually that Stratton almost thought they were sarcastic. It didn't sound like a head of state managing an international nuclear crisis. It sounded like a sleepy local sheriff reporting to a mayor on the matter of a missing gold medal pig from the local county fair.

There was no intensity. No sense of gravity.

No *sincerity*.

"Mr. President," Stratton began, "you are rolling *thousands* of troops and heavy armor across the Georgian border—"

"For security!" Nikitin broke in. "We do not yet know what other weapons may lay in this cache or who may be interested in them. No risks can be taken."

"On the contrary, you are taking a *huge* risk by deploying heavy fire-power into a sovereign nation. Forgive my bluntness, Mr. President, but you'll understand if America is hesitant to take you at your word following your predecessor's aggressions in Crimea and Ukraine. The similarities are striking."

A very long pause filled the speaker. Nobody around the table spoke or even dared to move. Stratton looked to Easterling, but she only stared at the phone.

At last: "Russia is not at war, Mr. Acting President. Not at this time. We are doing whatever is necessary to secure the region—and the world, for that matter. As I said, we will keep you updated. Now if you will excuse me."

Nikitin hung up without so much as a goodbye. The phone simply cut off, and the operator announced the disconnection as though anyone needed to be told. Stratton banged his hand against the table but withheld a curse. Leaning back, he scrubbed a cheek course with razor stubble and just stared at the phone. Thinking.

"He's lying," Yellin said. "When it looks like an invasion, and sounds like an invasion, and smells like an invasion, it's an invasion."

"So where does that leave us?" Gorman retorted. "You want to roll over there and go to war with Russia?"

Yellin flushed. "Madam Secretary, I don't pretend to know the first thing about international diplomacy, but where this matter concerns military strategy, I would appreciate a little deference."

"What's that supposed to mean?" Gorman said.

"It *means* we're at freaking DEFCON 2," Kline snapped. "And that maniac is rolling tanks into a sovereign nation only a hundred miles north of a NATO ally!"

The conversation spiraled as Gorman attempted to jump back in, and Easterling flailed to regain control. Other members of the cabinet were arriving now. More aides crowded the room.

Stratton tuned them all out and snatched up the nearest phone handset. The operator picked up immediately.

"Get me Langley," Stratton said. "I want to speak to Director Aimes."

The phone went silent. The buzz of conversation continued, both Kline and Gorman speaking over each other from across the table. Stratton simply stared at the screen as the long column of vehicles continued to churn southward.

They would reach the Georgian capital of Tbilisi before lunchtime in Washington. It was dark in the Caucasus, but the satellite could measure their progress by their headlights. That satellite would pick up muzzle flash, and detonating ordnance also.

But there was none. The Defense Forces of Georgia were making no apparent resistance. Russia was rolling right in.

"Yes, sir?" Aimes answered the line.

Stratton cut right to the chase. "What do we know?"

Short pause. "I can tell you what we've confirmed about Russian troop movements, but I think you're probably more interested in the validity of Nikitin's claims about the WMD depot."

"You're a smart woman."

Another brief pause. Aimes seemed to be wrestling with something. That only added to Stratton's unease.

Finally: "We have an asset, sir. Former Russian SVR. A ranking officer.

He's recently defected...sort of. To be perfectly honest with you, I'm not sure how much we can trust him."

"What's he saying?"

"He believes it's a false flag, sir. He thinks Nikitin is making a play to annex Georgia. The WMD thing is a fugazi."

"The blast in Panama wasn't a fugazi," Stratton said.

"No, sir. It wasn't. He..." Another hesitation.

"Spit it out, Madam Director. The nation doesn't pay you to pull your punches in a time of emergency."

"Am I speaking to you privately, sir?"

"You are."

"Our asset has...another theory. It's pretty outlandish."

"Hit me."

"He thinks...well. He believes the Panama bomb could have been Russian, not Soviet."

Stratton sat up. "What does that mean?"

"It means he believes Nikitin could have provided the bomb directly to Abdel, as a method of weakening us. That Nikitin has been influencing our instability for some time, with the eventual goal of launching Russian expansion."

"Into Georgia?"

"Georgia, yes...and beyond. It's just a theory, sir. Again, I'm not sure how much we can trust this asset."

Stratton pursed his lips. He was still staring at the screen, still tuning out the room. Weighing the implications of the unthinkable that Aimes had dumped on him like so much ice water. The prospect not only of Russia exploiting American instability, but of Russia *authoring* that instability.

The next question was obvious.

"If the theory were true, how would we prove it?"

"We need to know about the depot," Aimes said. "We need to know whether Nikitin is lying."

"You have a team?"

"Yes, sir."

"Deploy. Now."

12

Virginia

Aimes stood on the back porch of the safe house as she hung up with the acting president. In the trees beyond she could see the outline of a heavily armed CIA SAC operator keeping watch over the perimeter. Securing the asset in the house.

The asset that she didn't know if she could trust. And yet, like it or not, she was about to have to.

Turning back through the door, she found Reed Montgomery standing with his arms crossed in front of Ivan's chair, hitting the Russian with rapid-fire questions about Georgia. About the location of the weapons depot and the terrain around it. About what sort of ground forces the Russians would deploy to secure that site.

They were the questions of a field operator and a soldier, and they told Aimes that Montgomery was already bought in. She wouldn't have to sell him.

"Mr. Sidorov, you're confident of the location of this supposed WMD depot?" Aimes asked.

A soft grunt.

"And you can get there?"

A curt nod.

Aimes turned to Montgomery. "I'm deploying your team, Mr. Montgomery. How soon can you be ready?"

"I'm ready now," Reed said simply. He was already turning for the door, but then Turk broke in. The bulkier member of the Prosecution Force had stood in the background, alongside Wolfgang Pierce, just listening. Aimes had observed his body language intensify as the conversation with Sidorov unfolded. Turk seemed agitated, perhaps a little irate.

She hadn't invested much mental power into wondering why. Now she didn't have to wonder.

"Wait just a minute," Turk snapped. "We just got *back* from deployment. We've barely been stateside long enough to remember English. We won't be ready for another op until we've fully refit and planned this thing."

"So refit," Montgomery snapped. "We'll plan in the plane."

Again he turned for the door. Turk cut him off, ramming a hand against it and facing Aimes. There was a challenge in his angry eyes. Defiance.

"Just *what* exactly are you sending us to do?"

That was enough to stop Montgomery. He looked over one shoulder. Aimes thought quickly. It was such a vague request from the White House. Not at all the sort of clinical, highly calibrated mission she preferred to launch.

And yet it was unavoidable. Inevitable. It was the only path forward she could think of in such a demanding constraint of time.

"We need to know if he's lying," she said simply. "We need to know why the Russians are knocking on NATO's doorstep, before this thing can escalate. We need to know if that weapon was really Soviet, or if…"

"If it was Russian," Ivan finished. "It's okay, I am not offended."

Aimes's gaze snapped back toward her asset. She pinched her lips together. "Can you speak Georgian, Mr. Sidorov?"

Ivan curled his lip. "It's like speaking in donkey tongue. I barely understand it."

"So we'll need a translator." Wolfgang spoke for the first time, still standing in the shadows at the back of the room. None of Turkman's resistance radiated from his body language. He seemed as locked and loaded as Montgomery. "Madam Director?"

"I'll see what I can do," Aimes said. "It'll probably be a local. Somebody on the ground."

"The ground *where*?" Turk demanded. "We can't just parachute directly into Georgia with an entire Russian army crawling around."

No, Aimes thought. *You can't.*

"You've been to Turkey, Mr. Turkman?"

Dead silence. Aimes nodded and turned for the door. "Well, you're going back. You're going to see firsthand just how close this Russian army is crawling toward NATO."

Aimes departed the safe house in her own private SUV, leaving Reed to snap his fingers at Ivan, then turn for the front yard. Already his mind was spinning ahead to what operational functions would need to be performed before his team could depart.

All the equipment they would require could be found in the gym-turned-headquarters that the team operated just south of Nashville. It was close to the Leiper's Fork airport, where the CIA-issued private jet waited in a hangar.

The pilot was Kirsten Corbyn, a British RAF veteran recently turned CIA recruit. Her co-pilot was former US Air Force fighter pilot Kyle Strickland. Lucy Byrne, an old associate of Reed's and a former assassin herself, would manage the logistics.

Reed, Turk, and Wolfgang would form the strike team. Ivan would serve as their travel guide. It was a crude plan, but as Reed had already stated, they could refine the details on the flight eastward.

They just had to get their wheels off the ground.

Reed made it out the front door and halfway to the waiting SUV before Turk called out from the front porch. Reed ignored him and kept marching, gesturing for the CIA driver to start the engine.

He almost made it to the door before Turk grabbed him by the arm and yanked him around.

"*Montgomery!* Stop."

Reed's muscles tensed, sudden irritation flashing through the brain fog he'd fought for so many weeks it now felt like a part of him. His fists clenched and teeth gritted. He was spinning on Turk even as the bigger man released Reed's arm.

"*What?*"

Turk's face was beet red. He appeared completely blind to the presence of the CIA officers standing awkwardly around the driveway, or Wolfgang and Ivan watching from the safe house's slouching front porch. He stared only at Reed.

"What are we *doing*?"

It wasn't the question Reed expected. It flew out of Turk's lips with a confused contortion of his eyebrows, a pained frown. Reed's mind skipped, and then he spat out the first answer that surfaced from the mental muck.

"What do you think we're doing? Our *job*. Load up."

He turned for the Suburban again. Once more, Turk turned him back with a powerful twist of his arm. The bigger man closed in. His voice lowered.

"No, listen to me, Reed. Just listen to me. We need to talk about this."

"What's to talk about? You heard the woman."

"Yeah, I heard her. But I don't think you did. She has no *idea* what's going on here, man. She's dumping us into the heart of a developing war zone like a magnet on a string, hoping to pull something out of the muck. Do you hear me? This isn't even a clarified mission. She doesn't know *what* she's looking for. This is stupidity, Reed. This isn't what we do."

The irritation Reed had felt only moments before resumed in his chest, flushing a little hotter. Like the wash of a fever, ripping through his body. Turning his skin hot. Amping up his temper to confrontational levels in a moment.

"Seriously? A clarified mission? Was North Korea a clarified mission? Was Venezuela?"

"No they weren't, and I nearly left your dumb ass in both places because of it. Things aren't like they were then, Reed. You've got a kid, now. *I've* got a kid, and a family. I don't need the money. I don't—"

The irritation finally erupted into anger. Reed gritted his teeth and shoved close to Turk, speaking in a growl.

"So *stay home then*."

Dead silence. Nobody from the porch moved or spoke. The CIA driver remained frozen at the front bumper. Even the wind stilled. Turk looked over his shoulder to see the others watching on in silence. Then he rotated slowly back to Reed. His voice dropped to barely above a whisper.

"Reed, listen to me. I've got a bad feeling about this one. We're not ready for this op. We need to take a step back."

The words rang in Reed's ears like murmurs in a foreign language. Every syllable was clear. Every enunciation apparent. And yet none of it made sense. He couldn't compute Turk's argument any better than he could shut down the dreams or force himself into a good night's rest.

He closed his eyes and saw fire. He opened his eyes and saw a target. The *next* target.

"These thugs sponsored the attack that killed my child," Reed said at last. "They're going to die."

Then he turned and loaded into the Suburban, not caring whether anyone followed.

13

The Kremlin
Moscow, Russia

Makar Nikitin wasn't a politician during the formation of the Collective Security Treaty Organization, but in the years since, as the CSTO evolved into something of a gang of central Asian power—anchored, of course, by Moscow—he'd grown to better understand the benefits of an insiders' club full of small, seemingly inconsequential nations. Nations like Belarus, Armenia, Kazakhstan, Kyrgyzstan, and Tajikistan. All former Soviet states, and now standing as relatively independent nations, each concerned with a laundry list of petty personal agendas that paled in comparison to the once monumental aims of the mighty USSR.

Those were the glory days. The days when Moscow never asked for permission and never begged forgiveness. The days when the mineral resources of Central Asia and the oil wealth of the Caucasus served the Motherland without question or complaint.

At least, if they did complain, they never complained too loudly. Such grumblings could easily be interpreted as sedition, and the politburo stamped out sedition with an iron hammer.

Oh, for the days of unrestricted power and singular direction. It was the squabbling that brought down the empire, in the end. The indulgence of independence, of personality and nuance. In the next empire, none of the above need be tolerated. There would be one direction, one agenda. One vision, not just for Central Asia, but for the world.

Yet Central Asia, and the Collective Security Treaty Organization, would be the beginning.

Nikitin found representatives of each member state waiting for him in the sprawling conference room only three doors down from his executive office. It wasn't an accident that the "emergency" meeting he'd planned three months in advance would be held in Moscow. Belarus would kiss his ass and Kazakhstan was indifferent, but Kyrgyzstan could be obstinate, Tajikistan could be petty, and Armenia would be predictably alarmed, given her geographic proximity to the unfolding special military operation in Georgia.

None of that mattered. The CSTO itself barely mattered. They were simply window dressing to add an illusion of democracy to the proceedings. What mattered was the special guest—the seventh represented nation, who wasn't a member of the organization at all but had been invited to this meeting as a matter of *diplomatic courtesy*.

That nation was Azerbaijan, Georgia and Armenia's oil-rich neighbor and a part-time rival, full-time nuisance of Moscow. Their representative was none other than Elchin Rzayev himself, president of the Republic.

A piece of soiled toilet paper stuck to Nikitin's shoe.

"I thank you, my friends, for your patience." Nikitin kept his voice chipper as he barged into the room, coat tails flapping. Chin held high. Like he owned the room...because he did. The overweight, middle-aged men gathered around the table all hurried to their feet, a mix of uncertainty and alarm crossing their worn faces as the deluge of questions began.

Not all of them were in Russian. Some of the gathered heads of state spoke in their native tongues, with translators on standby. Nikitin ignored them all and stepped to the tea bar, mixing a cup of dark Russian tea with just a pinch of honey. A rare indulgence, but then, this was a day for celebration.

As he turned to the table, Leonid Zhukov, president of Belarus, greeted him with a warm smile and a soft handshake. There was no alarm in

Zhukov's face. Why should there be? Of the six men gathered to meet with Nikitin, Zhukov was the only one who had some prior knowledge of the events now unfolding in the Caucasus.

Not that he really understood those events or what eventual ambitions they were designed to stimulate. Zhukov—and for that matter, the entire state of Belarus—was one giant brown-noser, his face shoved so far up Russia's nether region that Nikitin doubted whether he could tell night from day. He was malleable, compliant, and not overly useful in most international concerns.

But when Nikitin needed to manipulate the CSTO, Zhukov's voice of support could be invaluable.

"My thanks for gathering on such short notice," Nikitin said, taking his chair and maintaining the chipper tone. "With events unfolding so quickly in the Caucasus, I felt it necessary to convene a meeting to discuss regional security."

Levon Petrosian, president of Armenia, didn't wait for the Tajikistani and Kyrgyzstani translators to finish their work before he fired back an alarmed bombardment, voiced in Russian and directed straight at Nikitin.

"Mr. President! We are *deeply* alarmed by this unprecedented and extreme deployment of Russian military assets into Georgia. I cannot fathom what misguided intelligence you must be acting on to justify such a show of force—"

Nikitin sipped his tea, tuning Petrosian out as the tirade continued. Already the Armenian was out of his chair, arms waving, sweat running down his face. The alarm—or fear, better put—was palpable, and certainly well placed. Moscow hadn't deployed nearly thirty thousand heavily armed soldiers so near to Armenia's borders perhaps since the collapse of the old Union, unless you counted the Chechen conflicts.

Armenia knew she was the smallest dog in the room. She would be the first to bark as a result. That didn't make anything Petrosian had to say particularly important.

"We share the concerns of our Armenian allies, Mr. President." It was the Tajikistani translator who spoke on behalf of his boss. The address was in Russian.

"It is deeply concerning for Russia to deploy so great an armed force without prior consultation with her allies. What is your explanation for this?"

Nikitin set the cup down, taking a moment to dab his mouth with a napkin. Then he raised a palm in a calming motion.

"My friends, please. Have a seat. There is no cause for alarm. Please…"

He gestured toward the chair Petrosian had abdicated. The Armenian president reluctantly sat down, still red-faced. Nikitin's gaze passed around the room, and he made a point not to focus too long over Rzayev, even though Rzayev was the reason for the meeting in the first place. The Azerbaijani president sat with his cold, lifeless eyes focused dead on Nikitin, unblinking. Unimpressed.

Unreadable.

It was one of the many reasons Nikitin needed Rzayev in the room for this meeting. The man was so difficult to gauge that nothing short of a personal interaction could ensure Nikitin's chances of keeping the Azerbaijani military at bay…at least for now. Unlike every other head of state gathered around the table, Rzayev was perhaps the only leader who could rival Nikitin in terms of raw ruthlessness and mental cunning. He was an animal. A brute. A solidified head of state who somehow managed to win election after election even while human rights activists from around the world decried the suppression of civic freedoms and the jailing of journalists in Baku.

Rzayev wasn't quite a dictator, not quite a despot. His grip on power was both absolute and mysterious, but the mystery was no great riddle to Nikitin. Rzayev maintained power by maintaining control of Azerbaijan's energy sector, one of the largest in the Caucasus.

It was a jewel the Soviet Union had once claimed as her own, and Rzayev knew it. That was what made him defensive—some might say trigger-happy. It was part of what kept him at odds with Moscow, always ready to threaten defensive action should Russia overstep her bounds.

Nikitin knew he needed to play the next twenty minutes very carefully if his unfolding strategy in Georgia were to have any chance of succeeding.

"The matter before us is indeed one of great concern," Nikitin said, taking his time. "This issue of forgotten Soviet weapons—weapons of mass destruction, no less—should be alarming to us all. You can be certain, I was deeply alarmed when—"

"Cut to the facts, Makar!" Petrosian broke through again, spittle flying across the table. "We *know* what you claim about the bomb. What we do not know is why you have chosen to deploy heavy armor and thousands of infantry into Georgia!"

Nikitin stared, unblinking. He gave the translators time to feed the message to their bosses. Then he took a breath.

"The matter of Soviet-era weapons of any sort, let alone WMDs, is of principal concern to the Russian Federation. Any instability in the region impacts us all, and as the leader of—"

"You are not the leader of the region, Mr. President. You are an ally only, and you owe us all an explanation for this dangerous aggression!"

The translators rattled quickly through the interruption, and Nikitin bit back the frustration boiling just beneath his skin. Dealing with Petrosian reminded him of dealing with the little German dogs his ex-wife used to enjoy so much. Those yapping, loud, obnoxious little vermin. He'd crushed the life out of one of them with his boot the day she left him.

He'd like to do the same with Petrosian, and in time, he would. For the moment, he needed to remain calm. Rzayev was watching him like a hawk.

"Mr. President." It was Zhukov who spoke, injecting himself into the conversation. "President Nikitin is attempting to answer your questions. You cannot expect the explanations you seek if you continue to interrupt him, can you?"

The appeal carried none of the derisive condescension that it would have had Nikitin voiced the words. Zhukov sounded downright reasonable.

Petrosian glowered a moment longer, then reluctantly settled back into his chair, face still beet red.

Nikitin resumed.

"As I was saying. The issue of regional security is of paramount importance to Russia. When Georgian President Meladze notified me of an unfolding investigation into a possible weapons depot left by the USSR, of course I offered my immediate assistance. When those rumors were confirmed, President Meladze became concerned of the proliferation of such discovered WMDs across his country. As you know, the depot we found is now empty. I offered the assistance of the Russian military and am now fulfilling that promise. Every element—"

"A treasure hunt? Really?" Petrosian scoffed. "You expect me to buy this, Makar? You do not need *tanks* to locate missing WMDs!"

Nikitin's back straightened, a little of the frustration boiling deep inside starting to seep out. Zhukov saw the shift in body language and opened his mouth to interject again. Nikitin cut him short.

"As I was *saying*, Mr. President. Every element of this special military operation is conducted in perfect adherence to the wishes of President Meladze and the people of Georgia. We are heavily armed because the possibility stands that the terrorist, Abdel Ibrahim, while dead, may have maintained alliances with similar extremist groups who may even now be returning to Georgia for the purpose of recovering additional weapons. With chemical weapons and even nuclear ones present in the countryside, it is *imperative* that all precautions be taken. Surely you can appreciate the necessity of regional security, Mr. President...your own country sitting so close to Tbilisi."

Petrosian's lips bunched. He looked across the table to the visiting heads of state from Tajikistan and Kyrgyzstan. Nobody spoke.

Rzayev was still zeroed in on Nikitin, those dead eyes searching like lidless spotlights. Probing Nikitin's body language. Measuring his intentions.

Nikitin knew what Rzayev was thinking. He was wondering whether he could trust the Russians. Whether twenty—and soon to be forty—thousand foot soldiers gathered so close to Azerbaijan's borders should be cause for alarm.

They were the concerns Nikitin wanted to assuage, but for now, Rzayev didn't speak. Petrosian jumped back in.

"President Meladze has signed off on this?"

Nikitin raised a hand. "Completely. I wouldn't dream of moving military assets across Georgia borders without his agreement."

"So *where is he*?"

Another question Nikitin expected. With Elchin Rzayev present at the meeting, it would be reasonable to expect Giorgi Meladze to be present also. But Giorgi Meladze couldn't be present. In fact, he couldn't be found at all. He'd been missing since…

Well. Since Nikitin had him killed.

"I am told Giorgi is unwell," Nikitin said. "That petulant stomach problem he deals with. He's in Tbilisi, in his residence. I'm sure you could get in touch with his office, if you like."

"I do not want to speak with his office, Makar. I want to speak with *him*. I want to know that Georgia has truly invited you to traipse across their countryside. That this isn't another Ukraine situation."

Bingo.

It was the accusation Nikitin had been waiting for. Hoping for. Biding his time for.

A wide-open door.

He sat up in the chair, face finally flushing, hand smacking in irate disbelief against the table. And then the tirade came—the pre-planned tidal wave he had rehearsed in front of the mirror two dozen times prior to this meeting. All the indignant disbelief. The frustration of a benevolent Russian leader, perplexed by petty obstinance after all that *he* had done.

Ousting his predecessor. Ceasing the war in Ukraine and drawing down Russian forces in the region. Rebuilding trust with Europe. Solidifying relations with CSTO members and funding the development of natural gas pipelines that poured millions of western dollars into the Caucasus—into *Armenia*. After all the effort, all the trust, all the sacrifice of Russian resources…

Nikitin didn't need to finish. Zhukov broke in right on cue, at just the moment that Petrosian began to shrivel into his chair, shame creeping across his face as the stern eyes of the Tajikistani and Kyrgyzstani glared down their noses at him.

A troublemaker. A wrinkle in the smooth seas of Russian support that had bolstered Central Asia into the most promising economic boom in decades.

Nikitin could have kept defending himself, but why bother? Zhukov was ready to play his lawyer.

"Makar, please. You have said enough."

Nikitin slumped back into his chair, swabbing sweat from his forehead and pretending to be winded. In truth, he was anything but. He was alive with energy, tense with emotional preparation.

He was watching Rzayev out of the corner of his eye and he thought... Rzayev was buying it.

"You must be insane if you actually think Russia is conducting an act of aggression." Zhukov addressed the Armenian president directly, his voice softening into disappointed disbelief. "What is better? To send five hundred troops and spend weeks sweeping the countryside, or to send thousands and have it done within the week? Do you seriously want a weapon of mass destruction lost so near to your own borders?"

It was a rhetorical question, but Zhukov waited with eyebrows raised. Petrosian, meanwhile, pivoted back to Nikitin. He squinted.

"The tanks?"

Nikitin feigned a disbelieving snort. "Is this what is bothering you?"

"You do not need tanks to search the countryside. I am no fool."

Zhukov opened his mouth. Nikitin held up an exhausted hand.

"The tanks support the infantry columns. Our logistical system made it easiest to send them together. But—"

Petrosian was tensing with an objection. Nikitin pressed on.

"*But*...if it bothers you so much, I will isolate them north of Tbilisi. It will be more difficult to move supplies once I fragment our mechanized divisions, but I am willing to do so. If it makes you more comfortable."

"It would," Petrosian said quickly.

"Okay. So I'll call back the armor and proceed with sweeping the countryside. Is this agreeable to everyone?"

Nikitin waited, knowing he'd already won. He'd obtained the rational, reasonable high ground. That bastion of argumentative advantage that no gutless person could assault.

Certainly, Tajikistan nor Kyrgyzstan nor Kazakhstan would. Their representatives spoke through translators, green-lighting their support for the continued operation. Zhukov voted in favor also.

Petrosian remained tense, lips bunched, gaze fixated on Nikitin.

"When you have completed your search, you will withdraw from Georgia?"

Nikitin lifted his cup, sipping lukewarm tea. Enjoying that gentle flavor of honey washing down his throat. The taste of celebration. He could see Rzayev out of the corner of his eye, and he could see that the Azerbaijani president had relaxed. His shoulders had loosened. The suspicion had vacated his eyes.

He had bought the entire spiel.

Nikitin shot Petrosian a reassuring smile.

"Absolutely."

14

The finalized paperwork lay on the counter. The bold figure printed in the bottom right-hand corner was officially official, as sealed by Banks's signature, her agent's signature, and the signature of the record label representative.

As of that moment, Banks April Montgomery was a millionaire. Or she would be, in a few days, when the initial advance on her record deal arrived via wire to her bank account. Jim explained that she would want to retain an accountant and a financial advisor as soon as possible. He had recommendations for both. There would be tax concerns and investment potential. All the nerdy little angles of the newfound wealth that Banks struggled to care about.

She didn't even care about the spending money. About a nicer condo—or a house in Franklin—or a nicer car, nicer clothes. First class plane tickets to a vacation on some island she'd never visited.

They were all things she'd dreamed of when the potential of stardom first became a reality, but those dreams rang hollow in the emptiness of the fifth-floor apartment. With Davy fast asleep in the second bedroom, Banks sat alone facing the window, looking out over the Nashville skyline, halfway through a bottle of merlot.

Questioning everything.

Where is he?

Looking back to the phone in her lap, Banks scanned down a list of increasingly desperate text messages she'd fired off during the past week, coupled with unanswered phone calls sent straight to voicemail. She'd been angry at first. Then hurt. Then paranoid.

But when four days became six, and six became ten, new terrors entered her mind. Thoughts of something much worse than another woman, or a wild drinking binge that had somehow landed Reed in jail. Now she was thinking about the uglier possibilities of real, significant harm for the only man she'd ever loved.

Reed could be reckless during his downtime. He liked to run his old Camaro far in excess of the speed limit. He liked to jump off of things that weren't made to be jumped off of. He liked to go dark, drinking himself into oblivion more often than not.

Had the demons finally bested him? Lurking out of their mental dungeons and dragging her husband into an abyss of absolute despair. A loaded gun and an empty bottle of whiskey. A dark hotel room in some grungy city...

It was too much. Maybe it was the alcohol or simply the developed pressure of days of anxiety, but Banks couldn't take it anymore. She lifted the phone and switched away from Reed's text message thread, away from his contact, and to a short list of favorites in her phone app. She tapped a name she swore she would *not* tap.

She gave into the paranoia, disregarding the fear of being labeled a controlling and crazy wife, and dialed Reed's best friend.

"Hello?" Turk answered on the second ring. He sounded exhausted and a little short tempered.

"Turk...uh...it's Banks."

"Yeah, I know. You okay?"

Banks fumbled, her throat suddenly constricting as she struggled for words. She knew what to say, but she still felt like an absolute fool for saying it.

She chugged the wine, draining the glass, and wiped her hand across her lips.

"Is...is Reed with you?"

"Uhm...yeah."

Relief cascaded through Banks's gut as warm as the wash of merlot she'd just gulped. Just knowing that Reed was in fact in the company of Turk answered a lot of questions and assuaged a lot of concerns. Turk was a good guy. He wouldn't put up with Reed catting around, and he wouldn't let Reed hurt himself, either. It was still possible that they were halfway up some radio tower, about to fling themselves into the dark with internet-ordered parachutes strapped to their backs, but at least Reed wasn't alone.

That didn't answer the question of why he had ghosted her, though, and as that thought rang back through her buzzed mind, the anger returned.

"I can't get through on his phone," Banks said, suppressing the frustration with effort. "Maybe it's dead?"

A short pause. Turk grunted. "Yeah, maybe. Hold on."

The phone shifted. A murmured conference was held. She couldn't hear words but she recognized Reed's voice.

She also recognized the wine of an airplane engine.

No way.

"Banks?"

Banks's heart jumped at the sound of his voice. She sat up on the couch, still angry, still indignant, but already feeling better.

"Where are you, Reed? Why haven't you answered my calls?"

The reply was slow in coming. She thought he might have been drunk, at first, but when Reed spoke, there was no slur in his words. They were perfectly flat. Lifeless.

"I've been busy. What do you need?"

Banks squinted, at once caught off guard and stung by the response. She sat forward on the couch, swaying a little as the wine did its work on her balance.

"I want to know when you're coming home. Davy's been asking about you. Where have you been?"

The same dead pause as before. Then: "I went to Virginia. Work stuff. Tell Davy I'll see him soon."

The phone shifted. Banks's stomach tightened in sudden panic as she realized he was about to hang up.

"Reed! Wait. Don't hang up on me."

His breathing remained on the line, but he didn't answer. Banks swallowed and looked across the room, eyes suddenly stinging. Confusion joining the frustration.

"Reed...what's happening? Why aren't you here? I...I haven't known..."

She choked and trailed off, waiting and praying that he would fill the silence this time. That he wouldn't leave her hanging.

No hint of emotion elevated his tone when he finally responded.

"I'm being deployed again. I'll be gone a week or so. I'll let you know when I'm back."

"Deployed? What are you talking about?"

"The terrorist thing. We're still working on it."

"What do you *mean* you're working on it? He's dead, Reed. You told me so."

The agonizing pause returned. She sat up, pushing hair back from her face. Forcing her head to clear.

"Look," Banks said. "I had that meeting today. With the record people? They signed me, Reed." She forced a laugh, not feeling any of it. "The money...it's all coming. It's in ink now. We're *rich*. You can quit, like we talked about! We can go to that island on the calendar. Bring Davy. Just get away..."

She choked again, hands trembling. Body quaking from the inside, sending tremors that ripped through her very soul.

She would shred that document in a heartbeat—give up all the money, all the fame, all the opportunity—if she could just fall into his arms. If he would just *be* there. Be beside her, holding her close, the way he used to.

But when Reed spoke again, it wasn't what she wanted to hear. It wasn't even what she feared she might hear. His words cut through the phone like bullets, ripping straight into her chest.

"I don't want your money. I've got a job to do. I'll call you later."

And then he hung up. The phone slipped out of Banks's hands as her vision blurred. The room swayed around her and those bullets struck again, sinking in deep this time. Burning.

She collapsed into her own arms and just sobbed.

15

Leiper's Fork, Tennessee

The flight from northern Virginia to rural Tennessee lasted barely two hours, but those two hours were dragged out in icy silence as Reed swigged Jack Daniels from a dirty glass and Turk sat in the tail of the plane, watching his best friend and longtime battle buddy literally cracking at the seams.

By the time the CIA transport plane dropped them off at the airfield in Leiper's Fork, Reed already had the wheels of deployment in motion. Ivan and Wolfgang were ready to go. Kirsten Corbyn arrived at the private hangar astride her Triumph Rocket 3 motorcycle, Lucy Byrne racing in just behind in a brand-new Mazda Miata.

Kyle Strickland—former Air Force fighter pilot and now a contract SAC pilot for the CIA—was on his way. The 2005 model Gulfstream V housed within the hangar and permanently assigned for the use of the Prosecution Force was already fueled and would be ready for takeoff within the half hour. All the field equipment anybody could imagine was stored in heavy-duty lockers behind the plane.

The pieces were already in place. The game was in motion. But even as Reed hung up on Banks and shoved the phone back into Turk's hand, he couldn't shake the nagging feeling deep in his gut that this wasn't like the other times. This wasn't like their last trip to Turkey, their hectic mission in Venezuela, or even that idiotic tour through North Korea.

Turk could feel it in his very bones. He could see it reflected in Reed's bloodshot eyes. Call it a premonition, or an intuition, or just common sense. Everything was moving too fast, and Turk had to put the brakes on.

"Montgomery!"

The night air was torn by jet engines as the CIA SAC jet that had brought them back to Tennessee prepared for takeoff. Reed was already halfway across the tarmac, headed for the hangar where Corbyn was busy completing preflight checks behind the Gulfstream's windscreen. He didn't even pause as Turk called after him. The blatant disregard angered Turk. It ignited something hot and indignant deep in his gut.

He didn't deserve this.

"*Marine!*" Turk roared. "Stop and turn!"

That got Reed's attention. His boots ground to a stop on the asphalt, and he glowered over one shoulder. Turk closed the distance between them, the indignation boiling rapidly into something much more volatile. He couldn't remember the last time he'd been seriously pissed at Reed. He couldn't remember the last time he'd been genuinely pissed at anybody. It wasn't in his easygoing nature.

But everything breaks when it's pushed too far.

"Don't you walk off on me," Turk snapped. "I gave you room on the plane. Now you're going to listen."

Reed's eyes blazed, but he didn't march off. He turned instead, jaw rising as his head rocked back to meet Turk's gaze. Despite the semi-inebriated fire in Reed's eyes, he looked somehow...flat to Turk. Two dimensional, as though he were doped up. Spaced out.

It only added to Turk's unease.

"You got something to say?" Reed shouted over the thunder of jet engines as the SAC jet raced down the tarmac and took to the air. Turk waited for it to pass, taking his time and not breaking eye contact. Searching those glassy pools of emptiness.

It wasn't what he was used to seeing in Reed's eyes. The Prosecutor was a man who—for better or worse—left his rawest emotions on his sleeves.

Turk always knew when Reed was angry. When he was obstinate. When he was finished with something. Turk had spent much of their joint careers serving as a moderator of those emotions. An equalizer.

But now he could see nothing. Reed Montgomery was dead inside.

"Listen to me," Turk said, lowering his voice. "Please listen to me. I'm not talking as a soldier, I'm talking as your friend. Do you understand?"

No reply. Reed didn't so much as blink.

"There's something wrong with this mission," Turk said. "I can feel it in my blood. We're not ready. We don't know what we're stepping into. I'm asking you—I'm *begging you*—to call it off. Give us forty-eight hours. Get more intel from Langley. Let's do this on our terms. Okay? At our speed."

Long pause. From the gate of the airport, headlights flashed, and Kyle Strickland's Toyota Tacoma raced for the hangar. The team was fully assembled now.

Reed still hadn't blinked. His eyes gleamed red in the moonlight, reflecting everything and betraying nothing.

"We have *families*, Montgomery," Turk said. "I have a wife and a daughter. You have a wife and a son. We can't afford to be recklessly throwing our lives around any longer. We have to *think*."

Long pause. Reed still made no sign that he'd even heard the words. He looked perfectly flat, like a zombie.

"Reed?" Turk questioned.

Reed's jaw clenched. His gaze turned hard.

"They *killed her*," he whispered.

A lead weight descended into Turk's stomach. He swallowed. He nodded once. "I know. But you got him, Reed. You got Ibrahim."

Reed blinked once. His eyes turned moist. Then his teeth clenched. He shouldered his backpack and turned for the hangar.

"Montgomery!" Turk started after him, shouting across the tarmac. "You *got him*. Ibrahim is *dead*."

"And now I'm gonna kill the rest of them," Reed snapped.

Turk stopped halfway to the hangar. He folded his arms, eyes burning. He swallowed.

"I won't do it."

Reed stopped. He looked back. "What?"

"I won't go. If this is the way you're gonna play it...you gotta play it alone. I won't watch you destroy this team."

Dead stillness descended over the airfield. Reed's lips parted. He stared.

Turk waited, hoping. Reed's jaw closed.

"Fine by me," he growled.

Then he marched for the hangar, leaving Turk in the middle of the airfield.

Something vaguely hot crept through Reed's chest as he reached the hangar—something a little like hurt, or frustration, or maybe raw anger. He attempted for a moment to clarify it, but he couldn't break through the fog that had descended so deep into the recesses of his mind as to numb his very body.

He left Turk standing on the tarmac, and Reed knew that he should feel troubled about it. But he couldn't. He couldn't feel anything except the dying burn of Jack Daniels and the growing hum of adrenaline in his veins. Of a new mission, ready to unfold.

Of new targets, ready to gun down.

Entering the hangar, Reed found Wolfgang and Ivan carting gear into the Gulfstream. Kyle Strickland had parked his Tacoma next to Corbyn's Rocket 3 and was already in the jet's cockpit, arguing with Corbyn about preflight procedure. Bent over a table, surrounded by bright red medical packs, Lucy Byrne was the only one to notice Reed's arrival. She looked over one shoulder and studied him with calm green eyes, her gaze switching once toward the parking lot. A low rumble marked the start of Turk's modified Jeep Gladiator. The truck roared out with a bark of tires.

Lucy looked back to Reed, a question on her face. Reed wasn't in the mood to answer questions.

"Everybody ready?" Reed barked.

Ivan grunted an assent. Wolfgang waved two fingers. Corbyn and Strickland ignored him and continued to argue, growing more animated by the moment. Only Lucy approached, a medical bag slung over one shoulder, loose auburn hair draping over her back. Her voice was as calm as mountain water rolling over smooth stones.

"You okay, Reed?"

The question reached his brain but didn't quite compute. Reed focused on Lucy until she blurred out of focus, just a blob of subdued earth-tone clothing and scarlet hair. Reed's chest tightened, and suddenly he didn't see Lucy at all.

He saw the field. The hilltop. The tree.

And his daughter.

"*Daddy?*"

"Reed?"

Reed blinked. Lucy returned to his view. He swallowed and turned for the plane.

"Fine, LB. Let's roll."

16

The morning dawned bright and cold over Washington, finding Acting President Jordan Stratton already present in his vice-presidential office, surrounded by empty coffee cups and printed briefs. The night had been long and relentless, and Stratton hadn't slept a wink. The problems at hand were simply too overwhelming.

First and foremost, what to do about Russia. That was a question Stratton punted to Secretaries Gorman and Kline, ordering them to draft recommendations for confronting the Russians with diplomatic pressure featuring a military undertone—whatever that meant. Stratton didn't even know. The bulk of his energy and creative focus was all bent on what he still considered to be the bigger problem. The problem that would bring both himself, and perhaps the nation, into an early grave if it weren't solved.

That was the problem of domestic instability. Rampant inflation and even more rampant fear. Failing industry and social unrest, boiling just beneath the surface. America was rolling into an emergency room, hemorrhaging from half a dozen mortal wounds. Stratton had to find a way to

rush her through triage and stop the bleeding before petty things like
Russian aggression and rogue acts of nuclear terror no longer mattered.

Before the Lady Liberty herself bit the dust.

Jill Easterling assisted him, the two of them barricading themselves in
the office and unplugging the phone as crumpled notepad paper gathered
on the floor and the coffee turned cold. By six a.m., Stratton was no closer
to an answer about how to solve America's problems than he'd been twelve
hours prior, but he did have an idea of which problems to attack first.
Whether by token assault or real impact, it had yet to be determined.

But at this stage, if there was one thing Stratton believed more than
anything, it was that *any* action would be better than no action. The
country desperately needed to see strength from their leader. Unless and
until Muddy Maggie Trousdale emerged from the shadow of death, that
leader was him.

"Call a press conference," Stratton said, heading for the door. "We meet
in thirty."

As a single woman, Maggie had little use for the majority of the fifty-
five thousand square feet that constituted the three floors of the White
House, and Stratton kept a standing wardrobe in the guest suite on the residence floor. A cold shower, a shave, and a fresh suit brought life back to his
blood and focus to his tired mind better than any amount of caffeine could.
Joined with a bagel and a glass of filtered water, Stratton felt as ready for
battle as he could expect to feel after barely sleeping in three days.

"Good morning, everyone. Please be seated." Stratton took the podium
at the end of the press conference room and turned to face the bank of
cameras and reporters gathered beyond. It hadn't been difficult to assemble
them. Many were already present in the West Wing, eager for a crumb of
news to leak from the generally silent administration. Breathless for an
update on Maggie. On the state of the nation. On a burgeoning
international crisis.

On anything. Stratton had left the media hungry for too long. Now he
had to feed them with care before they made a meal out of subject matter
he couldn't control.

"I'll get straight to the point. First, an update on the president. Her
condition is currently stable, and doctors are optimistic about her

continued recovery. We expect her to remain under the care of Walter Reed for the time being while treatment measures are pursued. I'll update you when we know more."

"Is the president in need of a transplant?"

The question exploded from the back of the room. Stratton shot a look toward his right, where Farah Rahman, Maggie's press secretary, stood in the shadows. Rahman stepped in without hesitation, pivoting an iron glare on the crowd.

"Please hold all questions until the acting president has completed his address."

Stratton consulted his notes. Then he cleared his throat.

"The second matter I'd like to address this morning concerns the stability of the American economy and our own domestic security. While the Trousdale administration continues our efforts to find solutions for continued global trade following the Panama Canal attack, we're also bending the resources of the executive branch against domestic concerns. Effective this morning, I'm issuing a letter of request to congress recommending a six-month suspension of all federal gasoline taxes to help fight the increasing cost of fuel. In concert with Congress's expected cooperation, I am also authorizing the immediate release of two million barrels of crude oil from the Strategic Petroleum Reserve to help stimulate the energy market. Further, my office has sent another letter of recommendation to the Federal Reserve recommending the increase of the federal funds target rate to help combat widespread inflation. All of these policies, working in cohort, are expected to help stabilize our developing economic situation."

Stratton paused and looked out over the crowd of reporters, scanning blank faces and parted lips. Nobody stirred. Nobody took notes. Everyone simply stared, waiting on the edge of their seats for...what?

He'd just given them the solution. The laundry list of anemic but actionable policies he would implement by sunset to help stop the bleeding. It wouldn't fix the problem. Not even close.

But it was *something.*

The looks in the strained faces of the press corps said otherwise. It was as though he were speaking Latin. He looked back to his notes and opened his mouth, ready to deliver the next phase of his spiel. All the details about domestic security and Americans getting back to work. National Guardsmen to be deployed to schools to assuage the fears of parents, and federal assistance of local authorities at ports and borders to prevent the intrusion of further threats.

Technical things. *Practical* things.

But not what the press corps needed to hear, Stratton realized. He could see it in the fear in their eyes. These were some of the most politically astute men and women in America. People who appreciated word salads and knew how to deconstruct them.

If they were lost, how lost was the rest of America?

Stratton flipped his notes face down and placed his hands on the edges of the podium. He dug deep. He pictured Maggie at this stage, all those times she'd refused a prepared speech and spoken from the heart. Those moments when she'd made the most impact.

What would Maggie do?

"My great-uncle was stationed in San Diego when the Japanese bombed Pearl Harbor. My father was serving in the Chicago state legislature when the Soviets parked nuclear missiles in Cuba. When the energy crisis hit. When Reagan was shot."

Stratton paused. Weighed his next words...and then pressed ahead.

"I was studying at Dartmouth on 9/11. I watched on live TV as the second plane struck the tower. I remember people crying...calling their parents. Panicking."

Another pause, this time for effect. He wanted the memory to sink in. He wanted everyone watching from all around the world to remember where they stood when flames erupted from the World Trade Center like dragon fire. To remember what it *felt like.*

The terror. The loss. The rage.

"I'm not going to stand here today and pretend like I have all the answers," Stratton began again. "I'm no superhero. I can't turn back the clock. The road before us is rough and bloody. America now stands at the brink of catastrophe in a way that—I'll admit—feels unprecedented. Cataclysmic, even."

Stratton raised a hand slowly, index finger pointed outward. His jaw locked. "But *it is not.* Whatever you're thinking, feeling, fearing...we've been here before. We've faced unthinkable loss, hardship, and brutal pain. What sets us apart in a world full of collapsing societies and absolute despair is the simple reality that Americans *refuse* to stay down. Our tenacity and relentless belief in our own values has brought this nation out of the fire and onto ever higher ground since the day we declared independence."

Another theatric break. Stratton knew what he had to say now. It wasn't a command, a plan, or the heroic declaration of a triumphant savior.

It was a plea. An appeal.

"In times of great crisis, we're reminded of the words of JFK—to ask not what our country can do for us, but what we can do for our country. Today, my fellow Americans, your country needs you like never before. She needs you to leave your home. To bravely proceed to your place of business, to your school, to your town square. To defy the scourge of terror and the oppression of fear and to *be* an American. Not because it's safe, or easy, but because liberty is *worth* the sacrifice. America needs you to look dead into the eyes of the challenges we face and to *defy* them. To spit in their face and refuse to acknowledge that any scum-sucking thug could for a *moment* ever tell us how to live or what to fear or who to be. We will not be afraid to go to work or to send our children to school. We will not be disabled by economic distress or international turmoil. We will sink our fingers into the throats of our enemies and *choke them out*...because we are free. We are relentless. We are unbreakable. We are America."

Tears moistened Stratton's eyes as he finished the spiel, and he wasn't the only one. The haunted faces of the press corps had grown perfectly motionless as Stratton spoke. Eyes turned red. The men blinked and the women dropped their faces. Nobody spoke in the stillness that followed. Stratton looked directly into the first camera he saw.

"I need you, my fellow Americans. Your country needs you. Don't let her down."

Then he ducked his head, retrieved his worthless notes, and exited the press room without another word. Easterling waited outside, her own eyes moist as she fell quickly into line behind him. Rahman took the podium and resumed control of the press conference, but the usual storm of questions was reduced to a mere murmur.

Stratton tuned it all out. His mind grew hard and cold as he returned to his vice-presidential office and rammed his way in. He sat at the desk and tugged his tie loose.

Easterling stood across from him. She still hadn't spoken a word since leaving the briefing room.

At last: "That was perfect, sir."

Stratton nodded slowly. Then he poured himself a glass of water from the pitcher next to him and guzzled. He set it down with a thump.

"What's next?"

Easterling consulted the iPad in her hands, although Stratton doubted that she needed to. She was ready with a response.

"Moscow is refusing to surrender evidence of whatever weapons depot they claim was breached in Georgia. They've reduced international communication to vague press bulletins. Meanwhile, the Collective Security Treaty Organization met yesterday, and every member state except Armenia has since issued a statement of support for Russia's military actions in Georgia. Whatever Nikitin's up to...he's already achieved momentum in doing it."

Stratton pondered, lips pinched together. Thinking. Not about the speech or even the situation with Russia, but about Maggie. His gut had told him to take a trick out of her playbook with the press corps. He wondered what other tricks she might have used with the developing international turmoil.

It wasn't the battle he could afford to fight. Not yet. He still needed to stall for time.

"Contact Ambassador Carrie," Stratton said. "Have her call an emergency meeting of the UN Security Council. We're going to raise the issue of Russian military aggression."

"I'm not sure how much that will help. Maggie tried that strategy during the Air Force One crisis. Russia refused to play ball."

"We don't need them to play ball," Stratton said. "We just need to force their hand into making a statement. If we give Nikitin enough rope...he might just hang himself."

17

Aimes never imagined when she ascended to the highest directorate in the American intelligence sector that she would ever actually be reviewing the fallout of a nuclear weapon deployed against the Free World, but sitting behind her desk on the executive level of CIA headquarters, that was exactly what she was doing.

Spread before her were a dozen different reports from forensic research teams on the ground in Panama, all of them venturing as close to ground zero as possible as they worked to recover whatever hard evidence could be obtained. The question was brutally simple but crucially important. It was the same question Russia claimed to already answer, but the White House doubted.

The question of *where* Abdel Ibrahim's nuclear weapon had come from.

Aimes was no expert in the field of nuclear physics. She didn't need to be. The CIA had an army of such experts on the payroll, either contractors or direct employees, and all of them were working overtime to dig through the mounting piles of data, searching for any tangible clue as to the bomb's origin.

The problem, of course, was that bombs have a way of destroying their own evidence, and the blast that had sent Colon, Panama, back into the Stone Age was a horrific example of destructive potential. Estimated to yield twice the output of the bomb that shattered Hiroshima, the weapon was undoubtedly atomic, not hydrogen, and already the ground team had established characteristics of the blast that were indicative of an old design. Something quite possibly dating back to the 1960s, or even before.

Perhaps the kind of thing somebody had lost. If the Russians were to be believed, the Soviets had lost it. But none of that was certain, and it needed to be. The only thing that was certain was the carnage. Aimes scrolled through digital pictures snapped by remote photography drones only a few hundred yards from ground zero and couldn't deny the sting in her eyes.

It was like looking at pictures of a war zone. Of genocide in Africa or earthquake devastation in Haiti. It was absolute. Crushing. Horrific in the most extreme sense of the word. Homes had been incinerated and streets rolled up like broken carpets. A hospital collapsed to mere ashes. Dockside warehouses were vaporized and cars reduced to crumpled balls of contorted sheet metal.

And the shadows...the shadows were there. Just like after Hiroshima, human bodies were printed against concrete backdrops as bright white silhouettes, present for a moment, and gone for an eternity. An entire community simply...erased.

Aimes's vision blurred and the iPad trembled. She focused on one shadow sprayed across a low stone wall and couldn't help but notice how small it was. Not an adult but a child. A young child. The smudge beside her might have been a dog.

Nobody would ever know.

Setting the device down, Aimes scrubbed her eyes and forced herself to clear her mind. She had a meeting in ten minutes. More analysis of the developing situation in Georgia. More questions. More fragments of intelligence leaking in from assets scattered across the region.

It was critical material, and yet it somehow paled compared to bigger questions. Questions that had kept her up literally all night long. Questions about the claims of Ivan Sidorov.

What if the Russians supplied the bomb?

It was such a wild, unthinkable suggestion that she hadn't wanted to accept it. She wanted to write it off as the bizarre, tin-hat concoction of a frazzled and bitter old Russian who had been disenfranchised by his country. The thought of a modern, civilized nation actually concocting a plot so insane, so bold and destructive, was more than she could wrap her rational brain around.

And yet there was the question. The foundational question that Aimes always asked whenever evaluating any series of confusing events.

Who stands to benefit?

Would Russia benefit from a devastated Panama Canal? Would they benefit from social turmoil inside the United States? Economic instability in the West?

A broken presidential administration?

No. It was too crazy. And yet...there was something about that line of inquiry. Something that rang vaguely, horrifyingly true.

Nuclear weapons don't grow on trees, after all. The weapon in Panama had come from someplace. If it hadn't been found in a forgotten Soviet weapons depot...then where?

Aimes reached for her phone. She dialed Silas Rigby's office. Her youthful deputy director answered immediately.

"Yes?"

"I want you to get in touch with the team in Panama."

"I just got off the phone with the managing case officer. No update so far. They're running tests but—"

"Call him back. I want to know if they can estimate the age of the weapon used."

"What do you mean?"

Aimes thought slowly. She measured her next words.

"Ask them to assume that the weapon wasn't old. Ask them if they could prove that it was modern."

"We already know it wasn't modern. The weapon was atomic. Pretty crude based on modern nuclear standards."

"I'm not talking about the design. I'm talking about the *construction*."

Long pause. "You think...somebody could have emulated an old design?"

Aimes thought again. She weighed the value of speculating.

She decided it was too soon.

"Just ask them, Silas."

18

Rockville, Maryland

James O'Dell parked the government-issued Chrysler sedan in the back of the lot and fast walked to the lobby. A receptionist offered to guide him to his destination after checking his ID and confirming his appointment. The office suite in question sat near the top of the multi-story glass-faced office complex. O'Dell's leather-soled shoes smacked the tile like gunshots as he trailed the receptionist, ignoring her polite questions about his day and her comments about the cooling weather.

He could only think of Maggie. If he closed his eyes, she was there. If he slept, she was there. If he ate or worked or tried to drown himself in blaring jazz music, she was always there. Reaching for him, begging for help. Desperate for the lifesaving exchange of a new liver.

When at last the receptionist guided him to an executive office, O'Dell proceeded through the heavy wooden door without waiting for permission, ushering himself into a sprawling room with windows overlooking the Maryland countryside. The floor was smooth carpet, the furniture modern and bright. A tall Native American woman with long black hair stood behind the desk, a phone cradled against one ear. Her gaze snapped toward

O'Dell—and the receptionist who trailed him—but she remained calm as she completed the call.

O'Dell remained standing, just across from the desk, impatient and demanding.

The woman hung up the phone and forced a smile.

"Mr. O'Dell?" She extended a hand, tilting her head for the receptionist to leave. The door closed behind them and O'Dell shook once. The woman's hand was warm against his palm, contrasting with the chilled touch of Maggie's skin.

Now pale and papery. Barely alive.

"Please have a seat," the woman gestured to a chair, then turned for a coffee bar. "Cream or sugar?"

"I'm fine, thank you." O'Dell descended into the chair with a muted grunt, his aching, tired body ready to collapse against the floor if he should let it. He hadn't slept more than eight hours in the past three days—combined.

All those long nights of phone calls, emails, and internet research. It had all led him here, to the top floor of the Health Resources and Services Administration, into the office of that administration's director—Winona Nightcloud. Truth be told, O'Dell had never heard of the HRSA, let alone its director, three days prior. He knew almost nothing about their purpose or operations. He only knew that the HRSA was the chief government agency responsible for the assistance, regulation, and oversight of the Organ Procurement and Transplantation Network. There was a middleman, he'd read. A private nonprofit, the United Network for Organ Sharing, who managed the day-to-day functions of the Transplantation Network. That also didn't matter to O'Dell. He couldn't get a meeting with the UNOS on short notice. He *could* get a meeting with the HRSA, and its director—perks of sharing an office in the same building with the acting president. Stratton didn't know about his meeting. Easterling didn't even know. But it was Easterling's office who had booked it for him, and the pressure of that office that had so quickly cleared a space on Nightcloud's schedule.

"I understand you're the official White House liaison to the medical team overseeing the president's recovery?"

Nightcloud sipped coffee, beautiful brown eyes peering at O'Dell with guarded openness. She hadn't been told why the official White House liaison wanted to meet with her, but she wasn't stupid. Surely she had guessed.

"That's right," O'Dell said. "I'm here to talk about finding the president a liver transplant."

Nightcloud nodded, lowering the coffee cup. "I thought you might be. I contacted the UNOS ahead of time to get an update. The president is third in line for a liver transplant. That's an improvement over earlier this week, when she was fifth. One patient passed away, regrettably, and another was downgraded based on medical need. The president's outlook is positive."

"How long?" O'Dell's voice remained flat. He didn't have time for courtesy, but Nightcloud didn't appear perturbed. She shook her head.

"We have no way of knowing, Mr. O'Dell. It could be tomorrow. It could be a month. It all depends on how many donor livers become available."

O'Dell gritted his teeth. He'd heard that answer before, from Dr. Fletcher. It wasn't what he'd driven all the way to Maryland to hear again.

"That's not good enough," he said. "I want you to bump the president to priority one. The next liver that becomes available goes directly to her, no questions asked."

Nightcloud kept her large brown eyes fixated on him, unblinking, one hand wrapped around the cup, the other flat on the table. The moment lingered, and frustration boiled into O'Dell's blood.

"Did you hear me?"

Nightcloud set the cup down. "Who are you, Mr. O'Dell?"

"I'm the White House liaison—"

"No, I know what your title is. I'm asking *who* you are. Because you clearly don't have any particular medical expertise, and what you're asking me to do is not only impossible, illegal, and unethical; it's immoral."

O'Dell's jaw locked. He leaned close to the table, lowering his voice to something between a threatening growl and an intent plea. He himself wasn't even sure.

"Madam Director, you are speaking to the president's representative. I'm telling you that she will *die* without a transplant, and—"

"There's nobody on this list who won't eventually die without a transplant, Mr. O'Dell. That's the nature of the entire system. The two people ahead of the president are, I assure you, in much worse condition, with much less time to waste."

"But *they* aren't president of the United States."

"No, they aren't. And fortunately for them, that doesn't matter. We don't judge priority based on job title or social status. Priority is established based on an ethical metric of medical need, time on the waiting list, and other objective factors."

O'Dell gritted his teeth. The frustration he'd initially felt at Night-cloud's rejection was now overflowing into something closer to desperation.

"Who are they?"

"I'm sorry?"

"Who are the other two ahead of the president? I want their names and phone numbers."

For the first time since the meeting began, Nightcloud's perfect composure faltered. Her brow wrinkled, outrage creeping into those beautiful native eyes.

"You can't be serious."

"I'll call the families. We'll make an arrangement for them to waive their status."

"Mr. O'Dell." Nightcloud sat bolt upright in the chair, the coffee cup smacking the desktop. It should have been enough to make O'Dell flinch, but he was too tired to flinch.

Too singularly focused on the task at hand.

For her part, Nightcloud had flushed. She stared unblinking at O'Dell, indignation radiating from her posture like rays of the sun.

"I'm going to excuse your outrageous request based on the stress of your office and your apparent exhaustion." Nightcloud's voice was tight, cutting like a bullwhip. She spoke through her teeth. "Allow me to be perfectly clear when I state that the privacy of donor patients, the integrity of the priority list, and the integrity of this office are *not* matters for discussion."

Her lips pursed, and the indignation hardened into a glare. She gestured toward the door. "I'm going to ask you to leave now."

O'Dell stood in a rush, suit jacket snapping, but he didn't turn away from the director. He glared down at the desk, bending the full weight and fury of the maddened desperation inside of him against her, and dared her to blink.

Nightcloud didn't blink. And she didn't speak.

"If the president dies," O'Dell growled. "Her blood is on *your* hands."

Nightcloud stood, chin rising with gentle poise. Her voice was calm. "And if she lives, Mr. O'Dell, she will live by the moral system established by law, just like the rest of us. Now kindly get the *hell* out of my office."

O'Dell didn't argue further. He barged through the door and exploded to the staircase, ignoring the elevator. His heart thundered as he took the steps two at a time, hurtling toward the bottom. Head pounding. Thoughts racing.

Already planning his next step to save Maggie.

19

Nobody commented on Turk's absence during the long flight across the Atlantic, but Reed knew that everybody noticed. Spread out around the worn cabin of the Gulfstream, Wolfgang and Ivan slept, Lucy read a medical textbook, and Reed drank Jack. Not enough to drive himself into full inebriation, but just enough to excuse the mental fog clouding his brain as something other than emotional distress.

By the time they finally reached the Middle East, he'd achieved that perfect balance of sustained drunkenness that was just strong enough to numb his nerves but not nearly enough to compromise his fighting edge. It was a skill set Reed had refined over decades of practice. A method of self-preservation that would eventually kill him, either by liver failure or eroded reaction time, but it still felt somehow better than the alternative.

Mental clarity.

Reed wasn't aware of what arrangements Langley had made for the passage of the private airplane into Turkish airspace. The last time he had entered Turkey, it had been via HALO jump, dropping out of the side of a CIA-issued Gulfstream and plummeting toward the crash site of Air Force One under the cover of night.

Turk had been with him back then. The mission was to recover the flight recorder from the wreckage of Air Force One. The Turkish government hadn't wanted American intervention within their borders then, and Reed suspected that they didn't want it now, either. He doubted that the CIA was declaring the true purpose of the jet as it touched down at Sabiha Gokcen Airport and taxied toward the private terminal. Strickland intercommed from the cockpit to direct everyone to stay in their seats and keep the weapons out of sight. They wouldn't be departing the plane. They wouldn't be processing through customs. If all went according to plan, they would only be on the ground for under an hour, just long enough to fuel up...and collect a passenger.

Reed sat halfway down the length of the plane, settled into the seat with a loaded SIG P226 Legion tucked next to his leg, a round in the chamber. Wolfgang sat across from him, eyes closed, one hand tucked beneath the edge of his signature pea coat. Reed had no doubt that there was a gun hidden there. Ivan likely had one also. He sat in the tail of the plane with a glass in one hand and a half-empty bottle of vodka resting in the seat next to him. Lucy had abandoned her textbook and retreated to the aft cabin. Maybe she was sleeping.

Or maybe she was praying. Lucy like to pray. She'd found religion during the chaotic and scarring years that had passed since her tenure as an assassin for hire. She often appealed for divine intervention.

But despite the number of highly competent, heavily armed men, and even despite Lucy's promise of having God Himself on their side, Reed felt oddly exposed. Vulnerable. Isolated.

It was the first time in *years* that he'd embarked on a mission without Turk at his side. The big Tennessean had accompanied Reed through firefights in half a dozen countries, going all the way back to their mutual tours of duty in Iraq as Force Recon Marines. Reed had saved Turk's life, on more than one occasion, and Turk had saved his.

But now Turk was gone, and not only did that leave Reed feeling exposed, it left him feeling a little betrayed.

At least, as much as he could feel anything. Mostly, he just felt numb. That incessant cloak of darkness that closed over his mind and swallowed his consciousness. He still couldn't sleep—not without the nightmares. He struggled to focus on any positive train of thought.

The only thing he could clearly picture, the only thing that served to assuage the anxiety, was the thought of a next target. Something to sink his proverbial teeth into and to shred to pieces. Something to exorcise his demons with.

If the Russians had truly supplied Abdel Ibrahim with his weapons... well. They'd do as targets.

From the front of the plane, the cockpit door slid open, and Corbyn appeared, running long fingers through dark brown hair to straighten it after the disruption of a headset for so many hours. Strickland remained in the co-pilot chair, arguing with somebody over the radio who apparently barely spoke English. The subject of the dispute seemed to be the arrival of a fuel truck.

"We're wheels up in forty-five," Corbyn announced. "They're only expecting us to be stopping for fuel. Our official flight plan routes us for New Delhi next."

Reed nodded once, but he was barely paying attention. In the months since he had met Corbyn, he'd quickly come to trust her abilities not only as a pilot but as an espionage operative. The British Secret Intelligence Service had trained her well. The flight path from Istanbul to New Delhi would carry them directly over northeastern Turkey, only miles from the Georgia border.

A slight technical mishap could be arranged there. Something that required Corbyn to temporarily put the plane down in some rural stretch of dystopian mountain wasteland where Reed, Ivan, Wolfgang, and their translator could bail out.

They only needed the translator.

"LB!" Reed kept his gaze on the window as he called toward the aft cabin. Lucy didn't keep him waiting. The door slid open and she stepped out in sweatpants and a sweatshirt, barefoot with an iPad in one hand. She settled into a seat across from Reed and worked her fingers across the screen.

"He's on schedule," Lucy said, without waiting to be asked. "Ten minutes out."

From the cockpit, Strickland muttered a curse and called back to Corbyn. "Truck on the way. They tried to jack up the price."

Reed extended a hand, and Lucy passed him the iPad. He rotated the screen around and swept his gaze over the personnel file it displayed. The picture was black and white, but the face was clear. The man's name was Davit Güneş. Georgian father, Turkish mother. He was thirty-six, five feet, five inches tall, chubby, and sported a grizzly-looking black beard.

Under the "Prior Military Service" tab, the descriptor read: "NONE." Under "Prior Governmental/Intelligence Service," the descriptor also read "NONE." Under "Relevant Professional Skills," the descriptor read: "Electrician."

Reed looked up from the screen, shooting Lucy a glare. "Are you serious?"

Lucy shrugged apologetically. "It's the best they could do on short notice. He's contracted with the agency for eighteen months. They say he's been reliable."

"He's going to be dead," Wolfgang interjected, taking the iPad.

"Yeah, about that." Lucy suppressed a smirk. "Langley asked for you to kindly...*keep him alive.*"

Reed snorted. "Langley can make passionate love to themselves."

"You know, that's not as funny as you think it is," Lucy said.

"Who said I was trying to be funny?"

"Here he comes." Ivan spoke for the first time from the back seat, kicked back with his vodka glass recently topped off. Reed bent his neck and saw the man approaching from across the darkened tarmac. He walked with a sort of half shuffle. As though he were partially dragging one leg. There was a messenger bag slung over one shoulder, and he kept looking back as he walked, as though he expected somebody to be following him.

"Why is he limping?" Reed asked.

Wolfgang scrolled on the iPad. He snorted. "Seems he's got a bad knee."

"Well, isn't that nice. He's a gimp like you."

Reed felt Wolfgang's glare on him but ignored it. He gestured for Corbyn to open the jet's door even as a fuel truck approached the wing. Güneş reached the steps with another paranoid sweep of the airfield, running his hand quickly through his beard and peering upward but not ascending the steps.

"Davit Güneş?" Corbyn called.

"Shhh!" Güneş held a finger to his lips, glowering at Corbyn. "Do not use my name."

His voice was raspy and tense, so heavily accented that Reed could barely understand it. Corbyn shot a glance over her shoulder, cocking one eyebrow.

"Get his clearance code," Reed said simply.

Corbyn turned back to Güneş and repeated the request. Güneş leaned forward and spoke in a conspiratorial whisper, barely audible over the rumble of the fuel truck.

"John has a long mustache."

From the back seat, Ivan snorted an inebriated laugh. "Are you serious?"

"Seems Langley has a sense of humor," Lucy said. "He checks out."

"Get him on the plane," Reed said.

Corbyn gestured Güneş aboard and the little man ascended the steps. He passed through the open door a full inch below Corbyn's line of sight, and she shut the door behind him. Then he turned to face the cabin with a happy, semi-silly smile.

"Good evening." He bowed, one hand supporting the messenger strap on his shoulder. Reed didn't return the greeting. He simply snapped his fingers and gestured to the bag. Wolfgang tore it off Güneş's shoulder and proceeded to dump it out on the floor amid a storm of dismayed objections from the newcomer. Reed simply jabbed a finger to the seat next to Lucy.

"Sit."

Corbyn pushed Güneş into the chair, and Güneş sat as Wolfgang sifted through the contents of the bag. There was a change of clothes, a toothbrush, some sort of dense bread wrapped in a cloth, a folding knife, a notebook rubber-banded closed with a pen, and one small handgun tucked into a worn leather holster.

Wolfgang tugged the weapon out and cleared the action. It was a Soviet made Tokarev, heavily used and not well maintained. Chambered in 7.62x25mm, with an eight-round detachable box magazine.

Not much of a weapon. Not in Reed's estimation, but Güneş seemed possessive of it. He reached for the gun even as Wolfgang tilted the muzzle into the light to squint into the now-empty chamber.

"You're all gunked up, my dude. Ever heard of a bore brush?"

"What's in the notebook?" Reed gestured, and Wolfgang passed it to him. He'd barely got the band off before panic crossed Güneş's face, and he reached to snatch it away. Reed recoiled and Corbyn placed a strong hand against Güneş's shoulder, pinning him into the seat.

"Please. It is private."

"Uh-huh." Reed flipped the cover open. Then blood rushed to his cheeks. The contents were indeed private, but not in the way he expected. In place of notes, he found photographs tucked against the first page. Four of them.

They all depicted a Middle Eastern woman of about Güneş's age. She was dark, with long black hair.

She was also naked.

Reed closed the book, dropping it back onto the pile of personal belongings. He turned back to Güneş. The man's face was crimson. Reed chose to ignore the awkward moment and plow ahead.

"You speak Georgian?" he demanded.

Güneş nodded once.

"You know something about the landscape north of the border?" Reed pressed.

Another nod, this one a little more tentative. It made Reed wonder what the CIA had told Güneş about his pending mission. Clearly, the man knew something about thousands of Russian troops pouring into Georgia—Reed could see the apprehension in his face. Maybe he hadn't actually expected to be deployed north of the border.

Craning his neck, Reed looked into the back of the plane, facing Ivan for the first time. The big Russian was still reclined in the seat, gently rotating the vodka in the bottom of his glass as he stared at Güneş, brow slightly wrinkled. After a long pause, he glanced to Reed and grunted.

"He'll do."

Reed turned back to Güneş.

"You like to make money, Mr. Güneş?"

"Yes..." The voice was tentative.

"Outstanding. You're coming with us."

20

Tbilisi, Georgia

Anton Golubev had served as Makar Nikitin's right-hand man since the two of them had worked together in the old KGB, but it wasn't until Nikitin ascended to the office of deputy prime minister of Russia that Golubev earned the nickname that would stick with him like a tick on a Siberian wolf.

The title of *fixer*. The nickname *Ghost of the Kremlin*.

It turned out that Golubev loved to kill people almost as much as he loved to drink and rape Chechens. More than amusement, it was closer to a hobby—something he practiced and developed. Back in the days when Nikitin's presidential predecessor had been kicking down doors in Ukraine and—allegedly—disposing of his enemies under questionable circumstances, Makar Nikitin had taken notes. He understood the value of having an agent of chaos working in the background, able to eliminate political adversaries and nosy reporters at will.

Likewise, Nikitin also understood the value of unspoken, unprovable truth. There would never be hard evidence. Nothing that could trace back to the men responsible or leave Nikitin vulnerable to his enemies. But everybody knew who gave the orders and pressed the triggers. Everybody knew that slit throats weren't really the result of enraged prostitutes, and tumbles in front of city busses weren't really the product of slick sidewalks.

Anton Golubev was behind them all, and he didn't really care who knew it. His hobby had grown into a sizable obsession, and he relished the terror he unleashed as much as the actual bloodshed. He was more than a ghost. He was a messenger of death, with a wicked smile on his face.

Maybe that was what made him and Nikitin such perfect partners. Nikitin did all the scheming, and Golubev managed the dirty work. It was just the way he liked it. He didn't have to *think* too much.

Nobody wants to have to *think* too much when they're pursuing a hobby. It's a recreational thing. And in the heart of the Georgian capital of Tbilisi, there was *plenty* of recreation to be had.

Golubev had arrived only hours prior, but already whispers of his presence had ripped through the seat of Georgian government, echoing down the corridors of power and unleashing a stir. The Georgians knew of the Ghost of the Kremlin, at least by reputation. They were immediately—and quite reasonably—uncomfortable with his presence, especially with the continued absence of their own president, Giorgi Meladze. Questions were starting to be asked. Murmurs of true alarm.

Golubev didn't care. Russian soldiers had already streamed into the countryside by the tens of thousands, Russian armor leading the charge. In another twenty-four hours, Georgia's fate would be sealed, long before she knew what was even happening. That was all part of Nikitin's role in the "special military operation."

Golubev's role, if he did say so himself, was decidedly more interesting. He could hardly wait to get started.

In the back of a temporary field headquarters Golubev had erected in a commandeered Georgia public library, a private office awaited him. The room was small and quiet, with a simple desk and a single satellite phone. The phone rang even as he closed and locked the door, settling into the creaking desk chair with a restrained sigh.

The chair was Soviet in origin. So was the desk. So, for that matter, were the aches and pains that ran up his legs and his spine as he sat. It was all so much a part of the heritage of Georgia that the mark of the USSR couldn't be ignored by a blind man.

Heritage, yes. And destiny.

Golubev answered the phone.

"Da?"

"You have arrived?" Nikitin's voice was distorted by distance and encryption, but Golubev recognized it. He grunted by way of response.

"The Americans are calling an emergency session of the security council," Nikitin continued. "They intend to force a statement on our activities. I expect them to have broad international support. We are running short of time."

"We are ready," Golubev said. "My men are in position."

A brief pause. "The target?"

"I have chosen."

A gentle grunt. "You may proceed, my friend."

Golubev hung up without further comment. He stood with a little effort and returned to the door. Across the hall, another room waited, illuminated by flickering fluorescent lights and occupied by tall bookshelves and sagging tables, all laden with cleaning and maintenance supplies. It was the storage room of the library.

Ten men also occupied the room, all dressed in pitch-black clothing, Grach handguns strapped to their thighs, armor plates held in carriers across their chests. AK-12 rifles held in two-point slings, dark berets pulled low over their scalps.

They were Russian *Spetsgruppa* "A"—Alpha Group. A detachment of the Russian FSB, itself the successor of the KGB, Alpha Group was one of Russia's most elite special operations and counterterrorism units. Or at least, it was supposed to be.

Some of Alpha Group had been repurposed, under Golubev's direct supervision. They had been hardened, washed through level after level of intense screening to ensure absolute loyalty and dependability. Complete ruthlessness and a relentless dedication to the mission at hand...whatever that mission may be.

Golubev liked to think of them as Double A's...the Alphas of the Alphas. The supremes. He could send them straight against the gates of Hell, if he so desired, and they would go.

They'd likely win, also.

"Are we ready?" Golubev addressed the question to the lone officer in the room. The man simply nodded.

Then Golubev proceeded to the table at the middle of the room, where his men had cleared the clutter away, allowing room for a large tablet computer. The tablet displayed a map of the region, with Georgia at the heart, Armenia to the south, Turkey to the southwest.

And Azerbaijan—loaded with oil and natural gas fields, mineral reserves, and strategic naval bases along the Caspian Sea—lay directly east.

Golubev studied the map and reviewed the two targets he had prese-lected—one effective but conservative. The other more effective but also more ambitious. It all depended on how well the first phases of the special military operation went.

Thus far? They had proceeded without a hitch. Everything was going splendidly. They had plenty of time.

Golubev pointed—not to the small target. To the big one.

"Green light. We go."

21

Davit Güneş wasn't happy about his CIA assignment. Apparently, the agency had misled him about the exact physical demands—to say nothing of the risk to life and limb—that the mission would require. That didn't surprise Reed in the least. He was used to the CIA lying and manipulating, and anybody like Güneş who had been dining on their gravy train for years in exchange for petty regional intel should be also.

What Reed was most concerned about, if he was concerned about anything, was the concept of charging headlong into a highly dangerous landscape mired by potential combatants and unpredictable factors while trailing an out-of-shape, overweight Turkish electrician behind him.

Then again, if everything hit the fan, those limitations wouldn't be Reed's problem. They would be Güneş's. The only thing that mattered now was getting across the border as quickly as possible and moving north before the Russian army, still penetrating southward, could cut off access altogether. To add a further wrinkle to the situation, Turkey—itself a member of NATO and no great friend of Russia—was actively deploying

military assets to their border with Georgia, just to remind Russia not to get
too close.

The Prosecution Force needed to move quickly to slide through that
gap before it was too late. That left Reed in the awkward position of dragging along Ivan because he needed intel, Wolfgang because he didn't fully
trust Ivan, and Güneş because nobody else could speak Georgian.

"Ninety seconds!" Corbyn shouted from the cockpit as the Gulfstream
screamed ahead, nose dipping down, losing altitude rapidly, but not yet
decreasing in speed. The airstrip where Corbyn would park the jet wasn't
actually an airstrip. It was just a long stretch of empty roadway, broad
enough to leave a yard or so on the outside of the landing gear and straight
enough to provide takeoff space for Corbyn to get back into the air.

The Turk's didn't know that any American assets were in play. This
flight wasn't supposed to stop at all, not until New Delhi. It was a race to get
back into the air before anybody knew what—and who—had been left
behind.

Reed double-checked his chest rig and tugged on the straps. They were
tight, locking an armor plate against his sternum along with six fully
loaded magazines of 5.56 NATO ammunition to feed the M4 rifle he cradled
in his arms. The SIG P226 Legion was strapped in a drop holster to his
thigh, and a KA-BAR knife, a flashlight, a med kit, and two fragmentation
grenades rode his belt.

In his pack was enough food to keep himself alive for a week and enough
water for thirty-six hours. Wolfgang was similarly equipped, but Ivan opted
only for a Glock 17 handgun, one spare mag, and an oversized bottle of water.

"I am not soldier," Ivan said with a grunt. "Somebody else do the
killing."

Reed shot Wolfgang a look, and Wolfgang waved a hand dismissively.
Reed turned next to Güneş. The electrician was busy stuffing everything he
could into a backpack—water, food, spare magazines for weapons he wasn't
even carrying, and that notebook full of nudies from the girl back home.
Reed muttered a curse and started snatching stuff out of the bag, throwing
it across the floor as the plane's engines wound back and the nose dropped.
Güneş scrambled to retrieve his things and Reed shoved him aside.

"Water and food. No weapons. I don't want you popping off shots and blowing my kneecaps out."

He shoved the bag into Güneş's arms, then resumed his seat and braced himself against the chair in front of him as Corbyn guided the plane in for the final approach. Reed couldn't see anything through the still-darkened windscreen, but it felt like the plane was moving much, much too fast for a landing.

Apparently, Strickland agreed.

"Ease off the power," the co-pilot advised.

"Not yet." Corbyn's voice was crisp and calm. Almost relaxed, as though this were an afternoon cruise in a convertible.

"You're coming in too hot," Strickland said. "You're gonna rip the landing gear off. Ease off the power!"

"Not yet," Corbyn repeated, now pushing the yoke to nose the airplane down. Reed's stomach flipped and he sank his fingers into the chair's armrests, impulsively glancing left to the seat across from him.

Where Turk should be. Only, Turk wasn't there. The absence sent a strange wave of instability rolling through Reed's chest, as though he were staggering on the deck of a small boat in a big storm.

Again the Gulfstream's nose dropped, and Strickland shouted a curse.

"What the—" He grabbed the yoke, seizing control. The plane jerked as the two pilots fought each other. Power bled off, and the aircraft dropped what felt like fifty feet, all at once. Reed's stomach hurtled into his throat. He gritted his teeth and the landing gear touched asphalt. A scream of rubber against pavement ripped through the cabin. Strickland shouted. Corbyn cursed. The plane bounced up, then came down again—hard. They hurtled forward, bags and weapons rattling across the floor and Reed's stomach conducting somersaults. Güneş cried out in Turkish. The plane struck again, and this time it stayed down. The back end fishtailed a little and the nose dove as Strickland laid on the brakes.

They screamed to a jolting halt, and momentary silence settled over the cabin.

Then the war erupted. Strickland tore his headset off and Corbyn descended into her trademark British cursing. The engines were still running and Reed's head spun, but nobody from the cockpit seemed to notice.

"What the bloody hell was that? You trying to get us killed? You don't ever steal control in a landing! I'm the bloody captain. You hear me? *I'm the captain!*"

"You're a crazy fool is what you are! You ever landed a plane on a roadbed before? You were gonna drive us straight into the ditch! I swear, I don't know where they found you, but I'll be *dead* before I fly with your dumb ass again!"

Reed ran a hand over his face, tuning out the noise as Wolfgang moved for the door. It opened with a heavy *thunk* of the latch, and the stairway lowered into the darkness outside. As Reed passed the cockpit, spittle blasted from Strickland's lips and coated his arm. Corbyn sat in the pilot's seat, sunglasses slid all the way to the tip of her nose, tongue stuck out like a four-year-old child.

"Hey!" Reed shouted, slamming a fist against the cabin doorframe.

Strickland went quiet. Corbyn's tongue disappeared. Both pilots pivoted toward him, waiting for him to pick a side. Reed didn't pick a side.

"Where are we?" Reed barked.

Outside the open cabin door, he couldn't see anything in the pitch blackness. Wind howled around the aircraft's wing tips, smelling of dust and jet exhaust.

"Roadbed in northeastern Turkey," Corbyn said. "You're twelve klicks from the border."

Reed lifted his pack and headed for the door, dropping out onto busted asphalt. Looking both ways, he couldn't see the horizon. He couldn't see any city glow. Only the landing lights of the Gulfstream marked their position on a narrow highway, riddled with cracks, vacant of vehicles.

There were no people. No animals. Just desolation and silence, broken by the hum of the jet engines.

Wolfgang and Ivan reached the ground behind him, Güneş trailing last of all. Without a word, Reed waved once at the plane, indicating for Lucy to close the door. Then he led his three counterparts quickly off the road and dropped into knee-high grass, already dying as winter moved in.

Behind them the engines thundered again. The plane strained against its brakes as Corbyn prepped for an aggressive takeoff.

Then the wheels broke free, the engines dumped fuel, and the plane rolled quickly away down the asphalt. A moment later it was nosing up and reaching toward the sky, already pointing eastward again, toward New Delhi.

Reed watched it go, breathing easily in the cool night air. Despite the weight of the gear on his back and the armor plate dragging against his chest, a strange sense of calm washed over his body. Almost relaxation. It was so warm and so welcome, he couldn't identify it at first. It felt like the moment when painkillers kick in and the agony goes away. When the buzz hits, and all those busy thoughts just fade.

It was focus. It was clarity. It was stillness in his exhausted mind. Reed blinked once, and just like that, the fog he'd fought for weeks evaporated. He could *see* again. He could *feel* the moment.

And what he felt was a thirst for action.

Sweeping away from the road, Reed nodded once to Wolfgang, and then he stepped deeper into the grass. The city of Ardahan lay only five clicks to the northeast, closer to the Georgian border. There would be vehicles there, Reed knew. Opportunities to hot-wire a truck before they turned north into Georgia.

With a hodgepodge team at his back and the mission dead ahead, Reed Montgomery led the way.

22

Williamson County, Tennessee

The house on the western edge of Franklin was one of those generic-not-generic, cookie-cutter-but-totally-unique builds with a stone facia, a two-car garage, and a postage-stamp yard encircled by a decorative steel fence. The patio was overhung by an awning, leaving just enough shade for Turk to sit by himself on generic outdoor furniture and slowly smoke cigarettes while he overlooked the backyard.

It was almost empty. Just green grass that needed a trim, with a few scattered nuggets left behind by the frou-frou terrier that Sinju had adopted. Baby Liberty was too young for yard toys, but there was a swing mounted to a metal frame that she loved for Turk to push her in.

The hallmark of the backyard was the little memorial garden Sinju had planted against the fence. It consisted of a small water feature, several colorful flowers, and an engraved granite slab with her dead mother's name on it.

The mother Turk had been unable to save from the ravages of North Korean tyranny.

Gently thumping ash from the end of his cigarette, Turk sat with a sweating bottle of beer in one hand that he had yet to take a sip of. There were additional cigarette butts on the ground around his boots, but he didn't so much as flinch when the front door opened and the yapping of the frou-frou terrier signaled Sinju's return.

Baby Liberty laughed at something, and Sinju prattled in Korean—probably talking on the phone to one of the South Korean expats she'd made friends with in Franklin. It made Turk happy to hear her talking in her native tongue. Sinju had mastered English quickly, but he never wanted her to forget her heritage. He wanted Liberty to grow up in its shadow. To appreciate American freedom the way only a survivor of brutal oppression could teach her to appreciate it.

The phone call ended and Sinju called his name. Turk barely heard her as he lifted the cigarette to his lips, drawing slowly. As he stared at the memorial garden, he could remember the gunshots. The mud. The darkness that closed over the beach even as US Navy SEALs stormed up behind them, joining the fight against North Korean soldiers.

Turk had nearly died on that beach. So had Sinju, and her father.

So had Reed Montgomery.

The door creaked open next to Turk, and Sinju poked her head out. "Turk?"

He didn't look up. He didn't hide the cigarette. He stared at the garden and he saw the storm clouds gathered over Pyongyang. The lights of the Hotel of Doom. The threat of nuclear holocaust hanging over the world like a blanket.

"Turk?" Sinju's voice softened, and Turk finally looked up. She stood in the doorway with Liberty on one hip, the dog bursting past her to go urinate on the swing set. Their gazes met, and Turk's eyes suddenly blurred. Sinju's face softened and she pushed outside, leaning down to wrap him in a hug. Turk extinguished the smoke against his ashtray and wrapped his arm around her. Then he took baby Liberty and kissed his daughter on the forehead.

She was beautiful. More like her mother than her father, thank God. Clear-eyed and always smiling. Always bright. When Turk fell in love with Sinju, he thought that nothing could ever rival that passion.

He was wrong. So very, very wrong.

Sinju settled into the chair beside him and smoothed her skirt. It was floral and loose. It matched her gorgeous Korean complexion perfectly. Her dark gaze swept over the cigarette butts on the patio, but she didn't say anything. She simply watched while Turk cooed to Liberty, nestling her in the crook of his arm while the child's big eyes blinked ever more slowly.

At last, Sinju said: "Where is Reed?"

She knew what question to ask. She'd known that Turk had gone to Virginia with Reed, and maybe she expected something more dramatic to follow. Sinju was nobody's fool. She also didn't ask many questions.

She took things as they came, like an iron wall. Unbendable, unbreakable. One of the many things Turk loved about her.

"Overseas," Turk said simply.

"Another mission?"

Turk nodded.

"And you?" Sinju's next question took Turk by surprise. Not the nature of it, but the tone of it. She sounded suddenly demanding. He looked up and saw her chin held high, lips pursed.

"I'm here," Turk said.

"Why?"

"Why what?"

"Why are you here?"

Turk blinked. It wasn't what he expected. He sat up, Liberty now sleeping in the crook of his arm.

"Because my family is here."

Sinju remained impassive, chin still elevated, eyes dark and unblinking. He waited, but she didn't say anything.

"What?" Turk demanded.

No answer. Sinju looked away. Turk gritted his teeth.

"Hey. Don't do this. I came back to take care of you. I came back to be *with* you. I thought that was what you wanted."

Sinju folded her hands. She looked at the garden. Turk waited, but still there was no answer. It made him suddenly angry. He wanted to snap his fingers.

"Hey," Turk snapped.

"What do you see?" Sinju asked, still looking at the garden.

"What?"

Sinju pointed. "*What do you see?*"

Turk looked out to the garden. He saw the flowers, the little rocks. The babbling fountain and the granite marker.

"I see a memorial," he said.

Sinju finally faced him, still pointing. She shook her head. Her large eyes turned moist, and she blinked hard. She lowered her arm.

"No. You do not see a memorial. You see a *reminder*. My mother died in Korea because she was too afraid to resist. She would rather have had comfort than freedom. It is like you say—freedom is not free."

Turk gritted his teeth. He raised a finger. Sinju cut him off.

"No! No, you do not argue. You do not argue. You are soldier, not politician. You fight for us. This is the man I married. He is not coward."

"Coward? Are you kidding me? You think I'm here hiding?"

"Aren't you?" Sinju demanded.

A lump rose in Turk's throat. He opened his mouth. Then he closed it. He shook his head slowly.

"He's losing it, Sinju. Reed is losing his edge. He's going to run his team right off a cliff. I got *out* of the military. We said we were getting *out* of that business."

"And I want you out of that business," Sinju said. "But family comes first."

"This is my family!" Turk's voice cracked. Liberty flinched in her sleep. Sinju's dark eyes softened a touch, and she leaned forward out of her chair. Her hands closed around Turk's. She squeezed softly. Her voice dropped to barely above a whisper.

"So is Reed."

The words landed like bunker busters. Turk's chest caved in and his face dropped. He clutched Liberty close, and Sinju's forehead pressed against his. She touched his arm. For a long moment she said nothing, and Turk just inhaled her scent, pressed up close to her warmth. Drowning himself in it.

And knowing, whether he liked it or not...she was right. It had haunted him from the moment he stormed out of Leiper's Fork, leaving the Gulfstream and the team to their own devices. He'd known, as much as he hated it, that he was leaving something behind.

More than people. A duty. Not to America, and definitely not to the CIA. To something much deeper. To a brother waylaid by forces far darker than whatever petty geopolitical powers were now at work in Georgia.

"I'm sorry," Turk whispered.

Sinju pulled him close and squeezed. He felt her tears on his neck as she whispered back.

"Don't be sorry. Be brave."

More simple words. But they struck just as hard. Turk lifted his face and kissed Sinju on the forehead. He squeezed her arm and passed baby Liberty off to her. Sinju continued to cry but she smiled at him. She leaned back in the chair and cooed to Liberty, stroking the child on one cheek. Singing softly to her in Korean.

Turk stood and shook out another smoke. He lit up and walked to the edge of the yard, near the garden. He placed a phone call to the blocked number that he knew rang to a telephone in an office building in Langley.

The operator picked up. His contact. His governmental concierge.

"Yes, sir?"

"I need a flight to Istanbul."

23

The little deli at the corner of F Street and Ninth Street was a guilty pleasure for FBI Director Bill Purcell. Only a block away from the J Edgar Hoover Building, where he'd spent most of his life since graduating from Quantico nearly four decades prior, Purcell had made friends with the ownership and had a standing order for a pastrami with Swiss cheese that never disappointed.

During the earlier parts of his career, before he rose to the highest post in the Bureau, Purcell frequented the shop two or three times a week, but since the crushing weight of the directorship had descended on his shoulders like a wrecking ball, he was lucky to get his pastrami with Swiss delivered to his office more than twice a month.

Actually making the walk to the deli had become a semiannual pilgrimage at best, but with everything unraveling in Washington, and more pressure than ever descending upon his office, Purcell felt the need to step away.

He needed to clear his head. He needed a moment by himself, just to breathe, and to *think*. Not just about the ongoing Bureau investigations into the origins of Abdel Ibrahim's terror attacks, or the wave of violent crime sweeping the country as desperation and fear cloaked the nation, but about smaller, somehow more sinister questions.

Questions like *what*, exactly, had become of former CIA Director Bill O'Brien.

Purcell peeled the top off his Italian roll and squirted spicy brown mustard from a bottle, relishing the savory odor of the fresh, hot pastrami. There was a pickle spear, also, and a sliced apple. Lemonade would wash it all down. The meal was so tantalizing, Purcell's mouth actually watered as he spread the mustard with a knife.

He was going to enjoy this. He was going to barricade the pressures of the Hoover building from his mind, just for a moment. What was an emergency now would still be an emergency in twenty minutes.

Purcell closed the sandwich and crushed the roll together. He took the first bite—always the best bite—and groaned a little at the sublime flavor of artisan bread, premium sliced meat, and gourmet cheese. It was better than sex.

"Mr. Director! Fancy meeting you here."

The voice was bright and chipper, jarring Purcell from his deli bliss as his gaze snapped toward the door. A tall man with thick brown hair stood there—broad shouldered and healthy-looking, he wore a premium black suit with a United States Senate pin on one lapel and a red power tie tucked behind the jacket.

Mid-fifties, but he commanded the vibrancy of a much younger man. He looked...lithe. Very comfortable in his own skin. Like a rock star.

Purcell lowered the sandwich and wiped his mouth as the man approached the table, still beaming a high-wattage, can-I-count-on-your-vote smile. He extended a hand and Purcell half rose from the chair to shake it, his own flabby grip lost amid the crush of the bigger man's powerful fingers.

"Pastrami, huh? Great choice! I'm a club man, myself. Turkey, bacon, lettuce, and tomato. Regular mayo, not light. But don't tell the wife."

He winked, and Purcell returned to his chair while trying not to let his irritation leak out into his features. He hadn't immediately recognized the senator when he first barged into Purcell's delicatessen sanctuary, but long before that crushing handshake, the memory clicked.

It was Matthew Roper, three-term senator from Iowa. Former collegiate football star, and a rising star amid the Democratic party. Purcell had likely met the man on occasion, although no particular conversation stood out. All he really knew about Roper was that he chaired the Senate Select Committee on Intelligence.

And, more importantly, that he was interrupting what was meant to be a desperately needed hiatus from the workday. No such thing, in Washington.

"Mind if I pull up a chair? It's funny I should bump into you. There's actually something I wanted to ask about."

Roper pulled up a chair before Purcell could object, settling down and calling over his shoulder to the young Greek guy working the counter.

"One club, extra turkey, regular mayo. And a beer, if you have it!" Roper turned back to Purcell, still smiling. "Don't tell," he said.

Purcell wasn't sure what it was that he wasn't supposed to tell, but it didn't matter. He hadn't been given a chance to speak yet.

"Busy day at Hoover?" Roper asked.

Purcell saw his opportunity and charged for it like Roper might have charged a gap in an offensive line.

"Extremely, actually. I don't mean to be rude, but—"

"Bud Light okay?" the Greek guy called.

"Sure. Long as it's American!"

Roper laughed at his own joke, and the clerk brought the beer. Purcell restrained a sigh and sipped his lemonade, finally resigned to the fact that Roper wasn't leaving. He hadn't ascended to the top of the food chain at the FBI for nothing, after all. This wasn't a chance meeting. Whatever brought Matt Roper into the deli that day, he wouldn't leave until he got it off his chest.

"You guys faring okay with all the extra work?" Roper asked. "Anything the Senate can do to support?"

Roper said it as though he were the chair of the Senate Judiciary Committee, not the Intelligence committee. Purcell appreciated neither the condescension of the question nor the intrusion of it.

"We're just fine, Senator. How are things on the hill?"

"Oh, you know. Another day, another bloodbath."

That brought an additional chuckle from Roper. His sandwich came, and he took a massive bite. Bacon crunched, and Roper groaned.

"Wow. I see why you like this place. That's fantastic!"

Purcell squinted, lemonade halfway to his mouth. He never recalled telling Roper—or anyone save the secretary who ordered his lunch, for that matter—that he liked this deli. Roper made the comment as though it was a callback to a previous conversation.

It somehow made Purcell uneasy. He decided to give up on a peaceful lunch and go on the offensive.

"You said there was something you wanted to discuss, Senator?"

Roper nodded, grunting through a full mouth. He held up a finger, then swigged his beer. When he finally swallowed, the smile had at last faded. He looked serious.

"Right. Yes. Actually, Mr. Director, I'm sort of surprised you haven't already called me about it."

"About?"

Roper cocked an eyebrow, as though he couldn't believe Purcell didn't know. He leaned a little closer and lowered his voice.

"*O'Brien.*"

A tingle ran up Purcell's spine, but he played it cool, remaining relaxed. He cocked an eyebrow of his own.

"O'Brien?"

Roper smiled, but this time it wasn't the vote-catcher smile, it was more of a smirk.

"Oh, come now, Mr. Director. There's only one O'Brien at the top of your agenda, and he drowned in a pool in his own backyard. Allegedly."

Purcell looked back to his plate, spearing an apple slice with a plastic fork and taking his time. He still couldn't tell if Roper was broaching the subject of the recent death of Victor O'Brien out of a hunger for idle gossip or if something less transparent was at play.

Regardless, it didn't matter. The answer would be the same.

"I can't comment on an ongoing investigation, Senator. Your office is welcome to submit an official request for information, if you like."

Another snort from Roper. He was no longer eating. He wasn't smiling, either.

"O'Brien died at a pretty unusual time, wouldn't you say? Right before he was set to testify to my committee about criminal misconduct of the president."

Purcell looked up, suddenly irritated by the comment. As though he were being schooled on his own investigation. "*Alleged*," he said.

"Yes, of course. *Alleged* criminal misconduct. All the same, I thought you'd want to interview my office. You know...to consider a motive."

"There's no motive in fate, Senator. When you drink too much and fall into your own pool, you drown. That's how life works."

Roper rocked his head back and forth, as though he were weighing the argument but not quite buying it.

"What if he didn't trip?"

Purcell set the fork down. He wiped his mouth. "Is there something you want to say, Senator?"

Roper held up a hand apologetically. "No, I'm sorry. I'm not insinuating anything. Obviously, you're the investigator. I'm just saying that O'Brien was set to testify about some *alleged* matters of corruption inside the Trousdale administration. Serious allegations, they seemed. My office was supposed to receive initial discovery documents the very next day after... well. After he drowned."

"Your point?" Purcell pushed. He already knew, but he wouldn't be the one to voice it.

"No point, Mr. Director. I just wanted to be sure your office had all the available facts as you pursue your investigation. You know...leaving no stone unturned and all that."

Roper's smile returned. Purcell remained ice cold, the unspoken barb in Roper's last comment sinking in deep. Not because Purcell really cared about what any senator who didn't sit on the Judiciary Committee but because, someplace beneath the stress and pressure of the hurricane ripping through his office...Purcell had questions of his own.

"I appreciate your concern, Senator."

Roper smacked Purcell on the arm and stood, dropping two twenties onto the table.

"Lunch is on me, Mr. Director. You enjoy that sandwich, you hear? There's a lot of hours left in the workday."

Then Roper winked and turned for the door, leaving Purcell thinking that whatever his actual purpose in the chance-not-chance encounter, it had very little to do with concern over the fate of Victor O'Brien.

24

Ambassador Tracy Carrie had served as ambassador to the United Nations since the Brandt administration—the predecessor to the Trousdale administration, which now felt terrifyingly close to the predecessor of the Stratton administration. Working under three de facto presidents had brought a string of challenges a mile long, with conflicting leadership styles, expectations, and policy concerns.

But what really made her job difficult—what kept her hair turning gray and her nights sleepless—had little to do with who was calling the shots from the White House. It had everything to do with the UN Security Council, and particularly the four permanent members of that council who joined the United States with veto power: the United Kingdom, France, China...and Russia.

It was because of that veto power that Carrie knew her special resolution requiring Russia to immediately surrender all evidence of forgotten Soviet-era WMDs found in Georgia would be shot down long before it reached the end of the runway. If Russia *wanted* to surrender such evidence, after all, they already would have, and if they didn't want to, all they had to do was veto the resolution.

But despite the inevitability of that defeat, Carrie understood the power of proposing the resolution and putting Russia on the spot. It was a strategic move on behalf of the United States. America could expect the other three permanent members of the security council, along with the ten non-permanent members, to vote alongside them in a demand for the surrender of evidence. That demand, while ultimately toothless, would place Russia in the predicament of having to justify themselves. Of having to explain why they claimed to know things but weren't willing—or able—to prove those claims. It was a game of chicken, and Carrie was determined to not be the first to blink.

She entered the security council chamber with aides at her back, Armani shoes clicking on her feet. Carrie liked nice shoes. They gave her a feeling of standing on a powerful foundation, as though the style and exclusivity of the brand somehow gave her a diplomatic edge. She represented the United States, after all. The richest, most powerful nation in world history.

She had to act the part.

Assuming her position behind the United States sign on the left side of a giant circular desk, Carrie waited while the session was called to order by the council president, French Ambassador Margaux Renard. The first order of business for the emergency meeting was to address the member nation which had called it—the United States. Carrie was given the floor, and she stood behind her microphone.

"Thank you, Madam President. Distinguished ambassadors and members of this council. The United States has called this emergency meeting of the United Nations Security Council to address a recent and alarming development in the nation of Georgia. Following the detonation of a nuclear weapon in the Panama Canal, which is still under investigation, Russia has declared that the weapon used was Soviet in origin, taken from a forgotten arms depot in Georgia and detonated by the terrorist Abdel Ibrahim. Subsequently, tens of thousands of ground troops of the Russian Federation, accompanied by a significant number of tanks and combat vehicles, have penetrated the Georgia border and are now sweeping through the country. While there is no evidence of Georgian resistance to this dramatic military action, the deployment of these troops bears all the hallmarks of an invasion and a military occupation of a sovereign nation. To complicate matters, Russia's claimed motivation for what the Kremlin is terming a 'special military operation' is to secure any additional WMDs which may have been discovered alongside the bomb used in Panama, and yet they are unwilling to substantiate these claims with hard evidence of their findings."

Carrie stopped, sipping water from her glass and strategically looking across the circular table to Russia's seat, where Ambassador Maxim Belov leaned over his desk, staring intently at her with unblinking eyes. There was no sign of a challenge in his face, but she could feel the rebuttal brewing.

All well and good. Time to hit him with the punchline.

"For the purpose of global security and in order to hold the Russian Federation accountable for her military actions, the United States is proposing a resolution which would compel the Russian Federation to surrender any and all evidence they have assembled concerning a forgotten Soviet weapons depot in Georgia. In addition to serving as the foundation for any discussion as to whether this so-called *special military operation* can be justified, it will also serve every member nation to know what weapons may have been stored in this depot and what threats they may pose. The United States moves that such a resolution, as prepared and submitted to this committee ahead of this emergency meeting, be immediately voted on for adoption, so that the pressing nature of these concerns may be addressed without further delay. Thank you, Madam President."

Carrie resumed her seat, and Renard leaned into her microphone. She spoke in French, but translators working in real time in the room converted her words to English via the earpiece Carrie slipped on.

"The council thanks the ambassador from the United States for her voice on this matter. Would the ambassador from the Russian Federation wish to make a comment before the motion proposed by the United States is put to a vote?"

"Yes, Madam President," Belov responded in Russian. "We would."

"Very well, the ambassador from Russia has the floor."

Belov consulted his notes, taking his time. When at last he looked up, he didn't look to Carrie. He looked instead around the table, down the long line of permanent and non-permanent members, maintaining an expression of absolute gravity and sincerity, despite the fact that Carrie had no doubt Belov couldn't care less about her "concerns."

It was the mark of a skilled ambassador.

"Members of the council, distinguished representatives and ambassadors. I deeply regret the tragedy of the recent detonation of a nuclear weapon in Panama—the first such detonation of a nuclear weapon in anger since the United States' use of atomic bombs in the Second World War."

Carrie resisted cocking an eyebrow, remaining perfectly still in her chair. The jab didn't surprise her. It was exactly the sort of tactic a man like Belov would attempt.

"While the loss of life and the resulting economic devastation is horrific, of one thing we can all be sure. We do not yet know what we do not yet know. The details of this attack, the motives and methods of the terrorist Abdel Ibrahim, and the exact source of the weapons he used are still matters under thorough investigation. As I speak, authorities in the Russian Federation are indeed pursuing leads into the question as to whether this weapon may have been Soviet in origin. This investigation, however, is a work in progress, and what details we have confirmed—while alarming—are still limited. The Russian Federation remains stalwart in our aim to secure the region, and by so doing, to ensure continued global peace. We object to the insinuations of the United States that our dedication to verifying certain facts prior to presenting them to this council is in any way an indicator of deception or calculation. We assure this council that the moment such facts are confirmed, Russia will present these details in full. Thank you, Madam President."

Belov looked to Carrie, his face expressionless. Carrie stared right back, and Renard resumed her microphone.

"Are there any other members who wish to make statements prior to a vote on this matter?"

No answer.

"Very well. The draft resolution proposed by the United States will now be put to a vote on a matter of adoption. All those in favor?"

Carrie raised her hand alongside the UK, France, and all ten non-permanent members. Belov's arm remained down, as did the arm of Chinese Ambassador Liu. No doubt China was planning to abstain from the vote, Carrie thought. That was typical of China, always eager to play the neutral party and buddy up to whoever would pay them the most.

"All those against?" Renard asked.

Belov raised his hand.

And then so did Liu.

Carrie's back went rigid, and ice entered her veins. Her gaze snapped to the face of the Chinese ambassador, but he was fixated on his notepad. She could feel the United Kingdom and France both looking her way, but she couldn't afford to betray her surprise by acknowledging their own.

"Abstaining?" Renard asked.

No hands went up.

"Very well. The total votes are as follows: thirteen votes in favor, two votes against, no votes abstaining. The draft resolution is defeated, due to the negative votes of two permanent members of this council."

Renard smacked her gavel against the desk.

Belov smiled.

25

The Turkish/Georgian Border

Reed's team located a vehicle on the outskirts of Ardahan. It was an early 2000s model Nissan Patrol, a four-door SUV set on beefy off-road suspension with dents pounded into every body panel and a crack racing through the windshield. The truck sat behind a fuel station on the outskirts of town. The station was closed for the night, and it took Reed all of two minutes to defeat the door lock with a lockout tool, then hot-wire the ignition. The engine rumbled to life and he powered it around to the front of the fuel station, where Wolfgang had already cut the lock on an outdated fuel pump. They filled the tank, put Ivan and Güneş in the back seat, and then Reed turned north for Georgia.

Riding in the passenger seat, Wolfgang kept his rifle pinned between his knee and the console as he worked a satellite phone. Wolfgang switched the device into speaker mode and dialed. It rang only once before the controller picked up on the other end.

"Eagle's Nest. Clearance?"

"Echo-Charlie-Echo-seven-eighty," Wolfgang called back. "Prosecution Force inserted and proceeding to target. Requesting connection of live drone feed."

Reed wrestled the Nissan along a busted providential road as the controller responded with a quick "standby." The Nissan was already locked into four-wheel drive, but the suspension was battered and abused by decades of heavy use in rural Turkey. Each pothole and rut send bone-jarring shudders ripping up Reed's spine, gear rattling in the cargo area.

Reed ignored it, the focus and exhilaration he'd felt the moment he departed the plane seeping deeper into his consciousness with every kilometer that ground by. It was more than excitement and deeper than thrill. It was an intrinsic, magnetic force that dragged him ever closer to the action, ever closer to the promise of gunfire.

He'd given up trying to understand it, and given up trying to apologize for it. It felt so good to simply feel, and not overthink, that nothing else mattered.

"Drone connection authorized. Live feed pending. Standby."

Wolfgang dug an iPad housed in an armored case from his backpack. It flicked on and he accessed a navigation app. The feed from the Air Force reconnaissance drone the CIA had deployed out of northern Iraq to fly forty thousand feet over the rough Turkish landscape was slow in coming, but when it finally connected, it featured not only a night-vision-equipped view of their position but also an infrared-enhanced grid. Bright red dots marked the location of Ardahan fading behind them, while the expanse of the borderlands ahead was illuminated only by a single heat signature.

It was the border crossing—three klicks away, situated along the beaten Turkish road and staffed by both Georgian and Turkish authorities.

"Crossing dead ahead," Wolfgang said. "Detour in four hundred yards. Eagle's Nest, requesting zoom."

Reed clenched both hands around the wheel and kept the Nissan pointed toward the border crossing, his foot jammed into the accelerator to drive the speedometer up toward the ninety kph mark. His headlights were off, rendering the path ahead only navigable by the NVGs snapped down over his face and the guidance of the drone.

"Right turn in three...two...mark."

Reed yanked the wheel right on Wolfgang's signal, leaving the road and rushing through a shallow dip before the tires grabbed rough foothill soil and pulled the Nissan fully off-road. From the back seat, Ivan grunted like an old man and Güneş yelped at the slam of bottomed-out suspension, but Reed powered on. Wolfgang clung to the iPad and called for another three hundred yards directly up the side of an aggressive slope. The landscape was semi-mountainous, with arching green hills covered in thick, chest-high grass dropping at random into jagged ravines. Reed couldn't see anything through the grass save the green-tinted horizon beyond. He was left completely in the hands of Wolfgang and the Air Force drone to keep them from taking a wrong turn and flying straight into an abyss. The Nissan's tires dug in and shredded the dry soil, hurtling them two hundred yards above the roadbed in mere seconds. Güneş shrieked from the back seat and Ivan shouted for him to shut up. Reed followed Wolfgang's directions to pull a hard left, and the Nissan exploded through a shallow ditch to land on a mountain roadbed.

Or maybe it was a goat track. A shepherd's path. Whatever the case, it was little smoother than the open terrain they'd just left and still overgrown with grass.

"Ahead one klick," Wolfgang said. "Ravine to your left. Hug the right shoulder."

Reed guided the Nissan along the mountain wall to his right and glanced once through the driver's-side window. Three or four kilometers away and several hundred yards beneath him, he could see the border crossing. It glowed like the sun in his night vision, illuminated by security lights on either side of a lowered gate. On the Georgian side there was a bridge, stretching thirty yards over the churning Kura River.

It was the river they had to cross. There was another bridge, located by a CIA satellite earlier that day four miles further down the goat track. It wasn't an official crossing. It was more like the goat track version of its larger twin up the road, designed for pushing herds of farm animals and making village trades with neighbors from the north and south. It was wooden, probably homemade, and certainly not designed for the bulk of a heavy SUV.

But for all that, it appeared unguarded, and beyond lay another busted highway, leading north into Georgia. The goat track bridge would have to be their intrusion point.

"Four klicks," Wolfgang said. Then the satellite phone crackled.

"PF, be advised. The Air Force has identified a contact on the roadbed beyond the target bridge. Two vehicles, possibly military, moving south at speed."

Reed breathed a curse. Wolfgang lifted the radio.

"Eagle's Nest, please advise on ETA of contact."

"Standby."

Reed wrestled the wheel of the Nissan through another run, forced to slow as the back tires kicked up a mini avalanche of rocks and loose soil. It erupted over the cliff to their left, and then they were diving into a narrow valley with mountain ridges rising on either side. Reed knew the bridge lay dead ahead at the bottom of the valley, even though it was lost beyond a dip in the road.

The headlights, however, were perfectly visible. They pierced the night from the Georgian side of the river, powering south directly toward the goat track bridge. Reed didn't need an ETA from the CIA to know that the oncoming vehicles would reach the bridge before they could, but it came crackling through the sat phone anyway.

"PF, be advised. Oncoming vehicles are confirmed to be Georgian military trucks. Personnel unknown. Will reach bridge ahead of your ETA."

Reed stepped on the brakes, and the Nissan ground to a stop at the entrance of the valley. Engine rumbling, headlights still off, he wiped sweat from his chin and watched the trucks churn steadily onward.

They were coming in fast. Too fast for the busted road. It was indicative of an emergency response, and it made him wonder...

"What've you got?" The question was addressed to Wolfgang.

"They're headed for the bridge," Wolfgang said with a shake of his head.

"I realize that. I'm asking what my options are."

Wolfgang panned and zoomed on the drone feed. The trucks neared the bridge and slowed. Spotlights snapped on and scanned the northern bank of the Kura River.

"They saw something," Reed said. "Something keyed them off. Wolfgang?"

Then the sat phone crackled. "PF, be advised. Turkish patrol vehicle

departing border crossing and moving eastward along the river toward
your position. Time to arrival estimated three minutes."

Reed cursed again and dropped his foot off the brake. There was no
going back. They would be lucky to turn the heavy SUV around at all
without dropping it into a ditch or rolling off a cliff. Through his NVGs,
Reed saw a low patch of ground with more chest-high grass rippling
beneath the wind and bending toward the riverbank. There was a low spot
there, where the river looked wider and shallower than the rest of its
rushing stretch. Maybe forty yards instead of thirty, and even from so far
away, the current seemed to slow.

The Nissan rumbled and lurched as it left the goat path, front bumper
dropping almost immediately as the tires dug into sandy soil. Reed jammed
his foot harder into the accelerator and the truck surged. From across the
valley, the headlights of the two Georgian military trucks reached the
bridge and stopped. The spotlights swept two hundred yards in either
direction. Reed aimed for a portion of the river three hundred yards west of
the bridge—far enough to remain out of the spotlights but close enough to
avoid colliding with the incoming Turkish patrol.

Hopefully.

Wolfgang saw what was coming and called over his shoulder.

"Get the gear off the floor!"

Ivan moved to lift the backpacks out of the cargo area and into his lap.
He tossed one at Güneş and the little Turk grunted as it landed.

"What's happening? What is he doing?"

"American stuff." Ivan laughed. "Were he Russian, he would have
rammed straight for the bridge."

Reed ignored the commentary and surged onward, hurtling through
divots and over ridges, thrown at times toward the ceiling, shockwaves
racing up his spine. He was conscious of the noise his truck produced and
knew the Georgians would hear it. They might confuse it for the incoming
Turkish patrol, whom they were certainly communicating with, but that
cover wouldn't last for long.

"Cow! Cow!" Wolfgang shouted from the passenger seat and Reed
yanked the wheel to the left, narrowly missing the animal as it bellowed
and lurched out of his way. The river was only two hundred yards away. He

could see the Turkish patrol a mile to his left, headlights bouncing as they proceeded toward the goat bridge. The Georgian spotlights continued to flick over the surface of the river and the bank beyond.

Reed focused on the water line, slamming on the brakes of the Nissan as the front tires crossed onto pebbled sand only yards from the river's edge. He still didn't have his headlights on, but he could see the water clearly through the NVGs. It was moving slower than it had upstream, yes, but not by much. Black ripples washed against the banks as the current swept downriver toward the bridge, maybe hard enough to push the truck when he entered.

He should have turned farther upstream. Given himself additional buffer from the sweeping spotlights.

Too late now.

Reed grabbed the floor lever and rocked the Nissan into four-low—crawler mode. Then he stomped the gas. The engine surged but the vehicle rolled forward slowly. Front tires reached the water and dropped in. He could hear it sloshing against the undercarriage. The body rocked, and Ivan spoke from the back seat.

"Did I ever tell you of the time I drove a tank into the Moskva River?"

"I remember you taking a swim in the Moskva River," Wolfgang muttered.

Dark curses rumbled in Russian from the back seat. Reed ignored them and clung to the wheel. The back tires were in now. The water pushed against the door panels, and he could feel the tires slipping.

"No, this was another time. Long before I was cursed to meet you. It was a new Soviet tank, with a better engine. I was an officer in the Red Army at this time. I requested an opportunity to test it."

From upriver the Turkish patrol's headlights bounced. Reed turned in that direction as the water line reached the bottom of his window. The nose of the Nissan was almost fully submerged, meaning that the radiator was now mostly underwater, but the engine chugged on. They closed toward the middle of the river and the tires slipped again. Reed could feel them being pushed sideways—toward the bridge. Toward that Georgian military patrol.

"I guess the new motor got away from me," Ivan continued. "I ran right off a bridge! Into the ice. It sank, of course. One person died. The tank was ruined. I blamed it all on the Red Army private sitting next to me! I think they sent him to the gulag."

Ivan bellowed with laughter, and water rushed in from beneath the dash. It splashed across Reed's boots and saturated his pants. He looked left and saw the Turkish patrol only a hundred yards away from drenching them in headlights. To his right, they were much closer than that from being swept into the range of the Georgian spotlights.

"You should drive faster," Ivan commented casually.

"You think?" Reed shouted. He jammed his foot harder into the floor. The engine gargled beneath the rushing water, and the front wheels spun. For a moment, he thought they'd lost traction altogether. In mere seconds they could be stranded, or worse, swept downriver toward the bridge.

In the back seat, Ivan directed Güneş to hold his backpack higher over the water now filling the floorboards. Wolfgang raised his M4 and pivoted the muzzle toward the window, ready to engage the Georgians on the bridge if the truck slipped into range of their spotlights.

Reed clung to the wheel and closed his eyes. Not praying. Not doing anything but hoping.

The motor churned harder. Icy cold water washed up to his thighs. Then the wheels grabbed again, and the front bumper rose from the water. The Nissan inched forward, scraping toward the Georgian bank.

Ivan cheered from the back seat, and water washed toward the cargo area. Another yard, and then it began to drop away from the hood. Reed could see the far bank in his NVGs. Ten yards. Then five.

"Turks incoming!" Wolfgang called.

Reed didn't bother to look. He stopped the truck the moment the front tires rose out of the water and yanked the floor lever back into four-high. When he stepped on the gas again, the engine rushed higher and the wheels spun.

"They hear us!" Wolfgang shouted, pivoting his attention toward the goat bridge. The spotlights were flicking rapidly now, only twenty or thirty yards from spilling over them. The Turkish patrol behind them had stopped and men were piling out.

Reed didn't care. He saw the path ahead. The tires caught again, and this time the Nissan rocketed out of the river. Water rushed from the floor-boards, and they hurtled onto the far bank. In seconds they were rumbling up a low incline, headed into the Georgian side of the valley.

Reed looked over his shoulder and saw the Georgians and the Turks, still clustered around the bridge, still searching madly for the source of the engine noise.

But the Prosecution Force had already slipped through. They had reached Georgia.

26

"The *Chinese*?" Stratton made no effort to hide his surprise or frustration as he held the phone to his ear. From New York City, Ambassador Carrie remained calm on the other end.

"Yes, sir. They voted alongside the Russians."

"You said they would abstain."

"I expected them to, sir. They usually would. This is very unexpected."

Stratton leaned back into his chair and ran a hand over his face. His mind spun, but it was already too tired to make sense of complex geopolitics. It wasn't something he was fully updated on. Not something he considered himself an expert in. This was Carrie's realm.

"What does this mean?" Stratton said simply.

"It certainly hinders our ability to pressure the Russians. From the Chinese perspective, it could be a vote of defiance. If they think we're wounded, they may be testing the waters to see just how wounded. They may have voted alongside Russia just to rattle our cage. I can't imagine they honestly support Russia concealing evidence while they occupy a sovereign nation."

"Unless they've already seen the evidence," Stratton said. "Russia could have given them an inside look in exchange for the negative vote. A way of solidifying support."

"That's possible, sir."

"What are your next steps?"

"I'm remaining in New York for now. I'm going to attempt to meet with the Chinese ambassador. Ambassador Belov is ignoring my calls. I'll keep you updated."

"See that you do."

Stratton hung up and pinched his lips together. He was alone in his vice-presidential office. Paperwork was piled up everywhere. His computer was cluttered with open windows, a metaphoric reflection of his mind.

I need clarity.

Lifting the phone again, Stratton buzzed Easterling's office.

"Get in here."

He hung up and dug in a drawer, locating a yellow legal pad. It was cluttered with notes, but he tore the top sheet off. Next he found his favorite pen—a Visconti Homo Sapiens in ballpoint. It was jet black, made of actual basaltic volcano lava mixed with resin.

One incredible pen, with one incredible job to do.

The door opened, and Easterling stepped in. Stratton motioned for her to shut the door and sit down.

"The Chinese voted alongside the Russians," he said. "We don't know why, but it's safe to say our friends in Moscow are up to something."

"Next steps?" Easterling asked.

Stratton tapped the Visconti against the legal pad. "That's why we're here. We do not leave this room until we have a plan."

27

Reed made it thirty miles inland before the sun broke the horizon over eastern mountain ranges and spilled across the Nissan. It was cold in Georgia, barely fifty degrees, and not warming much with the sunrise. Gray clouds obscured the bulk of the sky, thickening as Reed finally pulled the Nissan off a rural road and shifted into park.

They were still ninety miles from the Georgian capital of Tbilisi, but now that they had penetrated well inside the border, the Air Force had been forced to retract the drone. There was too much danger of the aircraft being detected by Georgian—or Russian—air radar the closer inland they penetrated, and Langley was concerned about touching off a powder keg.

Langley was apparently unconcerned with leaving the Prosecution Force without overwatch in a hostile landscape.

"There is a daba about five kilometers from here," Ivan said. "Up in the mountains. Good place to ski."

"What are you, a tour guide?" Reed demanded. "What's a daba?"

Ivan sighed theatrically. "*Daba* is a settlement. A small town, you might say. Bakuriani is a ski daba. A ski town. For tourists."

"What's your point?" Wolfgang pressed.

"The point is that Russia is here for one of two reasons, as we agreed. Either they are here to locate and recover WMDs…or they are here to seize the country. In the second case, they would seize Bakuriani. It is of strategic value due to its position in the mountains. It would command primary roads."

Reed sucked his teeth, considering. It seemed like a rabbit trail to him, inspecting ski towns instead of cutting right to the heart of Georgia and routing toward the alleged weapons depot.

Then again, he was growing increasingly uneasy with rumbling through the mountains, plowing ahead without any certain knowledge of whether a Russian tank column lay around the next bend. A bird's-eye view could be helpful.

"You know how to get there?" Reed asked.

"I have skied there since I was a child," Ivan said. "Turn left at the next road."

Bakuriani sat in a dish between rolling mountain peaks, all of them covered in dying vegetation and tree cover, and several of them already topped by early snowfall. From an elevation of eight hundred or a thousand feet above the daba, Reed left the Nissan parked amid the trees, engine still running, and bailed out with his M4 swinging from the end of a one-point sling. Wolfgang followed, and Ivan racked his Glock 17 before unfolding his bulky frame from the back seat.

"What about me?" Güneş asked, a hint of alarm leaking into his voice.

"Stay here," Ivan said. "Try not to get eaten by the wolves."

Ivan added an animal grin to the end of his recommendation and slammed the door. Reed couldn't resist a smirk of his own as Güneş peered wide-eyed through the dirty window.

Maybe he had more in common with the big Russian than he initially guessed.

Setting out across the beaten dirt road, Ivan led the way amid the thick undergrowth, pistol hanging at his side, his oversized nose flexing as he inhaled the forest scents. He fell into easy step along a narrow deer track, and Reed followed behind while Wolfgang walked sideways, keeping a lookout over their six. The sun had fully risen, but the blanket of gray clouds obscured it from view. Reed tasted humidity on the air that made him think of rain, but the sensation that dominated his mind wasn't the clouds, or the smells, or the taste.

It was the sounds. He heard the rumble of heavy engines long before they broke out of the trees—chugging diesels and rattling tank tracks. Voices shouted in the distance, and a rifle crack was followed almost immediately by the burst of automatic gunfire.

Ivan descended onto his stomach ten yards from the edge of the tree line, and Reed and Wolfgang followed suit. They fanned out, wriggling amongst the sticks and beneath the brambles, edging all the way to the beginning of a small clearing.

It was a picnic spot, resting just ten feet beneath them with a small pavilion and a metal picnic table. There was a fire pit also, with a grate and a heap of ashes. Trash blew against the dying grass, and a path led away from the pavilion, down the slope to a block of apartment complexes. And then the city.

Bakuriani wasn't a big place. Ivan had accurately described it as a "settlement." A town, in Americana. Small buildings rolled across the valley floor, nestled up to the edges of the mountains exactly like any ski town in Colorado. The streets were narrow, the buildings multilevel, the cars appearing as little gray dots.

And the Russian military sticking out like dog crap in the snow. Reed dug a powerful set of Swarovski binoculars out of his pack and settled in behind them while Ivan and Wolfgang did the same. They all lay perfectly silent for a while, just studying the landscape. From his position on the highest point of the slope, Reed could see all the way to the heart of the town, a small patch of open asphalt spread in front of a ski lodge and a row of retail stores. The little gray dots of vehicles were joined there by a crowd of tightly packed bodies, all lined together across the street, like a wall of human bodies.

Standing in front of them, its giant barrel jutting high above their heads and toward the sky, was a Russian T-90 main battle tank. Russian soldiers clogged the streets around the tank, appearing as smudges from so far away, but under Reed's trained eye he could still appreciate the strategy of their movements. They were breaking apart, moving quickly from door to door. As he swung the binoculars across the city, mapping more distant streets and much closer ones, he saw more of the same. Assault vehicles, Tigr trucks, and two additional tanks had deployed throughout the city. Soldiers were kicking down doors, barging through homes and retail shops. Twice in the passage of five minutes, the familiar pop of a handgun or the belch of a shotgun was answered by the thunking rattle of a Kalashnikov rifle fired into the air.

Smoke rose from one apartment complex. One of the T-90s rolled right over the nose of a minivan, tearing through a privacy fence as a crowd of school children fled in front of it. Screams rent the air, joined into one collective voice of desperation.

Reed's stomach twisted, and he lowered the binoculars but couldn't take his eyes off the daba. It was like watching a train wreck in slow motion. Disaster, and unthinkable tyranny, unfolding right before his eyes.

"They're not looking for WMDs," Wolfgang whispered.

"No," Ivan said. "They are not. They are here to take everything."

28

"We've got something!"

Silas Rigby was speaking even as he crashed through Aimes's office door. She choked on coffee and hurried to wipe her mouth as her deputy director burst into the room, face alight with triumphant excitement, an iPad held up in one hand. The door swung automatically shut behind him, and he advanced right to the desk.

No hint of trepidation in approaching his boss. No thought of formality or decorum.

Aimes's efforts to break down the walls of bureaucracy inside the agency were proving fruitful. Maybe a little *too* fruitful.

"We've *got* something," Rigby repeated.

Aimes swallowed her coffee. She jabbed a finger at the chair across from her and tore tissues out of a box to wipe her face. Rigby sat down, virtually radiating nervous energy. He was like a kid on Christmas morning. He was barely holding himself together.

"Start again," Aimes said, finally collecting herself. "What are we talking about?"

"Isotopic analysis," Rigby said.

Aimes blinked. "What?"

The triumphant smile broadened across Rigby's boyish face. "I hadn't heard of it either. It's something one of the contractors explained."

"*What* contractors?"

Rigby blinked. At last he seemed to remember the context of his excitement. "Oh, right. We're talking about the blast team researching in Panama. Remember you asked me to have them estimate the age of the weapon? Not the age of the design, but the age of the construction."

"Right." Aimes nodded. "Now I'm tracking. What did they find?"

"Well, that's where the isotopic analysis comes in. Essentially, a nuclear blast leaves isotopes—chemical elements—behind, like a sort of fingerprint of the radiological elements used to create the blast in the first place. I'm fuzzy on the details, but the key point is this: isotopic analysis can be used to prove what type of nuclear material was used in a given bomb. It's a relatively straightforward process, apparently. They were already working on it."

"And?" Aimes prompted, feeling a punchline coming.

"And the bomb was an enriched uranium weapon, almost certainly. Very similar to Hiroshima, but larger. Probably late 1960s in design, possibly Soviet but it's really too early to tell."

"Okay. We already suspected that. What's new?"

Rigby's smile faded. He sat back in his chair and swept his glasses off.

"What's new is isotopic analysis can also determine the approximate *age* of the nuclear fuel used in a bomb. It's a lot of science, but essentially as enriched uranium fuel ages, the isotopes develop what are called *daughter isotopes*. Examples would be thorium-231 or protactinium-231. These are both natural byproducts of the decaying process, and we would expect to find them among the radioactive debris following the detonation of a very old bomb. A bomb that was built in the late sixties or early seventies."

"So the bomb *was* old."

Rigby shook his head. "That's the thing. Like I said, we'd expect to find those daughter isotopes in the aftermath of a very old bomb. *But we didn't.*"

A dull chill ran up Aimes's spine. She sat forward. "So..."

"So the weapon detonated in Panama was based on an early Cold War design, but the fuel used was younger. *Much* younger. Potentially...brand-new."

29

Diyarbakır, Turkey

The CIA-issued Gulfstream hadn't landed in New Delhi or even proceeded very far in that direction after departing the busted asphalt roadbed in northeastern Turkey. Corbyn flew just over the border of Armenia before banking the plane like a fighter jet and turning back westward. The target was Diyarbakır, a major Kurdish metro center in southeastern Turkey where the Prosecution Force B-Unit, as Lucy called it, could refuel their plane at a small private airport and remain on standby for word from Reed.

It wasn't what she wanted. If Lucy had her way, she would have deployed alongside Reed. That would have taken her out of the plane—*away* from the constant, childish arguing between Corbyn and Strickland —and most importantly of all, it would have put her alongside Wolfgang.

Lucy wasn't sure how the romance first developed. She'd met Wolfgang years prior, and there had never been any particular spark that she could recall. To be fair though, in hindsight, she'd been pretty self-involved back then. It was really no wonder she hadn't detected his interest, but now that she had returned to the team and encountered Wolfgang again, the attraction was undeniable.

Better still, it was mutual. Nothing hot and heavy. Nothing reckless and sensual. Just a sort of quiet comfort that Lucy felt whenever she was near Wolfgang, and Wolfgang seemed to mirror. They started hanging out together. Wolfgang rented an apartment in Lucy's building outside of Nashville, and they watched movies. They played games. They walked Tennessee trails and attended small concerts.

There was no conversation about the past or extensive joint analysis of the extensive physiological damage they both suffered from. No conversations about politics, or the future, or anything more serious than what was for dinner. Lucy didn't ask about Wolfgang's hopes and dreams, and he didn't ask about her fears or insecurities.

They just enjoyed one another, as friends at first, and then as something more. Lucy wasn't sure where it was headed and she wasn't sure if she wanted to know. She put the brakes on when she felt like it, and that wasn't too often. Neither of them were kids any longer. Neither of them felt any crazed urges to be wild and reckless. They hadn't slept together and she felt no pressure to.

But there was chemistry. A gentle magnetic draw. She liked being around Wolfgang, and now that he was someplace downrange, and Lucy was stuck inside the Gulfstream listening to Corbyn and Strickland bicker about landing protocols, all Lucy could do was think about him.

And wish she was with him.

"What I'm saying, genius, is there's a *system*. Do you hear me? *A SYS-TEM*. You don't just whip the thing like a dang Corvette!"

"Well, maybe you don't, but some of us have a bloody sense of moxie."

"*Moxie?* What does moxie have to do with anything?"

"It means I've got *style*, mud brain! *Panache.* Flair. Zest. Spirit. *Zing.*"

"*Zing?*"

"Yes, zing! I guess they don't teach that in the Air Force academy. No room for zing when your ass is as tight as a washboard. I'll bet you haven't experienced any zing since you were twelve years old zinging yourself off to your arithmetic teacher."

"Excuse me?"

"You heard what I said!"

Lucy slammed her book down with an extended groan, but nobody from the cockpit was paying any attention. Marching across the aisle, she unlatched the door and announced her intention to get some fresh air.

The two pilots made no acknowledgment. The argument about landing procedures had denigrated into a pissing contest about sexual conquest. Corbyn was screaming about Swedish men with barrel chests and Strickland was defending the virtue of his junior high math teacher—a little too passionately.

Lucy pushed through the doorway into the crisp air outside and stepped onto the tarmac. The early morning sun spilled over the single airstrip. As she circled to the back of the plane, Strickland and Corbyn's argument fell mercifully out of earshot. She could see all the way to the end of the runway, with the Turkish countryside spread out beyond.

It was beautiful. Very calm, with tall grass bending in the wind and occasional vehicles passing on the highway. Not much else to see. The airport was encircled by a fence with a small guard shack occupied by an overweight Turkish official with a paperback novel and a box of donuts. He looked happy.

It made Lucy smile.

Lifting her face toward the sky, she closed her eyes and breathed a silent prayer for the safety of Reed, Ivan, the Turkish interpreter, and Wolfgang. Maybe...especially for Wolfgang. She knew her God had a plan for the mission at hand. She believed nothing was random.

She also enjoyed the comfort of asking Him for divine intervention. It gave her a sense of calm. A grounded confidence that whatever happened next...it was all part of the plan.

When Lucy opened her eyes, there was a vehicle pulling up next to the guard shack. Sunlight glinted off the windshield, obscuring her view of the occupants. It might have been a taxi. She couldn't be sure.

But as she watched, the car pulled away from the shack. It turned toward the parked Gulfstream and accelerated. Lucy's heart rate accelerated with it, and she edged backward toward the aircraft. There were a number of planes parked at the little airport. Any one of them might be the target of the car.

But no. It was headed straight toward her. Lucy turned quickly and rushed back to the steps. She climbed into the plane, once again engulfed in passionate argument—now about stamina between the sheets.

"Guys!" Lucy called.

No break in the argument.

"*Hey!*" Lucy snapped. "Somebody's coming!"

That finally got their attention. Strickland bent to peer through the Gulfstream's window, while Corbyn went directly for her backpack, producing a Glock 17 and racking the slide.

"What are you doing?" Strickland demanded.

"Grabbing my zing," Corbyn snapped. "I'd suggest you grab yours, but I know it's so small."

Strickland flushed. Lucy ignored them both and returned to the door, Corbyn on her heels. The car pulled right up to the base of the stairs.

"Easy..." Corbyn whispered, keeping the Glock out of sight.

Lucy raised a hand to shield her eyes, and put on a smile.

Probably just an airport official.

The back door of the car opened. A man got out. A *big* man. Well over six feet tall, heavily muscled, wearing sunglasses. He slammed the door and turned toward them.

Lucy's heart lurched, and she rushed down the steps. It was Turk. She wrapped him in a hug and Turk stumbled, pushing her quickly back.

"Lucy."

Lucy regained control of herself and leaned back. Turk's chin rocked down, his face strained as he pulled the sunglasses off.

"Where's Reed?" Turk said, voice taut.

Lucy's stomach tightened, and she released him. She shook her head.

"He's already downrange."

30

Reed parked the Nissan on the outskirts of the Georgian capital and all four men bailed out. It was even colder amid the mountains than it had been in northeastern Turkey, but the steady drip of adrenaline seeping into Reed's bloodstream kept him warm and focused.

They had passed *a lot* of Russian soldiers on their way northward, even as they skirted away from main highways and dabas and stuck to the back roads. Many of those back roads ran along ridges and around mountain peaks, offering sweeping vista views of the countryside. It was from those observation points that they easily tracked the tide of Russian armor and fast infantry, closing from town to town and leaving detachments behind at every key intersection.

Ivan was right, Reed decided. This wasn't a search and recovery mission, it was very evidently a total occupation by a foreign military. What was strangest about it all, however, was the total lack of resistance on the part of the Georgian Defense Forces. On occasion, their mottled green uniforms contrasted with the darker green of the Russian military, but the Georgian soldiers seemed disoriented and lost inside their own country, rushing to calm panicking civilians and to clear streets ahead of the oncoming Russian tanks.

It was as though they were directly collaborating with the invasion. Submitting to it.

"Bending over," in Ivan's words.

By the time the four of them reached the outskirts of Tbilisi, the presence of Russian assets was too extreme to allow the Prosecution Force to proceed in full combat gear without being noticed. Reed stopped at the edge of a city park and peered out toward the core of the city, where smoke rose toward the horizon. Another burning building, or perhaps a car. Random shots cracked off also.

"They will take the government buildings," Ivan said calmly, as if he'd seen this a thousand times before. Maybe he had. "There is a tower that houses the Ministry of Defense. It is much like your Pentagon. If this is an invasion, the Russian forces will seize it. It is a good place to start."

"Shouldn't we head to the arms depot?" Wolfgang asked. "Sounds like you're leading us into the hornet's nest."

Ivan snorted. "There is no arms depot. Just an empty place long forgotten by time. We find the Russian command, and we may find a suitable intelligence source."

"Intelligence source?" Wolfgang cocked an eyebrow.

Ivan smiled. "All birds sing when you light them on fire."

"What does that mean?" Panic edged Güneş's voice as he huddled behind a tree, too afraid to even look out across the city. Before Ivan could answer, Reed took charge of the conversation.

"Ivan's right. It would be quicker to interrogate somebody than to keep sneaking around hoping for a lucky break. We'll leave the rifles and packs here. You and I will go in. Wolfgang, watch the translator."

"Are you kidding me?"

Reed was already tugging the chest rig over his head as Wolfgang objected. His rifle, backpack, drop holster, and spare magazines all found their way into a pile next to Güneş. Only the SIG P226 Legion, the KA-BAR knife, and the Swarovski binoculars remained, the first two tucked into the small of his back beneath his jacket and the last dropped into his pocket next to the compact messaging device he would use to communicate with the rest of the team. Ivan followed suit with his Glock 17, and in seconds the pair of them appeared no more military than any of the hundreds of civilians crowding the streets as distressed mobs, pushing against the lines of Georgian military and shouting at the passing Russians. It was organized chaos in Tbilisi—exactly what Reed would have expected, given the circumstances. They would blend in easily enough.

"I'm not a babysitter," Wolfgang growled, leaning close to Reed.

"Good thing he's not a baby," Reed said. "Try to keep him alive. We might need him later."

"Da," Ivan said, flashing his wolfish grin toward Güneş. "Perhaps we will need bait to draw out the Russian wolves."

Güneş paled. Reed simply turned toward the park. Together he and Ivan stepped out of the trees, into the sunlight.

Into the city.

It was a four-mile trek across the city to Georgia's Ministry of Defense building, and Ivan seemed to know the way. He walked easily, shirt untucked, grizzled face defying the cold wind as he and Reed melted into the crowd. Reed noted Ivan's gaze moving in short, systematic sweeps of the landscape on every side, pausing from time to time on Russian soldiers or pockets of agitated civilians. The tension in Tbilisi was rising to palpable levels as the objecting cries of civilians were suppressed by the barked orders of armed men.

While the Georgian Defense Forces continued to appear bewildered and overwhelmed, the civilians seemed fully aware of what was happening, and they weren't having it. When a burst of automatic gunfire rent the air from a hundred yards ahead, screams burst from the crowd and a tidal wave of bodies churned up the sidewalk toward them. Ivan shifted deftly to the side, leading Reed down an alley between tall gray apartment buildings. Aggression slipped into Ivan's stride as the gunfire repeated, rolling with the familiar *thunk thunk thunk* of a Kalashnikov rifle, immediately joined by more screams.

"Real humanitarians," Reed muttered. "The locals seem grateful."

Ivan glanced over his shoulder, sneering. "Remind you of Iraq?"

Reed stopped mid-stride. The Russian smirked. Then he bent a little as they approached the next intersection. They were passing out of the heart of the city, nearing a river that divided downtown from what Reed assumed to be uptown. Wide, muddy water churned slowly beneath bridges heavy with foot traffic and vehicles. A makeshift barricade of humanity had been erected to block the passage of a pair of Russian Tigr trucks, and a confrontation was underway.

Reed noted the heavy machine gun mounted to the roof of the lead Tigr, manned by a Russian infantryman in full combat gear, and knew how the confrontation would end.

"We must hurry," Ivan said, leading the way back onto a main street. He fast walked amid the gathering crowd as everyone surged toward the mouth of the bridge. A few dozen of the braver civilians had even approached the sides of the Tigr trucks and were shoving against them, rocking them on their suspension. A trio of Georgian soldiers tried in vain to pull the people back from the Russians, but mob mentality had overtaken any thought of self-preservation. Even as the Russians barked through bullhorns, ordering the people back, more of them flooded the street.

Ivan pushed through the crowd and Reed kept tight on his heels. They circled the Tigr trucks and reached the bridge. Forcing their way against the stream of civilians, they fought across the river and reached the north bank even as the crowd of protestors swelled in size.

Ivan ignored the tumult and turned eastward along the river. He started to jog, apparently unconcerned with being identified. Every Georgian soldier or cop who passed was now headed straight for the bridge, pale terror saturating their faces in the morning sunlight. Despite his initial revulsion at Ivan's jab, Reed couldn't deny that it did feel a lot like Iraq. Like those days when he was nestled behind a sniper rifle, someplace high above a dusty city, while a detachment of infantry went door to door.

A humanitarian mission. A search and recover op. So much pain and chaos.

"Here," Ivan said, finally slowing but not stopping. They walked along the riverbank, with trees crowding the sidewalk to their left. Beyond that tree line stood a tall glass building with red-and-white Georgian flags fluttering from its top. There was a steel gate and a guardhouse standing in front of it, with another pair of Russian Tigrs parked directly across the street, joined by two Georgian Defense Force Humvees. The entrance of the military compound was situated on a corner, impossible to approach or observe without standing directly in view of the guardhouse, now occupied by a half dozen Russian soldiers.

But once again, the protestors were ahead of Ivan and Reed. They had gathered in a knot across from the gate, fists raised and steady chants directed at the defense building. Ivan slipped into them with ease, and Reed followed him. The noise was so loud he couldn't hear himself think, but the view of the defense building was clear. Ivan stopped beneath an oak tree and crossed his arms, dark gaze sweeping across the building's grounds and beyond the Russian soldiers standing at the gate. Those soldiers made no effort to engage the protestors, but a trio of Georgian cops worked the line with arms outstretched, pushing the protestors away from the street and motioning with their hands for everybody to remain calm.

Nobody remained calm. The tension Reed had felt before was verging on panic, and if he put himself in the shoes of the men and women on every side, he could understand why. This was their home. Their capital city. The heart of their own country. An occupying force had moved into it almost overnight—but not just any occupying force, it was a force Georgia had only very recently divorced themselves from.

This had to feel like unbelievable déjà vu to those old enough in the crowd to remember the Iron Curtain, or even the Russo-Georgian War of 2008. It was easy to see why they would be desperate.

It was less easy to understand why the Georgian Defense Forces *still* weren't putting up a fight.

"There," Ivan snapped, arms still crossed. Reed followed his gaze to a detachment of Russian soldiers departing the entrance of the Ministry of Defense building, walking in a tight knot toward the Tigrs. Or, at least, he *thought* they were Russian soldiers. Unlike those troops that now guarded the gate, these men weren't dressed in dark green uniforms but in pitch-black ones with berets cocked over their skulls. They wielded AK-12 rifles fit with red dot optics and flashlights, chest rigs hung heavy with spare magazines and armor plates. Russian flags adorned their arms, and knotted into their midst, barely visible, a man in a black suit marched. He was short and dark, with eyes that reminded Reed of empty pits. A scar rippled up one cheek, and he walked with a slight limp.

Even from a distance, Reed felt a chill in his blood at the man's face. Not because he recognized him as an individual but because he recognized him as a persona. The type of man that Reed had encountered in the worst corners of every society he'd ever visited. A viper. A dog. A vicious, flesh-eating monster.

The kind of man to whom money and power were only the means to a much more sinister end—cruelty for the sake of it. Bloodshed as a way of life.

"Hell's angels," Ivan breathed.

"Who is he?" Reed spoke without taking his gaze off the knot of black-clad soldiers. They had reached the Tigrs now, and the dark man was boarding without a single glance at the crowd of protestors.

"Anton Golubev," Ivan said. "They call him the Ghost of the Kremlin. The fixer. He is Nikitin's right-hand man."

"And the death squad?" Reed asked.

"Alpha Group. Special forces. We created them in the seventies to serve as a military wing of the KGB. They are like...well."

"Like Nazi SS," Reed finished. "Storm troopers."

Ivan shrugged, still watching the soldiers. They had fully loaded into the Tigrs now, and as the big engines roared to life, the standard Russian soldiers in dark green were moving to clear the protestors away. Behind them, back across the river, the heavy *chock chock chock* of a machine gun ripped through the air, joined by horrific screams of pain and terror.

But Ivan didn't look away from the pair of Tigrs as they rolled slowly onto the street. His jaw locked, and something like boiling rage ignited just behind his gray eyes.

"If Golubev is here, there is much more at play than occupation." Ivan looked to Reed. "We must follow him."

31

Trailing Golubev was easier said than done. The Tigrs had to move slowly due to the mob of so many civilians in the streets and the bullying presence of the Russian soldiers working to overpower them. But even with the frequent delays, the armored trucks rolled ahead faster than Reed and Ivan could keep up with on foot alone. They made it half a dozen blocks, moving gradually northward away from the river, before the roadway finally cleared and the Tigrs were able to accelerate. Reed slowed to a walk, breathing hard as the pair of trucks blazed through an intersection and continued toward the city outskirts.

"Plan B?" Reed gasped.

He was answered by the shatter of window glass over his right shoulder. Ivan had just driven his bulky elbow through the driver's side window of a boxy little sedan with a long nose and a short trunk. Reed didn't recognize the make or model, but the implication was clear. Ivan dipped his hand through the busted window to unlock the door. Reed circled around to the passenger side and Ivan let him in.

Already the big Russian was crowded behind the wheel. The car smelled of stale cigarettes and sour food, trash gathered in the back seat. The doors groaned as they slammed closed. Ivan's thick hands disappeared beneath the dash.

"Lada Riva," he said. "I lost my virginity in one of these. Pounded her so hard I blew a tire. Ha!"

Wires tore from the underside of the dash. Ivan stripped them with his bare teeth, hot-wiring the ignition in record time. The little motor coughed to life, sounding something like an army of hamsters trapped inside a Tupperware box. Then Ivan slammed the shifter into first gear, and they were off. The Lada rumbled over the pavement, a blown-out muffler howling as Ivan swerved around oncoming pedestrians. The Tigrs were only barely visible, a mile ahead and topping a hill.

"You should drive faster," Reed jabbed.

Ivan grinned, and the Lada howled. They hurtled through the same intersection the Tigrs had passed through only a minute prior, catching a little air as they lurched over the crown of the road. An oncoming pickup truck blazed past, and a horn blared. Ivan yanked them back into the middle of their lane and dropped his big head beneath bulky shoulders to gain a view ahead.

The Tigrs were nowhere in sight.

"Right turn at the next intersection," Reed said.

"How do you know?"

"Big trucks have bad turning radiuses. I saw them swerve left just as they were topping the hill. They were preparing to turn right."

Ivan accepted the guess with a mere grunt and pushed the Lada to max speed—maybe fifty miles per hour. The overworked engine smelled of burning oil, and black smoke clouded the rearview mirror. With every pothole and rut, the entire suspension system rattled as though it was about to fly apart. Reed looked over his shoulder to check for pursuers and couldn't help but wonder how in the world a man Ivan's size had pounded anybody in the narrow back seat of the undersized sedan.

Off topic.

Ivan hauled the wheel to the right, and the Lada leaned as it slid around the corner. A pair of Georgian army infantry stood at the intersection, AKM rifles held helplessly over their chests as they stared wide-eyed at the oncoming car as though they'd never seen a Lada before. Then they were gone. Ivan took them down the next hill, the buildings rapidly thinning out on every side as they passed from the core of the city into the outskirts.

Hills and low rolling mountains covered in dying vegetation surrounded them on all sides. Cars parked on the street forced them into the middle of the road, and an oncoming Georgian military Humvee nearly blocked their path. Ivan forced the Lada through a gap to its right-hand side, and then Reed saw the Tigrs again.

The pair of heavy Russian trucks had topped the next hill, rearview mirrors glinting momentarily in the sunrise before they dropped into the next valley. Still a mile ahead, but the gap was closing despite the scream of the overworked hamsters.

"There!" Reed pointed.

"I see them!" Ivan downshifted and rammed his foot into the floorboard. They began racing up the next hill, and Reed instinctively checked the SIG pressed into his spine. It would be a pitiful defense against Russian Alpha commandos armed with automatic Kalashnikovs, but hopefully the situation wouldn't devolve to that.

They just needed to get close enough to see where Golubev was headed. Then they could regroup.

The Lada started up the next hill. The engine was so overworked that Reed could feel the heat of it pouring through the floorboard. The tachometer strained and Ivan downshifted. Behind them the core of Tbilisi had already faded into the rearview, and Reed was hyperconscious of the fact that the Tigrs could have stopped just over the hilltop, barricading their path, the Alphas ready to gun them down.

But the Tigrs hadn't stopped. The Lada topped the hill with a howl, and morning sunlight spilled through the windshield. Reed looked ahead into a sprawling valley packed with the European equivalent of subdivisions—rows of tight streets, small houses, and little cars. The neighborhoods moved with the land instead of being carved into it, homes rising and falling with the gentle hills and stacking right up next to another mountain ridge.

The highway they drove on wound down the outside of the neighborhoods, moving north and east around the edge of the valley. Reed's gaze snapped left, and he saw the sunlight glinting off the mirrors of the Tigrs again. They had gained ground while the Lada fought to get up the hill. Even as Ivan turned the car into the valley to pursue, Reed held up a hand.

He could already tell where the two armored Russian vehicles were headed.

"Slow up."

"I see it," Ivan replied, relaxing off the accelerator. The Lada calmed, and they rolled into the valley. The Tigrs disappeared over a low hill, but Reed no longer needed to guess where they were headed. The military encampment built across a sprawling field at the end of the valley was constructed of dark green tents and occupied by camouflaged vehicles, but for all that, it seemed to be making no effort to conceal itself. It sprawled out right next to the neighborhood, with a cloud of dust rising from the churn of military vehicles chewing up the loose dirt.

And hanging above it all, high atop a flagpole like a beacon of domination, was the tri-bar flag of the Russian Federation.

Ivan left the highway and swerved into the neighborhoods, weaving slowly toward the end of the valley. Every time they rose to the top of a low hill, Reed could see the encampment, growing larger each time. It looked to be the field headquarters of an infantry detachment—a very large one. The tents were all infantry style, designed to keep foot soldiers out of the elements, and there was even a barbed-wire perimeter and a trailer-style mobile command post.

"Didn't take you guys long to settle in," Reed muttered.

Ivan shot him a sideways scowl and stepped on the brakes at the top of the last hill. The Lada slid next to a curb, its front bumper positioned half a mile from the makeshift gate of the encampment—a wide hole between tangles of barbed wire. Reed drew his binoculars while Ivan fell into automatic surveillance mode, keeping a lookout for any Russian or Georgian military patrols that might take issue with two unidentified males parked in a car spying on a military outpost.

The sun was still bright, and the dust hanging in the air obscured Reed's view, but the Swarovskis were excellent binoculars. With a little adjustment, he could see clearly.

He didn't like what he saw. The encampment was infantry, just as he suspected, but nothing about the thousands of ground-pounding Russian troops dressed in dark green, armed with modern variations of Mikhail Kalashnikov's timeless design, spoke to a search and recover mission.

Beyond the AK rifles and the rows of Russian T-90 main battle tanks and armored troop carriers, he noticed at least half a dozen Tornado-G rocket trucks, fifteen Akatsiya self-propelled artillery pieces, and four Hokum A type attack helicopters.

The rocket trucks, artillery, and helicopters were all shrouded beneath camouflage netting, obscuring them from satellite or surveillance drone view, but it seemed clear to Reed that much of the equipment was ready for immediate action. He slowly lowered the binoculars and turned to Ivan. He didn't say anything. He just cocked an eyebrow.

Ivan yanked the binoculars away with an irritated curse and took his own turn surveying. He chewed a lip as he looked, a low growl rumbling in his throat.

"Nineteenth Motor Rifle Brigade," Ivan muttered. "Battle tested, deployed during the Ukraine offensive. Accessorized, it seems, with support from the air forces."

"How many men?" Reed asked.

"Eleven thousand, at full force. This seems to be most of the brigade. I would guess that there are at least two other brigades elsewhere about the country. Anchor points to hold key objectives. Small detachments will break off from them to seize such tactical objectives as Bakuriani."

"So this isn't a temporary invasion," Reed said. "It's a full occupation."

"Da." Ivan lowered the binoculars slowly, blinking. Reed glanced sideways and saw something moist glimmering in the old Russian's eyes. Ivan shoved the binoculars back and turned quickly away. Reed chose to give him his space and took another look.

There was something near the makeshift gate of the encampment that had drawn his attention. Soldiers that stood awkwardly outside the barbed wire, dressed in full battle uniform, but not the uniform of the Russian military.

No. These were Georgian Defense Forces. They wielded AKM rifles and were positioned to protect the gate, but they didn't seem to be tactically engaged. They stood awkwardly, rifles held down, faces turning at the approach or departure of every Russian vehicle.

They seemed...bewildered. Overwhelmed. Confused.

They weren't putting up any sort of fight.

"Company," Ivan growled.

Reed quickly lowered the binos as Ivan shifted into gear. Both men remained relaxed, rolling down the hill and taking a quick right turn as another Russian Tigr hurtled past. A message played from a bullhorn mounted to the Tigr's bumper. The broadcast was in Russian, and Ivan didn't offer to translate, but Reed didn't really need him to.

He could guess what it said. It would say what any occupying army would want to say to a terrified and confused populace.

Stay calm. We are your friends. This will all be over shortly.

More lies.

"What is the next play?" Ivan said, driving the Lada amid a cluster of tightly packed Georgian homes with no destination in mind.

Reed's brain had already spun ahead to that question. He dug a hand into his cargo pocket to retrieve the compact messaging device. The next play was locked and loaded.

"We rendezvous with Wolfgang," Reed said. "We need the interpreter."

Ivan cocked an eyebrow. "The Georgian Defense Forces?"

Reed nodded. "It's time we find out why they aren't shooting."

32

Reed contacted Wolfgang while Ivan located a vacant house at the end of a long street, about four miles from the Russian military outpost. There was a sign posted out front that Ivan thought was a "for lease" sign, but Ivan read Georgian about as well as he spoke it. Reed only cared that the two-bedroom, one-bathroom home was empty and far enough removed from the remainder of the neighborhood to obscure some of the noises that would soon be bleeding through the thin windowpanes.

Once Wolfgang was notified of the location, Ivan and Reed once again departed the neighborhood, rumbling in the stolen Lada back to the end of the valley near the encampment. The car was hidden in the parking lot of a small city park, with tall trees overhanging its roof. Both men bailed out, weapons concealed beneath their jackets, the sun now blazing down from the high noon position.

"Distraction?" Ivan asked.

Reed fished a cigarette lighter from his pocket and checked the flame. Then he lifted his chin toward a fuel station situated at the end of a cul-de-sac, the storefront closed up, a sign posted to explain temporary closure. There were two pumps, both outdated and worn, but appearing in working order. The nearest other buildings stood fifty yards to either side.

Plenty of room.

Ivan grunted his approval. They set off down the sidewalk with hands at their sides, remaining calm but relentlessly alert. From the core of the city, several miles to their left, a distant clamor of distressed voices merged into a steady buzz not unlike the hum of a hornet's nest only moments after a boot is smashed through it. There were no pedestrians on the neighborhood streets. No children playing in the park or gathered in the schoolyards Reed and Ivan had passed on their way toward their makeshift safe house.

The city felt at once dead and at once ready to blow. House and apartment windows were covered over by curtains. Tension hung so tight in the air that Reed felt suffocated by it. With every rumble of a heavy engine, he and Ivan slid off the street to take shelter in the shadows of a tree or a home.

Russian patrols were everywhere. They had saturated the city with light trucks, each of them loaded with members of the Nineteenth Motor Rifle Brigade. But even though they were armed to the teeth and looked ready to raze the city to the ground, no shots were fired. The Russian army was simply rolling right in, setting up shop, dispersing their equipment and digging in.

Without one hint of resistance.

"Is the Georgian Defense Force weak?" Reed asked.

They were almost to the fuel station. Ivan had produced a folding knife from his pocket and flicked it open with a snap. He snorted.

"They are not a paper tiger, if this is what you mean. They have resources and equipment. They are well trained."

And yet they're doing nothing.

Reed pivoted right as they stepped beneath the awning of the petrol station, his gaze sweeping automatically left and right to survey the surrounding streets and the field behind that station. The streets themselves were empty, but a quarter mile across that field lay the outskirts of the Russian military outpost.

The Georgian Defense Forces he'd noted outside the barbed-wire gate now stood in between the petrol station and the encampment, right where he wanted them.

Without waiting for permission, Ivan dropped to a knee next to one of the fuel pumps and went to work with his knife. Machine screws backed out and dropped over the concrete. Reed kept one hand near his pistol and again swept the streets for any sign of police or military personnel. His eye caught on a window where the curtain parted. The home was eighty-plus yards away, but he could see the small face peering out at him.

A child. Not more than ten years old, with bright blonde hair that framed a pale face. An adult appeared and yanked the child away from the window, and the curtain fell.

Reed gritted his teeth, hot rage building somewhere deep in his gut. He looked back to the fuel pump just as Ivan slashed the outdated wiring mechanism which operated the electric pump, and bypassed the valve. The razor-sharp blade sliced through the thick rubber of the fuel hose, and an instant later the air was flooded with the pungent stench of raw gasoline spilling across the concrete.

Ivan got up quickly and advanced to a trash can between the pumps. He fished out a small fast-food carton and flipped it to Reed.

The carton was red, made of thin paper. The inside was greasy and smelled of fries. A familiar golden arch logo was printed across the face. Reed crushed the container as fuel continued to gush across the concrete. He and Ivan both took several steps back. The lighter flicked, and the corner of the carton ignited. Reed lowered it gently onto the concrete, about five feet from the edge of the growing pool of gasoline.

Then both men turned and sprinted down the street. They made it one block away from the petrol station before the fuel reached the burning carton. A hot rush of flames raced to the gushing fuel hose, and then fire spread across the parking lot and toward the locked retail store. Within seconds, a full-blown inferno had captured the station and was licking up the walls of the building, consuming the pumps and pouring clouds of black smoke into the sky.

Reed and Ivan knelt behind an oak tree at the edge of the park and watched as the fire developed. The binoculars were back in the Lada, but Reed didn't need them to know that the Georgian Defense Forces gathered outside the Russian encampment had noticed the flames and were reacting predictably. A knot of them had already broken away from the others and were jogging toward the station, rifles held in low ready, distressed faces now fixed on a new kind of threat.

"You know their insignias?" Reed asked.

"Da."

"We want an officer. Somebody who knows which way is up."

Another thirty seconds ground by. A buzz in Reed's pocket signified an incoming message from Wolfgang, but he didn't bother checking it. Wolfgang was likely reporting that he and Güneş had secured a vehicle and were en route.

Now it was time to secure their intel source.

"Him." Ivan jabbed his chin toward a soldier standing slightly apart from the others, a bewildered look on his face as he regarded the burning petrol station. He carried an AKM rifle and wore the mottled-green uniform of the Georgian military, with twin green patches on his shoulders. Each of those patches bore twin gold stars.

"What is he?" Reed asked.

"Junior officer. Similar to your lieutenant."

"That'll do. Get the car."

Ivan departed without complaint to get the Lada, and Reed crept out of the shadows of the park. He shouted toward the burning petrol station.

"Officer!"

Nobody responded. The rush of the flames was now overwhelming, joined by the wail of an incoming fire truck.

"Officer!" Reed repeated.

At last the lieutenant turned, looking over one shoulder. Wide and disoriented eyes fell over Reed, but he didn't seem to know what to say. Behind him the enlisted members of his detachment were busy creating a perimeter around the blaze, beckoning on the fire truck and generally doing a lot of nothing.

There wasn't much they could do.

"Over here!" Reed called, waving.

The lieutenant squinted. Reed beckoned again, then pointed toward the park, faking alarm. He gestured to the fire, then back to the park. He tilted his head and ran in that direction.

He knew the lieutenant was following him without needing to look over his shoulder. Heavy boots crunched on the ground. Reed swerved around a tree and ducked into the shadows even as the Lada backed into a parking space twenty feet away.

There was nobody else nearby. All attention was now zeroed in on the burning building and the bright red fire engine racing toward it.

Ivan appeared from the driver's seat of the Lada. He circled to the trunk. The lid snapped open.

Then the lieutenant rushed around the tree, rifle still held across his chest, wide eyes darting about for sight of Reed.

Reed grabbed him by the collar and spun him around without any effort to take control of the rifle. There was no need. Long before the junior officer had any idea what was happening, Reed was smashing his forehead against the oak's rough bark. The collision sounded like a melon striking concrete. The guy's eyes rolled back in his head and he went limp. Reed grabbed the rifle as it fell and took the man's shoulders. Ivan took him by the ankles. The guy swung like a dead body as they heaved him toward the Lada, then folded him into the trunk.

Reed took the Jericho 941 sidearm from his holster before slamming the trunk lid. Then he and Ivan were both piling back into the car, and the overworked engine whined. They turned east, away from the fire and the chaos it had unleashed. Within minutes, they were pulling back up to the makeshift safe house. Ivan circled around behind it. Reed gained access through the back door that he had already broken through on their initial visit.

They set the still-unconscious lieutenant on the floor of the dark living room and tied his hands with his own belt. Then Reed stood over him, arms folded, and waited for Wolfgang.

33

Wolfgang and Güneş arrived half an hour later, parking a battered Opel Vectra next to the Lada. Güneş got out with his head ducked, turning paranoid eyes toward the Russian encampment that he had no doubt seen while topping hills on their way to the safe house.

Wolfgang grabbed his arm and corralled him through the back door, ordering him to shut up whenever Güneş opened his mouth.

Inside, Reed and Ivan had descended onto the brick hearth of the little fireplace to eat a late lunch of dry power bars and warm water. The Georgian lieutenant was also awake, having surfaced from his temporary unconsciousness and proceeded directly to screaming for help.

Reed stopped up his mouth with one of his own socks and cuffed him across the face hard enough to stun him. That shut him up.

As Wolfgang stepped into the living room, his gaze fell over the officer, and semi-disbelief, semi-disgust passed across it.

"What did you do?"

Reed wasn't entirely sure whether the question was directed at him or Ivan. He didn't much care. He only needed Güneş.

"Get over here."

Reed snapped his fingers and gestured to the floor across from the imprisoned officer. Güneş complied with rushed, almost panicked alacrity.

Descending onto the floor, he looked with wide eyes between Reed and the Georgian lieutenant.

From four miles away, the fire engines continued to wail. Reed thought he heard the growl of Russian Tigrs also, but when Wolfgang peeled a curtain back to check the street, he reported nothing to be alarmed about.

"We're gonna interrogate him," Reed said, addressing Güneş. "You tell him that if he screams, I'll cut his throat. Got it?"

Reed drew the KA-BAR knife from his hip and flashed it across the lieutenant's face. The officer's eyes grew wide and he began to squeal behind the putrid sock. Güneş rushed to translate, and the officer nodded quickly.

Reed lowered the knife and squatted next to the man. He yanked the sock out, and the lieutenant gasped for air. Ivan closed in and folded his arms but didn't bend to the prisoner's level. He just waited.

"What's your name?" Reed said flatly.

"Uh...Davit?" Güneş said uncertainly.

Reed gritted his teeth. "Not *you*, idiot. *Him*."

"Oh, yes, yes." Güneş nodded quickly and translated the question into Georgian. The lieutenant spat back an answer.

"Badri."

"His name is—"

"I got it," Reed said. "Ask him what his unit is."

Güneş translated, and Badri shot back a detailed spiel about his military post, the regiment he was attached to, and his particular job. He was a cop, it seemed. The Defense Forces of Georgia equivalent of a US army MP. Reed glanced up at Ivan with a question in his eyes, and Ivan nodded once.

The information sounded legit.

"Ask him what's happening with the Russians."

Güneş posed the question. Badri hesitated, wide eyes darting from one face to the other. Ivan had yet to speak in his presence, a strategy Reed assumed was probably meant to prevent Badri from knowing that there was another Russian in the room and making him suspect that he was being interrogated by some of the occupying forces now crawling all over his country.

Maybe that strategy had backfired, however, putting Badri further on edge. He didn't seem willing to talk.

Reed didn't have time for that. His right hand popped out like a striking snake, cuffing Badri across the cheek hard enough to send his skull smacking against the wall. Eyes rolled back and blood spurted from his nose.

"Answer the question," Reed snapped.

Güneş translated. Badri choked and gasped.

"He wants water," Güneş said.

"He'll get water when he talks."

Footsteps tapped across the room and Wolfgang appeared, shoving a bottle of water toward Güneş. Reed put a hand up, and Wolfgang shot him a glare.

"You're proving nothing, Reed. Let him drink."

Güneş took the bottle and fed Badri a few swallows. The Georgian gasped. Reed repeated his question, and this time Badri spoke without waiting for the translation.

"He says they are here looking for weapons of mass destruction," Güneş said. "The Russian military has come to Georgia because of rumors of a nuclear bomb found in an old Soviet weapons depot."

"Is that true?" Reed asked.

"I do not understand," Güneş said.

"Is it true that a weapon was found in an old Soviet weapons depot?"

Güneş translated. Badri shook his head, mumbling with both water and blood slipping down his chin.

"He does not know," Güneş said.

Wolfgang stepped in again, speaking quietly.

"Ask him why the Georgian Defense Forces haven't put up a fight. Ask him why they're allowing an invasion."

Güneş repeated the question. Badri's face dropped and he began to cry. Murmurs escaped his lips and he shook his head again.

"He doesn't know," Güneş repeated. "He is just a low-level officer. He—"

Reed didn't allow him to finish. Something deep inside of him had escalated to fever pitch, like the squeal of a silent whistle that drives a dog crazy. It had been building in him all day long, and listening to the mumbled, incoherent excuses pouring from Badri's lips finally brought that tension to the breaking point.

Springing across the floor, he grabbed the lieutenant by the shirt collar and slammed his head against the wall. The first blow struck him in the face, and his nose crunched. The next landed on his eye socket, hard enough to leave a dent in the drywall behind his head. Badri cried out in pain, but Reed could no longer see a junior officer of the Russian defense forces pinned beneath his grasp, taking his abuse.

He saw Abdel Ibrahim again, and the blood spraying across the wall was the blood of the terrorist who had taken his daughter's life. With every ounce of the strength in his trembling body, he wanted to crush that face. He wanted to obliterate it. He wanted—

Both Ivan and Wolfgang caught him by the shoulders as he readied his next swing. Ivan muttered something in Russian, and Wolfgang growled through his teeth.

"Enough, Reed! Back off!"

The combined muscle was enough to pull him off balance. Reed slammed into the floor, head spinning. Wolfgang shoved him back, and Badri slumped against the wall. Snot, blood, and tears streamed down his face as he quaked, struggling with his feet to push himself farther away from Reed.

His back was against the wall. Wolfgang abandoned Reed and approached Badri. The Georgian squirmed and cried out again. Wolfgang held up a finger.

"*Quiet.*"

Güneş repeated the command. Badri swallowed and continued to shake but no longer cried. Wolfgang repeated his question from only seconds earlier, and once again Güneş translated it.

Badri's wide eyes darted from Wolfgang to Reed, and then to Ivan. He'd no doubt heard the Russian speak. He would have recognized the familiar sound of the invader's language. Now he had a decision to make.

Reed sat quaking on the floor, fighting to catch his breath. He shouldn't have felt winded after so little exertion, but his body was strung out, alive with tension again. Ready to snap.

Once more, Wolfgang repeated the question. "Why aren't you resisting?"

This time, Badri finally answered. He spoke slowly, swallowing back blood, his voice trembling with pain. It took effort, but he got the words out. Güneş translated.

"He says there was a special executive order from the office of the president—President Giorgi Meladze. The order required the Ministry of Defense to comply with all directives and actions of the Russian military. The order was explicit. Georgian forces were to make no resistance to Russian forces. Russian forces have come in peace, to assist Georgia."

"You're telling us he simply ordered you to all stand down?" Wolfgang pressed. Güneş struggled with the question. Wolfgang reworded.

Badri shook his head and rambled on for a moment.

"He says that Defense Forces of Georgia are to cooperate with friendly Russian forces here to help secure the country against imminent nuclear threat."

"Are Russian forces in command?" Ivan entered the conversation for the first time.

Badri received the question and shrugged.

"He does not know," Güneş said.

"Ask him how peaceful it is when Russian forces gun down protestors in the streets." Reed spat the line and turned blazing eyes on Güneş. When the question was translated, Badri resumed crying. His shoulders fell, as did his face. His whole body quaked, and Wolfgang glowered at Reed.

For a moment nobody said anything as the information was assimilated. Reed wasn't sure if he believed Badri's story, but he was pretty confident that Badri believed it. A chain of command had informed him of the direction of the president.

To lay down in the road and let the Russians run right over them. *Unbelievable.*

"Where is he now?" Reed said finally.

Güneş squinted. "Who?"

"Their president. This guy Meladze."

Güneş posed the question. Badri swallowed hard. His answer was brief. Güneş turned back.

"He has vanished."

34

The city was dark in the early hours of the morning, but still alive with the ceaseless noises of commerce and governance that ground on around the clock. Rushing cars, honking horns, and the clamor of voices in late-night restaurants.

One of those restaurants was a twenty-four-hour cafe called the Capital Social. Situated only blocks from the seat of American government, the carpet was maroon, the lights turned down low, and the booths quiet. The menu was a mix of French and American gourmet cuisine, with prices that James O'Dell found personally offensive. It was the sort of food he didn't understand and didn't want to understand.

But he wasn't here to eat. In fact, he didn't even plan to order. He accepted the default glass of water and kept waving the waiter off, seated in a booth at the back of the room where he could maintain a full view of the door.

O'Dell was tired. Beyond tired. He couldn't recall the last time he'd slept a full night. Days? Maybe a week. He'd caught cat naps a few times a day and fueled his body with caffeine pills to push through. He knew it was a short-term solution with a long-term cost—that he was already burning the candle at both ends and working his way dangerously close to the center.

But none of that mattered. His own physical health, strength, his very life. It was all secondary. The job that kept him awake day after day, churning on, fighting for a solution, would motivate him until his dying breath.

He owed her that. He owed her everything.

The front door creaked open, and a tall guy in a gray jacket stepped in. His hair was cut high and tight, like a military cut, but this guy wasn't military. He was more like a blinking neon billboard, proclaiming a one-word message: *cop*.

O'Dell lifted a hand, and the guy saw him. He bypassed the maître d' and ascended two steps into the dining room. A moment later he slid into the booth with his back to the door, dropping a file folder on the table. He grunted.

"You got expensive tastes."

O'Dell ignored the comment and took the folder, flipping the cover open. The top document bore a photograph, a name, and a complete profile. Jeffrey Simmons Jr. of Cleveland Park. Thirty-six years old, a registered sex offender recently released from FCI Allenwood Low, in White Dear, Pennsylvania. Six years for rape.

O'Dell flipped past the introductory page and scanned the next report. It was also about Simmons, but it didn't detail his criminal activity. Instead it focused on medical details...things like whether he was an alcoholic or a substance abuser, what his blood type was, and any diseases or genetic defects he was known to have. Things the prison doctors at Allenwood Low would have needed to know.

It was a lot of information.

"That's everybody in a fifty-mile radius who matches your parameters," the cop said. "Eighteen records in total. There's another fourteen or fifteen possible suspects in northern Virginia and a half dozen in Maryland."

O'Dell ignored the comment and shuffled through the next two stapled documents. Heather Clemmons, a convicted drug dealer. And Stephen Rutger. A child molester. Each file contained medical reports, with all the relevant details. There were eighteen files in total, just as the cop had promised.

O'Dell flipped the folder closed. "Good work," he said simply. Then he shifted toward the edge of the booth.

The cop held up a hand. "Wait. Just...help me understand. Why did you need the medical records?"

"I already told you. There's been a credible threat on the president's life."

"Right, but usually the Secret Service would contact us via the MPD liaison."

"This isn't a usual threat." O'Dell's voice remained flat and cold, inviting no further inquiry. The cop pressed ahead anyway.

"But the medical files?"

O'Dell slid out of the booth. He reached into his pocket and dropped a hundred-dollar bill on the table.

"Get yourself some dinner, officer. Your country thanks you."

Then he turned and headed for the door. Folder pinned beneath his arm. Eighteen names on his mind.

35

Tbilisi, Georgia

The interrogation of Lieutenant Badri proceeded for another twenty minutes, but Reed had already heard everything he needed to hear. It was evident to him that the junior officer—and much of the Georgian military, likely—knew absolutely nothing about what was actually happening inside their own country. Even if they wanted to resist the tide of invaders, it was much too late. They'd lost the initiative. Russia had blitzkrieged them and established strategic control.

Georgia had put her head right through a noose and didn't seem to understand why.

Outside the temporary safe house, the sun was setting in the west, with only hours remaining until impending darkness. Reed retrieved the rest of his gear from the trunk of Wolfgang's captured Opel and spread it across the home's kitchen counter. The SIG Legion joined his M4 rifle, all his extra ammunition and food. It was more than enough for what came next.

Wolfgang and Ivan left Güneş to deal with Badri and joined Reed in the kitchen. More power bars were torn open, and Wolfgang kept watched through a slit in the curtains. Thus far, no Russian forces were going door to door to root out infiltrators.

That was likely because they didn't *expect* any infiltrators.

"You shouldn't have hit him," Wolfgang said, turning away from the window. "He was about to talk."

"Yeah? So this way, he talked quicker."

"Good grief, Reed. Have some heart. His country just got *invaded*."

"Exactly," Reed said, gaze snapping up from the counter. "And he didn't do a thing about it. He's a coward."

"Hell's angels," Ivan broke in. "Stop being children. This is not America. This is not Russia. This is a small country with a very small army. Nikitin would have planned this for months—his military was ready to move quickly. There was nothing Georgia could have done even if they had fought. It would have been a bloodbath."

"Better to die free than look like him." Reed jerked his head over his shoulder, toward Badri. The lieutenant was sobbing again, bent over with Güneş huddled next to him like a mother hen.

"Either way, what is done is done," Ivan said. "Russia has taken military control of Georgia. President Meladze is missing, which is shorthand in the world of Nikitin for *dead*. We can only assume the intentions of Moscow are to annex the country. What we do not know is why."

"Why else?" Reed said. "Power. You said yourself that he wants his old Soviet Union back. Georgia was a part of that Union."

"Da, that it was. But you are missing my point. Obviously Nikitin would like control of Georgia. But this is only part of what he desires. The end of his game is to control everything—as much as he can. He will plow ahead to take the world, if he is allowed. Whatever happens now, you can be sure, another move is coming."

"We're off target," Wolfgang cut in. "We're not here to unravel Russia's intentions. We're only here to validate or disprove their claims of a forgotten weapons depot. That claim could still be true. The bomb in Panama came from somewhere."

Ivan grunted in condescension. "A week from now, it will not matter whether the claim is true. Russia's hold on the region will be absolute. There will be no way to know the truth, regardless."

"So we have to move now." Reed grabbed his backpack and slung it back on. The M4 rifle slid into his hand. He turned for the back door.

"Wait," Wolfgang called. "What are you doing?"

"What do you think I'm doing? I'm going to find that jackass we followed in the Tigr. The guy from Moscow. If Badri doesn't know what these thugs are up to, you can bet he does."

This time Ivan laughed out loud. It was a rolling, disgusted sound. "You are going to kidnap Golubev? Please, American. Be serious."

Maybe it was the further disparagement in Ivan's tone, or just the frustration of the situation, or the continued numbness that pounded through Reed's head, always dragging his thoughts and feelings down to a base of the lowest common denominator.

Maybe it was the thought of Banks and Davy, back in the United States. The uncomfortable reality of how little Reed missed them. Of how he no longer saw his family when he closed his eyes.

He only saw that bloody face—the face of Abdel Ibrahim. And wished he could keep pounding it.

Whatever the case, Reed's frayed nerves snapped again, just like they had with Badri. He slammed the rifle down on the counter and turned back.

"You got a better idea, big guy?"

Ivan cocked an eyebrow. Wolfgang held Reed's gaze. From the living room, Badri's sobbing abruptly ceased. The house felt very still.

"You are hot stuff, cowboy," Ivan said. "But you are not hot enough to capture Anton Golubev. The man will be surrounded by Alpha Group at all times. You'd need a small army. And besides, even if you capture him, he will not talk. He is the coldest man I've ever met, and this includes myself. You could beat him to death before he would break."

Reed gritted his teeth. "Again I say...*do you have a better idea?*"

Ivan thought. He scratched a cheek. Then he nodded.

"If the claims of a Soviet weapons depot are false, the Russian military leaders must know. It is a question that would impact their entire strategy. There will be several such officers in the camp. Any of them could be captured and broken."

"So we're kidnapping people again?" Wolfgang raised both eyebrows.

Ivan smiled. "Do you have a better idea?" He may have been trying to mimic Reed's voice, but the attempt was so bad, Reed couldn't even tell.

"Where do we find them?" Reed said. "These officers."

"Inside." Ivan tilted his head toward the camp. "There will be a mobile headquarters. I will show you, but not now. We must wait for the dark."

Reed sank his teeth into the inside of his lip, savoring the pain as it broke through his mental fog and provided clarity. Focus. He processed the problem at hand and reached a decision.

It was as good a plan as they could hope for.

"Update Langley," Reed said, addressing Wolfgang. "We go immediately after nightfall."

36

Diyarbakır, Turkey

Turk wasn't sure what he expected after boarding a last-minute flight to Istanbul, then taking a puddle-jumper aircraft out to the small private airfield where the CIA informed him that the Prosecution Force was sitting on the tarmac. He didn't have any details of their present activities. He should have known he wouldn't find Reed sitting on his hands, wasting time. It wasn't like Reed. For that matter, it wasn't like Turk.

And yet he was now forced to do exactly that. To sit on his hands in the back of the Gulfstream, waiting—and hoping—for an update from Reed's ground team in Georgia. Trying not to stress. Trying not to kick himself for hanging back in Leiper's Fork instead of joining the team from the start.

Trying not to overthink...and left with precious little else to do.

It had been years—most of his adult life, in fact—since Rufus Turkman had put his feet on the ground in the morning and not been concerned with the welfare of Reed Montgomery. From their first encounter in the United States Marine Corps, when Uncle Sam had signed young Turk to be Reed's spotter downrange in Iraq, to all the tumultuous, often agonizing years that had followed.

Even when Reed Montgomery was a criminal on the run from the federal government, and Turk was a member of the FBI task force assigned to capture him, Turk couldn't escape from the responsibility he felt to watch Reed's back. It was deeper than military loyalty or the camaraderie of men who had been shot at together. Deeper even than the friendship they had developed in foxholes across northern Iraq, battling ISIL while they tracked NFL games from back home and made outlandish bets on their outcomes.

There was a magnetic attraction Turk felt toward Reed that defied explanation. Not a romantic one. Nothing like that. It was the draw a ruthless warrior feels toward a relentless leader. The compulsion that drew good men like Turk out of their homes and onto the battlefield to fight on behalf of ruthless men like Reed.

It wasn't something Turk was necessarily proud of. In fact, if he was honest, it was something he could live without. Certainly, life would be easier—and a lot safer—if he didn't feel compelled to follow Reed straight into the jaws of hell. Maybe that was why he'd become so angry when Reed yet again announced his intentions to throw himself, and his team, against a faceless enemy. Maybe that was why he put his foot down.

But no. Turk knew it was deeper than that. He was as concerned about his own safety and happiness as the next guy, but he'd never minded following Reed before. He'd literally thrown himself off TV towers alongside Reed, just for the thrill of it. There was a deeper, darker force at play in Turk's trepidation that he couldn't shake, and the more he thought about it, he didn't think the mission itself was the problem.

It was *Reed*. And what was changing inside of him.

"Hey...you look like you could use a sandwich."

Turk looked up from the back seat of the jet, where he sat reclined, gazing out the open window into the Turkish afternoon. Corbyn and Strickland had both left the plane to purchase food and have one tire on the landing gear replaced. It was leaking after the rough landing on the busted road, and Strickland was ready to have a conniption over it.

Corbyn was much less concerned. She never seemed to be very concerned about anything, but she went with him to get the tire, the two of them arguing the entire way.

Now it was just Turk and Lucy on the plane, and it was Lucy who offered him the sandwich. Turk looked up to see the petite redhead extending him a wrapped sub role with turkey and bacon poking out. He didn't think he was hungry, but just the sight of the bacon made his stomach growl. Turk tore through the plastic wrapper as Lucy placed bottled water on the tray table and sat down across from him.

One bite in, and Turk's brain erupted in a euphoric dump of dopamine.

"Sweet merciful goodness...where did this come from?"

"I made it," Lucy said cheerily, leaning back in her chair.

Turk snorted. "You know, we never used to eat this good before you came along."

That brought a grin to Lucy's face. "What can I say? A logistics officer is good for more than booking hotel rooms."

Turk finished the sandwich in another four massive bites and licked mayo off his fingers. Then he drained a bottle of water in one long pull and burped. Lucy cocked an eyebrow.

"I see we're not much on table manners."

"Don't usually have time for them. We're usually being shot at."

He looked back out the window, watching Corbyn and Strickland now locked into an argument with a Turkish mechanic. The issue seemed to be the tire. Turk couldn't tell who was arguing with whom.

"You're worried about Reed, aren't you?"

Turk's gaze flicked away from the window. Lucy was staring right at him, small hands folded in her lap, perfect calm engulfing her face. Turk opened another bottle and sipped water.

"Always dangerous going downrange," he said.

"Yep. But that's not what you're worried about."

He faced her again, and Lucy remained relaxed, like a military shrink performing a psychiatric evaluation. Turk had endured them before. They always made him nervous and irritable.

Somehow, Lucy didn't make him feel that way. She made him feel calm.

"He doesn't handle domestic life well," Turk said slowly. "He doesn't know how to switch it off."

"The violence?"

"The need for the violence."

"I've been there."

Turk narrowed his eyes. Took another sip. It suddenly occurred to him that he knew very little about Lucy Byrne. She'd always just kind of *been there*, since Reed's emergence from the criminal underworld. Turk knew that she'd been an assassin at one point in time. Not anymore.

Now, he wasn't really sure *what* she was. A logistics officer, by title. A medic in training. A heck of a sandwich artist, apparently. But...

"Why are you here?" Turk said. It was a blunt question, but he didn't regret it.

Lucy smiled. "To make sandwiches, apparently."

"Something tells me you're good for a lot more than that."

A soft shrug, but no answer.

"Is it Wolfgang?" Turk asked.

That got her attention. Lucy turned stiff and blushed a little.

"Wolfgang?"

"Come on." Turk rocked the bottle back again. "I may not be a rocket scientist, but it's not much of a riddle. I see the way you two dance around each other. Every time we assemble in Leiper's Fork you arrive together. Seems like Wolfgang is hardly ever in New York anymore."

Lucy hesitated, then shrugged and smiled, as if there was no point in lying. "He's good to be with."

"So don't apologize for that. We all need somebody."

"Is your somebody Reed?"

Now it was Turk's turn to be caught off guard. He set the bottle down and didn't answer.

"I didn't mean it that way," Lucy said. "I just meant, you asked me if I was here for Wolfgang. Are you here for Reed?"

Turk looked back out the window. The argument had concluded with the mechanic. He was rolling a cartload of tools toward the plane, coming to jack up the wing and unbolt the wounded landing gear.

But Turk wasn't thinking about landing gear. He was thinking about Reed...and what had changed inside of him.

"You ever touch darkness, Lucy?"

"How do you mean?"

Turk faced her again. "I mean, have you ever stepped into a place so completely black, so totally empty, that it saturates your very soul? Sucks the life out of you? Drags you into an abyss so deep, you forget who you are?"

Lucy's eyes grew distant. She inhaled slowly...then nodded. "I have."

"I've brushed up with that feeling," Turk said. "In Iraq. In the FBI. In North Korea and Venezuela. Places where I've seen some really, really ugly stuff. I've touched that darkness, but I've never slipped into it. Not quite."

"But you think Reed has."

"Do you?"

Lucy pursed her lips. She seemed to be thinking very carefully about her answer. At last, she said: "Do you believe in God, Turk?"

It wasn't the answer he expected, but maybe he should have. He'd seen the little Bible Lucy toted around. Seen the tiny gold cross neckless that sometimes swung into view when she wore lower necklines.

It was a simple question, but Turk wasn't sure how to answer. So he stuck to the truth.

"I'd like to."

"That's a good place to start."

"What's that got to do with Reed?"

Lucy bent away from the table and fished across the aisle into a small leather bag she carried like a purse. The Bible appeared and she rested it on the table. She didn't open it.

"I met God while I was in rehab. I'm sure you've heard people say that before. Like, they met Jesus. Everybody has their own experience, but for me, it was pretty literal. Like, I was trying to kill myself. And then God was there."

Turk said nothing. Lucy tapped the Bible.

"I never understood the world around me until I read this. I'm still not sure that I do. But when you look at life through a spiritual lens, there's some clarity there."

"What do you mean?"

"I mean it's a war. Not a metaphorical one or a theoretical one. The world, all of history, all of life is literally a cataclysmic clash between the powers of goodness, love, and truth, and the powers of darkness. The same darkness you described. It's a spiritual conflict that spills over into the physical realm. All the death, the pain, the betrayal, the bloodshed. It's all a part of the bigger war going on behind the curtains."

"Armageddon?" Turk asked, not quite hiding the sarcasm in his voice.

Lucy's gaze rose, and she nodded. There was no sarcasm in her face. No hint of humor. She was dead serious.

"That's exactly what I mean."

Turk set the bottle down, the humor melting from his mind. He stared and said nothing. Lucy folded her arms and looked out the window. She pursed her lips.

"You asked why I'm here, Turk? I'm here because we're all at war. I'm not exactly sure what my role is yet, but it won't be to sit on the sidelines. Reed Montgomery is a man who stands on the edge."

She pivoted back to Turk. Her next words cut like a razor blade.

"We have to keep the enemy from getting him."

37

Nightfall descended over Georgia, and Reed, Wolfgang, and Ivan departed the safe house. The question of what to do with Badri was a simple one to Reed. He wanted to hog-tie the Georgian soldier and abandon him in the safe house.

Maybe he would escape, maybe he wouldn't. Either way, he wouldn't endanger the mission, and Reed wouldn't have to directly put a bullet in his head.

Wolfgang objected, of course, arguing to set him free and roll the dice with his compliance. While Badri trembled against the wall and babbled in Georgian, Güneş struggling to translate, the two men argued. In the end, it was Ivan who settled the matter. He lifted Badri by the collar of his blood-stained uniform, pinned him against the wall, brought his face to within centimeters of Badri's, and growled a long string of Russian into his ears. Reed didn't understand a word of it, and he doubted whether Badri did either, but the menace in Ivan's tone was impossible to ignore, as was the cadence of a violent threat.

When Ivan finished, he cocked a fist and punched the soldier right in the temple—hard. Badri's eyes rolled back in his head, and Ivan dropped him. Then he turned to Güneş.

"You will load him in the car and drive outside the city. When he wakes up, kick him out and keep driving. We have no further use for you."

Ivan turned for the door, grabbing one of the M4 rifles off the counter as he went. Reed fell in behind him, and Wolfgang offered some final directions to Güneş. Details about which way to drive and what would happen to him if he sold them out.

Güneş didn't need to be warned. Reed could tell by his eager agreement to Wolfgang's instructions that the interpreter was only too happy to be leaving Georgia.

Outside the safe house, Reed, Ivan, and Wolfgang melted into the darkness well outside the city and listened to the voice of desperation rising from over the mountains, closer to downtown. Maybe the words were spoken in Georgian, but the meaning was universal. The Georgian military had followed orders and complied with the Russian invasion. Already that decision was biting them in the back. Scattered automatic gunfire and the blare of loudspeakers proclaiming pre-recorded messages told the story.

This was just like blitzkrieg. Russia was here to stay.

Reed glanced sideways as the truck blaring the loudspeaker message rolled slowly down the safe house street, headlights flashing across busted asphalt. Ivan's gaze was fixated on the vehicle, his eyes very hard and cold. Reed saw his hand flexing around the grip of the M4, and for the first time since agreeing to this mission alongside the ex-FSB officer, a worm of doubt entered his mind.

Could he really trust Ivan? He had no reason not to. But the heart of their mission had now swung directly into the path of Ivan's people.

As if he knew what Reed was thinking, Ivan spoke quietly through gritted teeth, still watching the truck.

"Before there is an evil empire, there must first be an evil man." He rotated to face Reed. "The first country he invades is his own."

With that, Ivan swung the M4 into low ready and turned to set off through the overgrown grass of a wide Georgian meadow. Reed glanced at Wolfgang and cocked an eyebrow. Wolfgang simply started after Ivan.

The path to the Russian military encampment led over low, rolling hills, three miles as the crow flies, but much longer via the meandering, circling path that Ivan chose. Reed elected to trust their Russian counterpart, content to let Ivan assume the risks of taking point while he held back and swept their flanks and rear. No sign of military personnel, Russian or Georgian, crossed their path as they ascended to the high ground and eventually looked down over the camp. It lay at the end of the valley, sandwiched between ridges, with clear access to both the outskirts of Tbilisi and the B9 highway. The strategic impact of the location was evident, but as yet the Russians didn't seem to be pressing their advantage. Instead, they were reinforcing. Fresh Tigr trucks, troop transports, and additional T-90 tanks were rolling in off the B9 in a steady stream.

Hundreds of them.

"I should go in alone," Ivan said. "I have a better chance of blending in. I will bring you a prisoner."

"Not a chance," Reed said. "I have to see this myself."

Ivan cocked an eyebrow and looked sideways. Then he simply grunted and led the way down the hill. The closer the three of them drew to the curled barbed wire encircling the camp, the brighter the generator-powered lights blazed down from the tops of high poles. Rows of thick green tents ran like city blocks along the backside of the camp, grass bending in the wind alongside them and soldiers moving in streams amongst them.

It seemed that chow time had arrived, and everybody was headed toward the mess tent at the middle of camp. When the three of them finally reached the curled barbed wire and squatted just outside it, there was no danger of being seen. There was nobody to see them. All the soldiers had moved away from the perimeters, a clamor of voices and clinking plates carried on the breeze from three hundred yards away.

"Rifles stay here," Ivan said.

"Are you insane?" This time it was Wolfgang who objected.

Ivan snorted. "I am not the insane one if you want to walk in there wielding American weaponry. It will be impossible to sneak. We must blend."

Wolfgang opened his mouth to object again, but Reed was already dumping his rifle. It wasn't like thirty rounds of 5.56 would do him much good against eleven thousand Russian infantry, anyway. Something in his numb gut told him that Ivan's plan was worth a gamble.

Wolfgang capitulated with an exhausted sigh, then Ivan was busy thrusting his rifle through the barbed wire, using it as a fork to lift the wire eighteen inches off the ground. Wolfgang dropped down and wriggled through, his prosthetic leg dragging awkwardly over the grass as his biological leg did all the work. Reed followed, then grabbed the barrel of Ivan's rifle and held the wire for Ivan to pass.

The Russian took longer than either of them, grumbling in grunting with each aching twist of his body. When he reached the other side, Reed lowered the rifle and smiled. Ivan breathed a curse in Russian.

"You are smug now, young man. If you are lucky to be old, you will learn."

Rifles on the ground, Ivan kept his body bent in a low crouch as he led the way through the bending grass to the first row of tents. They stood staked into the Georgian earth, tall walls and arching roofs reminding Reed a little of the GP Medium tents he'd occasionally used in Iraq. Standard issue, ready for any deployment. The Russian equivalent.

Circling to the end of the first tent, Ivan held up a hand and Reed and Wolfgang froze as the Russian bent his neck toward the entrance. The tent was illuminated only by the soft glow of an LED light strip, just bright enough to keep soldiers from tripping over themselves in the dark.

Ivan bent to look inside. He called a soft word in Russian.

No answer.

"Follow," Ivan said.

The three of them slipped inside the tent to find rows of cots were packed tightly together, green metal footlockers slid beneath each one. Ivan slipped down the row of cots, feeling the ends of each before randomly stopping in front of one and ducking to retrieve the footlocker housed beneath.

Reed identified the strategy and couldn't resist a grunt of respect. He moved quickly to the next row of cots and copied the procedure, running his hand along the ends of the cots, feeling the fabric. Inspecting for wear.

"What are you doing?" Wolfgang hissed.

"Tall soldiers wear tall clothes," Reed said. "Their feet also overhang the ends of the cots and wear down the fabric."

Reed found a cot with exactly the sort of worn fabric he'd been looking for and swung quickly to pull the footlocker out. It was unlocked, and a folded uniform lay inside, along with basic-issue toiletries and personal effects. A photograph of a very plain Russian girl with blonde hair, and a handheld gaming system.

Behind him, Ivan was already peeling his body out of the ill-fitting American clothes the CIA had provided, and dressing in the Russian infantry uniform he found beneath the bed. Reed followed suit, tugging on pants, jacket, and boots. Regiment patches on one arm of the jacket, and a tri-bar Russian flag on the other. It felt strange to wear, but not because it was a foreign military uniform. Just because it was a military uniform at all. It had been so long since Reed wore one daily that the sensation jarred his mind.

"Smells like BO," Wolfgang muttered, pulling uniform pants over his prosthetic leg.

"Smells like glory," Ivan replied, tugging a camouflage cap down over his ears. His face twisted toward Reed, and Reed couldn't deny that Ivan looked like a natural in the uniform. A little old. Very weathered.

But believable.

"Ready?" Ivan asked.

Wolfgang buttoned his jacket and dropped his old clothes into the footlocker. Lids closed, and Reed tucked his SIG into the small of his back, dropping the jacket over it. Then the three of them were headed back out of the tent, Wolfgang walking a little stiffly, Reed feeling totally out of place, and Ivan leading the way.

"I'm an enlisted officer," Ivan said, tapping his arm patch. "Like your sergeant."

"NCO," Reed said.

"Whatever. You follow and keep your mouth shut. I will keep us alive."

Ivan may have meant the words as reassurance, but Reed couldn't ignore the uneasiness that overcame his body the moment a pair of Russian soldiers stepped into the lane between tents, one speaking in the familiar cadence of a joke and the other laughing as they walked. Both men stiffened a little when they saw Ivan, dipping their chins. Ivan only grunted and kept walking, as did the soldiers. They breezed past Reed and Wolfgang without a second glance, and the conversation resumed.

"Dumb as rocks," Ivan muttered in English.

Ahead the glow of the camp core grew brighter as additional generator-powered lights blazed down over the mess tent. They passed the edge of a motor pool where Russian T-90 tanks and a pair of attack helicopters were parked, then they were right in the heart of the camp.

Soldiers were everywhere. Voices buzzed. Dinner plates clanged. It was at once exactly the same as every military outpost Reed had ever experienced in the Marine Corps and also completely different. The noise was the same, but the smells very foreign. Instead of overcooked hamburgers, bland beans, and acidic spaghetti sauce, he smelled...he wasn't sure what. Some Russian cuisine that didn't agree with him. There was music playing, which was familiar, but the music itself was Russian. A screaming metal band.

It was the thump of boots, the tides of men moving in semi-orderly lines, and that sea of green uniforms that took him back. If he wasn't hyper-conscious about the prospect of being discovered and shot in the head, he might even have felt nostalgic.

Ivan kept them moving through the sea of soldiers, tracking around the center of the camp and avoiding the long chow lines. Instead they slipped back into a maze of tents—not the barracks kind but the administrative sort. Medical, supply, and commissary, followed by a wide and muddy two-lane torn by the tracks of main battle tanks.

"Stay here," Ivan grunted.

"What?" Reed said.

Ivan flicked his wrist irritably, directing a finger toward a line of Russian infantry gathered outside the commissary tent, slowly filtering inside to buy candy bars and magazines—or whatever Russian soldiers bought while deployed. Reed hesitated at the edge of the two-lane, and Ivan marched right across, boots splashing. On the far side stood the command posts. They were all mobile trailers, all set up on hydraulic feet to stabilize themselves over the uneven soil. Russian infantrymen stood outside, AK rifles held across their chests, doing their best to remain alert.

"What now?" Wolfgang hissed.

"Get in line," Reed replied, shifting into the back of the commissary line and keeping watch over Ivan out of the corner of his eye. Additional music was playing from inside the commissary tent, providing a little noise cover as the line of Russians muttered amongst themselves and shuffled slowly ahead. In mere seconds Wolfgang and Reed were lined up with soldiers on either side, their mouths closed in tight lines as the column crept forward. It would be ten minutes or more before they actually reached the tent, but Reed's anxiety level spiked at every twitch of the soldiers standing ahead of him.

He didn't speak a word of Russian. As far as he knew, Wolfgang didn't, either. They were precisely one inquisitive comment away from having their cover blown, and the SIG pressed into the small of Reed's back wasn't nearly enough firepower to solve that problem.

Moving ahead half a step, Reed glanced left again to see Ivan standing next to the Russian sentries, bent over with a cigarette between his lips as one of them held a lighter. There seemed to be a joke exchanged, and one of the sentries laughed. Ivan rolled his head back and blew smoke through parted lips, his shoulders slumping in the familiar slouch of a nicotine addict overcome by relief.

It made Reed want a cigarette.

"*Izvinite.*" A hand brushed Reed's arm, and his gaze snapped back toward the line of men. The soldier standing in front of him had turned and tugged on his sleeve. The guy held a cigarette between his lips, a question on his face.

"*U vas yest' zazhigalk?*"

Reed's brain froze. He saw the cigarette and knew he should somehow understand how to respond, but his mind went blank. The fog took over. He simply blinked, and the soldier lifted his eyebrows, waiting.

"*U vas yest' zazhigalk?*" he repeated.

Reed's lips parted. The line moved ahead, but he didn't move with it. His boots felt locked into the mud, the world around him descending into a blur. His throat went dry, and his mind simply stopped.

It wasn't fear, nerves, or even uncertainty. It was just deadlock. Only one thought rang through clear: *Shoot him. Shoot him now.*

Reed's head dropped to his coat. He reached along his waistline, hand arcing toward his middle back. Already closing toward the SIG, fingers snaking around the hidden grip, reaching for the trigger.

Then Wolfgang moved. He pushed past Reed, something silver glinting in his hand. It sparked, and a yellow flame appeared. Wolfgang lit the soldier's cigarette with a grunt. The soldier inhaled and rolled his head back, just as Ivan had. He grunted.

"*Spasibo.*"

Then he turned, stepping ahead again. Other soldiers shoved past Reed, elbowing him as they moved. Reed blinked, and the fog parted. He realized he was still gripping the SIG, and he looked sideways at Wolfgang.

Wolfgang glared, teeth gritted. He looked once at Reed's spine, and his chin twitched sideways. Reed released the gun and removed his hand from beneath the jacket. He stumbled sideways, feet sucking through the mud. His head spun, and he felt suddenly dizzy.

But he didn't fall. He reached the edge of the muddy two-lane and shook his head to clear it. Wolfgang followed. Behind them, the line of soldiers kept moving. Nobody seemed to have noticed. Ivan was still talking with the sentries, fifty yards away.

"What are you *doing*?" Wolfgang spoke under his breath. Reed simply gasped for air, suddenly feeling as though he were out of it. He blinked, looking down the street. He didn't say anything. His attention tunneled again, like it had before. Wolfgang jabbed him in the rib cage and said something under his breath again.

This time Reed wasn't listening—not because his brain had deadlocked but because he saw something. Something he shouldn't have seen in a conventional military outpost. Something he'd seen far, far too much of in recent memory.

It was a pair of men, walking two hundred yards away, slipping between additional tents. Visible for a moment, and gone just as quickly. Maybe Russians, maybe not. It didn't even matter. What mattered was how they were dressed—not in Russian infantry fatigues but in bright yellow rubber suits.

Radiation suits.

38

Reed was moving long before Wolfgang followed his gaze to the end of the tents. Already, the guys in radiation gear were gone. They'd disappeared down another aisle, fading deeper into the camp.

But the glimpse was enough. Reed knew he couldn't have imagined it. One man held a hood under his left arm. The other man carried a bright red toolbox. They were walking with purpose, as though they were headed someplace in particular.

Not only that, but the collars of their exposed uniforms, visible for only a split second beneath the blaze of generator lights, were black, not dark green like the rest of the infantry.

They were the color of Alpha Group.

"What are you *doing*?" Wolfgang repeated the question as he caught up to Reed, slogging down the muddy two-lane. Reed ignored him and pressed ahead, SIG grinding against his spine with every stride, heartbeat accelerating as adrenaline dumped into his chest. The commissary tent was already lost behind them, and they were alone on the road. Russian voices faded beneath the squish of heavy boots in the muck.

Reed reached the intersection and pivoted left. He didn't see the Alpha soldiers in radiation gear, but it wasn't difficult to pick up their beaten trail as it wound amid crushed grass, framed on either side by additional tents.

Reed pressed ahead, and Wolfgang followed, keeping quiet this time. The farther they walked from the core of the camp, the dimmer the noises of the Russian infantry became.

Then they heard different noises. Also dim, but growing louder. They passed the backside of the command center on their left—those elevated mobile buildings on hydraulic legs. The tents to their right seemed to be mostly for supply and storage. Ammunition, likely, and food.

The sounds Reed heard from ahead were heavy and mechanical. A truck, or perhaps another Tigr. The chug of the diesel was unmistakable, and as they reached the end of the tents and the trail twisted to the right, Reed heard voices also. Speaking in Russian, calling short and terse commands.

Slowing at the last supply tent, Reed pressed his back against the canvas and eased toward the corner. It was much darker in this part of the camp than it had been near the core where all the generator lights blazed down from telescoping poles. The shadows bathing the space between the tent were inky black, allowing additional shelter as Reed neared the corner and slowly bent his neck to look around.

One final tent sat in the farthest corner of the Russian encampment, pressed right to the base of a mountain ridgeline that rose rapidly into a sheer rock face, like a wall. It wasn't like the dozens of GP Medium style tents spread out across the valley floor. This was much bigger, more like a GP Large, with high central support poles and a lot of guy wires to provide tension. Outside the tent on every corner, Reed immediately recognized the silhouettes of Alpha Group commandos standing in the shadows, dressed in full black, each wearing armor plates and cradling a rifle. Two of them were marked by the ember glow of cigarettes. All stood with their faces pointed outward, away from the tent behind them and the heavy-duty truck backed up to its entrance.

Behind him, Reed felt Wolfgang moving to gain a look around the edge of the supply tent. Reed shot a hand out and blocked him, digging his fingers into Wolfgang's arm to underscore his silent point. His gaze snapped past the Alpha commandos to the light streaming out of the tent, flowing around the rear of the truck. It was dim, sheltered by the heavy canvas cover stretched over the truck's cargo area. The vehicle was still running, the diesel engine chugging with a steady *clack clack clack*.

The gap between its rear and the interior of the tent was barely six inches wide. Reed could see only a sliver of the tent's interior, with no visible detail in the glare of the light.

But he saw movement. He noted the truck shifting as something very heavy was slid along its cargo floor. He saw two men pass across the six-inch gap, light reflecting off their clothes for just a moment.

The clothes were bright, rubbery, and yellow.

"Reed, six o'clock." Wolfgang's hissed warning preceded the mutter of voices from behind them by only a millisecond, but it was enough for him to retract his head back around the corner and look up the trail in the direction they had come. The footfalls were heavy, the voices Russian. They were only yards away, headed straight for Reed and Wolfgang's position, about to round the corner at any moment.

There was only one place to hide. Reed couldn't move forward without throwing himself into the arms of the Alpha commandos. He couldn't turn back without doing the same to whoever was coming up the trail. They had to get inside the supply tent, and quickly, but the door was on the far side.

Reed's hand swept beneath his jacket again and found the grip of his KA-BAR. The razor-sharp blade slid from its leather scabbard and pierced the tent's canvas wall. It slid through the thick fabric with ease, opening a four-foot slit in under two seconds. Even as the voices grew louder, Reed pulled the slit open and grabbed Wolfgang by the arm. Wolfgang ducked through the hole, his prosthetic leg dragging stiffly behind him. It caught on the bottom of the fabric, and he nearly fell. Reed heard Wolfgang catch himself on some object inside the tent. Wolfgang grunted and fell. Reed sheathed the knife and used his own boot to grab Wolfgang's prosthetic foot and push it into the tent.

But there was no longer any time for him to part the fabric and duck through. The soldiers were on him, rounding the corner and marching toward the truck. They were more Alpha commandos, both dressed in full black with drop holsters and Heckler & Koch MP5 submachine guns strapped to their chests. Reed instinctively loosened his shoulders and started walking, heading dead toward them even as they rounded the corner. He dipped his chin once in acknowledgment, just one soldier passing another. Nothing unusual in the slightest. He believed it, owned it, and prayed for the Alphas to do so as well.

But they didn't. They closed to within ten feet of him, and Reed moved automatically to the left, ready to pass them. He kept his strides even and relaxed, his shoulders back but not tense. The Alphas swung to his right as though they were going to let him pass. They continued a conversation held in subdued Russian. They crossed to within a yard of Reed.

Then the one on the inside stopped and cocked his head. He pivoted toward Reed.

"*Ey. Kto ty?*"

He might have been asking for the time or the score of a soccer match. Reed had no idea, and chose to ignore the question, continuing to walk easily. But the Alpha didn't back down, instead pivoting on his heel and shouting after Reed, his words punctuated by the audible *snap* of the MP5 switching off safety.

"*Ey! Stoy!*"

This time Reed was sure the man was *not* asking for a sports score. He ground to a stop but didn't turn. Without looking over his shoulder he could feel the muzzle of the MP5 lowered over his back. A weapon light flicked on as though to confirm the fact, spilling bright white LED glow over his shoulders. Reed gritted his teeth and turned slowly, raising both hands. The SIG still rode in the small of his back, impossible to reach without earning a three-round burst to the chest. He faced the Alpha and noticed the lead man approaching with the MP5 held at eye level, his buddy side-stepping to Reed's left in an obvious tactical maneuver—even as the lead Alpha closed, the secondary commando would maintain a clear shot.

"*Kto ty?*" The guy repeated, jabbing with the muzzle. Reed looked right, over the commando's shoulder. He saw the slit in the tent part, and half of Wolfgang's face appeared as a shadow. Then the muzzle of his 10mm Glock 20.

"*Kto ty?*" The phrase was repeated with the growling tone of a final question. The MP5 flexed, the weapon light rising to Reed's face. Blinding

him. He shielded his eyes with his left hand and dropped his right hand to
his side.

He sighed. "Do it."

"*Chto?*" the first guy said.

But the second guy was quicker. "Amerikanskiy!"

His MP5 rose off his chest even as the first guy tensed, finger dropping
over the trigger. Then Wolfgang fired. Two quick shots from the tent,
bursting like thunderclaps and spitting flame across the darkness. Hot lead
struck the first man in the neck and the back of the skull even as the second
guy reactively pivoted toward the newest threat.

Reed drew and both he and Wolfgang fired even as the second guy's
MP5 rose toward Wolfgang's position. The soldier was caught in a crossfire
of nine- and ten-millimeter slugs, taking multiple rounds to the face and
neck, just above his body armor. Then he was headed down, Wolfgang was
headed back through the slit in the tent, and Reed was dropping into a
kneel to retrieve the nearest MP5.

By the time he returned to his feet, the momentary silence that had
engulfed the camp following the storm of unexpected gunshots expired.
An alarm sounded. Voices shouted.

And the next wave of Alphas poured around the corner.

39

The drugs entered Reed's bloodstream the moment the first gunshots cracked. More than adrenaline, this was something far more potent. Biological or psychotic, he didn't know, but it hot-wired his mind in an instant. He could think, see, and feel perfectly. Every movement was automatic and smooth. He stepped over the fallen Alpha body and pivoted into the faces of the oncoming Alphas.

Then he flicked the captured MP5 to full auto and dumped the mag.

Thirty rounds of 9mm streamed from the muzzle in under three seconds, pinging against chest plates and ripping through unprotected arms and shoulders. Screams rent the air, and one soldier went down. Then Reed was flinging himself sideways, into an aisle between supply tents even as Wolfgang joined the fight with a trio of shots from his 10mm. There was no time for Reed to stoop and recover a spare magazine for the MP5. No time to think about anything other than dashing for cover. He was literally lost in the midst of a hornet's nest, and he'd just set off an earthquake.

The camp's emergency alarm continued to blare as Reed reached the next tent city intersection and hurtled right. Already the Alphas were opening fire around him, sending hot lead zipping through canvas and buzzing over his head. Reed dove into a squat, the SIG clutched in his right hand. A Russian supply soldier appeared from the opening of a tent, confused and disoriented. His right hand flailed for the Grach handgun strapped to his side as he spun toward Reed. One round from the SIG split his head open, and he pitched backward.

Then Wolfgang arrived. He lunged from the end of his tent and sprinted through the torn grass, reaching Reed's position just before the next storm of MP5 fire ripped over their heads.

"Are you freaking *kidding me*?" Wolfgang shouted. "You just *had* to wander off. You just *had* to—"

His rant terminated amid the sound of shouts and footfalls pounding the dirt. The alarm blared like a cadence now. Reed returned to his feet and broke into a sprint, turning away from the scene of the firefight behind him and heading directly for the core of the camp.

The strategy was brutally simple. He couldn't hope to fight all eleven thousand plus soldiers camped in the bottom of the Georgian valley. He couldn't fight half of them. His and Wolfgang's best hope for survival was to lose themselves amid the crowd—to shrink back into the cover of the uniforms they still wore.

It was a good plan, but the moment Reed skidded back to the busted two-lane where he and Wolfgang had left Ivan, that plan went out the window. There was no chance of slipping back into the swarms of soldiers like members of the crowd—the swarms of soldiers were gone. Whatever alarm had been sounded must have been a Russian infantry equivalent to the Navy's general quarters. There was no chaos, and there was no mob to fade into. Everybody was rushing to their posts, truck engines churning to life and long columns of infantry merging into unified clusters, like Roman centurions.

No, this was more than just a call to general quarters. This was something bigger. The soldiers were headed *out*, away from the core of the camp. They were headed into the city.

What?

Reed's gaze swept right, down the muddy road toward the sound of a T-90 tank engine roaring to life. He spotted Ivan standing next to the men he'd been smoking with, the big Russian's gaze blazing with irate disbelief as it locked with Reed.

And then Reed heard the Alphas again, shouting behind him. He spun left and shoved Wolfgang through the entrance of the first tent he found. It was another supply tent, laden with stacks of ammunition crates all stenciled with black Cyrillic. There was nobody inside, and Reed pressed Wolfgang behind him, raising the SIG to eye level and watching the door.

Soldiers churned by. Two dozen of them, all rushing toward the back of a Ural-4320 heavy-duty truck. They loaded inside, packed along tight benches, then the Ural roared away and another took its place. The next truck was loaded the same way. The soldiers just kept coming.

Reed turned away from the door and tucked the SIG into the small of his back again. Sweat dripped from his face, but the mental clarity that had brought the world around him into crystal-clear focus persisted. It was as though he were running in hyperdrive. Everything was so simple, so direct. He knew exactly what to do.

"Put the gun away," Reed snapped, shoving the ammunition crates aside and reaching the back of the tent. It was dark there, but it didn't take him long to find what he was looking for—a crate full of Russian-made AK-12 rifles, chambered in the infamous 5.45mm, with thirty-round mags housed in an adjacent crate. He loaded one and tossed it to Wolfgang even as Wolfgang concealed the Austrian-built handgun in the small of his back. Then Reed took a matching rifle and ratcheted the bolt. He pulled the Russian military cap lower down over his face and turned for the door.

"Wait," Wolfgang said. "Where are we going?"

"Truck," Reed said abruptly. "We'll get out of the camp and regroup. Ready?"

Reed closed near to the entrance of the tent. The column of Russian soldiers ready to load onto the next Ural were packed into the aisle between tents, barely eight feet to his right. The next truck was coming—muddy tires kicking up sod as the engine churned.

"I can't get up there," Wolfgang said. "They'll see the leg."

"Go first," Reed said. "I'll push you."

"Push me? What?"

"Go now!"

Reed grabbed Wolfgang by the shoulder and pushed him through the door just as the truck rolled past it. Wolfgang staggered in the mud but maintained control of his rifle, holding it crossways against his chest just like the infantrymen lined up behind him. Most of those soldiers wore full battle gear—body armor, helmets, sidearms. Reed and Wolfgang only wore the green fatigues, but nobody questioned them as Reed closed behind Wolfgang and pushed him toward the back of the Ural.

Heavy brakes squealed. Wolfgang's hand closed around the rear rail, and his natural leg bent to power him up over the bumper. He heaved and swung up. Reed pressed his shoulder against Wolfgang's butt and twisted, shoving him forward.

Wolfgang hit the truck's floor on his knees, and Reed swung up next to him. Behind them the tide of soldiers crowded the rear of the truck, swarming like ants. Wide eyes and pale faces—a lot of *kids*. They paid no attention to Reed as he and Wolfgang sat on the outer benches at the front of the truck, facing each other. Nobody noticed their lack of body armor or helmets.

Everybody was too focused on his own equipment, nervous emergency radiating from the enclosed bed of the Ural like the heat wafting off a nuclear reactor. Reed remembered what Ivan had said about this brigade being deployed to Ukraine, and he thought half of them must have died there.

The soldiers that now surrounded him were little better than high schoolers playing dress-up.

Gears ground, and the truck started forward again. They made it ten feet as Reed's heart thumped a steady staccato, then the Ural stopped with a lurch, and shouts rang outside the canvas covering. Harsh and demanding, all spoken in Russian. Reed's body tensed and he held the AK between his thighs, muzzle pointed toward the roof of the truck. It was dark inside the vehicle and already sticky hot. Rough breathing and mutters of concern rippled down the benches. Footsteps pounded the mud, and Reed looked across the aisle to Wolfgang.

Wolfgang sat perfectly still, iron gaze fixating on Reed with pure fury in his eyes. Then a flashlight snapped on from the tail of the truck, and a question was barked into it. Loud and demanding.

Reed's hand slipped down to the grip of his AK, index finger hanging only an inch over the trigger. Already the safety was off. Already he was rehearsing the mechanical movements necessary to swing his body away from the bench, pulling the rifle into his shoulder.

There were a dozen or more Russian soldiers inside that truck, and the oldest amongst them couldn't have been more than twenty-one. Reed didn't want to shoot them, but he would. He'd gun every one of them down—whatever it took to get out alive.

He waited, and the question was repeated from the end of the truck. Murmured answers returned. The flashlight beam played down the length of faces. It stopped over Wolfgang.

Once more the question was repeated. Wolfgang didn't answer. He sat frozen in the seat, rifle held between his legs. The flashlight beam didn't move, and the question was barked a second time, louder than before.

No answer. Wolfgang's lips parted, but he didn't speak.

Repeat what they said, idiot, Reed thought. *Do something!*

Boots ground against the rear bumper of the truck. The light twitched as somebody swung aboard. Reed looked behind the neck of the soldier sitting next to him and recognized the pitch-black sleeve of an Alpha Group uniform. The soldier was fixated on Wolfgang. He didn't recognize Wolfgang's face.

But he might recognize Reed's.

The Alpha took two steps down the narrow aisle, forcing his legs between the feet of the infantryman. The LED beam of his light settled over Wolfgang's face. Reed exhaled a mental sigh and lowered his finger slowly over the trigger of the AK, resigned to the inevitable.

It would be pure chaos when the first shot went off. If he was quick—and lucky—he could extricate himself from the truck before anyone really knew what was happening.

If he was quick.

The Alpha spoke again, repeating his question for the third and what sounded like a final time. His hand dropped over the grip of a Stirzh handgun affixed to his leg in a drop holster.

Reed wrapped his finger around the AK's trigger and prepared to fire.

40

"Stoy!"

The voice boomed from the rear of the truck only a millisecond before Reed pivoted the muzzle of the AK toward the oncoming Alpha commando. Jerking his head quickly to the right, Reed again looked behind the neck of the man seated next to him. He saw a hulk of a shadow standing behind the truck, all muscle and green uniform. Reed couldn't see a face.

But he didn't need to. The voice was impossible to misidentify. Ivan Sidorov swung into the truck and barked a short sentence at the Alpha commando. The commando barked back. Ivan waved his hand at the line of backlogged troops gathered behind the truck. Outside, the air was full of surging engines and shouting voices. A tank rattled back, so close it vibrated the truck's canvas top.

In the distance, Reed heard gunfire. A lot of it. But despite the growing chaos and Ivan's intensity, the commando wouldn't back down. He growled something and jabbed his light at Wolfgang. Ivan peered over the commander's shoulder, squinting at Wolfgang. Looking confused.

Then he growled what could have only been a curse. He shoved past the commando, his gaze flicking quickly across Reed. Then Ivan grabbed Wolfgang by the collar and shook him, shouting something in Russian. A swift blow of his right hand broke across Wolfgang's face so hard Reed winced. Wolfgang pitched backward and Ivan shouted again, shaking him.

The Alpha commando simply watched, and Reed wasn't sure whether he bought the charade—whatever kind of charade it was. Ivan hit Wolfgang again, and when the big Russian turned, Reed saw blood streaming from Wolfgang's nose.

Twisting back to the commando, Ivan rattled something off in what sounded like a more apologetic tone. He kept talking until the commando waved an irritated hand and snapped a single word.

Then the commando left, dropping out of the back of the truck. Ivan turned immediately back and grabbed Wolfgang by the collar, hauling him up. As he passed Reed, he jerked his head and snapped an order.

Reed stood and fell into line behind the flailing Wolfgang, wading between the tangled legs all the way to the tailgate. Ivan dropped out, pulling Wolfgang. Reed jumped, turning his back toward the column of men and ducking his head. The Alpha commandos were still busy sorting through them, shoving bodies aside and barking demands. Thus far, nobody seemed to have any idea what they were talking about.

"*Dvigat'sya!*" Ivan shoved Wolfgang ahead, and Reed followed alongside. They moved quickly through the camp, back amongst the tangle of barracks tents, all the way to the barbed wire. Ivan spoke in nothing but short bursts of Russian the entire way, while Wolfgang and Reed kept quiet. Nobody accosted them or stood in their way. No more Alpha commandos appeared. They reached the barbed-wire fence and Reed used the muzzle of the AK to lift the coils off the ground.

The transition out of the camp was quicker than the intrusion. Outside the fence, the three of them immediately sprinted for the tree line—Reed and Ivan stretching out and Wolfgang struggling to keep up on his prosthetic leg. They lost themselves in inky deep shadows and slipped beneath tangled tree limbs. Ivan led the way, heaving as he ran but not stopping until they were four hundred yards up the next slope, far enough away from camp to avoid any chance of detection.

At least for the moment. As Reed turned back and squinted through the dark, he marked the progress of the Russian army by the headlights of trucks and the sweeping spotlights of hovering attack helicopters. The entire force was deploying, surging out of the camp and headed into Tbilisi.

"*What was that?*" Wolfgang leaned over his own knees and spat blood, still heaving from the run. His nose bled, as did his bottom lip. He looked like he'd just tangled with a brick wall—and lost.

"That," Ivan growled, jabbing a finger into Wolfgang's chest, "was me bailing you out of very bad situation! Stupid fool. Can I not leave you for five minutes?"

"Me? Are you kidding? I didn't go anywhere. Reed went dashing after something and got us into a gunfight."

Ivan spat and turned to Reed. Reed ignored him. He'd left his binoculars with the rest of his American gear outside the barbed-wire fence. From nearly a thousand yards away, he could see very little detail of the Russian column, but the intent was obvious. They were moving in to take Tbilisi—more than a passive occupation. A forceful one.

"What's happening?" Reed demanded.

"They are mobilizing."

"I can see that. *Why?*"

"I do not know. Perhaps because a crazy American just opened fire next to their command post."

"That should result in *internal* security," Wolfgang said. "Not a deployment."

Ivan shook his head, watching the lights. Then he sighed.

"This was likely the plan all along. You may have triggered it early. Like I say, I do not know."

"What did you say to the Alphas?" Wolfgang asked, wiping blood from his face.

Ivan smirked. "I tell them you are a dishwasher wandered off to play hero."

"Dishwasher?"

The smirk grew into a grin. "In Russian army, dishwashing is saved for... the challenged ones." Another laugh.

Wolfgang squinted.

Then he got it.

"Wait. You told them I was mentally disabled?"

"Aren't you?" Ivan toed Wolfgang in the shin.

Wolfgang gritted his teeth. "So why'd you have to hit me so hard?"

"I didn't. I just wanted to."

Wolfgang looked like he was about to return the favor to Ivan. Reed interceded before he could.

"What were you talking to the guards about? The ones outside the command post."

Ivan's smile faded as his mind returned to the present. The lines in his face depended.

"We discuss incoming troops. Apparently, two more brigades are en route to Georgia as we speak. Combat infantry with supporting armor."

"When do they get here?" Wolfgang asked.

"I am not sure. I had to save your dumb asses before I could get that far. What did *you* find?"

Wolfgang left that one to Reed, raising both eyebrows. Reed recalled the truck backed up to that oversized tent. The commandos gathered around it, securing the perimeter. The yellow radiation suits.

Only one possible explanation.

"We found another bomb," Reed said. "And they're moving it as we speak."

41

Anton Golubev hauled the Russian controller out of the command post by his ear and shot him in the back of the head. The young man was still a teenager, with an embarrassing attempt at a mustache gathered on his upper lip, panic in his eyes. It had likely been an honest mistake when the Alpha commander radioed in for a camp-wide alert, and the controller had blasted the loudspeaker signal for deployment instead.

But once the mistake was made, there was no going back. Every infantryman in the camp knew to be on the alert for the signal to rush to arms and deploy into Tbilisi. It was a standing order. Only the higher-ranking officers expected there to be the sort of emergency which would drive the Russian military into Tbilisi, offering them an excuse to assume full military control.

That emergency, however, wasn't meant to happen until the next day, just after sunrise. The signal had been called five hours early, meaning that the soldiers now storming Tbilisi were dangerously out of sync with Russian ground forces distributed across northern Georgia.

All because of an idiot boy who pushed the wrong button. *Stupid.*

Whatever the case, the boy was dead now, and the Nineteenth Motor Rifle Brigade was seizing the city. They were already encountering resistance from scattered segments of the Defense Forces of Georgia who were now electing to break with the directives of their missing president and resist the invaders, but that wouldn't last long. By sunrise, the job would be done. Maybe the darkness was even an advantage. The only question that really remained was *what* had caused the Alpha commander to call for the emergency alert in the first place.

In one of the mobile command trailers at the core of the encampment, Golubev listened as the commander debriefed, describing the domino chain of events that directly preceded the radio call for the alert. There were gunshots, at first. Two members of Alpha group were found dead in the grass, shot through the neck and the head. So much for body armor.

But what alarmed Golubev the most wasn't the dead soldiers or even the prospect of enemy combatants penetrating the Russian base. They could very likely be rogue members of the Georgian Defense Forces. Foot soldiers who got lucky while jumping a couple of Alphas.

No, that wasn't the concern. The concern was *where* the Alphas had been jumped—only yards from that one particular tent, all the way in the back corner of the camp only yards from the truck which had just departed. That was plenty to alarm Golubev.

He ordered the Alpha commander back into the base to search every square inch of the valley floor, and Golubev barged out of the command trailer and into the surveillance trailer that sat next to it. Most prominently a center for the use and control of small surveillance drones, the trailer doubled as a security center for the Russian encampment. It was the central hub for the small collection of cameras posted at key points around the command center and the temporary airfield where the helicopter gunships had been parked.

Golubev ordered the lieutenant running the computer station to wind the tape back—even though Golubev knew it hadn't been called *tape* since the days of the old Union. He wanted a view of any and every camera posted around the vicinity of the camp nearest to that dark corner with the big tent. There were no cameras there, of course, but anybody walking that way would pass pretty close to the command post cameras pointed outward at the base. And maybe...

"Stop." Golubev pointed. "Right there. Scan back."

The lieutenant rushed to follow orders. Golubev leaned close to the screen and squinted as two dark figures dressed in Russian infantry uniforms broke away from a throng of soldiers lined up outside the commissary tent and wound toward that back corner of the camp. He quickly lost them, but something about their stance, their stride, their body language...it didn't sit well with him.

The lieutenant scanned forward again. Golubev watched the recording at three times the regular playback speed. He recognized the moment that fool controller had sounded the wrong alarm. He saw the panic sweep the camp, but only for a moment, because these soldiers had been trained well, and many of them were battle hardened from their days in Ukraine. They rushed for their combat gear and their rifles. They lined up to be deployed by trucks and armored troop transports.

And then...

"*Stop.*" Golubev growled the word, his own blood rising to an instant boil as the silhouette crossed the edge of the camera's view. The lieutenant had to rewind. He missed it, and Golubev shoved him out of the way. He took control of the computer and found the frame he was looking for, freezing the tape. He squinted.

And then the fire in his veins surged as though raw petrol were dumped onto it. The face was a mere profile, turned sideways. The figure wore dark green combat fatigues and moved toward the rear of a stopped truck. The camera caught his face for only a moment.

A moment was enough.

From his hip, Golubev's radio crackled. He tugged it free and mashed the button, ordering the speaker to go ahead. It was the Alpha commander.

"We found something," the commander said. "American built M4 combat rifles, near the perimeter."

"How many?" Golubev said. He already knew the answer.

"*Tri.*"

Three.

Golubev slammed the radio down and left the room. He rushed back to his command trailer. He locked the door behind him and slid into the chair behind a metal desk. He opened a briefcase and accessed a secure satellite phone—or, at least, a private satellite phone. A phone linked to a private military satellite, with only one possible number to call. Golubev input his passcode and dialed.

Makar Nikitin didn't keep him waiting. He answered almost immediately.

"Anton? What the hell is going on down there?"

"*Sidorov*," Golubev growled. "Ivan Sidorov. He's here, and he's working with the Americans."

42

The West Wing
The White House

Dawn broke over Washington, but it didn't wake Acting President Jordan Stratton. It couldn't. He'd never slept. Together with White House Chief of Staff Jill Easterling, the two of them had barricaded themselves into his vice-presidential office and worked through the night, scratching notes and guzzling coffee, searching for a solution.

The problem wasn't technical, or even strategic. The questions of how to put a reeling nation back on its feet, quiet the storms of fear, stabilize the economy, and confront what certainly appeared to be dramatic Russian military aggression were complex at face value, but at their core they all orbited around one singular principle.

The American people were on their ass. They'd been sucker-punched again and again and were now so dazed that they hardly knew which way was up. Stratton believed in his very bones that there was no threat on planet earth which could truly jeopardize the future of America, except America herself. A back-to-back world war champion should know something about digging deep and finding a way.

But first, Americans had to *believe*. They had to rally. They had to gather together and unite into the same unstoppable national spirit that had already overcome a civil war, a Great Depression, Nazi Germany, the Soviet Union, and Al-Qaeda.

All they needed was something to rally around. Something to *believe* in.

By the time Stratton reached the conference room, the vision had clarified. By the time the cabinet had fully assembled two hours later, trays of sandwiches scattered around and laptop keyboards clicking, Stratton knew he was onto something solid. Something certain. Unconventional, certainly, but very powerful.

If only he could sell it. That would be the tough part. He expected resistance, which was why he refused to begin his spiel until the entire cabinet was assembled.

At last the room was quiet, all eyes fixated on Stratton. He saw a lot of uncertainty in the faces of the younger aides. Absolute exhaustion in the eyes of the head secretaries. People weren't sleeping. They were eating poorly, and not enough. They were burning the candle at both ends and drifting dangerously close to total burnout.

Just like the nation.

Stratton looked sideways at Easterling. She nodded once, reassuring him. It was a good plan.

He turned back to the table. "Who here slept last night?"

Dead silence. Gazes shifted uncertainly.

"Who saw their family this weekend?"

Continued silence.

"Anybody eat a good breakfast?"

An uncomfortable shift of bodies against leather chairs circulated the room. Momentary confusion, then frustration played across several faces. Stratton expected it. It was all part of the foundation of his argument. He needed to lay the groundwork.

"Nobody slept, did they?" Stratton said. "No. I can see that."

Leaning back in his chair, Stratton drummed his fingers slowly against the table. Taking his time, letting the moment build. He knew everybody was fixated on him. He knew he had their attention.

"Can you feel it?" he asked. "Deep down inside. Someplace in your gut. Do you feel your body breaking down?"

Stratton raised both eyebrows and pivoted around the room. He stopped at random over Secretary of Transportation Stacey Pilcher. She blushed and looked away. Stratton didn't let her off the hook. He waited.

"I'm not sure what you mean, sir," Pilcher said at last.

"Well, let me drill down a little. I'm talking about that feeling in the back of your mind. The one that kept you up last night. That paranoia. Those unanswered questions. Will there be more attacks? Will the economy spiral? What about the stock market? Is my daughter safe at school? What the actual hell are the Russians doing? Is this war?"

Another pause. Stratton nodded. "I know the questions. They're keeping me up at night, too. I haven't slept well in days. But it's not a contest. We're all exhausted. Does anybody know why?"

Awkward silence. It seemed like such an obvious question. Stratton had hoped they would leave him hanging. Now he leaned forward.

"Because this room is the *bellwether* of the nation. What you're feeling, that fear and that uncertainty, that's just a hint of the pain that's ripping through this nation right now. The instability. The worm eating slowly away at the very fabric of who we are as a nation. You feel it because the *people* feel it. They're all asking the same hundreds of questions you're asking. They want to know about the stock market, and about the security of their children, and about gas prices. They want a plan and they want leadership. But I can tell you this. Every doubt they face can be boiled down into one simple question. Six little words. *Are we going to make it?*"

He let the question hang. He could see the restlessness again. The impatience of older secretaries who wanted to get down to business. Senior advisors who wanted to skip the motivational speech and get down to the meat of the matter.

But the meat of the matter wasn't policy. Stratton could feel that now. They had missed the forest for the trees.

"It is the duty of this administration to convince the American people, beyond any shadow of a doubt, that the answer to that question is a resounding *yes*. An absolute *yes*. An inevitable *yes*. Not because we have all the answers, but *they do*. Because there is no force on this earth that is more powerful than the unified spirit of the American people. Period."

Stratton stood. He walked slowly behind his chair and placed both hands on the back of it. He faced the room.

"Ladies and gentlemen, we are *failing* in that duty. As an administration, as a government, and as the leaders of the free world. We are allowing ourselves to get lost in a mire of policy and paperwork while we miss the forest for the trees. The people out there"—Stratton pointed to the window —"don't *need* policy and they don't *need* our permission to rise up. What they need is to *believe*. They need somebody to unify them. From this moment forward, that job and that job alone will be the sole agenda of this administration. Full stop."

He let the moment hang. At last Secretary Gorman spoke.

"I'm...not sure I understand what you're asking us to do, sir."

"I'm asking you to help them believe, Madam Secretary. I'm asking you all to help them believe, and to ruthlessly destroy anything that stands in the way of that belief."

More blank stares. Stratton nodded. He'd expected as much. Time to get relative.

"Okay. Let me get specific. With the assistance of Chief of Staff Easterling, I'm announcing a new initiative for this entire administration. We're calling it *American Spirit*, and you can think of it as a marketing campaign— but don't dare call it that. The concept is very simple. We're going to get out of the weeds and build a bandwagon. A simple campaign developed with the assistance of Congress, governors, thought leaders, celebrities... whoever we can get on board. Literally anyone. The idea is *one* America. One nation. One fight. We're going to shift the focus of political ire away from the guys across the aisle and outward to the forces of evil assaulting our democracy. We are going to rally this country the way Wilson rallied us for World War One and FDR rallied us for the sequel. Okay? I'm talking about *spirit*, here, not policy. I'm talking about *American Spirit*."

More blank stares. They still weren't getting it. Stratton felt like he was communicating abstract impressionist art theory to a room full of mechanical engineers—which was funny, because he'd never understood abstract impressionist art.

"I'm sorry, sir. I really don't know how to take practical action out of that."

The objection came from Stephen Kline, the SecDef. Stratton wasn't surprised. The man was always blunt.

"Fair enough," Stratton said. "Let's get practical. Here's what I want you to do. I want you to get on the phone with Congress and lobby a bill to have memorial pendants designed and manufactured for every active service member in the DOD. It'll be cheap and bipartisan. Make the design something that memorializes the terror attacks. Make it personal, make it red, white, and blue, make it a done deal by the end of the week. Call a press conference to announce it. Get families of some of the victims involved. Have your press office book you an appearance on a talk show. Beat the American spirit drum—endlessly. Share the belief. Got it?"

Kline blinked. His brow wrinkled and his lips parted. Stratton could feel the objection coming.

Then, it didn't. Kline closed his mouth. He rocked his head, then nodded. "Yeah. Okay. I can do that."

"Great. Now, Secretary Clancey." Stratton next addressed Paulette Clancey, secretary of the interior. "I want you to head up the national parks initiative of the American Spirit campaign. This is where we get celebrities involved. I'm thinking big events at all of our national parks. Concerts. Festivals. Red, white, and blue, and it's gonna be free. No admission charges. If you don't have the funding, we'll lean on Congress. This is bipartisan. We want people *out of their homes*. Celebrating unity. Standing together. Honoring the dead and defying the enemy. You get the vibe?"

Clancey blinked. She pushed her glasses up her nose. "Uhm..."

"Say it," Stratton encouraged.

"It's a nice idea, sir. I'm just wondering if things like concerts are a little...well..."

"Insensitive," Lisa Gorman said.

Stratton resisted glowering at the secretary of state. He shook his head. "That's exactly the *point*. It's not insensitive because America does not cower. We do not surrender. We will not let murderous thugs tell us how we spend our free time. That's not the American spirit."

Stratton looked around the room, eyebrows up, waiting for buy-in. He still wasn't getting it. The exhausted faces' flat expressions spoke to a spirit of brokenness, not hope.

If he couldn't inspire this room, how was he going to inspire the nation?

"Look," Stratton said. "I fully realize this comes off a bit..."

"Amateur?" Easterling said. The word landed hard but Stratton appreciated her for voicing it. Everybody had to be thinking it. Easterling knew when to yank the curtain back.

"Okay," Stratton said. "Amateur. Childish. Small potatoes. I get it, believe me. But just let me ask you one question. If you don't believe this country can rise from the ashes and stand tall in the face of the storm...why should they?"

Stratton gestured to the window, motioning generally to the open countryside beyond. The land of the free. He left the question hanging, even though it was rhetorical. He waited.

To his surprise, it was the gruffest, toughest, grouchiest man in the room who spoke first. General Yellin grunted from the end of the table, nodding his white-haired head.

"I like it! Smells like good old-fashioned war spirit to me. Give me a couple days to call some air bases and we'll put some air shows together."

Glances turned his way. A few eyebrows rose. A healthy pause.

Then Secretary of the Treasury Carmen Silva chimed in, shooting a smile Stratton's way.

"American Spirit, sir? I can get behind that."

A chorus of agreement circled the table, and Stratton returned the smile. He smacked the backside of his chair.

"American Spirit. Own it. Believe it. Make them believe it, too. Let's put this country back on its feet."

43

Langley, Virginia

Reports from Georgia reached Aimes's desk five minutes after she arrived on the executive floor of CIA headquarters. Rigby delivered them in person —not hard files but yet another iPad. Aimes slurped coffee and scanned quickly through the messages.

They were directly from the ground, transmitted by the Prosecution Force. Detailed assessments of Russian ground forces gathered outside Tbilisi were joined by notations from Ivan Sidorov that Nikitin's personal advisor and alleged right-hand man, Anton Golubev, was also present with the military.

All of that was interesting, and perhaps consequential, but it paled in comparison to the final report Reed Montgomery's team delivered—confirmation of the presence of a Russian radiation team. A tent hidden in the back of a military compound.

A truck with unknown cargo.

"It's all speculation," Rigby said. "We need them back inside that camp. We need photographs."

Aimes didn't reply as she tabbed away from the Prosecution Force's messages, accessing reports from her own satellite surveillance unit charged with tracking Russian military action in Georgia. That team had remained awake all night, doing their best to keep up with armed forces movements even in the dark.

It was easy enough to see the muzzle flashes and burning buildings that ignited around one a.m. local time amid the northeastern outskirts of Tbilisi. That military action quickly spread throughout the city as Russian armed forces deployed from outpost camps and took complete control of the Georgian capital.

It was warfare, plain and simple. The Defense Forces of Georgia finally seemed to be resisting the Russian invasion...but too late. Russia had already dug in. For all intents and purposes, Georgia had been seized in a matter of three days.

In that context...what did the radiation team mean?

She thought again of Panama. Of those eerie reports from the radiological team on the ground there—all that discussion about isotopes and daughter isotopes. About brand-new fuel.

"Ma'am?"

Aimes set the iPad down and lifted her phone. Her secretary picked up.

"Yes, Madam Director?"

"Get the White House on the line. I need to speak with the acting president, if possible. If not, I'll take the chief of staff."

"Yes, ma'am."

Aimes looked to Rigby. He stood with his arms folded, a question his face.

"Put the PF on standby," Aimes said. "I don't want this boiling over while we figure out what to do."

"But the pictures..."

"Standby, Rigby. I've known Reed Montgomery for a while. I want him riding the bench before he touches off World War Three."

44

Reed, Wolfgang, and Ivan recovered their hidden backpacks and retreated into the mountains even as total hell broke loose in Tbilisi. They could hear it spilling over the ridgelines and flooding open valleys—the crackle of small-arms fire blended with the occasional pound of a T-90 tank cannon. Smoke, carried by a crisp pre-winter breeze, smelled of burning wood and oil.

It tasted like war on Reed's dry tongue. He guzzled water from his canteen and pulled the Swarovski binoculars from his pack, sweeping the valley floor.

Nobody had followed them. The getaway was clean, in part due to Ivan's quick thinking and successful impersonation of a Russian military cop. In part because the Russian military was now fully engaged in open combat with the Defense Forces of Georgia.

The Georgians were resisting from all across the city...but the fox was already inside the hen house. The battle now unfolding was over long before it began.

"Word from Langley," Wolfgang called from his position beneath a tree, slouched against the trunk and still gasping for breath. Reed and Ivan had pushed him hard on his prosthetic leg. He'd kept up without complaint, but he certainly appeared winded.

"They want us to stand down and stand by," Wolfgang finished, lowering the messaging device.

"Of course they do." Reed swigged more water, swishing it inside his mouth and spitting it out this time to blast battle grit from between his teeth. He wasn't surprised by the CIA's direction. If he'd learned anything about working for Langley over the past two years, it was that the agency preferred to move much more slowly than the black ops teams they recruited. It might have been interpreted as prudence from the shelter of an office building buried deep in Virginia, but to Reed, standing on the front lines, it tasted more like cowardice.

"Give me the map," Ivan said, extending a hand to Wolfgang. Instead of a paper foldout, Wolfgang handed him another tablet, and Ivan's chunky fingers worked the screen. Reed watched, allowing his heart rate to calm and waiting for Ivan to speak. He still wasn't sure if he trusted the Russian, but he was certainly interested in what the old soldier had to say.

He'd snatched Reed and Wolfgang from the jaws of death, after all.

"Your CIA has marked Russian troop locations around Tbilisi," Ivan grunted. "It seems American satellites are as intrusive as ever."

Another long pause. Ivan picked his teeth with one dirty fingernail and squinted. Then he shook his head.

"We are missing the forest for the trees. Forgetting the Russian pretense of searching for WMDs, these forces are too extreme even for an occupation."

"What are you saying?" Wolfgang asked.

Ivan looked out over the valley. His oversized, smashed nosed twitched, and Reed thought he was inhaling that same odor of battle that Reed himself had noticed.

Funny how smells could so quickly unlock long-forgotten memories. Recollections of carnage and bloodshed. Thundering artillery and clacking ISIL AK-47s. At least, that was what Reed remembered. He wondered what memories the smell unlocked for Ivan. They clearly weren't good memories.

"He will not stop here," Ivan said at last. "This is only the first step.

Nikitin has taken Georgia by trickery, but his next target he will take by force."

"Turkey?" Wolfgang's eyebrows arched.

Ivan shook his head. "No. Turkey is NATO. This would trigger a world war. Nikitin is not yet ready for that. He will first solidify his position in the Caucuses."

Ivan pinched the tablet screen, zooming the map out. A greater view of the region was displayed in black, with white lines marking international borders and gray pools painting the expanses of the Black and Caspian seas.

Russia filled the northern portion of the map. Iran filled the southern section, with Turkey and Georgia forming a buffer between the two on the western side of the Caucasus land strip and Azerbaijan performing a similar function on the east. Sandwiched right in the middle, sharing borders with every nation except Russia, was Armenia.

Ivan tapped his finger slowly against the side of the iPad. He seemed lost in thought, his wrinkled and scarred face twisted into a frown of concentration.

At last, he looked up. "All of these countries were once a part of the old Union. If Nikitin wants them back, it will not be difficult for him to seize Armenia. Their president is weak and their army small, but there's not much value in Armenia. There's not much value in Georgia either, for that matter. Both countries already hang from puppet strings."

"So why bother?" Wolfgang pressed.

Ivan looked back at the map and shook his head softly. He breathed a Russian curse. "I can think of only one reason—the one nation that is worth capturing. The one nation that does not hang from strings." He pointed. "Azerbaijan."

Reed took the map and surveyed the landscape. Azerbaijan was about the same size as Georgia and Armenia combined. It stretched along the Caspian Sea, its capital city of Baku resting right on its eastern shore. Russia to the north—Iran to the south.

"They have oil, natural gas, and minerals," Ivan continued. "They have critical seaports and infrastructure. Their president is obstinate and clever —he's defied Nikitin many times, refusing to join the CSTO and complicating trade routes with Iran. It would be impossible for Nikitin to ever fully control the Caucasus so long as Azerbaijan remains free." Ivan nodded, seeming to warm to his own theory. "If Nikitin's plan is to lock down the region, he would need to capture Baku."

Wolfgang squinted. He cocked his head. "Wait. You're saying Nikitin is about to invade Azerbaijan? You've got to be crazy. There's no way he could justify that on a global stage. It would be Ukraine all over again."

"Not if he has an excuse," Ivan said. "Like the excuse he made for Georgia."

A chill ran down Reed's spine, and suddenly, he saw it. He knew what Ivan was thinking, even before Wolfgang voiced it.

"A bomb," Reed said. "A *nuclear* bomb."

Ivan nodded. "Just like WMDs in Iraq. A blank check authorizing total military aggression."

Wolfgang was already shaking his head. "I still don't buy it. They've already pulled that stunt once, and nobody believes them. Now they're sacking Tbilisi. Nikitin can't keep claiming that any country he wants to invade is illegally holding forgotten Soviet weapons. It's not enough justification."

"It will be if a weapon is detonated." The words left Reed's lips even as they were forming in his mind. It was so horrific an implication that he winced even as he said it, but the logic was all there.

Abdel Ibrahim. The Panama Canal bomb, its source still unidentified. The massive Russian military aggression into Georgia, clearly planned and prepared for months in advance.

It was chess, not checkers. So unbelievable that Reed easily bought it.

A *madman* at work.

"That's what we saw down there, isn't it?" Reed asked. "That team in radiation gear. You don't need radiation gear just to handle a nuclear weapon. Not a fully complete nuclear weapon. But we found similar gear at the warehouse in Beirut, where Ibrahim was handling the bomb that went to Panama. Why? Because it's not a conventional weapon. It's something special built, something shipped in pieces that has to be assembled before use."

"Something designed to leave the blast signature of an old Soviet weapon," Ivan finished.

Wolfgang snorted. "That's insane."

Ivan looked his way but didn't say anything. Slowly the disbelief melted off Wolfgang's face, replaced by something graver.

"He is fully insane," Ivan said at last. "And the more nuclear weapons that detonate for seemingly uncontrollable reasons, the closer we draw to open nuclear war. With full control of the Caucasus, Russia is anchored into the Middle East, and the momentum of expansion is much stronger than at any time in recent history. Another offensive in Ukraine, or even in Europe..."

"Suddenly it's much more plausible," Reed finished.

"It's *inevitable*," Ivan said.

For a while the mountainside grew quiet, nothing but the whisper of nighttime wind drifting amid the trees. Then Wolfgang spoke.

"So what do we do?"

Reed had been asking himself the same question, twisting the problem in his mind and examining it from every possible angle.

Really, there was only one angle that made sense. Only one answer which was logical.

"Contact Lucy. Provide the B-team with a full update and tell them to keep Langley in the loop. We're going back into Tbilisi."

45

The electronic messaging system linked to Langley and the Prosecution Force sitting inside the Gulfstream V chimed at ten fifteen p.m. Turk had drifted off to sleep while Corbyn played video games on a handheld device, and Strickland sat in his co-pilot seat with a paperback of Charles Dickens's best work, occasionally grinding his teeth and glowering at Corbyn whenever she cheered a high score.

Lucy sat by herself in the tail of the plane, her Bible spread across her thighs, all her computers open and spread out around the table in front of her. She was halfway through the Book of Esther—a story she never tired of reading—when the message blipped through. Not from Langley but from PF1. Reed's handle.

Shutting the Bible, Lucy sat up and called to Turk from across the plane. Her voice was calm but sufficiently direct to arrest everybody's attention. Already she was lost in the message, bright green eyes darting across the screen.

PF1: *BE ADVISED. RUSSIAN MILITARY ACTION THROUGHOUT TBIL-ISI. OBJECTIVE UNCERTAIN. POSSIBILITY OF FURTHER AGGRESSION INTO AZERBAIJAN. RUSSIAN RADIOLOGICAL TEAM OBSERVED. PRES-*

ENCE OF NUCLEAR WEAPON THOUGHT LIKELY. RETURNING INTO
TBILISI TO FURTHER INVESTIGATE. LANGLEY ALREADY UPDATED.
STAND BY.

Lucy read through the message a second time as Turk leaned over her shoulder, breathlessly doing the same. From the front of the plane, Corbyn and Strickland simply waited, books and video games forgotten.

At last, Turk looked up. "Warm up the engines. I want us wheels up in ten. We're gonna hover over the Georgian border."

The two pilots sprang into action without objection or question, sliding back into the cockpit and automatically falling into their preflight routines while Turk read the message again. He shook his head.

"What are we gonna do?" Lucy asked.

Turk retreated across the aisle, sliding into his seat. He locked the belt and breathed in deep. Lucy waited, observing the odd twitch of his fingers wrapped around the armrest. The pulse of the vein bulging from his temple.

Stress. And uncertainty.

"We're gonna get as close as we can," Turk said. "If I know Reed, when it's time to extract, he won't have time to waste."

46

Another meal of dry power bars and water were all the fuel Reed and his battered team could afford before they journeyed out of the hills and turned south toward Tbilisi. Still dressed in Russian military garb and wielding Russian built AK-12s, Reed felt only moderately better prepared to blend into the local environment than he had when he carried an M4 and wore generic black fatigues.

Russian soldiers were now being shot at, after all. The intensity of the fighting inside Tbilisi had escalated significantly over the last hour, with additional Russian troops surging into the city en masse. But despite the now fierce resistance of Georgian Defense Forces, the tide of the battle was clear. Just as Ivan had said, the Russians were too well dug in. The Georgians were scattered and leaderless, already surrounded right in the heart of their own city.

And there were more than Russian infantry and tanks to worry about. Rockets raced over the hills and landed in the city also, quickly spreading dots of hot orange fire across the skyline. Helicopter gunships raced low over rooftops and unleashed raking fire over any and every pocket of resistance. Artillery thundered from behind the next ridge.

No, this was most definitely not a search and recovery operation, but as Ivan noted, the escalation of hostilities in Tbilisi wouldn't stall whatever future plans Nikitin had in mind. If anything, they would accelerate such plans. When morning dawned and the Russian president was forced to face the world, he would no longer be able to claim that his special military operation was anything less than a full invasion.

Unless, of course, some other catastrophic event provided him with timely justification.

Regardless, if there was indeed a bomb headed east out of Georgia, there would be no way Reed and his team could locate it inside the city. The fog of war had descended, and miles of tangled Georgian streets would provide an endless maze wherein the Russian Alpha commandos presumably in charge of the weapon could easily lose themselves. If Reed and his team had any hope of outmaneuvering them, they needed to get *ahead* of the problem. They needed to get outside the city and onto the highway leading toward Azerbaijan. There was only one in this part of Georgia—the B4 Highway, which raced southeast between mountain passes and across the Khrami River before eventually leading to the town of Qazax, Azerbaijan.

Population: thirty-five thousand. Distance from Tbilisi: just ninety-eight kilometers.

"We need a vehicle," Ivan said, huffing a little as he jogged along a mountain trail. They were still a mile or more from the nearest outskirts of Tbilisi. Already the gunfire was growing louder—irregular pops of Kalashnikov rifles and the heavy *thack-thack-thack* of Russian machine guns. There was a helicopter also, circling somewhere high overhead, invisible from ground level. A tank cannon boomed over the empty battle-torn Russian night.

"How about something armored?" Wolfgang wheezed. He still hadn't complained about the labor of hiking the torn Georgian terrain on a prosthetic leg, but Reed could hear the strain getting to him.

Yes, they needed a vehicle. Sooner rather than later.

Ivan held up a fist at the end of the trail and Reed slid automatically into point, the Russian AK-12 held into his shoulder as he surveyed the field ahead. It was another park, with a soccer field and picnic benches. A hundred yards farther on, a pair of tall apartment buildings stood beneath a black sky, and on the street below a row of small sedans were parked together at the mouth of the apartment's parking lot, forming a makeshift barricade.

A noble effort, but it wasn't nearly enough to stop the grinding progress of a Russian Tigr as the heavy vehicle slammed straight through, brush guards shattering windows and windshields and hurtling the sedans aside. A moment later four soldiers were bailing out of the back while a fifth manned a machine gun mounted into the Tigr's roof. They went straight to the entrance of the first apartment building, beating on the door and shouting at the windows.

The words were Russian and the tones jovial. Almost celebratory. Reed glanced sideways at Ivan and saw the big Russian's jaw clench.

"The Tigr?" Reed asked.

Ivan nodded. "I will draw them. You come from behind."

Without another word, Ivan left the shadows and jogged through the darkness, circling left through the soccer field. In an instant he was out of sight, and Reed checked his AK. It was loaded with twenty-nine rounds, one more in the chamber. From the parking lot he heard the soldiers calling into the apartment building again, laughing now.

Their tones had become taunting.

"What are they doing?" Wolfgang whispered.

Reed was tracking Ivan's progress to the end of the field. He looked sideways at Wolfgang.

"Are you serious?"

Wolfgang's face remained blank. Reed shook his head.

"You got a lot to learn about war, Wolf. Let's move."

Ivan reached the edge of the parking lot and passed out of sight behind a tree. Reed and Wolfgang circled right, headed toward the road where the Tigr had entered from. The jeers of the soldiers had only grown louder as they approached the smashed line of sedans hurtled aside by the war machine. Reed noted little green stickers pasted to the backs of many of those vehicles—college stickers, he thought. Parking passes.

The occupants of the apartments were college students, and he could already tell based on the continued cat calls of the Russian soldiers standing outside that they must be female college students.

"*Ey!*" Ivan's voice boomed from the end of the parking lot just as one Russian soldier planted a boot into the apartment's front door. The kick wasn't enough to knock the door down, and all four soldiers wheeled toward the noise of the intruder.

Ivan walked with his rifle hanging at his side, his shoulders loose, no pretense of aggression in his posture. He rattled off a question in Russian.

Apparently, it was a suggestion of joining in on the fun. One of the soldiers laughed and beckoned him forward. Reed led Wolfgang silently out of the grass and across the concrete, bent low, to a position behind a smashed Nissan sedan. He laid his rifle over the trunk and crouched. Wolfgang assumed a similar position behind the twisted front end of a Lada. He grunted a little as he descended onto his prosthetic leg.

Ivan made another joke and pointed at the machine gun, then at the door.

The soldiers laughed and stepped back. From the top of the Tigr, the Russian manning its machine gun spun the weapon toward the door. A heavy bolt slammed closed. Reed caught a glint of glass from the apartment building's second floor and noticed a pale female face appear momentarily at its edge and then vanish. Ivan stepped to the front of the Tigr, AK at his side, held by the grip, and twisted his face dead toward Reed.

He nodded once.

The machine gun thundered, a heavy *thack-thack-thack* that ripped through the night air and completely drowned out the voices of Reed's and Wolfgang's AKs. Before anybody knew what was happening, all four Russian soldiers were plummeting face-first to the ground. The machine gunner caught the muzzle flash to his left and frantically pivoted the gun. Ivan swung his rifle up and fired it one-handed, blowing the guy's jaw and half his face away. From the inside of the Tigr, a shout burst through the open back door—the driver, fumbling for a weapon.

Reed was already on his feet, rushing across the parking lot, reaching the back door and firing again. The driver was halfway twisted around the front seat when he caught three rounds to the neck and face, just above his body armor. Blood sprayed across the windshield and he went down.

"Get their weapons!" Ivan shouted.

As the big Russian tore the driver's-side door open, Reed and Wolfgang hurried to strip the fallen Russian soldiers of AK-12 rifles, spare ammunition, fragmentation grenades, and Grach handguns. They all found their way into the empty floor of the Tigr's rear. The vehicle was set up to be a troop transport model, with rows of canvas seats facing each other along either side of the entirely enclosed rear, an open hatch for the machine gun, bulletproof windows with gun ports, and two seats up front. Left-hand drive, the engine still chugging. Reed pulled the body out of the machine gun hatch while Ivan tore the driver out of his seat. Bodies hit the concrete even as pale white faces appeared in the windows again, overlooking unexplained salvation with a mix of terror and hope.

Reed couldn't bring himself to face them. He knew there was nothing he could do to save them. The would-be rapists now lying in pools of blood in the parking lot would soon be replaced by thousands more, just like every other war. He focused instead on liberating the dead machine gunner of his body armor and pulling the rig over his own head. There were both chest and back plates—thick and heavy, offering basic protection against small-arms fire.

"Wolf!" Ivan called. "Ride beside me. You'll navigate."

Wolfgang clambered into the passenger seat and Reed slammed the dual rear doors. They thunked closed and he slammed the latch.

Then Ivan found first gear. The overweight Russian war machine churned, a heavy engine driving all-terrain tires over the body of the driver. They turned in the parking lot and faced back up the road toward Tbilisi.

And then they entered the war zone.

47

From his second-floor executive office, President Elchin Rzayev stood breathless in front of a TV screen and watched war erupt in Tbilisi.

The Azerbaijani State Security Service had kept him posted all throughout the evening and into the night concerning the buildup of Russian military equipment and personnel outside the Georgian capital. A brief phone call with the Russian ambassador to Azerbaijan had reassured Rzayev that the gathering of ground forces was a purely precautionary measure. That Nikitin's intentions were entirely peaceful. That Russia merely wanted to save the world from the prospect of misplaced WMDs.

Rzayev pretended to buy the sales pitch—not because he believed it for a nanosecond but because he was scrambling for time. His adversarial relationship with Nikitin was no secret. He'd brushed up against the new Russian president far more often and more violently than he had ever brushed against Nikitin's predecessor. At least the predecessor was honest about what he wanted—Crimea and Ukraine.

Nikitin was much slimier. Much more subtle and smooth, but Rzayev never doubted that Nikitin's imperial objectives expanded far, far beyond the failed offensives in Ukraine. He fully expected for Nikitin to resume Russian aggression in Europe.

He just never expected it to be in his *corner* of Europe.

From the desk behind him, Rzayev's phone rang for the umpteenth time that night. He snatched it up, ready for another update from his State Security Service. The Dövlət Təhlükəsizliyi Xidməti, or DTX, had monitored Russia's every move from the moment Nikitin first shifted troops into the Caucasus, two weeks prior. They knew the names of every brigade, the numbers of tanks and mechanized rocket launchers.

But the call wasn't from the DTX, it was from Rzayev's minister of defense, the chief officer in charge of the Azerbaijani military.

"The battle is lost, Mr. President. The Georgians are already collapsing. By sunrise the Russians will have taken Tbilisi."

A crushing weight descended over Rzayev's shoulders, pressing down on his spine as real as the massive rucksack he'd once carried as a foot soldier in the Red Army. Back when Azerbaijan was a proud communist member of the USSR—but really just an underling held under the thumb of Moscow.

Someplace deep in his stomach, Rzayev felt that pressure again. That sense of being subjected. Of being pushed around and commanded. It was why he always refused to allow Azerbaijan to join the CSTO. Why he resisted Nikitin and forged trading partnerships with the West.

It wasn't because Rzayev had any use for the squabbling brats of Europe and America or their armies of screaming human rights activists. It was because he knew how priceless Azerbaijan's independence was.

And how fragile.

"Are the Russians circling south?" Rzayev asked.

"Not yet. They're closing around the city. But once the Georgians are driven off the highways, there will be nothing left to stall their advance."

Rzayev bit his lip, evaluating. Calculating.

He could deploy his ground soldiers immediately—send them north to confront the tide of Russians streaming into Georgia. Tactically, that would be the obvious option, but strategically it might be a mistake.

It might be exactly what Nikitin wanted him to do—a presumed provocation that could be used as an excuse by the Russians to press their attack all the way to the Caspian Sea.

And that would be a tidal wave Azerbaijan couldn't hope to resist.

"Deploy a unit of reinforcements to Red Bridge and close the border," Rzayev said. "Put our air forces on full alert and marshal our reserves. Call me at the first *hint* of Russian forces moving out of Tbilisi."

"Yes, Mr. President. As you say."

The minister hung up. Rzayev moved quickly around his desk and mashed a button on the phone, calling for the operator.

"Put me through to Moscow," he said. "I want to speak to the minister of foreign affairs."

The secretary complied, dialing the number. Rzayev leaned back in his chair and wiped sweat from his forehead. He watched the TV, still playing reports from Georgian news media. The video depicted fires erupting across Tbilisi's skyline. Smoke and shudders of artillery thunder.

Rzayev gritted his teeth, recalling Nikitin's silky promises of peace in Georgia. Of a humanitarian mission. His fingers tightened around the phone handset, and he listened as it rang.

Over, and over, and over again.

But nobody picked up.

48

Langley, Virginia

"I just received a message from the Prosecution Force on the ground. They're requesting immediate drone support over eastern Georgia."

Silas Rigby's voice crackled with tension the moment Aimes lifted the phone. She looked away from her computer screen, the onset of another migraine edging into her brain as she looked through the floor-to-ceiling glass walls of her office, across the executive floor to Rigby's office. Her deputy director sat behind a bank of computer monitors, zeroed in on his screens, his phone switched to speaker mode.

"What do you *mean* they want drone support? Support for *what*? I put them on standby!"

"Yeah, well, they disregarded that. Montgomery, Sidorov, and Pierce are back inside Tbilisi. They're reporting a presumed nuclear threat. Sidorov believes the Russians may be staging a nuclear blast across the border in Azerbaijan to justify further military action."

"*What?*"

It wasn't the subject matter of military action that surprised her. The steady feed of CIA satellites reporting on the growing conflict in Tbilisi had been fed to the White House and the Pentagon all morning. The State Department reported total radio silence from Moscow. Aimes's phone was ringing off the hook with calls from her counterparts in London, Paris, Berlin, and Tel Aviv.

Everybody wanted the same answers, as quickly as possible. Everybody wanted to know what the *hell* was happening. But it wasn't the conventional warfare erupting inside Georgia for the second time in as many decades that concerned Aimes, it was the intel the Prosecution Force had discovered of a potential nuclear weapon.

The question of whether, in fact, there really *were* forgotten Soviet WMDs up for grabs in Georgia or whether the rudimentary intel streaming in from the research team in Panama supported Ivan Sidorov's much more sinister theory.

Whatever the case, Aimes had most certainly *not* deployed the Prosecution Force for the purpose of running a rogue operation designed to directly engage the entire Russian army.

"I'm only repeating what the messages read," Rigby said. "Sidorov has a theory about Russian Alpha troops moving a weapon into Azerbaijan as an excuse to spread the conflict. He believes they will detonate it."

"Sidorov?" Aimes barked. "Look, I don't *care* what Sidorov thinks. I only care about what he *knows*. He's an informant, not an analyst. What do they want drones for?"

"They want help locating any trucks headed east along the Georgian B4 Highway, bound for Azerbaijan. Sidorov thinks—well. Sidorov claims that the Azerbaijani town of Qazax could be a target."

A sudden digital chime from Aimes's computer arrested her attention from the conversation. She allowed Rigby to drone on about the Prosecution Force's messages as the email loaded on her screen. It was from the managing case officer she'd placed in charge of the Panama Canal investigation. After the developments concerning isotope analysis and fuel decay, she'd instructed the officer to update her directly moving forward. The subject line of his newest email was written accordingly: *UPDATE*.

Aimes cradled the phone against her shoulder and opened the message. She scanned the body quickly, and her blood pressure spiked.

Madam Director,

Be advised that further testing of the isotope debris recovered in Panama confirms my initial suspicion of probable fuel age. Fuel is confirmed to be younger than twenty years, and very likely younger than five. Source is uncertain, but isotope signatures are consistent with fuel known to be enriched at the electro-chemical plant in Zelenogorsk. Final confirmation will take some weeks, but current evidence indicates that the weapon was relatively new and almost certainly Russian in origin.

I will keep you posted as our investigation develops.

"Did you get that?" Aimes asked. She could see Rigby's email address copied on the message.

"Just finished," Rigby said.

Aimes paused just for a moment, the briefest hint of hesitation melting quickly as the implications of the email finally sank in. She could no longer deny them.

She had to take action.

"Authorize the drones." Aimes's attention switched from the computer screen back to the windows. She made eye contact with Rigby across the executive floor through his office window. "Connect with the Pentagon and deploy whatever the Navy and the Air Force have available. Link the feed directly to our operations center and notify me as soon as we're live."

"Understood. Anything else?"

Aimes sank her teeth into her lip. She knew what Rigby was asking, and she didn't want to say it out loud. She didn't want the liability.

But in a situation like this...she had no other choice.

"Contact the PF. We're taking them off the leash. Whatever they have to do...I want that weapon *found.*"

"Understood," Rigby said.

Aimes caught him before he could hang up. "Silas?"

"Ma'am?"

Aimes hesitated. She found herself wanting to swallow, but she resisted. She kept her voice calm. "Assemble a team in the operations center. I want satellite footage of Azerbaijan...just in case."

49

The Kremlin
Moscow

Makar Nikitin would have much rather been on the ground in Tbilisi, a weapon strapped to his side and the smell of burning gunpowder in his nostrils, but for the next phase of his plan he needed to remain right at the heart of Russian power. Whatever else happened over the next twenty-four hours, controlling the narrative would be as crucial as controlling the movements of his military chess pieces.

But in moments such as this, when the movements of those chess pieces fell out of sync with the careful orchestration of Nikitin's own plans, the anxiety poured in. The frustration. The desire to be right in the thick of it, calling the shots himself.

The Russian ground forces outside of Tbilisi had moved too soon, sweeping into the city hours ahead of schedule due to a mistaken alarm. That would have been bad enough by itself, but the storm of conflict in Georgia had triggered a complementary storm of phone calls pouring into the Ministry of Foreign Affairs—Russians chief state department. The west was predictably alarmed by the ignition of full hostilities in the Caucuses, and now Nikitin could only stall them so long before the entire fabric of his scheme failed altogether.

And that meant that the second phase of the special military operation —the *special* part—had to proceed without delay. Nikitin needed Golubev's team of Alpha commandos in their truck and rolling out of Tbilisi as fast as humanly possible.

From the operational center built deep into the core of the Kremlin, Nikitin hung up the phone and circled his desk, looking to the screen built into the far wall. He was alone in the room. He'd sent all the aides and cabinet members home for the evening while the bulk of his military advisors were gathered at the main military building—the headquarters of Russia's Ministry of Defense.

Most of those officials understood what would happen next. They shared Nikitin's opinions of the necessity of the action, or else they were smart enough to keep their mouths shut. Golubev's hold on the Ministry of Defense was now so absolute that nobody dared to question him, but there were still millions of people Nikitin had to sell on the necessity of what came next.

He had to sell the Russian people. And to do that, the special operation had to succeed.

Displayed on the screen was a black-and-white map of the Caucasus region. It was zoomed in over Georgia. A white dot blipped inside Tbilisi.

It was headed steadily southeast along the B4 Highway. The road was long and bumpy, leading between high mountains and through deep valleys. The border crossing would be only lightly defended. The Azerbaijanis hadn't yet deployed their military—Nikitin's sales pitch in the CSTO meeting had worked.

They would never see what hit them.

50

"B-team is in the air!" Wolfgang shouted over the roar of the Tigr's engine, reading off the messaging device clutched in one hand. "They're gonna hover over the Georgian border, on standby for extraction. Langley is deploying drones."

From the back of the Tigr, Reed braced himself against the wall and fought to keep himself upright. Ivan drove like a maniac, shoving the accelerator against the floor to power the Tigr around the southeastern swath of Tbilisi and toward the B4 Highway. They'd passed multiple other Tigrs and two T-90 tanks, but the Russians hadn't engaged.

They were too busy assaulting the scattered segments of Georgian soldiers desperately dug in to defend their capital city. If anything, Reed was more worried about the Georgians than the Russians. The Tigr marked them as invaders, not friends.

"How long for the drones?" Reed shouted as the Tigr exploded through another makeshift Georgian roadblock, hurtling sedans to either side.

"An hour! They're flying in from Iraq."

An hour.

Much, much too long.

Reed grabbed an overhead railing and climbed over the bloody floor toward the front seats. Every pothole, rut, and obstruction sent shockwaves ripping through his legs, forcing him to duck his head beneath his shoulders to prevent it from slamming into the armored roof.

"Left turn in half a klick!" Wolfgang called from the right-hand seat, a CIA-issued iPad propped up on his lap to provide directions. Through the narrow, bulletproof windshield Reed could see a highway paved by irregular pools of yellow streetlamps. They'd left the Russians behind and were now well behind the battle lines, moving through the outskirts of the city just north of the Kura River. The turn Wolfgang marked on the map was a bridge.

Reed could only hope that the Georgians hadn't yet blown it to hold back the invading Russian army.

As if on cue, a storm of popping gunshots erupted from the street ahead, and heavy bullets slammed into the front grill of the Tigr. The beast chugged on as muzzle flash marked the presence of yet another makeshift Georgian street barricade, this one built of heavier vehicles than the flimsy sedans they had already blasted through. Ivan downshifted the Tigr and clung to the wheel.

"Grab something!"

Reed placed both hands on the back of Wolfgang's seat and drove his feet into the floor. The front of the Tigr collided with a Nissan pickup and sent it spinning to the side. AK rounds slammed into the armored sides of the truck, sounding like hammer strikes against steel. Armored glass raced with cracks, but the Tigr never stopped. Ivan downshifted again and four-wheel drive caught against busted pavement. The Nissan pickup scraped along one side of the truck, and then they were through. Wolfgang called the turn and Ivan hauled the wheel left. Reed slammed into the Tigr's interior wall even as the final hail of bullets rattled against it. He could feel the lead striking the armored sides, thumping and ricocheting even as he fought for footing.

A hundred yards ahead, the bridge over the Kura River stood in the darkness, marked only by the Tigr's headlights. It was a two-lane and as of yet appeared undamaged by military ordnance. Ivan laid on the accelerator, and the hair stood up on the back of Reed's neck. He wasn't sure what it was—a gut feeling, or maybe the instincts of having been in situations like this so many times before.

Whatever the case, he turned back. He looked through the bulletproof rear windows and saw the flash of fire—a puff of smoke beneath dim street-lamps. His stomach twisted into a knot, and his heart slammed into his rib cage.

"RPG! Left! Left! Left!"

Ivan responded on cue and yanked the Tigr into the oncoming lane. The armored front wheel fender scraped against the concrete bridge barrier, and a rush like the blast of a hurricane roared along their right side. The rocket-propelled grenade missed the Tigr by only inches, obscuring the right-hand windows with black smoke an instant before it reached the end of the bridge and detonated against a light pole. Fire and thunder rent the air, shaking the bridge as the light pole came toppling down.

Ivan laid on the gas. The thick pine pole splintered across the Tigr's brush guard. Beefy, all-terrain tires leapt over it. Reed's shoulder slammed into the interior wall as the back wheels bucked upward. They struck the pavement again. Rubber bit asphalt. AK rounds pinged off the rear door.

Then they were across the river and outside the city. In the darkness ahead, a reflective sign marked the onramp for the B4 Highway.

Ivan upshifted and took the ramp.

51

36,000 Feet over the Turkish/Georgian Border

Corbyn laid on the power in their race out of Diyarbakır, not bothering with a flight plan as she ascended to cruising altitude and pushed the jet to full speed. They cleared northeastern Turkey quickly, Strickland arguing with Turkish flight authorities about the nature of their emergency flight path while Turk and Lucy sat in the back of the plane, surrounded by satellite-connected iPads and messaging devices, and waited for word from Langley.

They could now track Reed's position on the Georgian B4 Highway, just southeast of Tbilisi. He had turned on his locator beacon and was moving at an average speed of about eighty-five miles per hour, pointed toward Azerbaijan.

Whether he was headed in the right direction was still a matter up for debate. The CIA was working what magic they could manage with their satellites, but the high-level Air Force drones deployed from Harir Air Base in northern Iraq were still en route.

Now it was a simple matter of rolling the dice. If Reed's—or Ivan's—gut instincts were correct, they were better positioned now to intercept a weapon headed toward the Georgian border. Then again, if their instincts were correct, there was also a weapon to intercept.

"Message from Langley!" Lucy's voice popped with tension as she spun a laptop to face Turk. He squinted at the screen, reading quickly. The message was only two words, accompanied by a satellite link.

Possible target.

Lucy selected the link as Corbyn banked the plane into a gentle turn, keeping them right on the edge of the Georgian border but not crossing it. The link loaded slowly. A black satellite feed populated on the screen. It was grainy, with a white grid overlaying it to separate the mountainous landscape into sectors.

In the middle sector, a yellow circle closed around a nondescript blob on the road. It was too dark to make out details. A pair of headlights were all that was visible.

But the vehicle was a truck. That truck was headed southeast. And it wasn't Reed.

"Get an ETA for the surveillance drone."

Lucy's fingers rattled over the keys. She waited, then shook her head.

"Forty-two minutes."

Turk's mind spun. Despite the pressurized cabin of the jet, a weight descended over his chest a little like the crush of thin air high in the mountains. His entire body felt taut and tense. Electric somehow.

He studied the grainy satellite footage, flicking every few seconds as it was updated from a thousand miles into outer space. It wasn't clear enough to make out any details. Until the drones arrived, this was the best they could get. The target seemed to be moving at about fifty miles per hour, giving Reed the edge on speed.

But would he overtake it in time? Would it even matter, if this were just a random truck?

Reed needed to know. Not a guess, but a certainty.

Turk left the rear of the plane and swung toward the cockpit, head low to keep it from banging against the jet's ceiling. He found Strickland still arguing with Turkish air authorities, their accented voices barking in broken English through his headset as he fought to turn the volume down.

Turk put a hand on the back of Corbyn's chair and leaned in close. He shook her by the shoulder.

"Hey!"

Corbyn's face pivoted around. She took a hand off the yoke to lift the headset off one ear.

"What?"

"How low can you fly this thing?"

Corbyn squinted. "Huh?"

"We got a target, but we need to confirm. You wanna try some cowboy stuff?"

A broad grin stretched across Corbyn's face. From the co-pilot's chair, Strickland pivoted to join the conversation.

"Say what?"

Corbyn ignored him. "Zing baby! Let's do it."

Turk returned to the cabin, rushing back to Lucy. He pointed to the computer.

"Get the coordinates. We're going in ourselves."

52

From the command trailer at the heart of the primary Russian military encampment, Anton Golubev monitored the invasion.

It hadn't begun as planned, but as things had turned out, that didn't much matter. The Defense Forces of Georgia were fragmented across the country, completely unprepared to mobilize, and still confused about *what* exactly was happening. Giorgi Meladze's last act as president of Georgia had been an effective one. His order for full military cooperation with the "assisting Russian forces" had provided just enough of a window for Russia to dig in deeply across the nation.

Now it was too late to resist the overwhelming power of those gathered forces, rolling in like a tsunami. Already the capital city was fully under Russian control, with only sporadic small arms fighting across random neighborhoods. West of the city a much larger detachment of Georgian forces had dug in outside a military base and were making use of the heavy armor and artillery units housed there.

It was a nuisance, certainly, but the problem would only last for as long as it took Russian Su-25 close air support fighter jets to scramble and deploy Kh-29 air-to-ground missiles. Then the Russian infantry could sweep in, clean up the survivors, and take control of what remained of the base.

All said and done, this would be even easier than the sixteen-day Russo-Georgian War of 2008, and the results would be even sweeter. It was a testament to the power of eroding your enemy *before* you attacked him. Weakening his economy, his society, his leadership. Lulling him into comfort and apathy. Distracting him with internal drama and positioning yourself as his one true friend.

Just like Nikitin had done with Meladze for nearly a decade. Just like Golubev had done with the United States.

Pivoting away from the screens displaying maps of Russian progress across Georgia, Golubev retreated to the back of the trailer and took a seat behind an isolated desk. Only Alpha Group was allowed in this portion of the command post. The lone computer resting on the desk was accessed by password and a thumbprint reader. Golubev was the only authorized user.

The map displayed on the other side of the lock screen? It was a map of Georgia, yes, but not a map of the Russian military advance. At least, not the conventional one. Instead, the night vision feed supplied by a high-level Russian surveillance drone marked the progress of a single vehicle. Not a military vehicle, per se, but a repurposed civilian tractor trailer, with a snubbed nose and a long box trailer.

Inside that trailer were housed fully a dozen of Golubev's most loyal Alpha commandos. The cargo they protected was worth more than a hundred million rubles, but its destructive potential if prematurely discovered would do far, far more damage than the loss of that investment alone.

That was why the truck was so heavily protected. It was also why Golubev's anxiety levels had spiked over the last hour. Not because he doubted his men or doubted the mission. It was because Ivan Sidorov, long-time KGB agent, SVR officer, and one-time friend of Anton's, was now on the loose, and if Golubev knew anything about Sidorov, he knew that his old friend's destructive potential rivaled that of the nuclear device now rumbling eastward toward Azerbaijan.

The problem? Ivan Sidorov was no longer loyal to the motherland.

Lifting a secure satellite phone, Golubev once more dialed that lone number. Nikitin picked up immediately.

"Da?"

"I think we should consider another target," Golubev said. "Something closer."

"Are you out of your mind? What happened?"

"Nothing has happened. The truck is on schedule. But I have a feeling. It will be over an hour before the truck can reach Qazax. We do not know what Sidorov may have discovered...or where he went."

"Sidorov?" Nikitin's voice cracked with disbelief. "You cannot be losing your nerve to an old man!"

Golubev gritted his teeth. "He is much more than one old man, Mr. President. He is ruthless and intelligent. Trust me when I tell you that this is not worth the gamble. If the weapon is deployed someplace closer to the border, the effect will be the same."

Long pause. Golubev panned the map, searching the winding highway that ran southeast out of Georgia and through the northwestern corner of Azerbaijan.

It was an exceedingly rural part of the country. Just mountains and rambling roads. Very little populace to speak of. But there was one option.

"What do you suggest?" Nikitin said at last.

"There is a village on the road, just across the border. Shykhly Vtoryye. Thirty-five hundred people—"

"Thirty-five hundred?" Nikitin barked. "Are you crazy? I do not want some little village, Anton. I want a *real* target. How else do you expect me to sell this?"

"Death is death, Mr. President. You can sell it just as well either way."

"Not if the blast happens just across the border. Then it looks like an accident. Something leaked out of Georgia. We need the weapon deep inside Azerbaijan. We need no questions."

"Mr. President, there will be no questions—"

"No. This is not a discussion. The target is Qazax. We're going to hit that smug little prick in his own hometown. Do you understand me? *Make it happen.*"

Nikitin hung up. Golubev gritted his teeth and slammed the phone down. He ran both hands through greasy hair, heart thumping. Anxiety leaking through his bloodstream.

He could feel it in his bones. Nikitin was wrong on this one. Catastrophically wrong.

But there was nothing more to be done. When Makar Nikitin had the last word, it was the last word. All Golubev could do was watch the blip on the surveillance screen.

The truck chugged onward.

53

It was late afternoon when the phone call rang in from Langley. Stratton had taken up residence in the Oval, owning it as his workstation as he placed phone calls to congressmen and governors, old friends in the business sector, and even a few celebrities.

The conversations were all the same. They all orbited around the question of how America could get back on her feet. The problem of reigniting an American spirit pushed to the point of total collapse was a problem Stratton knew he couldn't solve by himself. The entire administration and even all of a unified Washington—if such a thing could ever exist—would fall short.

They needed leaders on every battlefront. Local government, commerce, and entertainment. They needed a unified front, and Stratton had to lead the charge. He needed to be a salesman.

He needed to rally the nation around American Spirit.

But even as the phone calls stacked up and a structure for the campaign took shape, another menace growled in the shadows of Stratton's mind. He monitored it via emails with Langley, paired with brief phone calls from the

Pentagon. News of the conflict in Tbilisi was reverberating around the globe, tremors of war carrying the flavor of Ukraine and Crimea. Syria, and Georgia in 2008.

And still...Russia had yet to make a statement.

When Stratton hung up the phone with a movie star from Los Angeles —some narcissistic kid who spoke exclusively in shorthand slang—he saw the call ringing through from Langley, and his stomach fell. Aimes had messaged him all afternoon. An escalation to a phone call couldn't be good.

Snapping his fingers, Stratton pointed to the door. All the aides gathered in the Oval hurried quickly out, leaving only Easterling. Stratton mashed the speaker button.

"What've you got?"

Aimes skipped the pleasantries and dove right in. "I've just received word from our team on the ground in Panama. We're still running tests, but preliminary results indicate that the bomb was of Soviet design and Russian manufacture. The fuel was young, possibly only a few years old."

Stratton leaned across the desk, his brow furrowed. "What does that mean?"

"We're not yet sure. But...a reasonable speculation would be that somebody recently constructed this weapon using an old Soviet design."

"And modern Russian fuel," Stratton said.

"Yes, sir. It seems so."

Stratton's stomach descended into knots. His mind raced, orbiting around the problem and searching for an answer other than the obvious.

No such solution presented itself.

"There's something else, sir. We have a team on the ground in Georgia, and they've identified a possible secondary nuclear threat in the region."

"What sort of threat?"

"It's a truck. We're tracing it via satellite south of Tbilisi, headed toward Azerbaijan. Cargo unknown. We'll have further details as soon as we can get drones on site."

"You think it's carrying a *nuke*?"

"We're not sure. Possibly. One of our informants on the ground believes that a false flag operation might be underway."

"You have proof?"

"Just speculation. But we're monitoring the truck's progress, and with your permission we may intercept."

Stratton looked to Easterling. She had stood from an Oval Office couch and approached the desk. Her face was taut and a little pale. He raised his eyebrows.

Easterling nodded once.

"Proceed to monitor and keep us up-to-date," Stratton said. "Are you in communication with the Pentagon?"

"Yes, sir."

"Have them formulate a response plan should your suspicions be validated. I'll stand by to review it."

"Thank you, sir."

Stratton looked back to the phone. "What do you mean when you say you have a *team* on the ground?"

Brief pause. "It's a reconnaissance team, sir. The one you authorized me to deploy to Georgia."

Stratton squinted. "They're in a position to strike the truck?"

"I'm not sure how many details you want, Mr. Acting President."

This time it was Stratton's turn to pause. He nodded to himself.

"Keep me posted."

Then he hung up the phone.

The acting president disconnected, and a wash of momentary guilt descended over Aimes. She hadn't really intended to mislead the most powerful man in the free world. It just kind of happened. And maybe it was for the best—for Stratton's best. Because Aimes already knew she was going to deploy the Prosecution Force to intercept that truck, with or without the White House's permission. Too much was at stake.

"What's the update from the ground?" Aimes said.

She and Rigby had departed the executive floor of CIA headquarters and now stood at the back of an operation's center planted in a secure-access basement. It was something like a movie theater, with a broad screen spread across one end, a field of desks and smaller computer screens organized in a row beneath it, and at the back of the room an elevated platform overlooking it all, with smaller desks for those in command—in this case, Sarah Aimes and Silas Rigby. They were joined by half a dozen other officers. The screen at the end of the room was a satellite feed, but the picture was grainy.

It was dark in Azerbaijan.

"We're losing the truck in the mountains," Rigby said. "It's only about five klicks from the border."

"And Montgomery?"

"Closing rapidly. About nineteen klicks behind it."

"How long until the drones are on site?"

"Twenty-nine minutes. They're just now crossing over Armenia."

Aimes nodded slowly, processing the math and knowing that the truth would rise to the surface the moment that truck reached the Georgian/Azerbaijani border crossing. She could see the border post displayed across the main screen—a small collection of buildings with a smattering of Azerbaijani military vehicles scattered around them. Apparently, the authorities in Baku had deemed it necessary to reinforce the Red Bridge border crossing. That was logical.

But what would happen when that truck reached them? Would they engage it?

Would the truck explode?

From the desk next to her, Rigby breathed a curse, and Aimes's gaze snapped his way. His fingers rattled across the keyboard.

"What is it?"

"It's the PF B-team. I just got word from their plane. They say they're going in."

"They're *what*? What the hell does that mean?"

Rigby smacked the enter key to send his message. Seconds dripped by. Then he looked up.

"We just lost signal."

54

The Russian-built AK-74 hung heavy in Samir's hands as he stood outside the border post and looked eastward. At two a.m., the night sky was pitch black, the air crisp as it poured down out of the mountains. Samir couldn't see very far beyond the Debed River into Georgia. The dim streetlights mounted high atop light poles poured yellow glow over the two-lane highway which connected the two nations, but outside that glow, all was inky black. The Georgian border post was lost around a bend in the road, shrouded by trees.

Having been assigned to the State Border Service and stationed at the Red Bridge border crossing for most of the past year, Samir was very familiar with the natural rhythm of sights, sounds, and smells throughout a lengthy shift spent standing next to the road with his rifle held across his chest. On a particularly quiet night, when the wind bent toward Azerbaijan, Samir could usually hear the voices of his Georgian counterparts at their guard stations.

Laughter. Engine noises. Occasionally, he could even hear music. But not tonight. Tonight the border post had remained totally quiet, fueling suspicions that whatever Georgian soldiers remained at their posts were housed inside their guard shacks, listening for updates of the fighting in Tbilisi just the way Samir and his fellow border guards listened with bated breath.

Russia was on the move. Fighting had erupted in Tbilisi. Georgia, the so-called "nuclear nation," was under assault. What exactly that meant for Azerbaijan, nobody knew, but President Rzayev had ordered the border closed and deployed twenty-five additional Azerbaijani soldiers to reinforce the half dozen members of the State Border Service already posted to the crossing.

Samir was proud of being an Azerbaijani soldier. Even though he'd dreamed of more glamorous duties than inspecting passports and searching truckloads of vegetables for possible contraband, there was something to be said for feeling like he was a frontline representative of his native land. It made him feel bigger than himself—a more meaningful existence than most poor village boys could hope to achieve. With a freshly pressed uniform on his back and the heavy rifle in his hands, he felt brave also. He felt dangerous.

But maybe not so dangerous that he resented the reinforcements. The twenty-five additional soldiers deployed by President Rzayev helped to ease the tension in his mind. He didn't really *expect* a Russian invasion. He knew the Azerbaijani Ministry of Defense must be monitoring the situation closely and would deploy additional troops to the border well ahead of any crisis.

But he was still nervous. Nausea still boiled in his gut, and he still caught himself slipping a hand into his pocket to randomly touch the picture of Aylin safely tucked inside. She wasn't yet his wife, but after this posting, Samir planned to propose. He would gather both her family and his. They would go to that little spot down by the river where he and Aylin had spent so many wonderful summer afternoons together. He would present her with the gold band his grandmother had given him. They would share an afternoon meal, and there would be music.

Nişan, it was called. Engagement to be married. A dream he had fantasized of since secondary school, when the brown-haired Aylin had first moved to his village. She was quiet. Bookish. Many found her to be awkward.

But Samir understood her. Aylin understood him. It was meant to be.

Cool air clouded in front of Samir's face as one of the new arrivals stepped outside to light up a cigarette. He offered a smoke to Samir, but Samir politely declined. He didn't smoke. Aylin didn't like it. It made him proud to be a man free of vice.

It made him proud to think of being *her* man.

The soldier next to Samir inhaled deeply and held the smoke. He breathed out. Then he squinted.

"Do you hear that?"

Samir didn't hear anything. He took a step away from the border post and listened carefully. The wind was blowing against them, toward Georgia, but as the breeze died and a stillness enveloped the valley, Samir thought he heard something over the gentle gurgle of the nearby Khrami River. It was a heavy, mechanical growl. The churn of a big engine.

And then a sound that couldn't be mistaken anywhere in the world—the blast of automatic gunfire.

The soldier dropped the cigarette, and Samir's heart rate spiked. He clutched the AK even as his comrade burst back into the border post and sounded the alarm. The gunshots from around the bend in the road ceased even as the engine surged.

Then the face of a heavy truck rounded the corner, dragging a trailer behind it. The left-hand windscreen was shattered. Samir couldn't see any faces beyond the glare of the headlights.

But as the truck's engine surged and the vehicle gained speed, Samir saw the barrel of a Kalashnikov rifle swing out from the side window. He saw the muzzle flash light the night. He heard the thunderclap of gunshots as bullets whizzed over his head and slammed into the border post.

He turned and rushed for cover.

Then the bullets struck home.

55

"Muzzle flash! I've got muzzle flash!"

Strickland shouted from the cockpit, and Turk rushed to the window. Corbyn banked the jet hard, dipping the right wing low toward the earth as they raced along the border. With his hands pressed against the fuselage, Turk peered through the window and down into the darkness.

There was a border post there—buildings on either side with a river winding along next to them. The highway was a two-lane, and it split as it approached each border station. A semitruck with a large box trailer pulled up in front of the Azerbaijani border post.

And muzzle flash lit up the night, both from the windows of the truck and the windows of the border post. As Turk watched, the back doors of the truck's trailer burst open and little dots bailed out, illuminated by the border lights. They spun around the tail of the trailer and faced the border post. A flash of bright orange was trailed by a split-second delay.

Then the RPG struck the border post and detonated with a blast so loud Turk heard it from seven thousand feet. In a blink the border post was gone and the jet was racing back into Georgian airspace. Corbyn increased the bank and tugged the nose around, swinging into a wide circle. Prepping for another pass.

"We're coming around!" Corbyn called.

"You getting this?" Turk directed the question at Lucy. She sat with her belt cinched around her narrow waist, locking her body into the seat. The computer slid sideways in her lap, and she pinned it down. She was typing, her face constricted with focus.

Then she shook her head. "It's no good. We've lost connection with Langley."

56

Georgia

Ivan hadn't let off the gas since they hit the highway. As soon as Tbilisi faded in the rearview, the storm of combat and incoming bullets faded with it, leaving nothing but empty blackness punctuated by streetlights. The highway was smoother than the busted asphalt of tank-smashed city streets, and they passed oncoming traffic on occasion.

Nobody stopped for them. Nobody attempted to confront them. Even a Georgian police car veered off the road, the two cops inside diving for cover as the machine-gun-equipped Russian truck hurtled by.

"Nine klicks to the border!" Wolfgang sat in the passenger seat, the iPad vibrating in his lap as he monitored the route ahead. Over his shoulder Reed could see the white line of the B4 Highway streaking amongst farmland and small villages before diving into Azerbaijan. Another river wound along the border, with twin border posts guarding the crossing.

That was all the detail the map provided.

"Any word from Langley?" Reed called over the roar of the engine.

Wolfgang tabbed to another screen on the iPad. "Nothing. They haven't responded to my last sitrep."

"And the drones?"

"I don't know."

Wolfgang tapped out a message and mashed the send button, but the messaging application failed to deliver. He tapped a second time. Still nothing.

"I think we're disconnected. I've got nothing."

Reed slid into the back of the Tigr, lifting his rifle from the floor. He'd already locked a fresh magazine into the receiver. Additional magazines, rifles, handguns, and grenades slid across the bloody floor with every turn. Through the open turret hatch, cold wind pounded the roof of the truck and beat through the interior, stinging Reed's face.

And still, the question loomed. Were they on the right path? Were they chasing a wild goose?

"Aircraft!" Ivan boomed from the driver seat, and Reed's gaze instinctively snapped toward the windshield. From a thousand yards he saw the plane racing dead toward them, marked by blinking wing tip and taillights, flying not more than a hundred feet off the ground and following the highway. Long before he could even think about diving for cover or lunging for the machine gun, the plane surged directly over them, a wash of jet thunder shaking the Tigr as the aircraft shot skyward.

"Hell's angels!" Ivan shouted, fighting to keep the truck on the road.

Reed's ears rang as he fought his way out of the seat, dropping the AK and scrambling for the machine gun turret. A PKP Pecheneg was mounted there. Belt fed and chambered in the ubiquitous 7.62x54r, it was the Russian version of the American thirty caliber. A light gun, completely unsuitable for taking down aircraft.

But given another eighty-foot flyover, Reed liked his chances.

Pulling the pin lock, Reed activated the swivel mechanism. The gun moved smoothly on a greased mount, swinging to the tail of the Tigr as the unidentified plane arced through the sky and turned back toward them.

"Keep us moving!" Reed shouted. "He's coming around."

The aircraft dipped. Reed saw a flash of white in the midnight sky. He couldn't make out a full profile, but he knew it wasn't a fighter jet. It was too large. Too slow.

But still a lot faster than the Tigr.

"Come on, you sucker," Reed breathed, one hand closed around the machine gun's grip, his finger drifting toward the trigger. The plane had dipped down to a hundred feet again, racing in from five thousand yards. As it came, Reed thought he detected a rock of its wing tips—up and down, up and down. He squinted, leaning over the top of the machine gun. The jet was barely two thousand yards away now. Streetlamps reflected against its underbelly. The metal was white, not military gray.

"Hold up!" Wolfgang shouted. "Don't shoot! It's B-team!"

Reed relaxed off the trigger just as the nose of the CIA SAC jet twitched upward, climbing aggressively and blazing over the top of the Tigr. His ears flooded with the thunder of the engines, so loud he thought his eardrums might rupture. He ducked inside the machine gun turret as hot jet stream washed over his back.

Then he was looking up, following the path of the jet into the air. Watching the wing tips rock again.

Then the jet turned south, along the road, and blazed ahead.

"Follow him!" Reed said. "They've seen something."

Ivan didn't need another invitation. He already had the truck running at max speed, just a little under ninety miles an hour over the narrow highway. Another village flashed past on Reed's right, and the jet circled a few thousand feet overhead. The wing tips rocked again, and momentary uncertainty edged into Reed's gut.

Was Corbyn trying to warn him of something? Rocking wing tips were a pretty vague signal.

"We're almost to the crossing!" Ivan said. "Stay on the gun."

Good idea.

Reed swung the PKP around to face forward and clutched the grip again. The wind beating against his face formed an incessant roar, worsening the ringing in his ears left by the jet. He only focused ahead as farmland enveloped them on every side. Light poles poured yellow glow over the road. The Tigr roared over the last gentle hilltop, and up ahead Reed detected a narrow bridge followed by a bend in the highway.

He breathed in deep, quieting his thoughts. Zeroed in now. The truck shook, and he looked once more to the sky.

The jet was rocking again. One final message. He had no idea what it meant.

"Here comes the border!" Wolfgang called.

57

"The truck has cleared the border!"

The Alpha officer from the end of the trailer called the update as Golubev studied the wall-mounted screen displaying the progress of that blipping white dot.

He didn't need to be told that the dot had reached Azerbaijan. The necessary pause was indicative of the firefight that the Alpha commandos expected at the Red Bridge border crossing. That pause had lasted longer than Golubev would have hoped, which likely meant that the Azerbaijanis had deployed reinforcements to the crossing. A response to the action in Tbilisi, no doubt.

Whatever the case, the dot was moving again. The Alphas had broken through and left the border post burning behind them. The radio message from the truck on the ground indicated that the mission was proceeding. The truck was now only thirty-four kilometers away from the Qazax.

Half an hour. Not more. Golubev bit a dirty fingernail and breathed through his teeth, zeroed in on the map. Willing the truck to move faster. To somehow reach its target sooner.

It was time to put this matter to bed.

"Sir!" The Alpha officer called again, and Golubev snapped a curse. *"What?"*

"We've detected an unidentified aircraft circling over the border post. It appears to be a small jet. We've tried hailing it, but it's not responding."

Golubev left the screen and thundered down the length of the trailer. He pushed the Alpha soldier aside by the shoulder and leaned down over the computer screen he sat in front of. It displayed a digital grid, translated from a temporary field radar system erected by the Russian army.

The blip on the screen was indeed small, but it moved much too fast to be a harmless private aircraft. No, this blip moved with the speed of a jet, and it moved close to the ground also. Sometimes as low as beneath two hundred feet, moving in tight and aggressive circles before turning inevitably south toward Azerbaijan.

"Azerbaijani Air Force?" Golubev demanded.

"We don't know. We wouldn't expect them to deploy into Georgian air space."

No, Golubev thought. *They wouldn't.*

But the Americans might.

Golubev gritted his teeth. "They're searching for the truck. Get on the radio with air command. I want four jets scrambled immediately. They are authorized to bring it down by any means necessary."

"What if it flies into Azerbaijani air space?" the Alpha questioned.

Golubev was already halfway back to his screen. He looked over one shoulder. "Then they *follow it.*"

58

The carnage was visible the moment the Tigr reached the Georgian border post. With windows blown out and steel bullet casings scattered across the asphalt, Reed didn't even need to see the bodies to know what had happened, but the bodies were there—three of them, laid out beneath the security lights.

As the Tigr hurtled past the guard post, Reed knew they were headed toward a lot more of the same. He could smell the familiar odor of burned gunpowder, rocket smoke, and fresh blood hanging on the air like a cloud. Ivan slowed a little to navigate the turn, and Reed swung the PKP to keep the muzzle fixated on the Azerbaijani border post.

The building burned. A tri-bar blue, red, and green flag flapped in the smoke atop a flagpole. Azerbaijani soldiers in full uniform lay bleeding and broken across the parking lot, their AK-74 rifles scattered amid a field of further steel casings.

But there were no dead Russian soldiers. No dead Alphas clad in all black. The enemy had swooped in and taken the Azerbaijanis by surprise, dumping copious amounts of firepower onto the border post long before anybody knew what was happening.

Complete, total violence of action. The Azerbaijanis had been massacred.

Reed rocked his head upward as the SAC jet raced over them at two thousand feet, banking gently and climbing to avoid the mountain peaks. It seemed to be loosely following the highway as it wound southward into Azerbaijan.

Ivan turned to follow it, the headlights of the Tigr bouncing as the brush guard shoved a parked pickup truck aside. The path ahead was clear, but very dark. None of the lights from the Georgian side followed them south. The highway rippled a little as a mountain ridgeline ran along their right and the Kura River snaked through farmlands to their left. They passed by a small village sandwiched up against the bottom of the ridges. Emergency sirens screamed and a duo of police cars blazed past, headed toward Red Bridge.

But nobody stopped them. Ivan kept the Tigr surging along at full speed, leaving the village behind and burying them amongst mountain ridges. The only light shone from the moon, Reed's eyes adjusting quickly to the dim. He kept his hand on the grip of the PKP, pointed forward down the highway.

Ready for the inevitable.

59

"Mr. President! The Russians have scrambled four aircraft from outside Tbilisi. They appear to be en route for our border."

From the end of a long conference table, President Rzayev stood with arms folded and watched the bank screens displaying maps of Georgia and Azerbaijan, the zones around Tbilisi marked with little red flags to indicate Russian troop movements. The aircraft his minister of defense now reported on were not actually visible on the screen. Azerbaijan didn't have any of the fancy military satellites that Russia so often used to spy on her enemies—and her friends. But within seconds of the minister's announcement, a small diamond symbol appeared just south of Tbilisi to represent the aircraft now being tracked by Azerbaijani military radar. Those aircraft were moving rapidly south away from Tbilisi—headed straight for Red Bridge, where only moments prior all communication with the armed forces deployed to the border had suddenly terminated.

It might be a coincidence. It might be a simple failure of radio equipment. But with Russian air forces racing straight toward them, Elchin Rzayev could no longer afford to be cautious.

"What kind of aircraft are they?" he demanded.

"We're not sure," the minister said. "Likely jet aircraft, possible Su-35 multirole fighters."

Rzayev gritted his teeth, sudden rage boiling in his blood and spiking his heart rate.

The nerve.

"Scramble the nearest aircraft we have. Put them right on the border." Rzayev turned to face his minister of defense, speaking now through his teeth. "If the Russians cross into our air space, *blow them out of the sky.*"

60

"I gotta climb! We're too close to the mountains."

Turk barely heard Corbyn's shout from the cockpit as the jet nosed upward. In the field of black beneath them, he couldn't see the individual mountain ridges, the small houses, or any other distinct features of the landscape. He couldn't even see the highway. He could only see two pools of headlights weaving southward, deeper into Azerbaijan.

The first ran about four kilometers ahead of the second. It was the semitruck, chugging right down the middle of the highway and laying on its brakes for every turn, as though the driver was taking care about whatever cargo lay housed in the trailer.

The second pool of light came from the Russian Tigr rushing along the same path, moving considerably faster than the semitruck and closing the distance between them. On one of their lower passes toward the Tigr, Turk had seen a lone figure protruding from the machine gun turret. He recognized dark hair and broad shoulders. An iron face.

It was Reed. The truck would be driven by either Ivan or Wolfgang. Whatever the case, there was no way to contact the vehicle. All communications with both Wolfgang and Langley had failed. Lucy was fighting with the computer but had thus far been unable to get them back online, her efforts complicated by Corbyn's vomit-inducing air maneuvers.

All they could do was rock their wings, desperately trying to warn Reed of the truck full of Russian soldiers who had so quickly slaughtered the Azerbaijani border guards. Now that the Tigr had passed through the border post, however, Reed would have seen that damage.

He should be warned. Hopefully. Either way, Turk wasn't about to wait around and find out.

Departing his seat, Turk fought his way forward to the cockpit even as Corbyn pulled the jet into another aggressive turn. Every time she did that, Turk's stomach surged toward his throat and he was reminded of sweeping in across hot, barren desert in the back of an Army Nightstalker Black Hawk.

Far from his favorite memories.

Turk shook Corbyn's shoulder to get her attention. "How far until the road straightens out?"

"Huh?" Corbyn pulled one headset cup off her ear as the jet leveled off. Turk pointed through the windscreen.

"Find level ground! I want you to put her down."

61

Reed saw the truck from two kilometers distant. It appeared as a flash of red taillights, glowing just for a moment at the end of a mountain valley, and then it vanished around the next curve.

"That's it!" Reed shouted.

"I see it!" Ivan laid the hammer down, pushing the top-heavy truck to its limits as it hurtled over the next rise. They were still rushing along at near maximum speed, far more quickly than their quarry could drive, but the frequent bends, rises, and falls of the mountain highway made it nearly impossible to estimate when they would overtake them.

There was always a chance the soldiers aboard the truck would see them coming. Stop around a bend and lay a trap—a land mine or an Alpha commando with an RPG—but there was no time to worry about that. The dead bodies stacked up at the border told the story of what sort of enemy they were dealing with. Whatever was aboard that truck, it needed to be stopped.

Another thunderclap of jet engines boomed through the valley, and Reed looked up to see the SAC jet blaze overhead, disappearing over mountaintops, pointed generally southward along the highway. Without communication, Reed had no way of guessing what the B-team's strategy would be, and he couldn't afford to worry about it.

He only needed Ivan to bring that semitruck within range of the PKP.

"We're closing!" Wolfgang said. "I've got them at fifteen hundred yards."

"I see them," Reed called. The nose of the Tigr rose out of the valley and onto a wide plain. Mountain ridges framed the horizon on every side, and the road straightened out for the next couple of kilometers. The truck blazed directly ahead, the taillights growing ever brighter as the thundering Tigr engine sucked them closer.

Reed wrapped his finger through the PKPs trigger guard and lowered his body to bring his line of sight behind the weapon's rudimentary sights. He added elevation to compensate for bullet drop. He lifted the belt of 7.62 ammunition with his free hand, leveling it off with the machine gun to reduce the chances of a jam.

His finger tightened around the trigger. Then he heard another sound.

Deeper than the howl of the SAC jet, and somehow so much more sinister, this new roar pounded in from behind, a tornado of vicious thunder. Reed's face snapped toward the sky as four aircraft blazed only a few thousand feet over the plateau floor, dark triangular shadows joined into a diamond formation.

Headed straight into the jet stream of the SAC jet.

Reed's heart rate spiked, adrenaline overwhelming his bloodstream with a numb surge of energy. The jets faded into the sky and the ground shook beneath their passing. His mind stalled, and he thought of the B-team.

Of Lucy. Of Corbyn and Strickland.

Of one quick missile strike.

But long before he could complete the mental image of instant death, a crackle of automatic gunfire ripped through the night air. Hot lead raced past Reed's head and pinged off the roof of the Tigr, whirring into the night. He looked up to see muzzle flash illuminating the now open back doors of the semi trailer—small-arms fire, spraying their position.

"What are you doing?" Wolfgang screamed. "*Shoot back!*"

Reed clamped down on the PKPs trigger, and the heavy gun thundered. Blazing white muzzle flash illuminated the roof of the Tigr, and empty casings locked into the belt feed poured out of the right side of the gun. Every sixth round lit up the night in a phosphorus hot glow, aiding Reed as he guided the stream of fire straight into the back of the truck, shredding the plywood walls of the trailer and dropping the first two men huddled inside. One body fell out and the other pitched back. The truck swerved on the road and one door clapped shut. Ivan accelerated and the gap began to close. Reed reduced his fire to two second bursts to keep the barrel from overheating, now aiming beneath the opening of the trailer, shooting for the tires instead.

He didn't want to dump too many rounds into that trailer. He didn't know what it contained.

Tracer rounds skipped off the pavement, and rubber exploded from the left side of the trailer. He'd ruptured at least one tire, but the trailer ran on multiple, and the truck hurtled on. The Tigr's engine surged and the gap again began to shrink. Reed leaned low to sight more carefully along the barrel.

Then Wolfgang's shout exploded from the truck's cabin. "RPG! RPG!"

Reed saw the flash illuminating the foggy interior of the trailer. Black smoke poured out and Ivan swerved the Tigr hard right. They hurtled off the highway at full speed and crashed through a ditch just as the rocket struck the pavement and detonated with a thunderclap. Asphalt and dirt exploded into the air and Reed's chest slammed into the PKP. The Tigr was hurtling across a torn Azerbaijani field, tires lurching over low terraces and sending Reed's rib cage slamming into the edges of the hatch as Ivan fought for control.

Speed bled away and mud erupted on all sides. Reed got a hold of the PKP and ratcheted the muzzle left, toward the truck. He braced one boot against the wall of the Tigr to keep his body from being thrown around and began to squeeze.

Then the thunder of jet engines returned to the mountain plateau, joined by an unearthly scream. Reed's gaze snatched toward the sky just as the SAC jet came rocketing over the mountaintops, fully illuminated by the blaze of its right-hand engine. That side of the plane's tail was on fire, thick black smoke dumping into the sky.

And just behind it, only a mile distant and closing like a cat racing toward a wounded mouse, was a Russian Su-35 fighter jet.

62

___

10,000 Feet above Azerbaijan

"Bloody hell! What was that?"

The force of passing aircraft ripped so violently near to the SAC jet that the entire airframe shuddered. Turk was back in his seat, strapped in for the rough landing he expected. His gaze flicked toward the window and the voice of heavy engines outside, but he already knew what he would find. He didn't need to be an ex-pilot to recognize the signature thunder of a jet fighter, and sure enough, there was a long and sleek aircraft matching that description racing just outside their right wing tip. He didn't recognize the model, but the red stars printed on the wing tips reflected moonlight as the aircraft banked.

Russia.

"Put her down! Put her down!"

Turk's shouts ripped through the cabin even as Strickland wrapped both hands around the yoke and barked a command at Corbyn.

"My aircraft!"

"What are you doing?"

"What do you think I'm doing? I'm trying to keep us alive! Or maybe you have dogfight training?"

Corbyn didn't, and for once she relented to her co-pilot. Strickland rolled the jet immediately to the left and added power, whipping it as though it were an F-16. Turk listened as the fuselage shuddered and creaked, seats popping and his stomach flying into his mouth. The nose of the plane raced upward and swung left. Turk had the sudden sinking feeling that they were suspended in midair, like they were about to simply plummet to the ground.

As it turned out, his instincts were right on the money. Another alarm blared from the cockpit, and a mechanical voice blared over the speakers: "*Stall. Stall. Stall.*" Then the jet simply dropped, alternating views of the night sky and the hard dark ground flashing outside the windows. Turk's stomach convulsed and bile exploded from his throat. The alarms continued from the cockpit and Corbyn shouted above the din.

"We're losing airspeed! Give me the stick."

Strickland flatly ignored her, pushing the nose of the jet downward. The SAC jet slid out of the spiral and converted instantly into a nosedive. Turk vomited again and slammed forward against his seat belt. His head smacked the chair ahead of him, and Corbyn screamed over the thunder of jet engines.

"I'm gonna take her down low and screw with their weapons radar," Strickland shouted. "Then we put her down fast and bail out. Understand?"

Strickland looked across the cockpit even as the alarms continued to chime. The windscreen was a blur of black—Turk couldn't see the ground. He could barely hear over the scream of the engines and the thunder of wind.

Corbyn sat frozen in her chair, wide eyes locked on the windscreen. Breaking his left hand free of the yoke, Strickland backhanded her hard across the arm.

"*Hey!* Do you hear me?"

That did it. Corbyn blinked and nodded rapidly. She placed both hands on the yoke but didn't fight Strickland's control. The jet plummeted onward, Strickland's calm voice carrying just above the scream of the alarms.

"We break at fifteen hundred feet. Understand?"

"Fifteen hundred, roger," Corbyn managed.

"Great. Stay with me. Who's got eyes on those jets?"

Turk spat bile and forced his face sideways to look out the window. The sky outside was almost pitch black, the moon lost someplace in their descent. He couldn't see the Russian fighters. He couldn't see anything.

"I've got nothing!" Turk called.

"Me either," Lucy chimed in.

"They must be behind us," Strickland said. "They'll open fire next. We're almost there. Hold on, everybody!"

Turk sank his fingers into the seat ahead of him and looked down the aisle into the cockpit. Strickland was pulling the jet out of the dive, raising the nose and bleeding off air speed. Through the windscreen Turk saw mountain ridges only a mile or two away, a hard plateau floor spread out beneath them. It looked reasonably flat in the dark, but he knew it was very likely riddled with ruts and holes, small terraces and obstructions. He blinked and his stomach tightened. Strickland had pulled them out of the free fall but they were still losing altitude—fast. The ground was rising like a hammer, and fresh waves of nausea ripped through Turk's gut.

He could handle being shot at. He could handle bombs and grenades and rockets. He could handle *fighting*, but this wasn't a fight. This was fish, a barrel, and a shotgun.

Turk wasn't the shotgun.

Glancing across the aisle, Turk found Lucy pinned into her seat with her head pressed against the back rest. Her eyes were closed, and her lips moved silently.

Not a bad idea.

Turk closed his own eyes and tried to form a prayer of his own. He saw Sinju and baby Liberty, and before any words would come, another sound blazed out of the darkness. A heavy thunder, followed almost immediately by an explosive grind. The Gulfstream jerked, and holes opened throughout the right side of the fuselage, some of them as large as milk jugs. In an instant, fresh alarms joined the chaos and the jet dropped right, snatching in the wind.

Turk smelled smoke. The grinding shrieks of metal scraping against itself continued. Another thunder of cannon fire blazed, and additional sections of the fuselage splintered into tiny shreds of aluminum. From the cockpit Strickland shouted.

"We lost the right engine. We're going down!"

The jet's nose plummeted again. Turk's stomach flipped. His gaze snatched left toward Lucy.

She sat calmly in the seat next to him. Her eyes were open. She smiled once, very gently.

Then the jet dropped like a rock. Turk looked through the cockpit and out the windscreen. The plateau floor was illuminated by the aircraft's landing lights. He saw a highway, straight but narrow, rising rapidly toward them. He saw the headlights of a big truck pointed their way, sucking closer by the millisecond.

They were headed straight for it.

63

The Gulfstream jet struck the highway a quarter mile ahead of the semitruck. Reed saw it as a flash of white erupting into a shower of sparks. Hot on its tail, running barely a hundred feet off the ground, was the Russian fighter. The Gulfstream hurtled toward the semitruck, nose spinning and chunks of asphalt exploding from the roadbed. The Su-35 nosed down, bringing its cannon in line with its wounded prey.

Reed swung the PKP muzzle up, above the semitruck, and clamped down on the trigger. Brake lights flashed from the semitruck and tires screamed. The machine gun thundered, hurling eight hundred rounds per minute at the incoming jet fighter. Smoke and debris filled the air. The semitruck turned and began to jackknife, now sliding sideways in its frantic attempt to avoid a collision with the oncoming Gulfstream. Ivan laid on the brakes. The Tigr jolted. The PKP chattered on, flooding Reed's ears. He tasted smoke and gunpowder and burning jet fuel.

Then the Su-35 rolled off, banking hard and nosing toward the sky. Afterburner poured from its tail and it vanished into the blackness. A split second later, the sliding Gulfstream collided with the nose of the semitruck in a colossal crunch of steel on steel, and both the truck and the aircraft came to a screaming halt, smoke billowing from the jet's burning tail.

Reed couldn't see the cockpit. He couldn't tell how much of the jet's fuselage had survived the crash. He only saw the doors of the semitruck hurtling open and black-clad Alpha commandos bailing out.

"Back up! Back up!" Wolfgang shouted from the cabin of the Tigr, and Ivan threw the truck into reverse. All four wheels ground. Reed swung the PKP into line with fresh blasts of muzzle flash erupting from every opening of the semitruck and pulled the trigger. The machine gun was *hot* now. Tracer rounds spun wide, accuracy diminished by a smoking barrel. Reducing his fire to short bursts, Reed zeroed the weapon on one target at a time and squatted beneath the short armor protection that surrounded the gun turret. Bullets pinged off the Tigr and ricocheted into the night. The burning jet continued to dump black smoke into the sky, and Su-35s screamed overhead.

It was total melee. The fog of war, dragging everything into a blur, but Reed was ready for it. He ignored the incoming rounds and kept the PKP going, gaze dropping to the ammo bin mounted to the machine gun's side.

He was almost dry. Another fifty or sixty rounds, and then the weapon would be out of the fight. He'd dropped two commandos, maybe three, but at least eight more remained.

"I'm almost out!" Reed shouted. "We gotta cover that jet!"

Ivan had already found first gear again and was spinning the Tigr around, circling the side of the semi and moving toward the wrecked Gulfstream. Through the smoke, Reed couldn't tell if anyone had survived. One wing was torn off and most of the right elevator was shredded away by cannon fire from the fighter jet. He thought of Corbyn, Strickland, and Lucy inside, bodies trapped in the smoke and growing flames.

No.

The Tigr ground to a halt next to the jet, and Reed pointed the PKP to the face of the semi. There was at least one Alpha commando hidden inside the cab, but the flat-nosed, cab-over design of the truck provided almost zero protection for him. The last of the 7.62 ammunition tore through the windshield and the sheet metal face of the truck, completely ventilating the cab. A short scream was quickly silenced, and blood sprayed across a vinyl seat. Reed abandoned the machine gun and collapsed into the interior of the Tigr, breathing hard. Wolfgang was already there, an AK-

12 pulled into his shoulder, two extra magazines protruding from his pockets.

"Give me a rifle!" Ivan shouted. "We've got to secure that truck."

Reed scooped another AK off the floor and hurled it forward.

"Jet first," he said. "Then the truck!"

Ivan nodded once, and Reed located his own weapon. Spare mags dropped into his pockets, but he didn't have time for anything else. Rushing to the back door of the Tigr, he tore the latch open and kicked the door back.

The night was pitch black, whatever ambient light might have spilled down from the moon or stars now completely obscured by thick curtains of black smoke. Everything smelled of burning jet fuel. The air itself was superheated, singeing his throat as he and Wolfgang dropped out of the back of the truck. Ivan exploded out of the driver's door and circled to the front of the vehicle. Infrequent gunfire clacked from the direction of the semi, and bullets ricocheted off the Tigr's armored sides.

Reed ignored the incoming rounds and bent at the waist, using the heat of the fire to guide him through the smog. He saw the flames a moment later, breaking through the smoke and rising from the right-hand wing. Burning fuel puddled on the ground, producing additional smoke. From someplace ahead, a voice croaked a cry.

Reed's eyes stung. His throat flooded with the smoke and he choked. The AK rode against his shoulder, one finger held over the trigger. He detected a shadow near the nose of the jet, and his finger constricted.

Then an English cry broke through the darkness.

"Bloody hell! Don't shoot!"

Reed dropped the muzzle of the AK and rushed another five yards. The figure clarified through the smoke—it was Corbyn. She'd made it out of a ruptured emergency hatch and fell to the asphalt. Her face was coated in crimson, blood streaming from a busted nose and a gash on her cheekbone. She slumped against the fuselage, quivering with pain.

"You hurt?" Reed shouted.

"Busted leg." Corbyn grimaced. "*Again.*"

"Where are the others?"

"Inside. Strick is unconscious. I don't know about the others."

"Hang tight."

Reed squeezed her shoulder as Wolfgang appeared like a wraith, screaming from just behind.

"Duck!"

Reed flattened himself against the jet's fuselage just as a barrage of gunfire erupted from somewhere near the semitruck. Bullets pinged off the jet's nose and Wolfgang returned fire. From the far side of the fuselage, Ivan joined in, screaming unintelligible threats in Russian at his invisible foe.

Reed turned for the emergency hatch—a three-foot-square section of the fuselage that popped out to allow access to the interior. He scrambled through, choking on smoke and landing just behind the cockpit. Black soot from the jet fuel fires had saturated the cabin, sticking to the windows and carpet, leaving precious little oxygen behind. Reed found Strickland slumped over in the co-pilot's chair, face bloody as it rested against the airplane's dash. He shook the pilot, but Strickland didn't respond.

"Lucy?" Reed called. "Lucy!"

A groan sounded from the back of the plane. Reed flailed through the darkness, tripping over fallen equipment and reaching the back seats. He found Lucy slumped over, blood running from her arm. He could barely see her face in the glow of the firelight leaking through the windows. Her eyes were bloodshot, disorientation consuming her face.

"Can you walk?" Reed asked.

Lucy blinked twice, gasping for air. She didn't answer, and Reed decided it didn't matter. He simply scooped her up, her petite body as light as a child's in his big arms. Staggering back toward the front of the plane, he reached the emergency hatch and shouted into the darkness outside.

"Wolf! Catch her!"

Wolfgang responded, and Reed fed Lucy through. Then he was turning back for the cockpit, already reaching for his KA-BAR to slash Strickland's flight harness.

That was when a deep groan resounded from the back of the plane. A choking, coughing sound, followed by a curse. The accent was East Tennessee. The voice familiar.

"Hey...jarhead."

Reed spun in the darkness, eyes burning, throat on fire. He shielded his eyes and squinted at the rear seats. He thought he saw a leg there, sticking out in the aisle. An oversized boot and bloody pants.

Reed's heart rate skyrocketed, crazed energy rushing his system. He hurtled down the aisle, tripping over fallen seat cushions and still clinging to the rifle. He reached the leg and recognized the boot. It twitched as he twisted around the seat.

And then he found him. Rufus Turkman lay folded over in a chair, a seatbelt cutting into his waist and blood dripping from his nose. One leg stuck out into the aisle, while the other was jammed awkwardly beneath the chair ahead of him.

Pain enraptured Turk's face, but he forced a grin when he saw Reed. "'Bout time you showed up."

A hot lump rose in Reed's throat. His eye blurred in the smoke, and Turk racked a cough. Snatching the KA-BAR knife from his belt, Reed slashed through the seatbelt, allowing Turk to fall into his arms with a pained grunt.

"You're a lousy fool, Turk! You should be at home warming the couch."

"What, and miss all the fun?" Turk's teeth gleamed with blood as he grinned.

Reed put an arm beneath his shoulder blades. "Can you walk?"

"I think so. Sprained ankle."

"Come on!"

Reed helped Turk down the aisle, half supporting him, half dragging him. They reached the emergency hatch, and Reed lifted him toward it.

"Get out of here! I'm getting Strickland."

Turk scrambled through the hatch, assisted by Wolfgang on the outside. Reed let him go and turned quickly back to the cockpit. The KA-BAR went to work on the flight harness, slashing through nylon. Strickland's head rolled. Reed braced him with one arm and finished with the harness. He pulled the pilot sideways out of the seat. He was halfway out of the cockpit.

Then the voice of hell returned. A blazing thunder from out of the sky —an inhuman roar.

The voice of a Russian Su-35's nose cannon.

64

Golubev observed the action from a camera mounted to the underbelly of one of the four Su-35s deployed into Azerbaijan. It was like a train wreck—like an action movie where a bomb went off in slow motion. The camera footage streamed from ten thousand feet, the jet banked into a constant circle to remain on target, and in the space of mere seconds...the entire mission went to hell.

First came the unidentified aircraft. As the Russian fighters closed to blow it out of the sky, the plane conducted an aggressive emergency maneuver, spinning out of their line of fire. The automated camera on the surveillance jet tracked it with ease as it spun toward the ground in a free fall. It almost looked as though it had been shot.

But then it pulled out of the spiral. It nosed down, breaking the stall. Lift returned to the wings but it continued to plummet, racing not back into the sky but dead for the semitruck.

Golubev screamed, slamming a hand into his metal desk. He barked at the Alpha officer to contact the Su-35s.

"Take it down! Take it down!"

They did take it down. The point jet rolled in directly behind the unidentified aircraft and laid on its nose cannon. Thirty-millimeter rounds shredded the sky and tore into the tail of the jet. Flames erupted from its right engine, and its right-hand elevator was blown away. Smoke flooded the sky, joined by flames.

But the jet didn't plummet. It continued to nose down in a near perfect approach, headed straight for the road.

And the truck.

Somewhere around the time the jet collided with the semi, a Russian-built Tigr appeared out of nowhere. It burst from the darkness, its roof-mounted PKP machine gun blazing. It engaged the truck and circled toward the wrecked aircraft. The Su-35s, meanwhile, streaked back into the sky to regroup and retarget, their pilots barking confused questions as the scene on the highway descended rapidly into a total war zone of burning jet fuel and flashing rifles. Complete carnage.

Nobody knew exactly what was happening. Nobody knew who had joined the fight in the Tigr or who had been shot down by the Su-35s, but what Golubev *did* know was that such details no longer mattered. The situation had run violently off the rails, leaving him with a very simple choice to make. Two brutal options.

He could scuttle the mission altogether, ordering the Su-35s to obliterate the entire scene with a barrage of air-to-ground missiles, effectively erasing the evidence but also costing him months of preparation and any chance of success.

Or he could detonate the weapon right where it sat. Evaporate the witnesses and press ahead with Nikitin's plan all the same. There would be no devastated city, of course. No thousands of dead bodies.

But did that really matter?

No. The choice was obvious. The mission was still paramount.

Golubev snatched up a handset and radioed the Alpha commander.

65

Reed dove for cover even as chunks of the jet's fuselage were blown into shreds, heavy 30mm rounds ripping through aluminum and steel as though it were paper, blasting away insulation and nearly cutting the aircraft in half. The door was blown off, and a massive gap opened in the fuselage only inches from Reed's boots. He scrambled toward the cabin as shouts erupted from outside the jet.

"Reed! Get out of there!"

Reed ignored the call and rolled onto his stomach, clawing his way back into the cockpit. He could hear the jet orbiting overhead, arcing into a circle for a second pass. All he could think was that he had to get away from the Gulfstream—take shelter by running toward the semitruck.

The Su-35 wouldn't fire on the truck. Not if that trailer contained what Reed thought it contained.

"Strickland! Let's go!"

Reed grabbed the pilot by his arm and pulled him out of the seat. Strickland was still unconscious, head rolling, face coated in blood. Reed rose to his knees and lifted his body over the jet's center console. His back strained, hot fire racing through his muscles. Outside, Kalashnikov rifles rattled like firecrackers in a coffee can, and overhead, the jet engine had faded out of earshot.

That could only mean the Su-35 had completed its circle and was now banking into a final approach. A killing approach.

"*Reed!*" The voice was Wolfgang's, calling through the smoke.

Reed ignored him and snatched Strickland out of the seat with a heave. The two of them landed on the busted floor of the jet and Reed kicked his way back from the cockpit. He reached the hole blown in the fuselage and turned toward a black sky.

He saw the Russian fighter jet arcing out of the blackness, its canopy reflecting the firelight from a mile away. The aircraft was descending rapidly, dropping toward its target. Aligning that deadly nose cannon with the wreckage of the Gulfstream. Preparing to fire.

Reed scrambled toward the door, dragging Strickland with him, already knowing he wouldn't make it. The fighter jet was almost on top of them. At any moment the cannon would spin, and if Reed was lucky, he'd hear the first burst of thunder before the bullets stitched their way across the mountain plateau and cut his body in half.

So this is it.

It was a strangely calm thought. Not a moment of panic. Just a moment of defiance.

Reed twisted toward the hole in the jet, still precious seconds away from lifting Strickland to safety. Instead, he simply gave up. He dropped the unconscious pilot and lifted a middle finger toward the sky.

A split second passed. Then the thunder came, all at once. A hot blast of flame erupted across the perfectly black sky, a plume of orange, yellow, and red as the Russian jet simply evaporated. It was there and then it was gone in a split second, the horizon temporarily illuminated by fire and falling shrapnel. Reed blinked, caught off guard, middle finger still extended. He gasped in smoke.

Then the scream of new aircraft ripped across the sky—not one but *six* fighter jets, painted in mottled shades of blue and gray, with red, green, and blue emblems on their wing tips. They blazed over the plateau floor at five hundred feet, then they were arcing toward the sky again, twin afterburners blazing.

"Oh hell yeah!" Reed roared, sudden adrenaline rushing his exhausted body. He hauled himself to his feet and dragged Strickland behind him, reaching the hole in the fuselage and tugging the limp pilot through. Out of the smoke, Turk and Wolfgang appeared, helping to drag Strickland away from the burning jet and off the busted highway. Reeds ears rang with gunfire from behind. He looked over his shoulders and recognized muzzle flash dug in behind the far wing of the plane—Ivan, no doubt. The gunfire was returned from outside the semi trailer, six or more starlights of muzzle flash spread across the plateau floor.

Nobody saw the evacuees amongst the smoke. They reached a field terrace twenty yards off the highway, freshly torn by cannon fire, and rolled Strickland over it. Lucy and Corbyn were already there, and Reed slid down the slope, gasping for air. His head buzzed. His teeth were packed with grit. His vision blurred.

But he was still alive—yet again snatched from the jaws of death.

"Where's my rifle?" Reed choked.

Turk was already on him, patting him down, searching for wounds.

"I'm fine," Reed choked. "Give me a gun!"

"You're *bleeding!*" Turk shook him by the shoulder. "Where are you hit?"

Reed looked down at his filthy body. The Russian military fatigues were stained by dirt, smoke...and blood. Had he been shot?

No. It was shrapnel. He felt it with his hands, buried into his thigh. Not a bad cut, but enough to stain his pants leg with blood. He hadn't even felt it.

"I'm fine! Treat Strickland. Where's my gun?"

Turk and Wolfgang exchanged a look. Lucy's medical bag lay on the ground alongside her, but her eyes were still wide, her gaze disoriented. She was shell-shocked and inoperable. Reed had seen it before, and there was nothing to do about it. Not as long as they were still being shot at.

"*Rifle!*" Reed barked again. He stuck out a hand.

Turk shook his head in exhaustion and shoved an AK-12 into Reed's grasp.

"You're impossible, Reed."

"You said you wanted the fun," Reed retorted, racking the AK's charging handle. "Here it comes!"

66

The dogfight circling high overhead was punctuated by the occasional thunder of nose cannons and the blast of detonating missiles as Reed scrambled back to the top of the terrace, rifle held to his shoulder. The muzzle flash from around the trailer had become more sporadic, but it wasn't because Ivan had made any progress. With Ivan effectively pinned down, the firefight had descended into a stalemate. Neither party could leave cover without risking total exposure to the enemy, but something told Reed that time was not on their side.

There was still unidentified cargo aboard the semi trailer, and nobody knew what would happen if that cargo were broadsided with a careless burst of Kalashnikov fire. Regardless, the Russians had to be deploying reinforcements by now. Reed had to upset the apple cart before they arrived.

"Can you run?" Reed shouted.

Turk looked pointedly at Reed's bloody leg. "Can *you*?"

Reed shoved him. "Pincer move. You two hold the block. I'll deliver the needle. Ready?"

Turk shouldered his rifle and nodded once. "Three...two...cover fire!"

Turk and Wolfgang unleashed a burst of joint AK fire, and Reed broke from cover. Sprinting right, he circled through the drifting smoke, rushing along the outside of the highway. His body was so alive with adrenaline that he couldn't even feel the injury to his thigh. He couldn't feel the headache he knew he should have from the smoke and noise. He couldn't feel a thing...and yet he felt everything.

Absolutely alive. Completely zeroed in. The brain fog was gone, and Reed was electrified. He felt like he could run forever—like he *wanted* to run forever. He covered a hundred yards in twenty seconds and came level with the tail of the trailer. The flash of gunfire out of the corner of his eye snagged his attention, and he instinctively dove back to the ground. Bullets slammed into the dirt and kicked up a spray, voices now audible from the rear of the trailer.

Russian voices.

Rolling left, Reed planted his elbows into the dirt and steadied the rifle. In a millisecond he had a target. It was a black shadow dug in behind the trailer, raining fire from a SAW-type weapon toward Turk and Wolfgang's position. Reed's sights settled over the guy's head. Three quick squeezes of a gritty AK trigger delivered death rounds right to the Alpha's skull, blowing him sideways. Then Reed was scrambling backward again, taking cover behind another terrace as bullets blew loose dirt and sand into the air. He looked left and saw Turk, illuminated by the burning jet fuel and rising over the top of the terrace. The gunfire Reed had drawn offered a momentary opportunity for the big Tennessean to advance, and he took it, sprinting all the way to the nose of the ventilated semitruck before sliding into cover behind the bumper. A split second later, gunfire blazed from beneath the truck, directed toward the Alphas dug in around its tail. The fresh pressure delivered a needle into Reed's backstop, forcing the enemy back into cover.

Then it was Reed's turn to play the needle once more. He scrambled over the top of the terrace and broke for the trailer, aiming for the now flattened rear tires where his feet and legs would be shielded from fire. Sweeping the AK left, he caught the first Alpha, on his way to shoot Turk in the back, with four shots to the neck and chest as Reed raced around the tail of the trailer.

The Alpha went down, and Reed stepped right over the body. On the far side of the trailer, the voice of Ivan's rifle grew louder as the old

Russian pressed the attack, narrowing in on the Alphas still dug in on that side.

Reed didn't know how many soldiers remained *inside* the trailer, but he had no doubt they were waiting for him. He might have tossed a grenade around the doorframe, but he'd lost his grenade while scrambling inside the wrecked SAC jet.

Besides. There was delicate cargo on the far side of that wall. Would a grenade set off a nuke? Would a rifle bullet?

Reed had no idea, but he knew he couldn't afford to find out. He had to eliminate the Alpha's outside the trailer first, then follow the attack inside of it. Dropping into a squat, Reed swung his rifle beneath the trailer's floor and spotted the muzzle flash of Alpha commandos spread out behind a terrace on the far side of the trailer, attempting and failing to provide a security perimeter. They were now caught between Reed to their left, Ivan dead ahead, and Turk and Wolfgang someplace in between.

There was no place to run. Nowhere left to hide. Reed dropped his front sight post over the first muzzle flash and engaged. Screams tore the air and Reed's rifle ran dry. He ratcheted in a fresh magazine and kept firing, gunning down the last man as he sprinted desperately for better cover. Rifles went silent and dirt kicked up into the air. One man scrambled to his knees and twisted to run.

Reed blew his legs out from under him, then shot him in the back of the head as his body toppled. Seconds later the gunfire ceased altogether, almost as though it were coordinated to do so. Reed gasped for air and swept the horizon with his rifle. His heart thundered so loud it sounded like a drumbeat outside his body. He inched his way beneath the trailer and looked both ways, finger held just off the trigger, body alive with tension.

The shadows of dead Alphas lay motionless on the ground. Reed couldn't hear the fighter jets anymore. He couldn't hear anyone shouting in Russian. Only the crackle of the still-burning fuel filled the air, all else having fallen deathly still.

And yet he could sense something...

The creek of plywood jerked Reed's attention to the underside of the semi trailer, and he rolled automatically left a split second before a burst of automatic gunfire shredded the flooring and smashed into the asphalt.

Dust and wood splinters clouded the air, and Reed fought to escape the underside of the trailer. The gunfire was indiscriminate and reckless, blazing at random through the trailer's plywood flooring. One bullet skimmed Reed's shoulder and another cut the toe of his boot. He didn't feel pain—he only felt the adrenaline. He reached the edge of the trailer and rolled out, returning to his knees and lifting the rifle.

He didn't fire through the trailer wall. There was still a nuke inside. Instead he rushed to the tail of the trailer and readied the rifle to pivot around the opening.

"Reed! Wait!"

Wolfgang's shout echoed behind him, but Reed wasn't listening. The battle fury had taken over. He spun around the back of the trailer and swung the rifle up. He stared into a darkened interior lit by flashes of fire. Continued splinters of wood erupted into the air as the soldier inside fired into the floor. Reed leveled his AK on the man and squeezed the trigger.

The second Alpha hiding in the shadows fired at the same time. The AK slammed into Reed's shoulder and the bullet raced toward the standing commando's neck. At the same moment, twin slugs from an AK in the shadows zipped toward Reed's chest. They made impact against his captured Russian chest plate with the force of a front-end collision from a dump truck. Air raced from Reed's lungs and he stumbled back. The sky spun overhead. He couldn't breathe.

Catching himself on the open door of the trailer, he broke his own fall and pivoted the AK one-handed toward the threat. The Alpha rose from behind a tall wooden crate and pivoted his rifle toward Reed—not his chest, but his face.

Then the walls of the trailer exploded in a shower of plywood shrapnel. Heavy AK rounds burst through them and caught the Alpha commando from both sides, blowing his face off and ripping through his neck. He jerked and dropped the AK, but Turk, Ivan, and Wolfgang kept firing. Fully a hundred rounds ventilated the rear of the trailer, busting through the wooden crate and pinging off metal. The commando went down and Reed heaved, still fighting to catch his breath. His chest was alive with pain. It felt as though he'd been crushed by the dump truck—run right over.

The muzzle of his rifle drooped, and then Turk was at his side. Reed stumbled backward and Turk caught him, shaking him by one arm.

"Reed! *Reed!* Are you hurt?"

Turk's voice sounded like it was coming from the other side of a fish tank. The world spun around Reed's head, and he felt himself falling.

Turk and Wolfgang caught him, while Ivan was already scrambling into the back of the trailer. Reed swallowed back the blood in his throat and gritted his teeth. He finally caught a lungful of air and found his voice.

"What were you thinking? You could have set it off!"

Turk squinted in confusion, then Ivan breathed a dismayed curse.

"Hell's angels..."

Reed, Wolfgang, and Turk looked into the trailer. Ivan stood over the crate, his battered old face peering down into it. Cheeks washed white. Eyes wide. Lips parted. It was the most horrified look Reed had ever seen on the stalwart Russian's ugly features. It was enough to dump adrenaline back into Reed's bloodstream, and he dropped the AK, pulling free of Turk and scrambling to the rear of the trailer.

One leg on the bumper. One hand on the bullet-blasted floor. He was up and inside the trailer in another second, barely breathing, agony still blazing through his rib cage, but it couldn't stop him. Turk and Wolfgang followed. They all reached the crate at the same moment and peered down into it. Wolfgang shone a light. And then Reed's blood ran cold.

It was a bomb all right. About the size of a large refrigerator, housed inside a lead box that had deflected the hail of AK fire unleashed on the trailer. The weapon was cruder than Reed would have expected, hastily thrown together with a grimy metal shell shaped like a giant coffee can.

But two features immediately caught his eye. The first was an LED display, counting slowly down from five minutes. Now four minutes, fifty-nine seconds. Then fifty-eight.

The second was a stamped logo printed into the case of the weapon. A logo in English, with a flag engraved over it.

The flag was the Stars and Stripes...and the English read: *USA.*

67

The four of them stood over the crate for another perfectly silent four seconds. Reed knew it because the clock reached four minutes and fifty-four seconds.

Then Reed's heart slammed into his chest, and his mind ratcheted into gear.

"*Go!*"

He spun and grabbed the first person he could—Wolfgang. A shove from behind sent The Wolf stumbling and flailing to the back of the trailer. Reed leapt out, chest still racing with pain at every breath. He nearly fell in the loose dirt, but he found a way to stay on his feet. Ivan and Turk hit the dirt, then all four of them were racing down the sides of the trailer. Past the bodies. Past the busted asphalt and sea of steel shell casings. Ivan went for the Tigr. Wolfgang, Reed, and Turk went for Corbyn, Lucy, and Strickland.

"In the truck!" Reed screamed. "Get in the truck!"

Tires ground and Ivan backed the Tigr toward the terrace like a drunk driver, slinging the front tires around and ramming the rear bumper straight into the earth. Reed slung the doors open even as Lucy and Corbyn turned wide eyes toward the trailer.

"*Into the truck!*" Reed roared.

That was enough to jerk their focus back into the moment. Reed and

Turk grabbed Strickland and hurled his still-limp body into the back of the Tigr. Corbyn struggled to climb in and Wolfgang shoved her from behind. Reed picked Lucy up like a rag doll and dropped her into a back seat. Turk scrambled over Strickland and extended an arm to help Wolfgang.

Reed entered the truck last of all, casting one look over his shoulder toward the semi trailer.

And the weapon he had no clue how to disarm.

Then he was slamming the rear door and shouting to Ivan.

"*Go! Go!*"

The four wheels of the Russian beast ground over the dirt. They launched out of the ditch and returned to the broken highway. The armored beast snatched to the left, breaking through burning jet fuel and erupting out of black smoke. They clipped the busted right-hand wing of the Gulfstream as the engine howled.

Ivan was working through the gears. The Tigr was climbing toward maximum speed. Nobody spoke as Reed's head pivoted back, looking through the narrow rear windows of the truck toward the glowing jet fuel fire that marked the location of the trailer. It was half a mile away already. Then a mile. His mind worked quickly to break down the math.

Four minutes of escape time at eighty miles per hour. How far was that? Five miles? Was that far enough?"

"*Faster!*" Reed shouted.

It was pointless. The Tigr was already wound out to maximum speed. They were diving down a slight incline, headed for a curve in the road. A mountain valley offered shelter not far ahead. Reed clung to the wall and the Tigr dipped. His heart pounded and his head spun. He couldn't see the jet fuel fire anymore. He'd lost all track of time. It could have been one minute or three. The Tigr shook and lurched as Ivan took corners way too fast, laying on his brakes and snatching the wheel. Reed slammed into the wall and Corbyn let out a cry as Wolfgang landed on her knee.

Seconds dripped by. The distance stacked.

And then, for the second time in just over a week...the world went nuclear. The blast shook the earth and illuminated the night sky as bright as day. Reed clung to the door handle of the Tigr as the shockwave ripped outward from the epicenter of death and destruction. It caught the back of the heavy truck and sent a shockwave ripping through it, hard enough to send Reed's back slamming against the wall while everyone scrambled for a handhold. The Tigr lifted off its right-hand tires, rolling to the left. Ivan shouted in Russian, and Corbyn screamed. Strickland's limp body slammed against Reed's leg.

Then the Tiger went down hard, and a thunderclap rent the sky. Reed lost his grip on the Tigr's wall and hit the floor. Turk crashed on top of him. Bright light flooded the truck's interior.

Reed pressed his hands against the steel floor, jerking his face toward the rear windows—toward the source of hot red light. It painted the sky as bright and vibrant as a Caribbean sunset.

And framed right in the middle of it all was a mushroom cloud.

68

"Blast! We've got a blast!"

The voice ripped across the CIA operations center as Aimes stood on the elevated platform, overlooking that movie theater screen. The visual she saw wasn't from either of the Air Force surveillance drones the Pentagon had deployed to Azerbaijan. They had both been shot down within seconds of a high-speed dogfight erupting between Russian Su-35 fighter jets and Azerbaijani MiG-29s. Now all that remained was the satellite feed from outer space...but that was enough.

She could see it. The eruption of fire and fury dominated the Azerbaijani plateau, flooding the satellite lens with light, but no color. Everything was black and white, adding to the sinister drama unfolding before her eyes like a train wreck.

Like a *nightmare*.

Snatching a handset off the desk in front of her, Aimes speed-dialed. Rigby had descended to the main level of the operation's center to direct the growing crowd of specialists populating the desks. He was still well within shouting distance, but Aimes didn't want anyone else to hear what she was about to say.

"Where are they, Silas?"

Rigby looked up from his desk, making eye contact. He shook his head once. "I don't know. We've lost them."

69

"We've got company!"

Ivan's bellow from the front seat of the Tigr reached Reed's ears even as the last of that horrible rumble faded over the horizon. The light had faded with it, sucked into an abyss of evil black smoke that blanketed the sky like an oncoming hurricane.

Now everything was dark. The thunder of the Russian motor overtook the roar of atomic hell from eight miles across the plateau—and then a third sound ripped through the night. That all too familiar snarl.

Automatic gunfire.

Bullets pinged off the nose of the Tigr and slammed into the reinforced windshield. Turk clawed his way off Reed's body and yanked Reed up by the plate carrier secured around his chest. All was chaos inside the back of the Tigr. Reed couldn't see anything other than the blink of muzzle flash directly ahead. Ivan downshifted and slammed on the gas.

Then the Tigr struck something—something organic and meaty. Screams ripped through the gun ports built into the armored walls, and the heavy tires crushed over flesh and bone. Then they were back on the road and Ivan was accelerating again.

"Azerbaijani army!" Ivan called. "There will be more. What is our plan?"

Plan.

Reed's heart thundered. His head pounded. If he closed his eyes, he saw the mushroom cloud. He could taste the acidic mixture of radioactive heat and melted sand on the air. His hands trembled as he fought to stabilize himself against a rear seat.

But one thought rang clearly through the chaos—one perfectly clear reality. His last image of the bomb.

USA.

"Get us off the road!" Reed shouted. "Find cover!"

Ivan didn't need to be told twice. The Tigr yanked to the right and lurched hard as they cleared a shallow ditch. A split second later a thunderous *boom* was followed by the whistle of an incoming shell streaking only yards over the top of the Tigr.

Tank, Reed thought.

"They've got armor," Wolfgang shouted. "They're coming in hot!"

Reed spat blood from a busted lip, an accelerated heartbeat pounding in his ears as his mind fought for a solution. Even in the context of the incoming tank fire and the rattle of small arms, the most pressing issue continued to be that picture of the bomb. That etched flag in stainless steel. Those three letters that spelled out an unavoidable truth.

Langley. The CIA had to know. Absolutely, immediately, whatever it cost.

Where is the messenger?

Reed pushed himself off the wall, crawling over Strickland's body and shoving past Corbyn. Fallen rifles, sliding spare magazines, and blood ran across the floor as the Tigr hurtled over a terrace, suspension groaning. Reed dragged himself through the dark even as Turk shouted from the rear doors, announcing the closing line of Azerbaijani soldiers.

"Wolfgang, where's the messenger?" Reed shouted over the thunder of the engine as he reached the front seats. He grabbed Wolfgang's arm and shook him. Wolfgang looked back, eyes wide, already shaking his head.

"I dropped it!"

"*Incoming!*" Turk called the warning just as the thunder of the Azerbaijani tank detonated someplace behind. Ivan yanked the truck to one side, and once more a shell whistled overhead. Reed fell to the floor. His face slammed against the backside of Wolfgang's seat and pain exploded up his jaw. He tasted blood. He fished across the floor.

And then he found it. The CIA's messaging device had slid beneath the front passenger's seat. Reed shoved Lucy aside to reach it. He drew it out and mashed the power button, whispering beneath his breath. Praying for the signal to return.

But the device wouldn't power on. The screen remained black. He smacked it against his palm, shaking it. Jamming the power button again.

Still nothing. Then he remembered.

EMP. The nuke would have released an electromagnetic pulse, strong enough to fry any electronics within several miles. The fact that the Tigr was still running was a testament to modern Russian military engineering, but the CIA device was clearly not up to spec.

"*Incom—*"

Turk never finished his next warning. The third tank round finally found its mark, landing with the force of a giant's right hook. In a split second a 125mm armor-piercing shell ripped through the back side of the Tigr's heavy armor. Blasting through one wall and out the other, it left holes large enough to push a wheelbarrow through before vanishing into the darkness. Turk fell forward with a choking shout, slamming into Reed's shoulder. The Tigr lurched sideways, left-hand wheels leaving the ground. Reed and Turk both went down, slamming into Lucy as the right-hand side of the truck struck the hard Azerbaijani earth, metal crunching and dust exploding through the shattered armor. The tank fired again, and the next shell blew through the engine block, shoving the truck sideways until it teetered over what felt like a precipice. Loose items slid against the overturned roof. Ivan shouted.

Then they were rolling. Like a child's toy thrown down a hillside, the Tigr struck the ground again and again, every unrestrained occupant slamming into walls and crashing into the upturned ceiling. Reed's back hit a chair and pain lanced up his spine. His face struck the floor and he choked. Everything was a blur. It was all jagged metal and tumbling bodies and broken cries, and it went on for what felt like an eternity.

When at last the Tigr stopped rolling, it lay upright on its wheels, but there was no chance the vehicle would ever drive again. Reed was pinned beneath Strickland's still-limp body, and dust clouded the air. From the driver's compartment, an agonized moan filled the truck, but there was no longer any engine noise. There was no longer any engine. Reed's ears rang and he clawed at his eyes. He fought to shoved Strickland aside, coughing and fighting for air.

Everything around him was a blur. His vision had been knocked out of focus. His head buzzed, and his arms went numb. He heaved and struggled to pull his legs free. He tasted blood on his tongue and touched more of the same as he flailed for a handhold.

The moaning from the driver's compartment intensified, but Reed couldn't identify the voice. He couldn't see anything in the mix of dirt and darkness.

The only thing he *could* understand was the squealing rattle headed toward them from across the plateau. It was an incoming Azerbaijani tank.

70

"We've got action!"

The useless voice returned to announce the obvious as Aimes fixated on the screen. The light of the nuclear blast had already mostly faded, but she didn't need perfect illumination to recognize the indicators of erupting conflict. Muzzle flash. The heat signatures of a truck moving southeast at speed, away from the blast.

And the heat signatures of several additional trucks and at least one tank moving northwest to intercept it.

"Zoom in!" Aimes shouted. "I want a better visual."

"We're trying, ma'am. There's a lot of atmospheric distortion. We've got debris from the blast headed this way."

Another thing Aimes didn't need to be told. Blast wind from the nuclear explosion was carrying an aerial tsunami of ash and dirt directly toward the site of the converging vehicles. Within minutes—maybe within seconds—Aimes wouldn't be able to see anything at all. The debris would blanket dozens of square miles, completely blinding her satellite.

Yanking her phone back up, Aimes speed-dialed again. This time the call was outbound. The Pentagon didn't keep her waiting.

"Yes?" General Albert Porter, chief of staff of the Air Force, answered with predictable directness. The situation demanded nothing less.

"I need more drones, General. ASAP."

"I don't *have* any more drones, Madam Director. The two you lost were the only ones I had within range."

"Well, I need you to *find some*," Aimes barked, ignoring Porter's jab about her culpability. "We've got World War Three erupting in Azerbaijan and I can't see a thing!"

Gritty curses from Porter. Then: "I'll do what I can."

He hung up. Aimes hung up. She leaned over the table and stared at the screen. Debris had already deteriorated at least fifty percent of the satellite view she'd had only a minute prior. The heat signatures of the oncoming vehicles closed into a tight knot. The truck they were chasing had turned off the road and hurtled across the rough plateau floor...and then stopped.

Was the Prosecution Force on board? Or were these Russians?

She didn't know, and likely, she never would. The Azerbaijanis had almost reached the stopped truck.

71

"Bail! Bail!"

Turk's ragged voice erupted through the back of the Tigr even before the dust had settled. Tangled on the floor amid fallen rifles and Strickland's limp form, Reed lay, ears ringing. He could barely see, and it hurt to breathe.

But that one clear thought still radiated through his mind.

USA.

"Reed! We gotta move!"

Turk's next shout jarred Reed out of his daze. He scrambled onto his knees as Ivan flicked on an LED light from the front of the truck, spilling cold blue glow across the interior. Agonized groans resumed from the front passenger seat, and it wasn't difficult to pinpoint them. They came from Wolfgang, and a quick glance in that direction revealed the truth.

Blood speckled the Tigr's shattered dash, and shards of twisted metal protruded from Wolfgang's leg. His *good* leg.

On the floor, Corbyn lay still, blood coating one side of her face. Maybe dead, maybe simply unconscious. Reed didn't have time to determine either way. From the driver's seat, Ivan fought to extricate himself from a twisted seat belt. Lucy had somehow remained jammed behind Wolfgang, breathing hard, both hands clenched around the backside of his seat. She was clearly still in shock, and now sobbing.

"We gotta get them out!" Turk called, shaking Reed's shoulder. "Help me with Strickland!"

Reed didn't move. Even as he swept the rear of the truck, overlooking the carnage, his mind worked like a computer through every possible solution for a relatively simple equation. He calculated the disabled bodies piled around him. The shout of Azerbaijani troops a hundred yards overhead, presumably lined up along the top of whatever steep incline they had tumbled down. He factored in the thick darkness outside, the dwindling volume of firepower left to them, the sweeping fallout of that nuclear bomb and the all-important truth hidden at the bottom of it all.

Russian soldiers and an American bomb.

The solution came to him and Reed's eyes watered despite himself. He wasn't crying. Not really. But as the crush of the moment and its inevitable conclusion descended on his shoulders, another truth burned deep in his chest.

He hadn't called her back. All she wanted was a phone call. A moment alone together. A bit of unity, of intimacy. Of availability. A soft word and a loving touch. A husband to hold her. Banks had supported him relentlessly. Faultlessly. Without hesitation or question.

And he had abandoned her. He'd abandoned his own son.

He hadn't even called to say he loved them.

"*Reed!*" Turk screamed right in his ear, shaking him. Reed planted his boot against the floor to stabilize himself and snatched an AK from between his legs. He shoved it into Turk's hands and spoke calmly, even as the shouts of Azerbaijani troops descending the hillside grew steadily louder.

"Take Lucy," Reed snapped. "Get into the dark and get as far away as you can. Find communication and connect with Langley. They have to know about the Alpha commandos in the truck. I'll hold off the Azerbaijanis while you run."

Turk blinked, confusion and automatic objection drenching his face. He began to shake his head. Reed shook him.

"It was *our bomb*, Turk! Or made to look like our bomb. The Russians are setting us up. If Langley doesn't get ahead of this, it's World War Three. You understand that? It's *World War Three!*"

Another shake of Turk's shoulder. The big Tennessean blinked. Reed pulled him close and lowered his voice.

"Lucy can run. If you try to take anybody else you'll never make it out. Get deep into the dark and lay low. Whatever happens, *do not* come back for us. Understood? *Get to Langley.*"

Reed pressed a hand against Turk's chest and pushed him gently away. Turk was crying now, heavy tears rolling down his cheeks. He swallowed and looked like he was going to object again...

But he didn't. Reed could see the acceptance in his eyes. The logic was too irrefutable.

"Thank you for having my back," Reed said. "You've always had my back."

Turk blinked hard. Then he slung an arm over Reed's shoulders and pulled him in close. Not saying a word. Not needing to. One battered soul gripping another at the edge of eternity.

"Tell Banks I'm sorry," Reed said. "I love her. I'll always, always love her."

Reed's vision blurred as sudden heat erupted in his chest. The world outside slowed for a moment and became strangely still. Then Reed shoved Turk away.

"Move," Reed said. "Don't stop and don't turn back!"

Turk cradled the rifle in one hand and reached out to grab Lucy's arm with the other. She still looked dazed and confused as she stumbled toward the back of the truck, passing Reed with wide eyes. Not saying a thing.

Reed offered a weak smile. A forced wink. Then he looked to Ivan, a question on his face. The big Russian still sat behind the wheel, the seat belt cut free, a rifle in one hand. He looked toward Turk and the hole blown in the back of the truck, but Ivan made no move to follow. He snatched the charging handle on the AK and nodded once. Wolfgang reached out a hand, grimacing against the agony of his shredded leg. Ivan passed him a handgun.

Then Turk guided Lucy toward the hole blown in the passenger's side of the Tigr. Outside, the air was alive with shouting voices. Reed could track the location of those voices forming a long line across the hillside, slowly constricting toward the nose and tail of the Tigr. Hoping to close it off from both ends and cut off any route of escape.

Scooping a rifle off the floor, Reed turned toward the gaping hole on the driver's side. He nodded once to Turk. The big man braced himself near the hole on the opposite side, one arm wielding his rifle. The other arm shepherding Lucy.

Then Reed screamed into the night. *"Go!"*

72

"I've got them!"

A technician working the operation's center floor shouted up to the executive platform as Aimes held a phone to her ear and swept her gaze over the satellite screen.

The phone was an open line to the Pentagon—the Air Force was refusing to deploy a drone into Azerbaijani airspace due to an increased fighter pilot presence. The satellite screen was still obscured by blast debris.

But now, for the first time in nearly ten minutes, a fragment of an opening through the fog became visible, with a row of concentrated heat signatures spread out along a jagged line at the edge of the Azerbaijani plateau.

The heat signatures were all vehicles. The little dots crawling slowly away from them were humans. But about a hundred yards away from that vehicle line lay another vehicular heat signature. Motionless. Maybe mired in a ditch or somehow disabled. It was impossible to tell with the low-quality visual.

Slamming the phone down, Aimes held her breath as Rigby stepped in beside her. The whole room became quiet as everyone stared at the screen. Waiting. Watching the little dots draw closer to that stranded dot of a vehicle, its heat signature rapidly cooling.

Then came the muzzle flash. Lighting up the black-and-white satellite feed in irregular blinks. Probably automatic fire, but the lens of the satellite only caught some of the flashes. They came from the line of dots closed in around the vehicle. They came from the vehicle, directed back at the dots.

They lasted maybe sixty seconds. Then a gust of wind blew in the next cloud of nuclear blast debris, and the view of the satellite was yet again obscured. The muzzle flash and the heat signatures all vanished. Everything was consumed in fuzzy black and white, like the distorted screen of an old television set.

And the Prosecution Force—or whoever was taking fire from inside that stranded vehicle—was lost.

73

Stratton's blood ran cold as the blast erupted across the screen. He stood at the end of the conference table, and nobody said a word. All eyes were fixed on the grainy CIA satellite feed, an imperfect picture of a perfect horror.

The bomb went off, and in his very soul, Stratton braced for the fallout. He slumped into his chair and barely said a word over the next half hour as phones rang and people shouted. The military was on full alert, braced for a possible order to transition into DEFCON 1. The Air Force stood by hundreds of ICBMs tucked into silos around the country. The Navy prepped their boomers to open fire at a moment's notice.

But Stratton wouldn't touch the nuclear briefcase situated next to his desk chair—the so-called *football*. He left the authorization codes printed on a quick-reference card tucked into his pocket. When Yellin requested authorization to launch fighter aircraft off of carrier decks in the Persian Gulf and the Mediterranean, Stratton refused.

He simply sat and stared at the eruption of radioactive death displayed on replay. Picturing the moment and knowing beyond any shadow of a doubt that the second nuclear blast inside of ten days had changed the world far worse than the first.

He wasn't sure how yet. He didn't know what the exact consequences would be and knew they would likely be slow in unfolding.

But the hurricane was coming. It was headed straight for American shores.

A fractured White House was all that stood in its way.

74

The Kremlin
Moscow, Russia

On the other side of the planet, Makar Nikitin watched a similar satellite feed from the comfort of his private office. A fresh cup of tea rested on a saucer in his lap. Nobody else was in the room.

The earth-shaking eruption of nuclear energy was much smaller than the bomb that had wrecked the Panama Canal. This was closer to a tactical-type nuclear weapon, yielding about ten kilotons, roughly half the size of the Hiroshima bomb. Immediate blast radius was restricted to a distance of about three kilometers.

But the point wasn't the destructive potential, it was the implication. The horrific reality. A *second* nuclear blast inside of ten days. The world was spiraling into chaos...and who was responsible?

Nikitin sipped tea and inhaled deeply, relishing the moment. The perfect silence of his office was such a juxtaposition to the devastation displayed on the screen that the reality of the bomb felt a little detached, as though it were all just make believe. A Hollywood film.

But this was a film he had written, a production he had directed. There was more than a little satisfaction in that, like a playwright watching his actors deliver an opening night performance. It hadn't been flawless—not even close. But despite the sudden, unexplained arrival of hostile operators, an aggressive private jet, and even the loss of three Su-35 fighter jets shot down by Azerbaijani pilots...opening night had been a resounding success.

The secure satellite phone on Nikitin's desk rang, and he mashed the speaker button. He already knew who was calling.

"It's done," Golubev said.

"The Azerbaijanis?" Nikitin asked.

"They're mobilizing their forces. A full deployment."

Nikitin nodded. He sipped tea. He stared at the screen, watching a replay of that white-hot flash. That eruption of unthinkable power.

And he smiled.

75

Washington, DC

The street was pitch black, with all four of the streetlamps that should have bathed the sidewalks in a warm, protective glow broken and nonfunctional. Cars were parked against the curbs, some of them resting on flat tires, and one even resting on blocks. The pavement was busted and riddled with potholes.

It was an avenue of the American capital that news cameras and tourists never visited. A backwater, forgotten by society and neglected by law enforcement—or, perhaps, *avoided* by law enforcement. And not without reason. Violent crime was commonplace in this district, both random and organized. That fact, coupled with the lack of quality schools or localized shopping and dining options, drove the rent well below regional averages.

It was exactly the sort of place where a disgraced middle school math teacher, convicted of nine counts of child molestation and forty-two counts of possession of child pornography, would take up residence after being released from a fourteen-year prison sentence.

It wasn't like Jacob Grover could find a high-paying job in the education sector anymore. He now worked at a warehouse, loading grocery store trucks for twelve dollars an hour. The apartment he occupied was a one-bedroom with a window unit for air conditioning and no backyard or parking lot. That was okay because Grover didn't own a car. He took the bus. He kept to himself. He was never visited by the beautiful Guatemalan wife who divorced him or any of their three children.

Grover was a loner. A reject of society. A man that, as far as James O'Dell was concerned, should have never been let out of prison.

Leaving his government sedan at his apartment, O'Dell took the train halfway to his destination, a cab for another three miles, and then walked the remaining four blocks. He figured that assortment of random travel would compromise the ability of any one camera system to track his entire journey.

Nobody would know that the president's special advisor was in the neighborhood. Nobody would recognize him as he strode down the side-walk, slipped into the darkness, and approached the apartment from its back door. There was a rusted barbecue grill there. A grimy block of patio, and brick steps covered in mildew. The screen door was torn, and the metal main door behind it both scratched and dented.

O'Dell took his time with the lockpicks, working with gloved hands. The deadbolt wasn't even fastened. He only needed to defeat the thumb latch. Then he was inside, stepping onto greasy linoleum and closing the door behind him.

The kitchen was small. The living room beyond it just as small. A TV played and a lone easy chair slouched in front of it. There were empty soda bottles and a bag of chips on the floor. Jacob Grover lay slouched in the chair in front of a coffee table, one arm draping over the side, his mouth hanging open as he snored.

O'Dell advanced to the table. He shifted takeout cartons to the side and sat down. He rested both hands on his knees and studied Grover for a moment.

The man was skinny. His hair long and unkempt. Drool slipped from his lips and dripped over a soiled T-shirt.

He looked...pathetic. As though he had discarded himself as much as life had discarded him.

Reaching into his pocket, O'Dell found the Rock Island Armory revolver he'd purchased off a street corner in Baltimore for a hundred bucks. It was built in the Philippines, chambered in .38 Special. He'd loaded it with five rounds of ball ammo, but he only expected to need one.

Resting his gun hand on his knee, O'Dell kicked Grover in the shin. It took a couple strikes of his leather dress shoes before Grover blinked sleepily, then slowly pivoted toward the TV.

When he saw O'Dell, he startled, sitting up rapidly and choking. O'Dell raised the revolver and spoke quietly.

"Don't move. Don't make a sound."

Grover didn't move—he kept both hands on the worn arms of the chair, fingers clutching the stained fabric. He didn't scream. He simply panted, his body alive with sudden tension. Eyes wide.

"Who—"

"I'll do the talking," O'Dell said. "You just sit. Understand?"

Grover closed his mouth. He swallowed hard. Then he nodded.

O'Dell looked to the coffee table next to him and located a pair of house keys and a wallet. He flipped the wallet open and pushed a District of Columbia identification card out of the transparent plastic sleeve. He held the card up to the dull glow of the TV.

"Jacob F. Grover...thirty-seven years old. Five foot nine. One hundred thirty pounds. Sounds like you."

Grover's lips parted. O'Dell twitched the muzzle of the revolver, and the mouth closed again.

"I guess DC identification cards don't display sex offender status," O'Dell said. "We print that kind of thing on driver's licenses in Louisiana. Nice big red letters. So everybody knows who they're dealing with. I mean, that makes sense, right?"

No answer. Grover breathed hard.

"I guess in this case it doesn't much matter, since I do know who I'm dealing with. You're Jacob F. Grover, former math teacher at a middle school in Silver Spring. A nice job. A nice school district. Plenty of rich little kids with big smiles."

Grover blinked. His eyes watered.

"Are you one of the fathers?" Grover managed.

O'Dell laughed. "Do I look like a guy from Silver Spring?"

No comment. O'Dell shook his head.

"No, Jacob. Those fathers contented themselves with the so-called justice system. Fourteen years in a cozy federal prison in exchange for destroying the souls of nine little girls. I'm curious...does that sound like justice to you?"

A tear slid down Grover's cheeks. His bottom lip trembled. O'Dell nodded slowly.

"I'll give you this. You've put in the work to get back on track. You volunteer three times a week at a local food bank. You work hard. You don't bother anybody. You don't smoke, you don't drink. You even became an organ donor..."

O'Dell tapped the DC identification card with one gloved finger. There was a little red heart printed in the corner of the card. Grover's gaze dropped to look at it, and he frowned. He was confused.

O'Dell wasn't surprised. But Grover wouldn't be confused for long.

"Here's the thing, Jake. If it were up to me, swine like you would never make it to jail. A pine box is a lot cheaper for the taxpayer than a concrete one, and just because those girls are still breathing doesn't mean they're still alive. Not like they were. As far as I'm concerned, you're a murderous pig, and down in Louisiana we subscribe to the eye-for-an-eye philosophy. Unfortunately, I don't get to make those rules. Not for everybody. But seeing as you've put in so much effort to turn your miserable existence around, I thought you'd be interested in an opportunity to finish the job. Accomplish something truly meaningful."

The frown intensified. Grover swallowed. "What...what do you want?"

"It's not what I want, it's what you want. You want to erase your disgusting legacy. You want to do a little good in the world...on your way out. And I've got just the opportunity for you. You see, your country needs you. Your president is dying of liver failure. She needs a transplant, and as of this morning she's next in line to get one, but in a situation like this, every hour counts. I've already checked your medical files, and it seems likely that your liver would be compatible. So..."

O'Dell reached into his pocket. He produced a small notepad and a pen. He laid both items in Grover's lap.

"Here's your opportunity to reverse your legacy. That's what the notebook is for. You can write an apology, a poem...a freaking manifesto, if you like. Whatever you want the world to remember you by."

"What...what are you saying?" Grover was sobbing now. His hands trembled.

O'Dell leaned forward. "I'm saying, Jacob, that you've got five minutes."

76

The West Wing
The White House

A breathless swarm of reporters waited in the briefing room as Stratton advanced down the hallway. Eyes burning, body so crushed by exhaustion that he knew the effects were visually apparent.

A fresh suit and a shower couldn't completely hide that. Nothing short of two days of sleep and a box of Cuban cigars could hope to make an impact. But the time to be concerned about his appearance or even his own health had long since passed. Stratton had rolled the dice, and he'd lost. The gamble of focusing on domestic issues had failed before it even got off the ground.

Russia and Azerbaijan were at war, and nobody really knew why. Ten hours after the detonation of the bomb, very little was known about it. Neither Moscow nor Baku had made a public statement.

But what Stratton *did* know was more than enough to fill in the gaps and make some assumptions. Langley's official report regarding the origins of the Panama Canal bomb had reached his desk earlier that same morning, declaring it to be a Soviet-era design fueled by modern Russian uranium. Regardless of whether or not the bomb in Azerbaijan was more of the same, the raw implications were crystal clear, and impossible to ignore.

Something other than simple religious extremism was at play. Something larger than Abdel Ibrahim and his hitherto unknown band of terrorists was hell-bent on destroying America...and they were willing to play dirty to get it done.

As Stratton turned to enter the briefing room, Jill Easterling caught him by the elbow. She pressed a note into his hand, and Stratton scanned it quickly.

Donor liver obtained for POTUS. Headed into surgery now. Will update.

Stratton nodded once and passed the note back. Then he stepped into the lion's den.

Nobody spoke as he took the podium. The press corps waited as Stratton pretended to be consulting his notes. In fact, there were no notes. Only an iPad with a blank screen. Stratton was clearing his head.

When at last he looked up, he faced a bank of thirty-odd journalists all crammed into the narrow room, eyes wide, faces pale. Hands frozen over notepads. Camera lenses staring blankly.

It was the face of the nation, gazing right through him. And it was terrified.

"Good evening." Stratton's voice started dry, and he cleared his throat. "Earlier today, at around two fifteen a.m., local time, United States intelligence and military officials confirmed the detonation of a nuclear weapon in the Qazakh-Tovuz Province of the Republic of Azerbaijan. While the exact nature of this weapon, those responsible for its detonation, and the destruction it rendered are still unknown, I can confirm for the American people that this weapon was not deployed by accident, and was, in fact...an act of war."

Stratton paused, but for once, nobody interjected. The press room was as deathly silent as a crypt. There was nothing for him to do but press on.

"As the US intelligence sector and the US State Department work to uncover details of this unthinkable event, we extend our thoughts and prayers to the people of Azerbaijan and those across the entire region who are impacted by this detonation. The United States stands ready to assist the victims of this attack in any way necessary."

Another pause. A deep breath. This was the moment of truth. Stratton looked dead into the camera.

"In the past twenty-four months, the United States has experienced an unprecedented level of internal and global turmoil. From the death of President Brandt to the attempted assassination of President Trousdale to the terror attacks of Abdel Ibrahim, and now the dual detonation of nuclear weapons inside of ten days. The cumulative damage to our national economy, national security, and national spirit from these catastrophes is impossible to overstate. We have been wounded beyond record. Waylaid beyond measure. Kicked while we are down, and left bleeding in the mud."

Stratton slowly raised a finger. He wasn't pointing at anyone. He was pointing at everyone.

"But hear me now, my fellow Americans. As of this moment, we are *finished* with lying in the mud. Whether these events are truly an unimaginable string of unthinkable coincidences or in fact the orchestration of a dark power bent on undermining our strength and compromising our ability to resist, the net effect is the same. To whoever deployed the weapon into the Panama Canal—be warned. To whoever detonated the weapon in Azerbaijan—be on notice. The United States is *not* disabled. We are here, we are alive, we are relentless, and if needs be..."

Stratton lowered his finger. He glared into the camera. "We will go to war."

FALLOUT
THE PROSECUTION FORCE THRILLERS Book 8

Two weeks, two nuclear blasts. The world is careening straight toward the abyss, and Washington is powerless to stop it.

After an emergency mission deep into war-torn Georgia, the CIA's elite Prosecution Force has vanished without a trace. The chain of events leading to their disappearance and the detonation of a second nuclear weapon in two weeks remains a mystery. Langley is paralyzed, unable to inform a scrambling White House desperate to prevent global war.

Leaders from both China and Iran have fallen off the map, and Azerbaijan is facing down the barrel of a two-pronged invasion. It's a tangled web no one in the free world can unravel.

But one man holds the answer to the riddle. Separated from his team, Rufus "Turk" Turkman knows the truth. The intelligence he holds may be enough to prepare America for the sucker-punch to come, but stranded in a war zone without communication equipment, Turk's options are limited.

Even worse, Turk knows the location of his captured team. They're in enemy hands and unlikely to survive. His choice is brutally simple: save his comrades or save his country.

The game is set, and the free world is barreling into a trap... with no idea of what's to come.

Get your copy today at
severnriverbooks.com

ABOUT THE AUTHOR

Logan Ryles was born in small town USA and knew from an early age he wanted to be a writer. After working as a pizza delivery driver, sawmill operator, and banker, he finally embraced the dream and has been writing ever since. With a passion for action-packed and mystery-laced stories, Logan's work has ranged from global-scale political thrillers to small town vigilante hero fiction.

Beyond writing, Logan enjoys saltwater fishing, road trips, sports, and fast cars. He lives with his wife and three fun-loving dogs in Alabama.

Sign up for Logan Ryles's reader list at
severnriverbooks.com